## ALSO BY STEPHANIE RABIG AND ANGIE BEE

*Blasphemers in the Garden of Eden*
*Faerietale (with Colleen Toliver)*
*Pale Moon*

## ALSO BY STEPHANIE RABIG

*Cryptids and Cauldrons: The Sisters*
*In The Darkness Find Me*
*Playing Possum*
*Winterbourne's Daughter*

Anthologies:

*Angels with Clipped Wings*
*Desert Journey and an Uncommon Road*
*Last Petal on the Rose*
*Santa Claws is Coming to Deathlehem*
*Shiver*

## ALSO BY ANGIE BEE

*Hazeldine – Vol. 1*
*Hazeldine – Vol. 2*
*Hazeldine – Vol. 3*
*Hazeldine – Vol. 4*
*Sorry, We're Dead: A Supernatural Noir*
*Sorry, We're Dead: Clover & Curses*
*The Lito – Vol. 1*
*The Lito – Vol. 2*
*The Lito – Vol. 3*
*Weird, USA – Vol. 1*
*Weird, USA – Vol. 2*

THE SEARCH FOR AVELINE 1

# SINK
## OR
# SWIM

STEPHANIE RABIG

ANGIE BEE

Printed in the United States of America
Second printing, April 2021

Zombeesknees Publishing / Blurb.com
www.theangiebee.tumblr.com

*To all of the ladies left out of the history books. We know you were there, even if others ignored or forgot you.*

# PARADISE ON EARTH

They always said Captain Harry Roberts had the Devil's own luck.

As a curtain of rain doused the rigging and sails, the only illumination the intermittent forks of lightning striking into the turbulent waves, Harry wondered if perhaps it had finally hit its limits. The deck tossed and bucked like an unbroken stallion – the wild to-and-fro-ing would have sent a lesser seaman careening over the railing. But the captain pushed forward doggedly, hand tight around the sea-slick wood.

"What's the status?" Harry screamed over the tempest, voice crying out between crashes of thunder.

"The hole aft is getting bigger, Cap!" the first mate reported, her usual sangfroid cracking. If asked before today, Harry would've said it'd be a frozen day in hell before Jo's steel of self-control would so much as bend; now the captain was half-tempted to check the tropical waves for icecaps. "The bilges are half-full and the level's only rising. If we don't find the eye of this storm or a harbor soon–"

The rest of the words were lost in an apocalyptic crack. The questing lightning had finally earthed itself in something solid: one of the three masts. There was a terrible, pungent scent of ozone and ruined wood, a chorus of screams from the crew in the adjacent rigging still trying to secure the now useless sails, and then the top third of the splintered mast gave way to gravity and fell. Jo threw an arm around the captain's waist and dove to the side only a moment before the timber cracked the boards they had been standing upon.

"Captain!" shouted the steerswoman over the chaos. "Captain, I see a cove ahead!"

"Aim true, Agnessa!" Harry ordered, standing and helping Jo upright.

"Aye, Captain!" The thin arms strained with the wheel, hauling the listing craft to the east. If it had been anyone but Agnessa standing there, Harry might have worried. But the steerswoman's slight frame belied a whipcord strength and a diamond-hard resolve. Lashed to the tiller with knotted rope, feet planted as firmly as if she was rooted there, Agnessa stared straight ahead through the storm as though she hardly noticed the pelting rain and wailing wind. When she was focused on her job, she never paid the slightest attention to anything else.

Harry Roberts was not superstitious. While other pirates carried talismans and steered clear of so-called cursed wrecks and paid soothsayers outrageous sums to foretell the luck of raids, Harry scoffed and listened only to the wind and the waves. She understood the sea and knew its dangers, and refused to pay any attention to omens and signs.

But not everyone in the crew ignored such things.

"Look!" shouted a voice from a crow's nest. "Did you see it?"

"See what?" came the rejoinder down on the

tilting deck.

"Just off the bow — a giant tail! Something is leading us into the cove! A sea serpent!"

"You're seeing things, Mad! There are no serpents in these waters!"

"I swear, Cap! I saw it! It's good luck, it is! We're being guided to safety!"

"And you've been hitting the rum again! You're imagining things, or seeing jetsam stirred up by the storm!" Harry caught at a swinging rope and hauled hard to pull up a sagging sailcloth. "I swear to Ol' Jones himself, Jo, that when we get through this and shipshape again, I'm tearing out Wrath's liver with my own two hands."

"As well you should, Cap," replied the first mate, once again outwardly unruffled as the ship scraped past an outcropping of coral that would have sunk a craft with a less deft steersman. "To break a parlay like that proves him the most dishonorable of fools."

"To think that I saved that cur's *life*!" fumed Harry, ducking as a chill wave doused them. "Twice! I should've let the noose have his dirty, rotten, double-crossing neck!"

"Turning his cannons on us was utterly uncalled for," agreed Jo.

"In a way, I guess you could say we were lucky this squall blew up," said the captain as Agnessa spun the wheel sharply, missing a half-submerged wreck that had clearly fallen victim to the treacherous reef they were now navigating. "Bloody hell, remind me to give that woman a kiss when we weigh anchor. She's got us dancing through this muck like it's a bleeding waltz."

"I'll just take a couple of those eagle egg rubies you've been hoarding, Captain," called the steerswoman. "You can save your kisses for someone you actually *want* to kiss."

"Good God, woman, how did you hear that over this roaring?"

"Your voice sort of carries, Captain."

"She has a point," said Jo. "And I believe the storm is abating."

A ragged cheer rang out as the black clouds roiling like oil overhead began to dissipate, weak gray sunlight shining through the drizzling rain. Almost immediately a rainbow cut across the sky, arching triumphantly over a beach that couldn't have been a more welcoming sight. The driftwood-dotted strip of sand would no doubt be golden when dry. The sagging palm trees looked to be heavily weighted with coconuts. And – by far the most lovely of sights – a clear stream trickled down from a volcanic hill lush with greenery, spilling over the black rocks and soaked beach into a small, misting waterfall.

"Weigh anchor, if it's still attached," shouted the captain. "Take stock of provisions and the state of the hold. Jo, I need a headcount immediately. And Agnessa, three of those rubies are yours, m'girl. Not even Davy Jones could've sailed through that reef in such weather. You're a credit to us."

"Just doing my job, Captain."

"Both lifeboats still accounted for?"

"They are, Cap," called Mad Maddie, sliding down a rope to land with monkey-like agility beside

Harry. "I volunteer for the landing party!"

"Of course you do," Harry smiled, pulling off a paisley-patterned headscarf and mercilessly twisting it to wring it dry. Next to be doffed was a leather coat made three times heavier with water, which was draped over a patch of railing. The boots felt half-full with brine, but there'd be time to empty them on shore.

Then Captain Roberts undid her long blonde hair from its salt-encrusted braid and threw back her head to laugh. "We made it through Wrath Drew's cannon fire, a typhoon, and the very teeth of the Devil! I'd like to see another crew manage so much in a day! Excellent work, beauties!"

Just beneath the waterfall, submerged to the nose, he watched the bustle on the ship...

And waited.

*~*~*

"I got the feeling we're being watched," Mad Maddie said quietly, an ominous edge to her voice.

"Mad, what the hell did I tell you?" Harry snapped.

"To not intone dramatically like something outta the worst kinda blue-faced tale," Maddie sighed, pulling up the hand she'd been trailing through the water. "But Cap, I really *do*—"

"Shut up and keep an eye on the shoreline if you're not gonna row, girl," came the sharp retort.

"Yes, Cap. No sign of any hostile locals, no sign of civilization, no sign of much of anything excepting lots and lots of driftwood and broken coral. That storm must've scoured the bottom of the seabed nice and clean."

"We'll make camp on the beach until I'm assured *The Sappho* isn't sinking in slow motion," Harry decided, hauling on her own oar. "But we all keep a sharp lookout about us. Jungles like this can hide any number of dangers, and after a typhoon that size all sorts of creepies may crawl out of the water to lick their wounds."

"I'm glad Great Krakens aren't native to this region," Jo said. "Don't fancy dealing with another one of those any time soon."

"Those sucker marks made you a hit at every pub, though, mate," said Lucky Franky, the usual twinkle flashing in his dark eyes. "Every wench from here to Tortuga wanted to hear how you got them."

"If you've got enough air to chat, you've got enough air to row, so *row*," ordered Harry.

"Don't pay her any mind, love," Maddie assured him in a carefully modulated undertone. "She always gets a little snippy when she's been double-crossed."

"Noted," he whispered back, giving her a smile that put his dimples on fine display.

With their combined efforts, it took less than a minute to haul both lifeboats high enough up the beach to keep them from floating back out with the tide. Maddie promptly scrambled to work with the tent canvas and stakes, trailed by Lucky Franky, swinging a mallet in one large hand and a heavy bag over his shoulder.

"Like a puppy," Harry said to Jo, fighting the urge to grin.

"Like a lost lamb," her first mate agreed. "An unlikelier pair you'd be hard-pressed to find."

The small crew had become adept at moving around one another, and they were all of them hard workers. The camp went from rudimentary to solid in no time. A fire pit was dug, lined with flat black stones, and prepped with scavenged driftwood that was drying quickly in the hot sun. A small city of tents sprang up and palm fronds were gathered, shook free of insects, and laid out as temporary mattresses. Buckets were filled from the stream and stew pots were set to boil.

"Lizzie, Zora, Katherine, bring down some of those coconuts and then see what kind of fruit the edges has to offer us. I'm gonna try that lagoon. Cast a line and see what bites – rather have fresh fish than pickled eel for supper tonight."

"Can we come, too, Cap? Me and Franky?" Maddie asked, springing up seemingly from nowhere. The baggy shirt she wore had slipped down one dark brown shoulder.

"Of course you can't. Fishing requires patience and quiet, Mad – two things you've never gotten the hang of. Why don't you and the boy just walk the perimeter and scout the lay of the land. Make sure we won't have any nasty surprises once night falls."

The girl looked somewhat crestfallen and her, "Yes, Cap," was more subdued than usual.

"Buck up, girl," Harry said, nudging her bared brown shoulder roughly. "I'm givin' you some time to get to know our newest recruit a bit better. I'm expecting you to take his full measure and report back on your findings."

"Will do, Cap."

Harry rolled up the legs of her trousers, undid most of the buttons on her baggy shirt, and adjusted the floppy hat she'd slapped on as soon as the clouds had parted and the sun had shone through. The heat was heavy, humid, and would be unbearably oppressive if not for the brisk wind rolling in from the waves and the cooling mist of the ocean's spray. She grabbed a rod from the pile of supplies beside her tent, made sure her silver flask of rum was still tucked into her belt, and set off towards the rockier end of the cove where the water was deeper.

"Mind some company, Captain?"

Harry didn't slow her stride, knowing the woman just behind her was more than a match for it. "You really did some magic getting us through that reef, Nessa. I'm proud of you."

"Thanks, Captain."

"You can call me Harry, you know," she teased. "You earned that right long ago."

"Sorry, Cap — Harry," the younger woman stumbled verbally. "Still haven't quite shaken the upbringing. Alvar and I had respect drummed into us by the time we were walking. You must always give a superior their full title and honors," she said in a sing-song cadence. "You must always defer to the social hierarchy, and bend your head in the presence of nobility. A lady curtsies and a gentleman bows..."

"Good thing none of us are noble," Harry snorted. "And you're the only lady on board, so don't waste time on curtsies."

"Don't think you can do a proper curtsy in breeches anyhow, Cap — sorry. Harry."

"Alvar is your brother, yes?"

"My twin."

"The one that showed you how to run a wheel?"

"Yes. He's in the Navy now."

"What colors does he sail under? We can steer clear of any ships with—"

"No worries on that count. He's currently sailing around the Horn of Africa, on a three year voyage with a ship full of scientists and botanists. We won't be crossing paths with him."

"Well, if we happen to find ourselves sailing for the Dark Continent, remind me to keep a weather eye out for him."

"Will do, Harry."

There was a large outcropping of rock that jutted over the lagoon like some accusatory finger, flat and smooth and with ample space for the pair to sit side-by-side and cast out fishing lines. They settled themselves carefully on the hot rock, dangling their legs over the edge, and dropped their baited hooks. The wind played with their hair, weaving the loose strands into knots, and dried the sweat on their brows.

Harry glanced over at Agnessa with a half-smile and lidded eyes. She was only a handful of years her junior but seemed much younger thanks to a closeted upbringing. The captain knew she came from money — her father was some financial genius in Sweden, something big in banking who owned a shipping company or three, and she'd heard the crew say something about her mother having been minor nobility, a blue-blooded name tied to large tracts of land. She certainly had the fine bones and elegant hands of a lady, a sharp chin and demanding dark eyes that could be quite arresting. Nearly a year at sea had darkened her skin to a uniform nut brown, bleached streaks of blonde throughout her dark hair, and had put thick calluses on her once-soft palms.

But even with the tan and rough hands, it was impossible to hide what the steerswoman truly was: a fine lady. She still spoke with the eloquent rounded vowels that were hallmarks of wealth, still had a graceful way of moving, as if she were dancing in heavy skirts. In comparison, Harry was a coarse character indeed.

She was fair where Agnessa was dark. Her pale hair had begun to go white in patches – not from age, as she was still only in her thirties, and not from shock, as Harriet Roberts was nigh unshockable. No, it was the constant sun and brine that was bleaching away the blonde. And while that same sun had made Agnessa brown, it did nothing to Harry. She didn't freckle, didn't burn, and didn't tan. Her skin remained so pale it was almost translucent, and she knew this oddity had added to her growing legend. Maddie had overheard another pirate tell his drunken mate that Captain Roberts was actually a ghost, a sea spirit that could make itself solid.

But no – Harriet Roberts was a flesh-and-blood human woman, not a siren in disguise or a vengeful spirit, though she wasn't above the occasional act of revenge. Her teeth were slightly crooked just like her smile, her nose was a bit snub, and her pale blue eyes could glitter with amusement, go flat and empty with anger, or flash with hellfire depending on the heat of the moment. She wasn't particularly tall and there wasn't much meat on her bones; all of her muscle was wiry as whipcord. Besides her pale skin and white hair, the most unusual thing about her was her scar: it ran nearly the full length of her left arm, a dark and jagged red line that bumped where the stitches had been uneven. Only Jo knew how she had gotten it – it had been an old scar by the time she became captain of *The Sappho*.

There were many stories about Captain Roberts and *The Sappho* – one was that all of her crew was undead and cursed, women that had been thrown overboard or murdered at sea. And there was some slight truth in that story: most of her crew had indeed been thrown overboard or cast aside by cruel sailors. Wenches who had tired of constant beatings, stowaways with murky pasts, sailors whose disguises had been compromised.

Agnessa was a rare exception: someone who had sought them out and demanded to join the crew rather than a woman rescued from the waves or brothels.

"Nessa, exactly *why* did you decide to go to sea?" Harry asked, breaking the serenity of the lagoon.

She was quiet for a long while, eyes focused on the striations of the rock they sat upon. "I didn't want to live the life society demanded of me. When Alvar announced his intentions to join the Navy, Father said it was time for me to marry. He'd picked out a husband for me, and a wedding date, and had already commissioned the finest dressmaker in Stockholm to make my gown. And I didn't want any of it. I had never met this man who would be my husband. And he was so many years older than me. I didn't want all the fuss of a wedding, or to wear any more uncomfortable dresses, and most of all... I did not want to become a broodmare."

She shifted, drawing up one leg and tucking it beneath the knee of the other. Her fishing line bounced slightly as she rolled her shoulders and settled her arms more comfortably across her lap. "I had an older sister. Agathe. She was seven years senior of Alvar and I. And she died in childbirth, trying to deliver a third child in as many years. I was in the room with her. I held her hand as she bled out across the bed – I watched the light fade out of her eyes. It was the same way our mother had died: massive hemorrhage. The same way our neighbor died, and the baker's wife. And I could not shake the fear and exhaustion and resignation I saw in Agathe's face, the same emotions I was sure must have been on Mother's. She died birthing Alvar, only minutes after delivering me, and I decided I would never share that fate. They always speak of what a tragedy it is when a war claims so many young men, and yet society cares nothing for the war women face – are *expected* to face! And so many times! It horrifies me and I want no part in it," she finished firmly with an obstinate jut of her chin.

"So you turned to piracy," Harry said. "I must confess, I agree with you: it's a far safer career choice. Much rather a brigand than a mother."

"I don't think you're a brigand, though," Agnessa said after a moment's silence. "Not in spirit, anyway."

"Says the woman who now owns three of the Spanish king's prize rubies."

"I mean, we're *technically* brigands, yes," she clarified. "What with the stealing and all. But we only attack ships that deserve it—"

"Or whose captains have irked me."

"Yes, who deserve it," Agnessa agreed. "And we honor terms of surrender and parlay, and it seems to me that we spend more time rescuing people than we do killing."

"You make us sound like a bleedin' charity."

"But we are, in a way, aren't we? Last month we sailed fifty leagues off course just to get that girl Topaz back home to her mother, *and* you gave her a bag of gold when she landed."

"You noticed that?" Harry said wryly. There was a gentle tug on her line and she resisted the urge to immediately reel it in, knowing it was only the first test bite. *Come on, little beauty, take another nibble...*

"I've got good eyes, Captain. And I also noticed..."

"Speak your mind, Agnessa. You know I want everyone to have a say."

"You're looking for something, aren't you?" A gust of wind threw her dark hair into her eyes, and she reached up one hand to push it back.

"Something more than just the next fight or bag of gold. Something more important. You and Jo both."

Harry had stilled to the point where she looked like a very unusual alabaster statue. Her shirt hung down over one shoulder to bare a large swathe of undeniably female chest. Her white-blonde hair was a tangled rats' nest beneath the shapeless brown hat, and her legs were caked with dried sand. "We're all of us looking for something, ain't we?" she said finally. "The fish here don't seem especially hungry, do they? Maybe we'll have to settle for eel and biscuits after all. C'mon, m'girl. What do you say to a short swim? Get the salt outta our hair."

She set aside her rod and line, pulled the shirt up over her head, and unbuckled her belt, sloughing off her trousers before taking a running leap from the rock with a shout of excitement. Agnessa sat frozen, mouth hanging open, for several seconds before she came back to her senses.

"You're a crazy woman, Captain!" she called down as soon as the pale head had resurfaced in the center of a rippling circle.

"Come on in, Nessa!" Harry crowed, slapping the water. "Cool you right off!"

"And you've *definitely* scared off the fish now!"

"Aw, I'm not that terrible to look at, am I? I've still got most of my teeth." Harry stretched out, closed her eyes, and backstroked in a lazy circle. A moment later, a splash to the right indicated Agnessa had taken the leap. "This is most certainly the life, ain't it?" she said when she'd resurfaced with a splutter. "Paradise. We may just have to make this little cove our usual berth. Wouldn't be too difficult to navigate the reefs in smooth weather, would it?"

"No, not now that I've gotten the lay of them," Agnessa confirmed. "Though most helmsmen would steer clear of coral like that."

"Perfect, makes it even more attractive. We'll see how the night fares. So long as no terrible beasties prowl out of the jungle or slither up the sand, I'll have a word with Jo about making the accommodations here more permanent. Sure we could craft a couple little huts, maybe find a nice dry cave to store provisions and gunpowder in."

Behind the curtain of the waterfall, he watched the two with interest. He'd seen humans before but these were different. They smelled different, and they moved differently. Their voices were higher, closer to the music of his sisters, and they didn't carry the same air about them. He decided they must be females of the species.

The humans he'd watched before had reeked of avarice and violence, the auras haloing them black like the tar and smoke they smelled of. And while the pale one carried a promise of violence and the ghost of a long-burning anger, there was nothing dangerous in her aura, and her companion's simply held the cooler green of satisfaction and contentment.

He listened to the way their bodies moved

through the water. They were clumsy, as all humans were, their legs flailing and thrashing in discord. They did not know how to swim with the rhythm of water's ebb and flow – it was something their kind had lost when they climbed onto the land. But the pale one swam better than he would have expected a human to swim, just shy of graceful. It was clear that she loved the water, that she was so familiar with it she could *almost* hear its music. She was unafraid and joyous, reveling in the element. He could hear that singing out from her heavy human bones.

And he was greatly intrigued to learn more. Perhaps an offering or two would be in order.

Still, he wouldn't reveal himself just yet. He did not *think* these female humans would harm him, but far better to wait and study them for now; they did greatly outnumber him. He slid back from the waterfall, diving down into the crevasse that connected directly to the stream.

*~*~*

"Glad you two are having fun," Jo called. "The rest of us have just been busy making camp, that's all."

"Come on in, Josephine," Harry laughed. "The crew won't be offended that the captain, first mate, and steerswoman are enjoying themselves a little. After this morning, we've earned a respite."

"Oh no, you're not getting me in there. I know your tricks, woman. You'll be dunking me the second I dive in. Now come on, it's time to get supper started. And where in the blue blazes are your clothes? I swear, you're worse than a child."

"What's the problem?" Harry said archly, squeezing the water from her hair. "We're all of us ladies here."

"Except for Franky," Jo reminded her.

"I'm sure Franky has seen plenty of female flesh," Harry retorted.

"Exhibitionist," muttered the first mate.

"According to my mum, we were all naked before we started sinning and knew shame."

"Don't you go referencing the Bible with me, Harriet Roberts," Jo said. "As if you're free of sin."

"No, but I am free of shame," Harry countered with a laugh. "Oh, thanks, Nessa," she said, taking the clothes she held out. "You're a peach."

"Speaking of: Maddie and Franky found a whole grove of fruit trees. She thinks this spot may have been a colony at some point – maybe the Dutch, they're always throwing farmers on Godforsaken rocks."

"No sign of any colonists still around?"

"No. And the trees are so overgrown and wild now, it must've been a couple decades ago. Perhaps they packed up and went home."

"Or died because of some terrible disease or vicious animal," Agnessa said darkly.

"It's not like you to be so doom-and-gloom," Jo said. "Whatever the reason, it certainly wasn't for a lack of food. If we'd been marooned, I don't think I'd have minded it much. There's plenty here to keep us going for months, if not years. And I see this lagoon's well-stocked."

"What do you mean?" Harry asked, looking up from belting her trousers.

"The fish you caught?" Jo gestured to a nearby rock. Six enormous fish were lined up on it, eyes bulging and blue scales glittering in the sun like polished gems.

Harry and Agnessa exchanged looks. "We didn't catch anything," said the former quietly. "I only had one bite, but naught came of it."

"Do brownies live in the Tropics?" Agnessa asked. "Maybe there's a little tribe of them here, with woven grass hats? Maybe they came with those hypothetical Dutch colonists and stayed behind?"

"Can't see brownies spear-fishing," Harry said thoughtfully, heaving up one of the fish and examining the precise punctures that had gone straight through its head, killing it instantly. It was heavy in her hands: easily a solid fifteen pounds. "Well, whoever left these here meant well. I say we take it as a good sign. Something on this island is leaving us gifts."

"I don't recognize the species, though," said Jo. "Perhaps they're poisonous?"

"Whatever left these is armed and probably quite strong. If it wanted to harm us, surely it would've already attacked. Agnessa and I have been alone for over an hour. Ample time to take care of us. No, I'm going to look at this as an unusual welcome rather than a trap. Nessa, why don't you take one and go on ahead."

She turned back to scan the peaceful lagoon.

The waterfall hissed, birds in the trees trilled and squawked, and somewhere nearby a monkey shrieked.

But there was no sign of anything larger, and no footprints in the dirt and sand around the rocks.

*~*~*

In the days that followed, he began to put names to figures. The tall one with skin even darker than his and long hair that was bound back in dozens of tiny braids was Jo; she was always close to the pale one, Harry, and their body language was confusing. Often, Jo deferred to Harry: she walked a step behind her, stood at her left shoulder, and let her speak first to the others. But there was also a sense of equality and familiarity between them. He decided they were lifelong podmates, perhaps raised by the same matrons, though he thought Jo was older than Harry. It was difficult to gauge ages with humans.

Jo's golden aura complimented Harry's usually fire-tinged halo nicely, and her movements sounded like the bells of sunken ships during storms. In fact, the entire group now settled on his beach was very musical — there was not a sour note among them, nor an oppressive aura. They were a rainbow-hued pod that moved easily around one another. They whistled and sang and laughed, as noisy as dolphins.

Agnessa was the one with a green aura and flute-like movements. Zora, the one with hair as blue-black as octopus ink and skin the color of sun-baked sand – she made him think of a sea-snake because she seemed to undulate when she moved, and spoke in short, sharp snaps. She had a hissing cadence to her. The others wore things he knew were called breeches but Zora did not: she wrapped red fabric around her waist, which fell to her knees, and had strung ribbons and gold threads around her belt. Coins and jewels and beads and shells and talismans hung from these, shimmering and clattering as she stalked barefoot across the sand.

Katherine was very large compared to the others, taller even than Jo, with brawny arms and sturdy legs, skin spotted like a leopard fish – he thought humans called such markings 'freckles' – and a thick braided coil of gold hair that she wound around her head like a crown. She boomed when she laughed, and barked like a seal, and had tattoos across her chest and arms. He had seen her heft up a huge barrel on one shoulder as if it weighed nothing.

The one called Mad had skin like his, a tawny brown, and hair like his, too: dark but streaked with gold. Her face and nose were long and broad and she smiled constantly. She was also in constant movement, running from tent to fire to water, a wild energy about her. She made him think of the spiny crabs that scuttled restlessly across the beach, or anemones that shot out brightly colored fronds when startled.

And there was a strange human who followed Mad around – he wasn't sure if it was male or female. Male, he finally decided, if only because of the way he smelled: a muskier scent than the others. Even muskier around Mad, who he decided must be his mate. He was called Franky, or maybe it was Lucky, or perhaps The Boy: the pod didn't use a single name for him. He had shaggy dark hair, tanned skin, and long legs that he didn't have complete control over. He stumbled and tripped a lot, almost as often as he laughed or smiled. His energy and aura complimented Mad's.

There were others, too, about fifteen total in the pod: Lizzie was bald with skin even darker than Jo's; Wilhelmina was missing her right leg beneath the knee and wore a carved wooden foot in its place; Marcella had a crescent scar across her right cheek; Hope always wore red; Euphemia was very old and very strange...

The more he watched them, the more he liked them. Every morning they would share a meal before heading back to their ship to continue repairs; every night they would tell stories or sing or play instruments around the fire. Harry was clearly their primary matron, and they all deferred to her without question, content to obey her orders.

Harry was the one he was most curious about. She was the most mer-like human he'd ever come across. He would swear that she could hear the ocean's song just as he could, because she would adjust herself according to its moods. One day she told her pod to stay ashore and hold off on repairs because there was a small squall approaching – this was true, but how could she have known? Humans couldn't taste the air and feel the seabed's vibrations, and it was a clear and sunny day right up to the moment the sky went black and crackled with thunder.

His matrons had always told him to avoid humans. To hide if he could and chase them away if he must. It was dangerous to trust them because they were notoriously selfish, greedy creatures prone to hunting and capturing his kind. "When they abandoned the water, they left a part of their souls behind. They became half-deaf," he was told. "That's why they hate us – because they know we can still hear the song of the sea."

But these humans seemed so happy and generous. They sang songs of their own, even if they weren't as beautiful as the songs of merfolk. And it had been many, many years since he had lost his pod. He had been alone for so long he had forgotten what it felt like to have the comfort of community; and now he watched another from afar and felt the ache of longing. Reason said that humans would be a poor substitute. That they wouldn't satisfy his need for companionship.

But he had never been fond of listening to reason.

*~*~*

"Cap'n, I'd *swear* on my foster mother's head that the hole's smaller today," Katherine called up from her harness, scratching her head. Her heavy accent always put Harry in mind of mountains and goats and women in funny white hats; by all rights, the very large woman currently suspended by ropes with a bucket of sealing tar should be shepherding a flock of woolly sheep through a valley right now, not living on a ship and maintaining its cannons.

Destiny was a very fickle thing, if it truly existed.

"We *have* been working on closing it for more than a week now, Kath," the captain pointed out helpfully, leaning over the railing to look down at her.

"Smaller than it was when we left it yesterday, I mean. See here? Where we brushed on the pitch for caulking? It looks as if someone's smeared something else here." She scratched experimentally at it with her thumbnail. "Something that's dried as hard as rock."

"Seeing as how that's what we want, and so long as it's watertight, I don't see a problem."

"Nay, but what in the hell is it? Who put it there? Mayhaps Agnessa's right and there's a very odd tribe of brownies living by these waters. Or wish-granting faeries."

"Have you been wishing on stars for our ship to be repaired?"

"Naught I, Cap'n, but I wouldn't put it past Maddie."

"Wouldn't put much past Maddie. Perhaps I'll leave a sentry onboard tonight, just to see if we can catch these unusual brownies in action. A shame we haven't any milk to leave them for their troubles," she joked.

The next day, Zora woke early and took a walk along the tide-line, scanning the jetsam as she did. She always kept an eye out for beautiful shells and stones; Tessa, her sweetheart in Bogo, liked to tease her about it. Said she had a magpie's eye and that if she wasn't careful her skirt would rip clean off under the weight of her treasures.

The sun was just cresting the horizon, turning the sky the rosy pink of a conch shell's interior, when she saw the chest. Judging by the barnacles encrusting the thick wood and the rust edging the hinges and lock, it had been submerged for years. It was too heavy and the sea had been too calm for it to have been simply tossed up by the waves. How it had appeared was a mystery no one could explain when she summoned the others.

Lucky Franky produced the mallet he had taken to carrying, Lizzie supplied a chisel from her bandolier of tools, and with a couple of quick blows he'd knocked the lock off and thrown back the lid. It had been a well-made chest: not much water had seeped inside, just enough to turn the copper coins green. The gold and silver still gleamed brightly enough, and the sprinkling of gems was a cheerful sight.

"Guess we won't have to worry about covering supplies next time we sail into a port," said Jo dryly. "And we none of us even had to bleed for this booty."

"It's the definition of a windfall," Harry agreed, crossing her arms and chewing her bottom lip thoughtfully.

"This place is magic, Cap," Maddie exclaimed, scooping out a handful of coins. "It's truly Paradise!"

"Maybe we actually died in that typhoon," suggested Wilhelmina cynically. "The ship sank, we all drowned, and this is Heaven."

"If this is Heaven, then why are you here, Wil?" quipped Marcella. "Thought you didn't believe in God."

"I just said I can't prove He exists. I can't disprove it, either. As a woman of science, I must concede that until proof presents itself, either theory could be true. I try to keep an open mind on all things, Marcella."

"Didn't you tell me a couple months ago that we used to be monkeys or something?"

"You're referring to Mr. Darwin's theory that—"

"Ladies, I've no patience for scientific debates right now," Harry interrupted. "Katherine, can you haul this back to camp?"

"Absolutely, Cap'n."

"Thanks."

"Afraid it's faerie trash? A bunch of rocks glamoured to look like coins?" Jo asked in an undertone.

"I don't really know what I think. We'll keep an eye on it — if it stays exactly as it looks for another day or two, it's probably safe."

"Unless there's a curse on it," piped up Maddie, almost gleeful. "Maybe it's from a ghost ship, or was a bloody ransom for—"

"Mad, I am searching your locker and burning any penny dreadfuls you've got in there," Harry threatened.

"Aw, Cap!"

"Should we be worried?" Jo continued as the crew followed Katherine back to camp to better examine the treasure.

"Nothing has been hostile."

"Yet. Perhaps regular patrols?"

"I've a couple suspicions. But for now, we'll just wait and see. After everything we've been through of late, I've no desire to plant a seed of worry in their heads. They're relaxing and enjoying themselves for the first time in weeks. I want this to last as long as possible."

*~*~*

Two days later, Maddie and Franky returned from a stroll − Harry took one look at the state of their hair and read between the lines − to announce they'd found a splendid cave that would be perfect for storage.

"The stream curves right up to it, but the cave itself is higher up on this little hill," Maddie explained earnestly as they led the way back, following the markers they'd cut into the bark of the palm trees. "The floor is a little sandy, but the rock looks solid and there's no damp or dripping inside, and it's not too awful big. Just the right size for a few barrels. And I bet we could rig up a door or something to secure it, so animals couldn't get insi−"

The sentence was cut off when she ran smack into Franky's back, teeth clicking down on the tip of her tongue. "Owwww," she mumbled, putting a hand to her mouth. "I think it's bleeding."

"Shhh!" Franky gestured sharply, shoulders tensing, and the group immediately crouched into the undergrowth, hands reaching for an assortment of blades and pistols. "Hear that?" he whispered, looking sharply to Harry.

It was just audible over the rushing of the stream a mere few feet ahead: a dragging sort of sound, as if something heavy was being pulled across the rocks. Her chipped sword in hand, Harry crept forward, reaching out her left arm to push back the leaves.

There was a loud splash – she even felt the spray on her face as she rushed forward. The rocks glistened dark and slick in the dappled sunlight but nothing surfaced from the churning water. Raising her gaze she saw the cave, maybe thirty feet further up at the head of a sloping incline.

And lying at its mouth was a sword, a far finer weapon than the one she currently held. The blade had been recently honed into a deadly sharpness and the basket hilt was polished to a mirror gleam. It fit her hand snugly, well-balanced and beautiful with a faint yet indecipherable design etched into one side of the steel.

"Another present?" Jo said dryly, eying the strange, wide drag marks in the dirt that stretched from the stream all the way to where the sword had been left. "No, don't tell me: a woman in the river threw it to you and said you're the one true king of England."

"I have no idea what you just said but I'm sure it was scathing and pithy," said Harry.

"It was a reference to the classic Arthurian legend, dear," Miss Euphemia volunteered cheerfully with a twirl of her parasol. Why she carried the thing no one knew: it was dotted with so many holes it no longer performed its intended function. "According to balladeers, the Lady of the Lake presented Arthur with a magical sword, signaling that he was indeed the prophesized king who would unite..."

While the schoolteacher-turned-scribe nattered on matter-of-factly to Katherine and Wilhelmina, who both nodded and ahhed politely, and the others examined the cave under Maddie's urging, Harry made a few experimental swings and stabbing motions. "This is a *very* nice blade," she said appreciatively.

Jo sighed.

"What?" Harry demanded.

"You and your toys," the first mate clarified, crossing her arms. "You don't even care where it came from, do you?"

"No. Because I know where it came from."

"Oh? Do share."

"Same place that treasure chest came from. Obviously. And people think you've the brains in this partnership," Harry teased. "Nessa?"

"Yes?"

"Just give me a rough estimate. How many wrecks do you think we dodged sailing into the cove?"

"Three for sure, Captain, but there's no doubt more. The reef system is a sprawling one and there are some sharp dips into crevasses."

"See, Jo? There's a plethora of shipwrecks to choose from. Someone's just been raiding old holds, that's all. And how's that map coming along?"

"Lizzie and I have covered the immediate area and we're relatively certain we've marked down the truly dangerous spots. Once the repairs are done, sailing out and back in shouldn't be a problem."

"Glad to hear it — did you think I was sending them out in that lifeboat every morning on pleasure cruises?" Harry asked Jo, experimentally hanging the sword from her belt. She liked the way it looked on her hip. "I hope I'm the sort of captain that plans ahead and has her crew's best interests at heart."

"I never doubted you," said Jo woodenly.

"Ooh, you know better than to tell lies, Josephine," Harry grinned. "Because lying is sinning and we all know how Jesus feels about that. C'mon, sweetie, buck up! Why are you being such a curmudgeon?"

"I would just prefer to know what's going on rather than accept a bunch of mysterious gifts blindly, without a single question."

"Oh, I've got plenty of questions. And I'll get answers soon enough. For now, let's take a gander at this fine cave Mad and the boy found us. Yup, that sure is a nice cave. Very cave-like. Well done, you two. Champion cave finders you are. Alright, everybody, back to the beach."

When everyone, Jo included, had filed past and disappeared into the jungle greenery, Harry hesitated beside the stream.

"I'd like to meet whoever's been so kind to me and mine," she said loudly, voice ringing out clear into the sudden stillness. "After all these gifts,

I'd feel downright rotten if I didn't at least thank you properly. I'd just like an introduction, that's all. Say... down at the lagoon tonight? At dusk? I'll be there, anyway, because I fancy another swim."

Then she turned on her heel with a jaunty whistle and set off back to camp.

*~*~*

He should be conflicted, and indecisive, and hesitant to do as she asked.

But he wasn't. In fact, he felt rather giddy. Harry was a clever one, that much was obvious, and struck him as a person of honor. His overtures of friendship had been accepted and it would only be right for him to now present himself for her inspection. He had a vague and hazy recollection of such rituals; he knew there was a certain order to the way a male won the approval of a female, ceremonies that must be observed if he wanted to formally join a new pod.

Because that was what he wanted now: to be a part of Harry's pod. There were things he could provide them, ways he could prove himself a productive and worthwhile podmate. He could share his knowledge of the island and its reefs, and he could lead them to all of its sunken treasures. He could teach them how to speak to the dolphins and seals that frolicked in the kelp fields, and how to swim among the flat-bellied sharks without fear, and show them the best fishing spots. And he could warn them of ill weather, or if other pods with hostile auras were approaching.

Speaking of...

Near the lagoon, there was a small patch of sand surrounded by large, nigh insurmountable rocks on three sides and the ocean on the fourth – it was here that he'd taken to sunning himself during the day, confident that none of Harry's pod would stumble across him without warning. He usually wriggled into the wet, warm sand until most of his body was covered in it, crossed his arms behind his head, and snoozed away the hottest part of the day, lulled by the lapping of the water over the fan of his tail and the squawking of the parrots in the trees behind him.

But today, there was something on the air. A smell of fresh smoke that did not come from campfires. It was the smell of recently fired cannons and guns, of those odd things humans put in their mouths to breathe out smoke like a volcano.

He straightened and pushed himself up from the comfortable sand, body tensing with alertness. Now he could hear it: another ship. Rigging and sails and the creaking of old wood. Shouts of anger and violence. It was not far away and coming closer – he may not see it yet with his eyes, but he saw it plainly enough with his ears.

With a sharp twist, he splashed into the shallows. He would go out to this strange ship and take its measure. He had time before his appointed meeting with Harry.

*~*~*

The sky was just beginning to purple when

Harry dipped her legs into the water. Unlike certain *other* pirates, she was a woman of her word. If she made a promise, she kept it, and she couldn't abide those who were late to appointments.

Still, dusk was a rather uncertain time. A transitional period. More of an hour than a precise minute. She could be patient for a while and just enjoy the paradise her crew was already feeling proprietary of.

Most people thought Harry Roberts was all action and little thought. And in some ways it was true: she often leapt before she looked, driven by pure emotion and wild energy, and she was more comfortable in the midst of a fight than in the planning of it. She frequently reacted on blind instinct and the urging of her gut. If the situation called for a long reach and extensive preparation, she tended to leave that in Jo's more than capable hands – mainly because she bored easily and would start to look for distraction.

But that didn't mean she was an idiot. She was observant and could draw conclusions quicker than most. She could decode a confusing map or tricky riddle almost as easily as Miss Euphemia because her brain was predisposed to fit pieces together into a larger picture. She made crack judgment calls when lives were on the line, usually to her benefit, and could take a person's measure so long as they weren't skilled at deceiving others (hence her misreading of Wrath Drew).

And, unlike most, Harry didn't suffer from blind prejudice. It was an unusual gift, given all she had been through. But ever since she was a child she had known to judge a person on their own merits.

Her crew may be almost entirely female, but it wasn't because she hated men – women had simply come to her first. When Agnessa had approached her in the noisy pub, she hadn't immediately dismissed her out of hand because of the lace on her dress and her soft hands; instead, she had met her eyes and seen a fire there she approved of. After discovering Maddie stowed away in the galley, a half-eaten apple in her hand, she hadn't cared that she was young and brown, only that she was desperate. What did it matter to her that Zora and Jo preferred the company of women, that Lizzie liked men, that Wilhelmina and Katherine enjoyed both, and that Franky seemed to like *everybody*?

And even after losing Aveline, she just couldn't look at every mermaid and assume the worst. Their species was no more wholly evil than humans; some pods would make slaves of humans, but then how many humans were enslaved by other humans? How many mermaids had been slaughtered by sailors?

She boarded slaver ships regardless of what country's flag they flew, but she would only kill merfolk that actively tried to harm her crew.

Which was why she was waiting so calmly and unarmed. Every overture had been a friendly one and the last gift had confirmed her suspicions. Only one thing would leave drag marks like that: a mermaid, and a large one at that, both because of the size of the marks and the weight of the treasure chest left three days ago. Harry knew that merfolk were, pound for pound, vastly stronger than humans, but to swim while carrying such a weight she had to be comparable to Katherine in scale. Most of the mermaids Harry had ever seen were lithe and slim, but the width of the drag marks suggested a much broader torso and tail.

Their mysterious friend must be an impressive lady, and Harry was looking forward to formally making her acquaintance.

No sign of her yet, though. Harry leaned back on her arms and chewed thoughtfully on a slice of sugarcane. Maddie had found the stand not far from the overgrown fruit trees Katherine had taken under her care. When the girl walked into camp just before supper with an armful of stalks, Lizzie had started laughing.

"Ya become a regular bloodhound, girl!" she'd crowed in her rich Caribbean accent, taking one and splitting it deftly, whittling it into narrow straws and passing them out so everyone could enjoy the sweetness. "P'haps ya got a bit of a dowsin' witch in ya."

"This place certainly seems to have everything we need," Jo said. "Food, water, gold, a mysterious benefactor who may have ulterior motives."

"No rum, though," Zora said, pointing out the fly in the ointment. "And no Tessa."

"And no handsome men with big appetites," sighed Katherine longingly.

"I won't stand such dissension in the ranks," Harry had said teasingly. "You can't all be getting stir-crazy already – it's only been two weeks!"

"But the ship's almost seaworthy again," said Marcella. "And the gold in that chest isn't doing anybody any good where it is."

"I'm gonna use my share to get a new hat," Maddie had piped in enthusiastically. "A big red one with an ostrich feather, and some new boots since my old're starting to crack along the heels."

"You don't hardly wear shoes anyway, Mads," Franky pointed out.

"They'll be my going-to-town boots," she replied. "For when I'm feeling fancy."

"You don't need new boots and a big hat to feel fancy," the boy continued brazenly. "You're fancy just as you are, love, with your hair in knots and sunburned shoulders."

"Awww, listen to that charm!" Katherine cooed in her deep voice, slinging an arm around Franky's shoulders and practically lifting him up.

"Romeo could not be sweeter to his gentle Juliet," said Miss Euphemia, looking up from her knitting and flashing a yellowed smile.

Harry had slipped away while the focus was on the blushing Maddie and the grinning Franky, leaving behind the babble of good-natured ribbing to keep her appointment. She could still hear them if she concentrated, a distant murmur mostly covered by the splashing of the waterfall and the hissing of the clear freshwater of the lagoon as it met the briny waves of the ocean at the inlet.

Making this a permanent hideout wasn't a half-bad idea. They could easily fortify a position closer to the volcano, perhaps put a cannon on the ridge with a watchtower. The reefs were tricky to navigate, which would keep most other ships away, and the little spot was too small and remote to tempt wandering colonists – Harry suspected that it was the size of the island that had put paid to the failed colony that had left remnants behind. Surely the community had just outgrown its bounds and sailed off in search of larger territory.

Other crews had their own islands or harbors. Why shouldn't *The Sappho*? If nothing else, this would be a good shelter to run to if things got too hairy out at sea, or if they had any wounds that needed licking. The ship was fully repaired; the caulking on the patched hole had seasoned enough to survive a quick voyage to Bogo. With their new-gotten gold, they'd be able to afford more building tools and supplies. She'd run the idea past Jo and the others tonight, put it to a vote, and perhaps in the next day or two they'd set out to spend some treasure and satisfy everyone's itchy feet.

The lapping of the water against her legs was as soothing as the cool breeze. Her eyelids grew heavier and heavier. She sank back to lie on the rock that still held the warmth of the setting sun, crossing her arms over her bared stomach as her shirt rode up. A handful of quiet, comfortable minutes trickled past.

A sudden splash woke her, the water cresting over her knees and soaking the rolled-up legs of her trousers. She pushed herself up with a grin. "So, finally we–"

"This was not quite what I had planned," said the surprising figure floating before her. No mermaid, after all — no, this was obviously a mer*man*. And in his arms with an unconscious woman.

A woman whose face was covered in blood.

"My name is Kaimana," he said quickly. "And she needs your help."

*~*~*

"We should not take her fully out of the water," Kaimana said.

"Why the hell not?" Harry demanded, adrenaline coursing hot through her blood, making her body demand action. "She looks half-drowned."

"She is more like me than you," he tried to explain, moving along the edge of the lagoon to a spot where he could lay her down so her legs remained submerged. "Water is a healing element. I truly believe it is the only thing that has kept her alive this long."

"Jo! Jo, the medic bag!" Harry shouted, trusting her first mate would hear. She had a captain's skill of being heard over storms and violent waves, and Jo had always had excellent hearing. "Good God, someone's cut out her tongue..."

"Stay with her, try to wake her," Kaimana said. "I have things to collect." Another splash, and he was gone.

"Can you hear me, miss? Just squeeze my hand if you can hear me. My name's Harry."

The whole crew huffed and puffed into view, Jo in the lead with the black doctor's bag.

"What the hell?"

"Where did *she* come from?"

"What's happened, Cap?"

"Not good, not good," Jo muttered, dropping to her knees on the other side of the girl, taking stock with a wince. "If we don't stop the bleeding, she won't last another ten minutes."

"How the hell do we stop bleeding like this?"

"Cauterization is the best way," Miss Euphemia said, voice shaking. "It closes the vessels and prevents infection."

"And how do you suggest we do that?" Harry snapped. "Stick a hot coal in her mouth?"

"Who did this to her?" Agnessa said, face pale. "It's barbaric."

"There're blisters in her mouth and throat, too," said Jo grimly. "Across her lips. It looks like someone made her swallow something caustic."

"And bound her wrists — see where the ropes burned her skin?" pointed out Katherine.

"That's torture," said Maddie, unusually subdued, the animation draining from her face. "Someone's tortured her."

Harry looked up sharply, alerted by the dull tone of Maddie's voice. "Mads, you look away. Breathe in and out. Lizzie, get her away from here. Now."

"Captain?" cut in Franky, looking from Maddie to Harry in alarm.

"Franky, go with them. Get her moving and talking and thinking about something else. Snap her out of it. Last thing we need right now is for Maddie to have one of her fits."

"She a berserker, boy," said Lizzie, pulling a barely responsive Maddie away. "If she breaks, she's liable to hurt us all an' herself."

"Maddie, let's go back to the fire, okay?" Franky said loudly, taking one of her hands and rubbing it bracingly. "You were gonna show me how to do that tricky knot, remember?"

"She's right, though," said Agnessa. "This girl's been tortured. By who?"

The water rippled and before Harry could give any warning Kaimana resurfaced, startling a scream from Zora, who staggered back and nearly knocked Marcella off her feet. Katherine pulled a curved dagger from her belt and started to lunge forward before Harry's arm went out and stopped her, knocking against her legs. "Peace, he's our mysterious friend. He's the one who brought her here."

"After he'd had some fun with her?" Katherine demanded, eyes narrowing.

"No. I swear I did no harm to her," Kaimana said, raising his hands in a gesture of submission. "When they threw her overboard, I pulled her to safety. I went for medicine," he continued, directing the last at Harry as he swam closer. There was a net-like bag over his tattooed shoulder. "Things to stop the bleeding."

"Don't waste any more time on talk, then," said Jo. "This girl's going to die if you don't do something now."

"Lift her head up," he instructed, pulling out a small corked bottle. "And someone else will need to steady her, because she will struggle."

"Why will she struggle?" asked Zora in a small voice.

"Because it will hurt," the merman said grimly. "But it is a necessary hurt – it will stop the bleeding."

As he poured the black liquid into the girl's mouth, her eyes flew open and focused on Harry's. Her pupils had contracted to the size of pinpricks. The dark irises, just a shade lighter than her pupils, were glazed with an agony and terror that struck Harry like a physical punch to the gut. It was a look that would linger in her thoughts and dreams for weeks.

Then the girl's body began to jerk and spasm, hands clenching and feet kicking out. A wordless scream rose up through the blood choking her, cutting the air like a razorblade. It seemed to go on for an unnatural length of time, far longer than any human could scream, an audible manifestation of all of the girl's pain and fear, emptying her body of everything.

Harry thought of the immediate aftermath of losing Aveline, of the fire in her injured arm and the despair on Jo's face when she heard the news. The sound raging from the brutalized girl was like a magnet, drawing out all of the bleakest, most painful memories inside her head. She looked over at Jo and saw the familiar face etched with a similar agony.

And then the scream ended with a sharp note of finality. The girl slumped back into Jo and Harry's arms, eyes rolling up to the whites.

"Jesus Christ preserve us," whispered Jo.

"What was that you gave her?" Harry asked, pushing past the old pain to focus on the situation at hand.

"A potion my matrons swore by," Kaimana said quietly, shoving the cork back into the half-emptied bottle. "It will stop any bleeding, even from mortal wounds. Made of jellyfish and anemone."

"Sounds like a poison," said Wilhelmina, face wooden and stoic. Behind her, Marcella and Zora were both crying, holding one another tightly. Everyone gathered was visibly upset; a couple of the women stepped away with hands over their faces and eyes bright with tears.

"It would be a poison to anything not of merkind," he said.

"She's not a mermaid," Jo said.

"No. But she is kin from the distant past."

Harry looked down at the unconscious girl. She wore a dress-like garment woven from tough green fibers – kelp, she realized – and there was a string of pearls and polished seaglass draped around her neck. The captain lifted the hand she had been holding and examined the fingers. The nail were unusually long and sharp, and the fingers themselves were–

"Webbed," Jo said aloud, looking up from the submerged feet. She reached over and brushed the girl's jet black hair back from her slightly pointed ears. "And gills behind the ears."

"She's a siren?" Katherine demanded, crouching down. "I thought sirens healed from anything short of cannon fire."

"Humans didn't do this to her, at least not

41

entirely," Harry said with conviction. "Her own kind must have done this. Another siren cut out her tongue, made her drink something corrosive."

"Yes, I believe so," said Kaimana. "I did not see and hear everything, but I think I caught enough. A sister pulled her to the railing of the ship and put her to the knife. She said it was a test of her sincerity. That it would 'seal the deal.'"

"Utterly barbaric," Wil echoed Agnessa's earlier horror. "And people say intelligent species are 'enlightened' and superior to dumb animals. I don't see the beasts of the field torturing and murdering each other out of greed."

Miss Euphemia edged closer. "We should clean the poor dear up. Bundle her up warmly now. After such pain and shock, she should be kept warm."

Harry glanced at Kaimana. "Is that alright? Or should she stay here? I confess to knowing nothing of sirens, so I defer to you on this."

"The potion has taken effect. The best thing for her now is to sleep, and this matron is right: she should be taken somewhere warm. Take this," he held out a rough box made of shells. "Put this salve on her lips and where the rope burned her wrists. And," he added as Katherine bent to gather the slim girl up in her arms. "Someone should stay with her. Many someones, if possible. She will need community when she wakes, else she may will herself to die."

"Poor chick, poor thing," Miss Euphemia murmured as she and the others followed Katherine back to the camp.

"Jo, can you please check on Maddie for me?" Harry asked.

"Are you—"

"Yes. Please, Jo. I just want a moment."

Harry sat on her heels and brushed the back of her hand across her forehead. Now that the initial shock and fear had broken her skin felt too slick and hot, as if from a bad fever. The breeze skimming inland over the ocean was chill and sharp, and she turned her shoulder to it. "You saw the ship she was on?"

"Yes."

"Did you see the name on its prow?"

"I cannot read human tongues," Kaimana said. "But I would recognize the vessel again, and some of the humans on it."

"Was there a skeleton carved on the prow? A hooded skeleton with a scythe?"

"I do not know what a scythe—"

"A curved blade on a long pole."

"Yes. This is the craft."

"Did you see a man with a patch over his left eye and a black coat? With a scar across his forehead and cheek?"

"Yes, I did. Their captain, I believe."

"Of course," Harry said quietly to herself. "Of course it was."

"You recognize this ship? You know this man?"

"I thought I knew him, up until two weeks ago when he almost shot me in the back. His name is Wrath Drew. He captains *The Charon*."

"He has a black, slick aura," Kaimana said, his

distaste audible. "Like oil over water. A contaminating force. I think he must rot everything around him, for his crew had tainted auras, too. And the siren who did this terrible thing – I saw hers darken even as she drew the blade. Evil is a corruptive influence."

"You saw all that?"

"Yes."

"Wish I could see things like that. Would make it a helluva lot easier to know who to trust and who to steer clear of." Harry paused, looking at him appraisingly for the first time in the twilight gloaming. "Is that why you've been leaving us gifts? Why you brought her here and trusted us to help her? You could see our 'auras' and knew we were decent?"

"Yes." He was returning her appraising look, utterly unabashed. Not that he had anything to be embarrassed about: he had just saved a girl's life, after all.

"I thought you were a mermaid," Harry said. "I mean, I've never seen a merman before. I've heard stories, but I thought they were just fairy tales. I didn't think your species had males."

"There are as many males as are needed," Kaimana said as if it was something that should be obvious, common knowledge. "We are not vital to a pod's health, not as matrons are, so there are fewer of us. Is this not the way with humans?"

"No, this is definitely not the way with humans. You haven't met many humans, have you?"

"You are the first I have actually spoken to," he confessed. "But I have watched many ships that

44

have sailed past."

"You speak remarkably good English."

"I was taught by my matrons. I know how to speak many human tongues – many pods have adopted human tongues, and communication is important when traveling across territory lines."

"Pods are like... tribes? Crews?"

"Yes. Like your pod." He gestured toward the camp, smiling.

"And where is your pod, Kaimana?"

His smile faltered. "Gone."

"There's no one else here? Just you?"

"Yes."

"How long have you been here by yourself?"

"I cannot be sure," he said dismissively with a shrug. "My people are not so accurate in the measuring of time. Have you enjoyed the gifts?"

"Yes, we have, thank you," Harry said, shaking her head slightly. "I'm sorry, my manners are awful."

"Well, the last gift I brought you was somewhat awful," he said. "You have every right to be upset."

"And I don't know if I ever said, but my name is Harry," she added awkwardly. "Though I'm sure you already know that, since you've been watching us."

"The one called Jo does not trust me because of that," Kaimana said. "And I am sorry to have caused her worry. But I was always warned that humans were evil. I had to be sure of you before I revealed myself."

"Kaimana, I understand completely. Plenty of

humans think the same of merfolk."

"You may call me Kai, if you wish," he said.

"Alright. Kai."

He looked to the horizon, where the moon was beginning to rise, huge and milky white. "Perhaps we could speak further in the morning? I will come to the beach, if I may, and see how the siren is doing."

"Of course."

"Thank you, Harry. This did not go as I had planned," he added dryly, echoing his first words to her. "But you cannot plan for everything."

"No, you cannot," she said, as he turned and swam away.

*~*~*

It was a subdued crew around the fire, most still shaken by what all felt would be the siren's final scream. If she survived the night after all she had been through, it would be a miracle. But Harry, usually the most doubtful of atheists, found herself daring to hope. The girl clearly had a strong will to live, else she wouldn't have lasted this long. And there had been something in her eyes, something unspoken but still eloquent, that told of a burning need.

Such fires were not easily put out.

Miss Euphemia and Agnessa had stationed themselves on either side of the siren in the tent they had converted into a hasty medical bay. While the older woman sang quietly and gently sponged away the blood on the girl's face and neck, Agnessa was smoothing the cream Kai had given them over her raw wrists.

"How could anyone do such things to someone?" Agnessa said, biting her bottom lip.

Miss Euphemia's song faltered. "Every heart has its share of darkness," she said after a pause. "Some hearts carry more than others, and those hearts crack easily, spilling out the darkness until it festers. The people that do these things, child, do them because they've rotted inside like a sick tree. They're hollow, and they like to fill that hollowness with someone else's suffering. Some say they only kill and maim for profit, but that's a lie. It's because they're hollow and dead inside. Greed's just another word for the darkness."

She squeezed the sponge in her wrinkled hand, watching the red water drip into the bowl dispassionately. Then she looked back at the slack, unconscious face between them. The almond-shaped eyes, the skin that had a touch of gold to mellow the sharp planes of her cheeks and chin. "My, but she's a beauty," she said softly. "Almost as beautiful as my girl was. Skin just as smooth."

"You have a daughter, Miss Euphemia?"

"Had, dear. Esther. Died of a fever when she was eighteen. I sat like this by her for a week. Until the Lord reached down and took her by the hand." She brushed back the inky hair plastered to the siren's forehead. "I wonder what her name is."

"She can't tell us. She'll — she'll never speak again," Agnessa said.

"There are other ways of telling a body something," said Miss Euphemia. "If she hasn't the knowing of writing, I'll teach her. Just like I taught Maddie."

"What should we call her until then?"

"I'll leave that to you, dear." She picked up the thread of her song, humming the melody as she washed the still face clean.

"Silence," Agnessa said finally, tending to her blistered lips. "Because sometimes a woman's silence can speak volumes."

*~*~*

The next morning, Harry set off down the beach at dawn. She had explained everything to the others before retiring, and they would follow in their own time. For now, she was hoping for a few more minutes alone with Kai to properly get her bearings. And she had set out so early in the hopes of beating him to the rendezvous.

But he was already waiting for her at the tide line. He was stretched out in the shallows, arms crossed behind his head and eyes closed against the sun. She slowed her pace, taken aback by the sight of him in full light. He seemed larger than the night before, and this was her first real glimpse of his tail: vibrantly scaled in blue, gold, and green. The scales mostly ended where a human's waist began, but it wasn't a strict line delineating fish from man; there was still a faint smattering of blue and green scales across his stomach and up his sides, a few dotting his arms the way freckles spotted human skin.

His unscaled skin was a tawny brown and liberally marked with black tattoos: small triangles covered his left arm from elbow to wrist in a repetitive pattern that mimicked the scales of his tail, and there were whorls and spirals over his shoulders. His hair was long and dark, small braids visible in the tangled loose mass, and he had a short beard and mustache. A white scar bisected one thick eyebrow and he wore several necklaces; some were metal chains and others of braided rope, from which hung a number of carved shells and animal teeth.

"I promise I will not bite," he said suddenly, lifting one eyelid and arching the scarred eyebrow.

"I know," Harry said quickly, trying not to look as though he had startled her. She bridged the last few feet between them and dropped down into a casual cross-legged seat. "The siren made it through the night. Miss Euphemia and Agnessa say it looks like she'll pull through – she woke up once, drank some water, and went right back to sleep."

"Sleep is good. The best medicine for her." He pushed himself up and picked up his net bag, which Harry hadn't even noticed lying beside him. "Though I do bring more medicines. This will help with the pain, and this with the burns in her throat and mouth. Tell me when she needs more of either – or I could show one of you how to make them. They are not hard to brew. After a couple of days she should be able to eat solid food again."

"You know a lot about treating these kinds of injuries?" Harry said.

"Yes," he replied calmly. "When merfolk go to war, they aim for the throat and tongues as often as the fins. Taking away our fins is a killing blow, but taking away our songs cripples us. Such tactics are often used to incite fear and punish acts of rebellion. The liquid the siren was forced to drink was probably coral snake venom and crushed lionfish barbs — such a potion will not kill us, but it does scar the throat forever."

"And artists think your people are sweet and romantic," Harry said.

"We are that, too," he said, suddenly breaking into a huge smile. How did he get his teeth so white? Maybe merfolk chewed on coral the way humans rubbed their teeth clean... "I see that your ship's repairs have been completed."

"Yes. I suspect you're partially to thank for that."

"Only partially. Does this mean you will be leaving soon?"

"Do you want us to leave?"

"No, I do not," he said readily. Harry was beginning to wonder if it was actually impossible for him to lie or dissemble. He'd be terrible at cards. "I was hoping you would stay for some time. This is a beautiful place, is it not? There is still a lot I could show you."

"Did you get *any* sleep last night?" Jo's voice interjected. Harry turned to see most of the crew approaching, Maddie yawning and rubbing her eyes.

"Don't mother hen me so much, woman," Harry replied.

"I wouldn't have to if you'd stop acting like such an impatient child," came the sharp retort. "So you're Kai."

"Yes."

"And you've been spying on us since we got here?"

"Yes."

"And after watching us for two weeks you left a shiny sword for Harry?"

"Yes."

"What were you *thinking*, man?" Jo demanded, sitting down beside her captain. "It should only take a glance to see that this woman has poor impulse control. And you hand her an even longer, sharper sword than the one she already had. That's like giving a pair of scissors to a five-year-old boy and challenging him to a race. Just begging for trouble."

"Those are mutinous words, Josephine Duveau."

"You just try to challenge me to a duel, missy, and I'll tan your backside with the flat of my blade."

"Do you *want* to spark insubordination in the ranks? When a crew hears its first mate talk back to their captain in such a fashion—"

"You saved Silence yesterday," Maddie said, looking at Kai. "First from drowning, then from bleeding to death. Thank you."

"Silence?"

"That's what we're gonna call her, until Miss Euphemia can teach her how to write and she can tell us her real name."

"A fitting name," he said.

"So what were you two discussing so earnestly?" Jo demanded.

"Whether we'd be leaving soon or not. Kai wants us to stay a while longer."

"Oh, Kai does, does he?"

"And I had actually decided, before the madness last night, to suggest that we make this place a regular berth. Take some of that treasure, stock up on supplies, and make a couple permanent fixtures on the beach and the ridge. I was gonna put it to a vote."

"That would be alright with you?" Agnessa asked Kai. "You'd give us permission for that?"

"Yes, but why must I give permission?" The merman was visibly confused.

"Because this is *your* island?" said Katherine.

"I do not own it. It is an island — it cannot be owned by anyone. It is part of my territory, yes, but I gave you permission to stay here long ago. The gifts," he explained. "And if I am to be a part of your pod, obviously this territory is now yours as well."

"Part of our pod?" Maddie said.

"He means our crew," clarified Harry.

"So you want to join the crew, too?" said Zora. "That may be a little tricky."

"Owning a pair of legs isn't a requirement to sail with *The Sappho*," said Harry.

"Or a womb," chimed in Franky. "I vote to let him join up — it'd be nice to have another bloke to talk to."

"But it would be a bit awkward, wouldn't it?" said Zora. "He can't exactly help out when we're boarding another ship or in the middle of a fight."

"Plenty of other pirates have deals with merfolk," Wil pointed out. "They can get up to enemy craft without being seen and pick up information, sabotage hulls, scout ahead for naval ships and dangerous reefs..."

"We all have our specific jobs," said Agnessa. "Zora, the Captain doesn't tell you to steer the ship because that's my job. Wilhelmina isn't expected to scale the mast and serve as lookout in the crow's nest because of her leg, so she works in the galley instead. Katherine mans the cannons rather than Miss Euphemia because Katherine's the strongest. So on and so forth. So why can't a merman be part of the crew in a way that best suits him?"

"Perfectly put, Nessa," Harry smiled. "From the way I see it, Kai's already proven himself a helpful addition. That gold you all have been so pleased about? Wouldn't be in your pockets if not for him. And that girl would be dead if he hadn't brought her here."

A chorus of nods and murmurs of agreements met her words.

"So we put it to a vote: all in favor of giving the merman a chance, raise your hand."

It looked unanimous – and then Katherine stepped out of the group.

"I'll say yea on one condition," she said solemnly, arms crossed over her ample chest as she stared down at a wide-eyed Kai.

"Yes?"

"You give me a tattoo like that one," she pointed at a tentacle-like swirl over his shoulder, made entirely of dozens of tiny dots.

"When would you like it done?"

"I'm free now," she said. "And I'd like it right

here." She lifted up her shirt, eliciting a splutter of laughter from Maddie and grins all around.

"I'll go find a few urchins," Kai said, unfazed, rolling over and into the water.

"Oh yes, I like him," said Franky. "Didn't even bat an eye!"

"A shame he has a fish bottom," Katherine said thoughtfully. "He's a very handsome top half."

"You really *are* desperate, aren't you?" scoffed Zora. "Cap'n, when are we sailing?"

"Dawn tomorrow. That should get us to Bogo in three days, if the wind fares well. But I'll need a volunteer or two to stay behind and look after the siren."

"Silence, Cap. We're calling her Silence."

"Silence, then. She can't be moved, and we can't leave her alone."

"I'm sure Miss Euphemia will want to stay with her," said Agnessa, speaking on her behalf. The old woman hadn't left the tent all night, not even once.

"I'll stay," said Wil. "I'd like to keep studying some of the plant life, anyway."

"And I'll stay," Maddie volunteered, only a second before Franky offered, "Me, too."

*They're becoming a right terrible twosome,* thought Harry privately. "Thank you. Mads, I'll pick you out a nice hat, alright? Franky, Wil, if there's anything you need, just say the word. And, Kai," Harry turned as he slid back out of the water, several spiny sea urchins protruding from the bag over his shoulder. "Would you stay close to the beach while the rest of us are gone, in case they need you or your medicines?"

"Of course," he agreed readily. "Now, Katherine." He pulled an urchin free of the netting, breaking a needle-like spine from it. "Which one would you like the design on? The right or the left?"

"Surprise me," she grinned, pulling her shirt off completely and sitting down before him amidst peals of laughter.

# RETURNING THE FAVOR

A shape loomed out of the darkness. Franky looked up sharply, arms full of wood, then relaxed with a whistle, shoulders slumping. "Oh, Cap, you startled me."

"Apologies, lad. Just wanted a word before we head out tomorrow on the supply run. And I've had the Devil's own time getting you away from your lady."

"Maddie's her own lady," Franky said, bending to pick up another fallen branch.

"I've no issue with it," Harry said. "So long as you treat her right and don't get her in the family way, anyhow."

"Hope's helping us with that," the boy said, utterly unruffled, as calm as if they were talking the price of silk. "What's on your mind, Cap?"

"I wanted to let you know I've made a decision about your status on the crew. I know I said you'd get three months probation, but I've made up my mind."

Franky straightened and met her pale gaze. "And?"

"You've a place on *The Sappho* as long as you want it, Franky. I've no lingering doubts about your abilities or loyalty. How could I, after you saved my life?"

The boy smiled wanly and adjusted his hold on the firewood. "Thank you, Cap."

"Don't thank me; I'm the one who owes you a

life debt. I've been waiting for you to mention it to the others, to brag — it's well worth bragging about, and you earned the right to — but you haven't said a word. Besides Jo, I don't think anyone else even saw what you did..."

*~*~*

It had just begun to rain. The wind was picking up, promising a proper typhoon, but Maddie had sighted *The Charon's* distinctive black sails at the rendezvous location. Captain Drew was signaling for them despite the turn in the weather, and it would have gone against Harry's nature to ignore it. So they had pulled up alongside the larger boat.

"Talk fast, Wrath!" Harry had shouted across. "We'll both of us have to run hard if we want to outpace this storm!"

"I have news, Harry," the pirate with the jewel-studded eyepatch said. "News of a certain mermaid tribe. The ones you've been lookin' for."

Harry hurried to the railing, Jo at her shoulder. They crowded Franky, who had been securing a loose rope. "Where, Wrath?" Harry demanded, face bright and sharp.

"I've even talked with their leader. I told them your story. Asked them if they'd make a deal."

"Was she there, Wrath? Did you see her?"

"She's there," he'd shouted, and Harry sagged against the railing, overcome by some powerful emotion.

"What are their terms?"

"Rather good ones," the other pirate said. And then he'd pulled out a pistol.

Franky moved out of pure instinct, reacting before his brain could even think. He'd grabbed Harry's arm and pulled her down just as the pistol fired with a blast of sparks and sulfuric smoke. The shot had roared overhead and Franky could've sworn he felt its passage by his shoulder.

Jo screamed to Agnessa, Wrath Drew bellowed a command, and *The Sappho* bucked away like a frightened gelding as the boom of cannon-fire filled the torrential air.

And they had sailed straight into the storm-swept reefs.

*~*~*

"You don't owe me a thing, Cap," Franky said quietly. When he closed his eyes, he could still hear the crack of the gun. "You saved my life, so I returned the favor. Besides – I would've done the same for anyone."

"Regardless," Harry said firmly. "I won't forget it."

"Cap?"

"Hmm?"

"What was that bastard talking about? The mermaids, the woman you were looking for?"

Harry paused, silhouetted by the flickering light of the campfire down the beach. "I'll tell you the whole story when we get back, Franky. You've earned the right to hear it."

# SILENCE

She dreamed of cold, unfeeling eyes.

From the moment she had first seen Wrath Drew, Echo had been glad that only one of his eyes remained. The look there was something she loathed to see from one eye, let alone two. She'd turned to her sister, intent on asking what in the seven seas she'd been thinking – to form an alliance with a group of sailors was one thing, but to work with those who would as easily betray as smile?

But Aria's expression had matched Wrath's, and fear had shot through her. Echo had opened her mouth to Command them, to order them to back away and let her leave, but Aria had recognized her intention – just the day prior, hadn't she laughed about how the two of them might as well reside in one mind, one heart? – and had struck.

Never in her life would she have dreamed that such pain was possible, let alone that her sister would willingly put her through it.

Echo sat up, *feeling* the blood pooling in her mouth again, and flailed uselessly at the arms that held her.

She heard someone curse, the voice a far cry from her sister's high, sweet sound, and reality crept its way back in.

She was on a cot in the humans' ship. The old woman, the one who had barely left her side – Euphemia, she'd said repeatedly, pointing at herself

– had her teeth bared in a grimace as she clutched tight to her arm.

She had hurt her.

Echo sat up, patting at Euphemia's arm worriedly, asking silently to see the injury.

"It's all right, Silence," Euphemia said. "Gotten worse from the ship's cat."

*Silence.* Yes, that was her name now. Trying to argue, all she got out was a strangled squeak. Euphemia relented, holding out her arm. Silence inspected the slash. Made by one of her fingernails – at least she hadn't tried to bite in the midst of her delirium. She pressed one palm to either side of it.

"What are–" Euphemia began, and then she paused, gaping down at her arm, as she watched the torn skin knit back together.

Silence winced as the pain from the scratch transferred to her own arm. She unconsciously rubbed at the spot, and Euphemia watched the gesture with sharp eyes.

"Did you feel that?" she asked, and Silence nodded.

"Remarkable," Euphemia said. "Wait until I tell Wil; she's fascinated by all the differences between yourself and the merfolk."

Wil, Silence thought. And all the others on the ship. That was how she could repay them; most likely why they'd rescued her in the first place.

She got to her feet, wobbly at first but her pace grew steadier as she left the room and wandered down the hallway. Euphemia stayed close behind her, starting to ask what she was doing and then trailing off, as if just then remembering that

Silence couldn't answer.

Silence came out on deck into the sunlight, blinking in the sudden brightness and wondering precisely how long she'd been asleep.

That was something to concern herself with later, she decided. Right now, she had favors to repay.

Right away, she caught sight of a tall, brown-skinned woman with a shaved bald head, who had a bandage wrapped around her left arm. Silence hurried up to her, resting a hand on the bandage. A cut, she realized a moment later when the pain came through to her own skin; probably one sustained in a sparring match. True fights rarely let their opponents go so easily.

"What did ya—" the woman asked, looking stunned. Silence gave her a smile in answer, regretting it instantly as the motion pulled at her sore lips. She hurried away, searching the others' faces and bodies until she caught sight of a tiny woman who was holding the helm with only one hand. The other hand she held gingerly at her side.

*Rope burn*, Silence thought, as she grabbed the young woman's shoulder.

"How did — Captain!" the helmswoman yelled. "Cap, you have to come see this! The siren's up!"

A blond woman with the sleeves of her white shirt rolled up to the elbow strode forward, inspecting her closely. "You sure you're ready to be up and around?" she asked. "Still look wobbly to me."

Silence nodded.

"Quite a talent, Cap'n," the black woman said, holding the now-useless bandage that had been on her arm. "Heard tales 'bout how sirens could heal from most any wound, but I didna know they could heal others. Look at my arm."

"Quite a boon," Harry observed. "Thank you, Lady Silence."

Silence nodded distractedly, her focus on the wide, thick scar on the Captain's arm. She pointed to it and then grabbed her hand, surprised when the Captain yanked away from her.

The siren retreated, afraid that she'd offended her somehow. Granted, such an old injury would take longer to heal, but it could be done–

"It's all right," the Captain said, rubbing at the scar. "This... this one I want to keep, that's all."

Silence tilted her head curiously, unsure as to why anyone would *want* to retain a reminder of something that must've hurt like death. But it wasn't her business, and given the look on the Captain's face, she wasn't inclined to explain.

Not that it mattered, she thought. Right now, the main thing that mattered was getting something to eat. Looking around at the faces of the crew, she was fading from seeing people she wanted to thank, to seeing people who would restore her energy quite nicely.

Dangerous path, Silence thought. She needed to get back to the ocean, find a large fish or an octopus; something big enough to assuage her appetite. Perhaps she would come back, just to let these people know that she truly was well. They had tended to her when leaving her for dead would have been perfectly reasonable, even going so far as to bring in jugs of sea water to the small room where she'd been kept, rubbing down her wrists and arms, leaving a damp cloth on her forehead to keep her connected to her ocean.

Yes, she decided. She'd come back, and heal them when need be. The sea was a dangerous place; she would make sure to the best of her ability that this ship remained safe.

Giving a quick nod of thanks, she turned and dove over the side.

The instant Silence submerged, everything went red. She felt the chemical burning away at her tongue, saw her blood surrounding her in the water as she opened her mouth in a soundless scream. Salt water mixed with the potion Aria had forced her to drink, and tears fled from her eyes as she struggled to swim but couldn't, couldn't remember anything, there was just the crimson water and she was drowning, choking on her own blood—

Then arms wrapped around her midsection and she grabbed hold of them, scratching and trying to pull them away as they both broke through the surface.

"Enough," Kai said. "You're safe. It is all right, little sister."

Some part of her recognized him, but a stronger part still tasted blood, and she snarled at him as he lifted her into the landing craft. The rough wood at her back was the furthest thing from the enveloping water, and some semblance of where she was finally came back to her mind.

Along with that came the realization of what

she had just done, and she quickly reached out, intent on healing the cuts she'd inflicted on his arms.

He shook his head, pulling back from her as much as the small craft would allow. "Don't," he said. "You need your strength."

But she didn't, she thought. What would she do with that strength? What had she ever done? Didn't any of them understand what she had done to countless people just like them? Why were they helping her now, if not to take advantage of her healing powers?

Suddenly unsure of her position on the vessel, she curled up in the corner of the landing craft, closing her eyes tightly against everything.

Silence knew it was foolish, but all she wanted was for her sister to hold her close again. She was already a siren with no voice; now she knew she could no longer even seek the refuge of the sea.

What use was she?

# THE GRAND TOUR

Silence had been on board for several days, but everyone was still on edge about it – including the siren. She hid herself away in the darkest corner of Miss Euphemia's cabin and stared out with bright, almost luminous eyes whenever someone approached her. She seemed to understand that they meant her no harm, that they had, in fact, been instrumental in saving her life, but she remained skittish and wary.

"All wounded, frightened things want to hide away," said Wil. "It's a natural preservation instinct to find a defensible position and go to ground until the pain goes away."

"She's not an animal," Maddie protested.

"Yes, she is," countered Wil. "And so are we. Humans, sirens, merfolk – we're all animals, like imps and fish and sheep. We just happen to have more sophisticated ways of communicating and more complex social rituals."

"When you get all intellectual like that you sound like a ponce," Maddie said in frustration. "Miss Euphemia, can I take her her supper?"

"Of course, dear. But don't crowd her. She'll come out in her own time."

A plate of diced, raw fish in one hand and a bottle of one of Kai's potions tucked under her arm, Maddie carefully climbed the ladder out of the galley and made her away across the darkened, quiet deck. Marcella was keeping watch up in the crow's nest; Maddie could hear the plaintive whistle of her bone flute. The girl knocked softly before unlatching the cabin's door, to give the siren fair warning before she pushed it open with her foot.

To Maddie's surprise, Silence wasn't hiding in her usual corner; instead, she was sitting on the bed, back pressed to the wall and knees drawn up under her chin. She also wasn't alone. Zora was sitting in a chair, legs tucked beneath her and hands frozen in mid-gesture.

"Hullo," Maddie said, stepping inside and nudging the door closed behind her. "Am I interrupting?"

"I've been trying to teach her signing," Zora explained.

"Signing?"

"Talking with your hands. My older sister is deaf and mute – I thought it would be helpful for Silence. Learning how to sign is a lot easier than learning how to write, I always thought, and Kai says some merfolk communicate this way."

"And how's it going?"

"Silence," Zora said slowly, making the corresponding gestures with her hands. "This is Maddie. She is nice. She brought you fish for supper. Are you hungry?"

The siren stared for a long moment, eyes flicking from Zora to Maddie. Then she hesitantly lifted her fine-boned, webbed hands. *Yes. Hungry.*

"She's clever as a cat," Zora said, pleased and proud.

"Here you go, Silence," Maddie said, holding out the plate. "It's tuna, just caught today, and I made sure no one cooked it this time. And this is one of Kai's drinks, for your throat. To make it feel better."

"Medicine for your mouth," Zora signed/ said. "From Kai."

*Kai*, Silence signed. *Maddie. Thank.*

She turned away as she ate, for which Maddie was privately grateful. She had seen how sharp and serrated her teeth were, and knew how awkward eating solid food had to be for her now. When the plate was clean and the bottle empty, Silence turned back to look at Maddie with her huge, expressive dark eyes.

*Maddie. Thank.*

"You're welcome. I'm glad you're feeling better, Silence."

The siren looked around the cabin. Pointed at Miss Euphemia's much-holed parasol.

"Do you want to know where Miss Euphemia is?" Maddie asked.

Silence nodded.

"She's in the galley with the others, finishing supper. I could take you to her if you like."

Silence looked apprehensive at such a suggestion.

"You don't want to see so many people at once?" Zora asked quietly, making the gesture for *too many*.

Silence nodded firmly.

"Alright. Then how about I give you a tour of the ship instead? The others are bound to have a bit of a tipple while they discuss tomorrow's course. Everything else will be quiet and empty for a while."

She hesitated, then nodded.

"Well, first things first," Maddie said with a smile. She was often tasked with giving new crewmates the Grand Tour, and she liked to do the thing properly. "This that we're in is the captain's quarters. See, Cap'n Harry used to sleep in here, back when she and Jo first got the ship, but the crew was a lot smaller back then. And when Miss Euphemia joined up, Harry immediately gave this to her. As the official ship's scribe and teacher, she needed all the built-in-bookcases, see? And there's her little desk, which is nailed to the floor so even in rough seas it doesn't get toppled, and there are little secured containers for all of her inks and quills and parchment. And Miss Euphemia being a bit older and frailer, she needed the bigger, nicer bed with a real feather mattress. Sometimes this is also the sick bay, because there's space for another cot, like the one we put here for you."

Maddie set the plate and bottle down on the desk and opened the door, urging Silence to follow her. The siren carefully unfolded her long, elegant limbs and crept after her, nearly hugging the wall.

In the evening darkness, the moon hidden behind a large cloud bank, the still and empty deck of the ship looked positively ghostly. Water slapped rhythmically against the hull. The sails fluttered quietly, half-furled for the night, and the looser bits of rigging swayed pendulum-like in the breeze.

"The crow's nest is up there," Maddie pointed up the huge main mast. Silence craned her pale neck to follow the gesturing finger. "That's usually my spot when we're sailing. I've got the best long-sight of anybody, so I usually see other ships and reefs way before anyone else. It's my job to keep a lookout and shout down anything approaching. Are you afraid of heights?"

Silence shook her head.

"That's good. That's a good skill to have when you sail on a big masted ship like this 'un. Maybe tomorrow you can come up to the nest with me and see what you think. The whole world looks different up that high, and I've made the nest into a cozy little nook. That's the big wheel that steers the boat; this little platform here is Agnessa's domain. You know which one Agnessa is?"

Nod.

"She's a tiny thing but up here she's a *queen*. She tells *The Sappho* what to do and she does it, no questions or arguments. I tried to turn this wheel once and it fought me like the Devil himself, but Agnessa knows just how to manage it. It's like magic. Right beneath us is the gun deck; it's a sorta half-deck where we keep the cannons. If you look over the railing right here, you can see the holes they fire from. I don't really like cannons. They're too loud and their smoke burns my nose. But every pirate ship's gotta have 'em, and they're Katherine's responsibility."

Silence made a sudden, unexpected gesture, stretching her hands high above her head and balancing on the tips of her bare toes. Maddie laughed. "Yeah, that's Katherine. She's the giant with all the tattoos. She could probably pick up one of these cannons all on her own. Don't let her size frighten you, though. She's really a big mama bear.

And this little room is where we keep all the messy, smelly things, like the tar and pitch and lime. The main hatch, over there," Maddie pointed down the deck, "leads straight into the galley. And the big hatch in the middle near the mast goes into the cargo hold. But this one, here, goes down into the sleeping quarters." The girl lifted the wooden door and started down the steps, confident of her footing even in the darkness. Silence followed slowly and carefully, a hand pressed to the wall.

Her eyes really *did* glint in the dark, Maddie saw. Red like a crocodile's. It was a little unnerving, but she rallied quickly.

"Most ships, the crew just sleeps in the cargo hold, in little hammocks strung out above the crates and casks. But Harry doesn't like hammocks — she calls them 'infernal torture devices' and 'a waste of perfectly good rope'. So instead we've got this," Maddie said, striking a match and lighting a nearby oil lamp, illuminating a very strange room. Built into the walls on either side were several niche beds, stacked on top of one another, the higher niches accessible by fixed ladders. In the middle of the wide room were two more ascending frames of similar beds, unusual pillars stretching from floor to ceiling. Each bed was just big enough for one person to lie down and roll over comfortably, but not spacious enough for anyone to sit up straight. Then again, this was a space solely intended for sleeping, meant for people who had plenty of space to be active during the day. By evening, all they wanted to do in here was close their eyes.

"See that bottom bed in the middle?" Maddie said with a grin, pointing. It ran nearly the full length of the room where the other beds only took up half the space, and had more headroom than the others. "That's Katherine's. She had to have the bottom one because she sleepwalks.

"This next little room is Hope's workroom. She needed her own space for all of her bunkum. Hope's a fortune teller and a witch," Maddie said in a secretive undertone.

The glorified closet smelled strongly of incense. A delicate mobile of red paper lanterns and silver bells dangled from the ceiling. Runes and Chinese characters had been painted around the door frames in white and a plush satin pillow took up most of the floor space. "She doesn't like anyone coming in here, so we'll just hurry through. She's got all these little drawers in the walls for her spices and magic ingredients, and that scroll there shows all the phases of the moon and the names of the important stars. Hope can read palms and chicken bones, and tell you your future just based on the planets. She's always carving little charms out of seashells and she only wears red, because red is supposed to be lucky and ward off evil. Hope's really big on warding off evil," Maddie added. "So don't be alarmed if you see her making the sign of the evil eye or chanting foreign lingo or if she tells you to turn around three times before throwing a cup of tea over your shoulder or something. She's always like that."

Maddie opened the next door and there was a sudden sense of great space. "This is the cargo hold – Jo calls it 'the belly of the beast'. It's pretty empty right now, since we just unloaded all of those supplies and things on the island. But we've always got the big casks of water and ale; that's the most important thing, not to run out of either of those when you're sailing. You can go a lot of days without food, but not very long without water or ale. Do you drink ale?"

Silence made a confused, questioning gesture.

"Ale's like beer? It's mostly water but it's got other things in it, too. Alcohol and herbs and that. It fills you up in a way water doesn't, and it can be safer to drink. Sometimes water goes bad, you know? Makes you sick? Wil says all sorts of swimmy invisible things live in water – when she told me that, I didn't drink water for a *week*. But because ale has alcohol in it, it's safer. Apparently. Though if you drink too much ale, you can get sick, too. Just a different kind of sick. It's confusing, I know.

"And over here's where we put all of Lizzie's big tools. This thing's called a lathe, and that's a press, and she's even got an anvil. Lizzie's family have been smiths for a couple generations – when her Pap died, she inherited all of his things and signed on with us. It's been real handy having her on board, cause smiths make all sorts of things: wheels and horseshoes and weapons. She repairs swords when they get bent or chipped, and rigged up that pulley system for the lifeboat so Kai can haul himself onboard whenever he wants."

Silence turned and was greeted by a wall full of knives and strange implements. She stepped away sharply, the back of her legs striking a long table bolted to the floor.

"Oh, it's okay, don't worry," Maddie said quickly. "That's all Marcella's stuff. She's our seamstress? She tans leather and turns animal skins into felt. Those big needles are for repairing sails and making holes in leather belts. She's even taught herself how to make boots and hats, though they're not very fashionable looking yet."

A burst of raucous laughter echoed into the mostly empty space. The two turned to the last door. Lamplight was gleaming through the cracks and edges.

"That's the galley," Maddie said. "Sounds like someone's telling a story — and sounds like Harry let them open a cask of rum. I can show you that later tonight, once everyone's asleep, if you want. It's where we keep all the food. That's Wil's domain. She's our cook."

Silence put a hand to her leg.

"Yeah, that's right, she's the one with the wooden leg. Once you're feeling better, she'll probably have all sorts of questions for you. Not many people get the chance to talk properly to a siren."

Silence's hand rose to her throat.

"Well, maybe not actually *talk*," Maddie amended quickly, flushing. "Sorry. I don't think a lot before I speak."

Silence put one hand over the other and made a wiping gesture. Then pressed a palm to her chest, over her heart.

"Does that mean 'it's alright'?"

Silence nodded.

"Thanks. Do you want to go back to the cabin now?"

The siren hesitated, glancing at the last door. Then she pointed, face pale and eyes wide but determined.

"You want to go ahead into the galley? Are you sure?"

Nod.

"Alright." Maddie knocked firmly at the door before cracking it open. "It's Mads. I'm bringing Silence in — she wants to see the galley."

The burble of conversation promptly ceased. As Silence stepped into the room, she fought to swallow her rising panic as multiple eyes fixed upon her.

"Don't gawp at the child," Miss Euphemia said, breaking the tension with her raspy yet kind voice. "Being stared at by you lot would give anyone the collywobbles. Hello, dear. Feeling better? I'm glad you've come down to see us."

Silence moved quickly to the old woman in the lace-fringed dress, reaching out an unsteady hand. Miss Euphemia took it with a warm smile, patting the back of it. "There, there, it's alright."

The conversation picked up again, some turning away so the siren no longer felt like the center of attention. The sole male in the crew, Franky, still stared openly at her — but no, perhaps his focus was more on Maddie next to her.

Silence could smell the pheromones

between them. They must be a pair bond. And the one called Wil was looking at her with open curiosity, but it wasn't threatening; it felt more like when a youngling sees something new for the first time and sizes it up. She was also sitting with her hands in plain view, laid flat over her knees, which was reassuring. Silence wondered if she understood and was doing that on purpose.

Now that her heart wasn't thrumming so painfully in her chest, she found herself admiring the long, crowded room. There was a metal thing built into the wall that exuded heat, and heavy pots and baskets full of leafy vegetables hanging from the ceiling. A giant cauldron sat in the corner, and boxes and bags and casks were stacked everywhere, giving off a number of interesting and strange smells. There was even a large cask in the corner from which a small lemon tree was growing – Silence looked up and saw that there was a latticed hatch above it that could be thrown open during the day, so the plant could get enough sunlight.

The crew was gathered around two long trestle tables, sitting on benches bolted into the floor, and there were wooden plates, cups, and metal cutlery spread before them. It must have been a very large tuna to feed everyone, though they had eaten their servings cooked and rubbed with spices.

"Would you like anything, dear?" Miss Euphemia asked.

Silence looked at her with wide, questioning eyes.

"Anything else to eat or drink?" she said.

She shook her head. Most of the smells here were interesting but unappetizing to her. She had been content with her raw fish – would have been more content had she caught it herself, but she was learning to make adjustments.

"Did Maddie give you the grand tour?"

She nodded, the edges of her lips curling up. The blisters were almost completely healed: the smile didn't even hurt.

"Maddie's a good girl, isn't she? She likes to feel useful and help people. You ever need anything, you can always ask her."

Someone slid down the bench towards them. "How's the patient doing tonight?"

Silence stared at Jo, with her solemn dark face and many narrow braids, and felt a little flip in her stomach. She ducked her head shyly, pressing a palm to her chest.

"I think that means she's doing well," said Miss Euphemia. "Did Zora show you that?"

Nod.

"I didn't know Zora knew signing," said Jo in surprise.

"Zora has some unplumbed depths, Josephine. She has a deaf sister back home. Got a little too into her cups a few shore leaves back and mentioned it to me. You know how to sign?"

"A little. You pick up things at ports. I'm glad you came to see us, Silence," Jo said, making the accompanying gestures. The sign for her new name was the first two fingers of the right hand pressed to the lips.

Jo had very full lips, Silence noticed breathlessly.

"Franky, Maddie, Lizzie, you're on dish-washing detail tonight," Harry announced. "Everyone off to the bunks. Jo, can you go relieve Marcella?"

"Aye," a chorus of agreement sounded out. Maddie flashed a grin at Silence before she started gathering up plates and forks.

"How about we go over your letters before bed, hmm?" Miss Euphemia asked, leading Silence up the ladder. "You're doing very well." The old woman noticed how the siren's eyes followed Jo as she started up the main mast, hands and feet moving smoothly and surely over the grips despite the darkness. "You like Jo, don't you, dear?"

Silence nodded.

The old woman smiled. "She's a fine lady, our first mate. There are worse folks to set your cap on. Just... don't let your hopes get too high." At Silence's glance, Miss Euphemia sighed and patted her arm. "Her heart broke a long time ago, and I don't think it's ever really healed. First love can be like that sometimes. You just never truly recover from it."

# FIRST LOVE

"*Cherie*, I simply do not understand this sudden attitude," Francoise Duveau said sharply, dropping another stack of plates into the steaming sink. "You have grown up with the Roberts sisters – you have always been friends!"

"Aveline's not the same girl she used to be," Jo said stubbornly, plunging her arms into the scalding water and attacking the dishes with a coarse cloth. "Ever since she went to study with that tutor she has airs and graces."

"Why shouldn't she? Aveline is a remarkably pretty, talented girl," the mulish teen's mother persisted. "That voice of hers will take her into very fine society, and she should have the manners and training to match."

"If she's so fine then why is she singing here? Shouldn't she be gallivanting off to London to croon for royalty instead of wasting time here with our sailors and drunks?"

"Josephine Marguerite, envy can be a very ugly thing."

Jo dropped a fork with a clatter and stared at her mother through the steam. Francoise would never be able to shake off her military bearing or commanding tone; she would always be a little too imperious to be a maternal figure who encouraged shared confidences. "I'm not envious of her, *mere*."

"You're not? You tell me you don't begrudge Aveline her new refinement and graceful manners?

You don't wish you had pretty dresses like her? You're not jealous of her aspirations to travel to great cities and sing for exalted audiences?"

"No," Jo said firmly, setting her shoulders and resuming her scullery work. "I just don't think she belongs here any more, and I wish she would leave already, if she's so eager to go. I don't want to see her singing for coppers if she's so convinced she's worth gold."

"What singularly odd pride you have, *ma fille*," Francoise sighed. "Three years ago you wept bitterly when she left. Now that she's come home you run out of the room the moment she steps into it. I do not understand you."

"I don't understand me, either," Jo muttered to herself as her mother left the kitchen to tend to a sudden outburst of shouting at the bar.

When Aveline had left to study with Madame Rochelle, watching her go had made Jo's heart feel as if it was splitting in two. In the three years since her departure, she had felt like half a person; as if she was simply going through the motions and surviving on ill-formed hope. She had not tried to stop her, because she knew what singing meant to her.

When Aveline wrote to say she was coming home, it had been like a window opening onto a sunny spring day after a long, dreary winter. She had counted down the days with anticipation.

And then the carriage had stopped in front of the pub and a tall, lissome girl crowned with a golden braid, dressed in red silk, and carrying a large traveling bag had hopped down. When Aveline had left at fourteen, she had been gawky and coltish. Now seventeen, she had the grace of a noble. The sweetness of her face had sharpened into solid beauty and the blue of her eyes had darkened to a sapphire tone.

The girl had come home a queen, and Jo felt like a vulgar peasant with her work-roughened hands, muscular arms, and penchant for breeches. Aveline had gone out into the world, had seen what lay beyond their little harbor village, and now when she looked at this place and its people she must see how small and grubby they all were.

How could Josephine Duveau ever compete with the glitter of London, Vienna, Prague, Venice?

It had been two weeks since Aveline had returned, and in those two weeks Jo had managed to spend only a handful of minutes with her each day. She used work as an excuse; claimed there were too many dishes to wash, trips to the market that had to be made, floors in need of sweeping. Anything to avoid a pitying or indifferent glance from the girl who had meant the world to her, and now had the world on a platter.

Jo had seen some of the letters addressed to Aveline – the postman often left everything meant for the street at the pub, where anyone could come and pick out their particular envelopes at their leisure – and had noticed the far-flung and exotic postmarks. Aveline had made a reputation in the public performances she had given just prior to coming home; tales of her angelic voice and equally angelic face had apparently spread to the very ends of the earth.

A lot of the letters were embossed with gold or silver gilt, with the initials H.R.H.

With a shoulder shaking sigh, Jo rinsed the last dish and set it on top of the towering stack. She scrubbed her hands dry on a towel, noting how odd her calluses looked now they were waterlogged and pruned, and ducked into the large pantry where the vegetables, dried meats, and preserves were kept. Her mother wanted to make five pies for the supper crowd and she wasn't entirely sure they had enough bottled peaches or cinnamon for that much filling—

"So this is where you're hiding today."

"I'm not hiding," Jo said obstinately. "I'm working."

"You never used to work this hard," Aveline said, leaning against the doorframe. She was wearing a long cotton gown today of a blue color that matched her eyes, with an old-fashioned empire waist and a hem that brushed against the floorboards. Her hair had been curled and twisted up into an artful pile of goldb— held up by dozens of pins, no doubt. She looked like she'd stepped out of a painting, or a dream, a beautiful lady whose sole purpose was to be decorative and alluring.

Jo's hands itched to touch her, so she shoved the willful things into her pockets. "I grew up," she said shortly. "I have more responsibilities now, especially since Father's been under the weather."

"Under the weather my eye. Your father has the constitution of a bull, and a voice to match," came the blithe reply. "I just saw him pick up two men without a hint of strain."

"Why did he pick them up?"

"Because one had a death grip on the other's ear – with his teeth – and it was the only way to part them before he succeeded in chewing through it."

"That'd be Nulty. He thinks he can solve every problem with a firm bite."

"I'd forgotten how wild this place could be," Aveline laughed, a musical sound. Everything about her was musical. "The places Madame took me were always sedate, quiet, and so very proper. It literally bored me to tears on more than one occasion."

"Oh? Would've thought you'd welcome the change of pace. Must've been like a breath of fresh air after our pungent hole in the wall."

"Jo, why are you being so negative? Everything I say, you either have to argue with me or say something spiteful. You never used to be this angry."

"Three years is a long time, Ave. People can change a lot in three years. We were children three years ago. Besides, how much do you even really remember about me, huh?"

"I remember the kiss," Aveline said quietly, so quietly she could almost tell herself she'd imagined it. But then her eyes flickered up from the floor and met hers, and she saw the way her pale cheeks had flushed rosy. "I remember that last night before I left, how you climbed through my window and sat on my bed with me. The things we said in the dark. Your hair was shorter then, and you had a black eye from a fight with Lewis Johnston, and you kissed me right before you left."

"Well, I don't remember any of that," Jo said,

turning sharply and grabbing the nearest jar of fruit. "And I think you should go."

"Why do you hate me now, Jo?" Aveline demanded, voice brittle with pain and confusion. "What did I do to make you hate me so much? I came back because I've missed you so much I can hardly breathe for the ache in my chest, let alone sing. Because I haven't been able to sleep properly in weeks, because you stopped writing to me after I told you the Queen's cousin came to hear me—"

"I stopped writing because I knew I would never be good enough for you, Aveline!" Jo shouted, slamming the jar back onto the shelf with a thump that rattled the wall. "I tried to make a clean break of it, for your sake, because you shouldn't feel an obligation to a nobody who works in a pub!"

"How very kind of you!" Aveline shouted right back, eyes flashing. "Presuming to know what's best for me, to know what it's in my heart! You've always been so clever, Josephine, so wise beyond your years! It must be so nice knowing what everyone else deserves! You must take a great deal of comfort from being so self-sacrificing and noble! I hope it keeps you warm at night!"

They stared at one another, chests heaving and faces flushed with anger. The noise of the pub beyond the kitchen seemed half a world away, a muffled echo drowned out by the thunderous heartbeats and twisting emotions in the tiny space.

They both moved as one, as if sensing an invisible cue, crashing together like a wave upon a rock. Jo buried her rough hands in the soft curls to the pinging accompaniment of falling hairpins as

Aveline fisted handfuls of her damp shirt. Mouth met mouth with a bruising, hungry force, clumsy at first before growing confident and sure as they indulged their long-denied passion.

Jo pressed Aveline back against the shelves, a hand sliding down her body to map the new curves and dips. Aveline sighed as her hands spanned Jo's hips, fingertips pressing into her backside. She rubbed against her, tentatively, the front of her dress bunching up with the motion.

"I love you, I've always loved you," Jo whispered in her ear, cupping a breast.

"I know it," Aveline moaned between feverish kisses. "I'll always love you, too."

They settled against the flour sacks, heedless of the white powder that dotted their clothes and billowed into the air. Jo reached beneath the dress with sure, steady fingers and Aveline cried out softly at her touch. She plunged her own hands into Jo's unbuttoned shirt, kneading and pinching as Jo stroked and rubbed.

As Aveline began to shudder, Jo covered her mouth with a silencing kiss, swallowing her release, suddenly mindful of how precarious their position was. At any moment, someone could open the pantry door, could find them in this compromised position–

"Do you know how long I've dreamed of you doing that to me?" Aveline murmured, voice unsteady but sated, her eyes heavy-lidded, the fans of her dark lashes fluttering with her aftershocks. "For *months*."

"We can't stay here," Jo said after the frisson

of absolute delight began to dissipate. "It's too public."

"Where?" Aveline demanded. "Where should we meet?"

"The cave by the tide pools," she decided in an instant. "Do you remember it?"

"Yes, where we used to look for periwinkles."

Jo dropped Aveline's skirt. Helped her straighten her dress and mussed curls, then quickly buttoned up her own shirt. "I'll tell my mother I have some errands to attend to. You go home and grab some blankets. I'll meet you there as soon as I can."

"Don't keep me waiting, Jo," Aveline ordered, daring another kiss before darting out of the pantry.

It was easy enough to slip away; there were others to serve the supper crowd that was trickling in, Aveline's mother being one of them. Jo ducked her head when she saw her, suddenly sure that her thoughts were stamped across her face for all to see. She took up a basket as a prop for her story, slapped one of her father's old caps over her braids, and hurried down the sloping street toward the market and harbor. She stopped just long enough to pick up a bottle of sweet wine for a couple bob before running on, down to the beach.

Aveline had made a comfortable little nest by the time she arrived and was already reclining on it, naked as a nymph. She'd unpinned her hair, too, spreading the gold curls beneath her, and grinned triumphantly at the glazed, dumbfounded way Jo stared down at her.

"You've seen me naked before," she said lightly. "We swam together often enough."

"When we were children. Before my thoughts turned in certain directions, before you grew so many curves," she said, dry-mouthed and dizzy. "You look like Aphrodite. All you need is a clamshell."

"Clamshells make very poor beds," Aveline smiled. "Come *here*, Josephine, I'm getting cold."

"I can see that," Jo said, eyes fixed on her pert, dark pink nipples.

"Come and warm me up."

When she'd shucked off her shirt and trousers and boots, she gathered Aveline into her arms half in awe. This was something out of a dream – in fact, she'd had this exact dream only last week, except they had been on the beach, beneath the blazing sun, flagrantly exposed to any passing eye. This private, hidden spot was better; it had always been theirs, a sanctified fortress, and now they were consecrating it in a whole new way.

Jo kissed Aveline's breast, suckling the hardened nipple into her mouth to graze it with the edges of her teeth in a way that made Aveline arch against her. Every gasp and moan was amplified as it echoed around them.

When both breasts had been thoroughly kissed to the point of painful sensitivity, she trailed her lips lower, across the flat stomach, over the soft navel, to the patch of wiry red-gold hair at the crux of Aveline's legs.

"Wait, wait," Aveline cried, pushing herself up. "Lay down here. I don't want to be the only one being touched."

Aveline's curls trailed over Jo's skin, the contrast between the gold and the black startling, as she drew down the length of her body. She seemed determined to note every freckle, every birthmark and pale scar Jo had accumulated in her rough-and-tumble childhood.

And as Aveline did so, she stroked and caressed with fingertips and palms and tongue, finding all of the unexpected spots where she was responsive. Jo never would have guessed that a wet kiss pressed to the inner crook of her elbow would have such a galvanizing effect on her.

"Spread your legs," Aveline said firmly, as imperious as a royal, and when Jo complied she was already breathless. "Oh, Josephine, do you even know what you do to me? The fantasies I've had about you over the years..." She slipped two fingers inside her, reaching for that hidden spot, and Jo's breath hitched loudly in her throat.

Aveline caressed, she rubbed, she thrust in and out, sliding deeper...

Jo was so close. Just a little more to the right...

And as if she could read her mind – and how many times had she suspected her of such a thing when they were girls? – her fingers shifted and there, just *there*, she reached the tiny spot that would unhinge her completely.

Aveline's smile was slow and a little feral; she could feel the way she was shaking around her hand, could see the tension in the line of her jaw and the thick lust in her eyes. She pressed hard, stroked firmly, in and out and in and out, and Josephine keened as the muscles convulsed around Aveline's fingers, as her body spasmed and dark breasts quivered.

"You said I looked like Aphrodite," Aveline whispered, kissing her slowly as she panted for breath. "You look like Cleopatra. Like some ancient queen. You should wear bands of gold and nothing else. You should be stretched out on an ivory couch, imperious with everyone but me."

"You really think I'm like a queen?" Jo said, unable to keep the edge of wonderment from her words.

Aveline's brow furrowed. "You're the most regal woman I know, Josephine," she said as if that should be obvious.

Jo laughed weakly. "And here I was thinking *you* were the royal one, too beautiful and refined and noble for the rough likes of me."

"You walk like you're wearing a crown, so steel-backed and straight shouldered. I always envied your way of carrying yourself. It's the sort of posture that demands respect and admiration."

"Suppose that's the benefit of being taught deportment by an ex-military mother," Jo said. She encircled the slimmer, paler woman in her arms and decided that she had never known real contentment until that moment. "Ave, I'm sorry for my behavior. I'm sorry I pushed you away and treated you so abominably."

"I understand now why you did it," she replied. "You always have enjoyed playing the martyr, Jo. The way you used to throw yourself on your own sword to get me and Harriet out of trouble, taking all the blame and punishment so we could escape whippings and eat nice warm dinners while you went to bed hungry. I just wish you could expect the best now and then. I wish you could try to be optimistic rather than realistic. ...And if you ever act so mulish with me again, I *will* slap you good and hard. Understood?"

"Understood," she said wryly. "God, I've missed you."

"I've missed you, too, darling," Aveline said quietly, resting her head on her shoulder.

# NON-SEQUITUR

"Your people are very funny."

Harry cracked open one eye and glanced over at him. She was starting to get used to his odd non sequiturs, but her curiosity demanded that she ask for clarification every time. "How so?"

"Clothing," Kai said, vaguely gesturing at her. "It is very hot, and you are sweating, yet you still insist on wearing constrictive fabric. It gets caught on things and you spend an awful amount of time in washing and repairing it, swearing all the while, and it costs you gold when you need fresh garments. It is very strange to me."

"Humans have a lot of social rules," Harry said.

"As do merkind."

"Okay, well, it's like how each of your necklaces means something? The shells and teeth represent things, so that other merfolk know that you're strong or have completed certain rituals, right?"

"Yes."

"So humans wear certain uniforms and hats to show their status to others. Anyone sees a hat like mine, they know I'm a captain."

"Miss Euphemia has many strange hats, though."

"Miss Euphemia is an odd duck and bucks all trends and conventions."

"She is a duck? How is she—"

"It's a metaphor, Kai, don't over-think it."

"Alright, I understand what you are saying. But by your logic, the only thing you truly *must* wear to show other humans what you are is your hat. You don't *have* to wear trousers and shirts all the time. But you still choose to. Why?"

Harry looked at him properly, eyes narrowed in suspicion. He always *sounded* so earnest and sincere, naive as a newborn, but she knew Kai was much sharper than he seemed. He couldn't be *that* innocent. He had to know what he was implying. "If you want to see me naked, Kai, you could just come out and say it."

"And if I did?" he countered guilelessly.

"I'd call you a cheeky blighter and threaten you with fifteen lashes," she said smoothly.

"Only fifteen? I must try harder."

It took all of her self-control, but she repressed the smile and maintained a stony glower even as he grinned shamelessly at her. Damn him for having a smile that white, and *dimples*, on top of all that muscle and wild hair.

It was downright appalling, really.

# SECURITY

"Kath! You all right, sweetheart?"

Katherine grinned, displaying bloody teeth, and tried not to laugh at the sight the two of them must make— herself, sixteen and gangly with it, knuckles split and left eye swollen shut; and Mari, a hundred years old if she was a day, reaching up on her tiptoes to pat her on the head and try to tilt her chin so she could look at the damage to her face.

"Not to worry, Mari," she said. "I'm still pretty as ever."

Mari rolled her eyes, and Katherine looked up as she heard footsteps clattering down the stairs.

"Ohhhh," Samantha groaned, hurrying to her. "Not *another* fight?"

"It needed done!" Katherine protested. "He was harassing one of the girls from Jenny's place!"

"And where was she?"

Katherine resisted the urge to look down at the ground and shuffle her feet. Samantha was Mari's daughter, and the madam of this brothel. Though she was now a head and a half taller than her, Sam still had the power to make her feel like a wayward child.

"At Flanigan's Bar," she muttered.

"How many times have I told you to stay out of those places?" Samantha asked.

"More than I can count?"

"I know you like the bars, and I know you like

the fights – don't give me that look, sit down."

Katherine sat. "But he was–"

"And don't tell me that whoever you hit had it coming, because I'm most certain that he did – but one of these days you're going to come across someone who can hit harder. You're stronger than you have any right to be, but these are full-grown men who've been in more fights than you have," she said, kneeling down in front of her. "Sooner or later you're going to lose the element of surprise that's gotten you through so far. And one of them will kill you. You understand?"

Her first instinct was to make a joke, but the solemnity and worry on Samantha's face stopped her. "Okay. I understand."

"Kath!" Hannah exclaimed, popping out from the kitchen. "Who'd you get this time?"

"Don't encourage her," Samantha said, and Hannah stuck her tongue out at her and plopped down in the chair next to Katherine.

"Some blighter who was getting handsy with one of Jenny's girls," Katherine said.

"Good," Hannah said. "Wish I could put the fear of God into those who need it. You know I had a client yesterday tried to wriggle out of payment? Said I was asking for the last of his money and judging from all the decorations in my room, I didn't need it anyway."

"Did he pay?"

"No more than the half he'd paid up front," Hannah said. "Don't worry, Kath, I told the other girls who he was; he won't be given any more business here. Alerted Jenny's and Rachel's places as well."

"Still!" Kath complained. "Hannah, you should've told me right away!"

"Why, so you could hold him upside down and empty his pockets?"

"I was thinking of threatening him until he saw sense, but your idea is so much better. Sam!" she exclaimed. "That's what I could do! I could be security here!"

"Katherine..."

"I could do it," she said stubbornly. "You know as well as I that the girls get an occasional bounder who needs his head introduced to the nearest wall."

"That doesn't mean you need to—" She looked at the expression on Katherine's face and sighed. "On one condition. You stop going to the bars."

"Agreed," Katherine said, grinning as she stuck out her hand. Samantha shook it, and then made a shooing motion with her hands. "All right, now go get cleaned up."

"Yes, ma'am," Katherine said, giving a salute and barely dodging the swat Samantha aimed at her shoulder.

*~*~*

The earliest memory she had was walking down the big staircase at this brothel that led into the main room, holding up the long, gauzy skirt of the lacy nightgown she'd snitched from Laila's closet, her cheeks smeared with rouge and about four layers of lipstick caked onto her mouth. She'd grinned as the girls caught sight of her and let out hoots of laughter, and sashayed down the stairs as best she was able until she'd tripped on the third step from the bottom.

Samantha had been there to catch her.

It was something the madam had been doing for years, both literally and metaphorically.

Katherine knew very little about her birth mother – she was one of the women who'd used to work here, albeit for less than a year; soon after she'd given birth to her, she'd disappeared in the night – and even less about her father.

But she'd grown up with a multitude of aunts and sisters, who'd held her when she'd skinned her knee on the rocks outside and told her bawdy stories and taught her how to cook (Colette); how to properly throw a punch so she wouldn't break her thumb again (Kumiko); that loving only women was a thing that happened (Aiman); that loving men and women both was also a thing that happened (Mina); how to write her letters and how to read (Mari); how to play the piano (Hannah)...

And there were so many other things, both big and small – how to treat most any minor illness or injury; how to hold her own in a verbal argument; how to recognize when following her impulses was a good idea and when it would get her into trouble (just because she didn't follow that skill often didn't mean she did not possess it); how to tell truth from falsehood; how to best get blood out of her underthings... And those all came from Samantha.

A good number of people, Katherine knew, would not have taken her in. Much less when they had a good-sized business such as this brothel to run. Samantha already had plenty on her plate, but she had chosen to adopt her herself rather than send her to an orphanage.

It was something Katherine was grateful for every day of her life, even if much of the time she felt too awkward to say it.

*~*~*

Three weeks later, she came home with her first tattoo. Samantha took one look at it, threw her hands in the air, and exclaimed, "I give up!" Later that night, she examined the design and asked her where she'd gotten it done, congratulating Katherine on choosing one of the more reputable artists. "Big Ace has rarely had a customer's arm or leg rot and fall of from a gangrenous infection," she said earnestly, grinning when Katherine's face blanched.

*~*~*

Leaving them was simultaneously the hardest and the easiest thing she had ever done.

Easy because she knew she would have a home with them again whenever she needed it, and that she was welcome to visit whenever she liked; because they were almost as eager for her to get out to sea and start writing them of her adventures as she herself was.

Hard because they were her family; because she knew everything that was here and nothing of what was out there.

Well, that wasn't quite true, Katherine thought, as she lightly chided Colette for crying even as she held back tears herself. She'd heard story upon story for years, both from the girls themselves and from the clients who came here, fantastical stories about pirates and sea monsters and buried treasure and the way the light played over the ocean at sunrise and how the sea could become as dear to you as a lover.

She'd just never experienced any of those things for herself.

Finally, she turned to Samantha, who beamed at her, the gray in her hair looking like streaks of sunbeams in the early morning light. Samantha opened her arms and Katherine hugged her, remembering a time when her head had only come up to the older woman's waist.

"Good luck," Samantha said. "And remember, no getting drunk when you're not with at least two or three other people you can trust. Folks get—"

"—shanghaied that way, I know."

"I expect a letter from you every month. And try to visit at least once a year, all right?"

"Especially if the ship you board has any handsome sailors!" Padma laughed.

"Would I board a ship that didn't?" Katherine said, pulling Padma into a hug.

"Easy!" Padma squeaked. "I intend to use this body later."

"Fine, fine," Katherine said, releasing her and

looking back to Samantha again. "I'll write and visit as often as I'm able."

"Good. And I expect plenty of stories about mermaids. Saw one when I was a little girl, you know. She waved to me." Samantha raised her handkerchief and blotted at her eyes, then waved Katherine away. "Go on then, before I really start blubbering."

Katherine pulled her in for one last hug, muttering, "Love you", before she turned and walked outside, heading for the docks, not daring to look back for fear her courage would leave her completely.

*~*~*

"You know, I like you. Remind me of Samantha."

"And who's Samantha?" the petite blonde asked before taking another drink of beer.

They'd been trading stories for close to an hour now, ever since Katherine had sat down at their table and offered to buy them each a drink if they'd let her know where they got their cunning hats. Samantha's latest hire, Hilja, adored hats and collected them to the point where her closet was almost overflowing; one that looked like theirs would make a fine gift.

"Madam at the brothel I used to work in."

Captain Harry choked on her drink. But to her credit, she merely looked surprised by the answer, not offended. If she'd been offended, then she and Katherine might've had to have words.

Katherine had run into a few folk on her travels thus far who seemed to think that the people who worked in brothels were lesser somehow, and if they didn't stop holding that opinion after she'd had a little 'discussion' with them, they at least knew better than to express such foolishness in front of her again.

"You get many clients?" the captain's first mate, Jo, asked curiously. "My experience, men tend to get panicky around a woman they think can beat them at arm-wrestling."

Katherine grinned. "Didn't work with the clients. Worked security. But I've had no problem finding my share of men. Or women, really."

"I imagine not," Harry said. She looked to her first mate, who nodded. "Actually, Katherine, we're in need of a bit of security ourselves. Could well use someone with your skill set on board *The Sappho*. Would you be interested?"

"Hell yes," Katherine said. "How's the pay?"

"Nothing to write home about, but you won't starve."

"Well, tell you what then," Katherine said with a grin. "You give me a little advance, and I'll buy you two another drink."

# WEATHERING THE STORM

"All right," Elias said, wiping rainwater off his face as he entered Anne's Arms. "Which one of you pissed off Poseidon?" The wind nearly tore the door out of his grip, and he cursed as he yanked it closed.

"What are you doing out in this weather?" Violet asked. "Thought you'd have enough sense to stay at the hotel!"

"And miss seeing you lot?" Elias asked, his gaze sliding to Tessa. She rolled her eyes, giving him a good-natured grin. Elias always came to her bed at least twice whenever his ship came into the Bogo port. He was pleasant enough in bed and entertaining to talk to, and over the years he'd graduated from mere client to friend.

"I know these are wonderful," she said, cupping her ample breasts, "but I'm not sure they're worth dying for."

"Think a fair number in here would disagree with you," Elias said, grinning as several of the other customers let out affirmative hoots and hollers.

"Priorities, lads, priorities," she teased, heading back behind the bar to fetch Elias his usual order.

Though she kept her grin firmly in place and her banter appropriately saucy, as the storm grew worse she couldn't help but worry, wondering where Zora was in the midst of this.

Was she sailing calm waters, far away from

where this current maelstrom raged? Or was she in the midst of something even worse?

Normally she could stave off the worry, but nights like this always drove home the plain fact that every time Zora left, it might be the last time she ever saw her.

She wasn't the only one who fretted during storms; Violet had a nephew out on a merchant ship, and any time a storm came up her jokes grew bawdier and her laughter grew louder, as if she could drown out the thunder itself. If Lucia was off-shift, then she baked, working her fingers to the bone in the Anne's Arms' small kitchen. One could always tell when she worried for her friends out on the ocean, because she would bring forward five or six pies the next day. If she was on-shift during a monsoon, like tonight, then she prayed, one hand carrying trays and the other hand wrapped tightly in her rosary. And Amelia painted like a dervish, staining her fingers and clothing with dabs of her oil paints.

Once upon a time, the worst thing Tessa had had to fear where Zora was concerned was an overzealous client. Though Port Royal had most certainly had its share of pitfalls – she'd had very little say in whom she took to her bed, and if they chose not to pay she hadn't had much recourse – but at least she and Zora had worked together, and after a night of smiling and giggling for men who were only too happy to believe they were honestly enjoying themselves, they could rest at each others' side, talking quietly about their dreams for the future.

Zora had spoken a time or two about traveling, but Tessa had assumed that meant she would take one or two voyages on a ship to get to a new location, and then stay there for a time. Never that she would make the ocean itself her home.

Now she heard stories about krakens and murderous pirates and wicked merfolk and had to stop herself from picturing Zora in the place of those stories' hapless victims.

Her own future plans had always involved a continuation of her job. She made very good coin, yes, but she also had expensive tastes – and she did love buying Zora sparkly gifts. And she had absolutely no intention of someday being an old woman who was dependent on the charity of others to keep a roof over her head. She wished to retire in good standing, and preferably with enough coin to help out other girls should they need it.

She had thought, often, of opening a brothel of her own. She hadn't told Zora about this yet; though she knew it was foolish, a base part of her held tight to the fear that because Zora had fled from this profession as soon as she was able, that she wanted her to do the same thing.

That she would be disappointed in her otherwise.

Zora would be the first to scoff at her for such fears, she knew, but they still weren't easily dismissed.

Probably because they came part and parcel with the job. Most of the women she'd worked with back at Port Royal who had been perfectly understanding about her taking a lover from among their ranks had changed their minds the moment Zora had joined *The Sappho* instead.

"Not one of us anymore," Amber had sniffed. "She's a sailor now. You mark my words, within six months she'll start complaining about your work and trying to bribe you to quit."

"Zora understands," Tessa had told her, back when she still found a point in arguing such things.

"Not for long, she won't. Any time a girl successfully gets out of the life, she starts looking down on us others for not doing the same."

Well, it had been four years now, and the look on Zora's face whenever she came into the Anne's Arms and saw her again was a greater reassurance than words could ever be.

Thunder crashed outside, rattling the windows and making the floor under their feet tremble, and Tessa took a deep breath.

Zora sailed with a fine crew. She had to trust that, in a few weeks or even months, she would walk through that door again.

# CHANGE IN LUCK

He'd always been "Lucky".

When he was five years old, he and his brothers were climbing a tree. Daring one another to reach for the next highest branch, then the next. Whoever climbed the highest would win a large honeycomb liberated from the neighbor's hives, not to mention bragging rights for a solid week.

Franky being Franky, he was always ready to push things to their limit. Agile as a monkey, lighter than his older brothers, he was confident the emaciated branch would hold his weight.

He was wrong.

And when it snapped, he experienced a sickening moment of complete awareness. That his confidence had been foolish. That he had been betrayed by his belief in his own immortality and was actually frail and breakable. In that moment, he almost saw bony hands reaching out for him.

But then his fatal fall was cut short. The rope knotted around his waist as a crude belt was snagged by a sturdier branch and he was jerked to a safe, if bruising, halt.

Most of the village had heard his shriek of terror and come running – there was no way to hide his brush with death. But when his mother's hysterics had subsided and after his father had smacked his backside beet red in punishment, everyone looked at him with something approaching awe.

Lucky Franky, they started calling him. Saved by a miracle. God Himself had stretched out a hand to catch him.

As he'd grown, his luck only improved. By the time he was twelve, the other boys refused to play dice or cards with him. Not because they suspected him of cheating – Franky was not the type who could lie convincingly; his eyes and voice gave away even the smallest of fibs – but because in his hands the dice always fell on sixes and the cards always ordered themselves in unbeatable runs.

Though he was as good-natured and friendly and trusting as the mark of a conman's dreams, no one could hoodwink him, either. It was a combination of his irresistible charm and that unfailing luck. A trader would set up a booth, have half of the village convinced about the sterling quality of his wares, then Franky would stroll up with a sloppy smile – and a little warning voice would start to whisper in the seller's head. *Steer clear of this one*, it would say. *Don't be fooled by that open face and rustic innocence*. The smart would heed the voice, those with a sliver of a conscience left wouldn't be able to ignore his innate kindness, and the stupid? Well, Franky would pick up one of their items and it would promptly fall apart, revealed as the shoddy fake it was. Word spread quickly, and before long Franky's village saw only the most honest of tinkers.

By the time he was fifteen, his luck was enabling him well in the lists of romance. He would smile at a girl, pay her a sincere compliment, and before he knew it they were in her father's barn, or enjoying long walks through the vineyards, or simply ducking behind the church after services. He always confessed everything afterwards to Father Giovanni, who would sigh and rub his temples and order suitable penances, which Franky would carry out to the letter and in a true spirit of contrition.

But then next Wednesday would come, and then next Sunday, and Franky would be back in confession with another name (or two) on his lips. The old priest frequently sent prayers of gratitude heavenward that Franky's luck extended far enough that none of the girls ever became pregnant, and none of the fathers ever found out and picked up knives.

Not long after his seventeenth birthday, his father came home with life-changing news. He had decided to finally follow a lifelong dream and buy a boat, go to sea, and try his hand at fishing far out beyond the coast. He was tired of the drudgery of farming and he had always loved the sea. With his brother and best friend as partners, the three of them had enough to cover the initial costs for a small craft. And if Franky would join them, they should be able to divvy up the work into manageable portions. Plus, it wouldn't hurt to have his by now infamous luck on their side.

Unfortunately, on his eighteenth birthday, Franky's luck finally ran out.

The storm appeared out of nowhere. One moment: cheerful sun and smooth seas. The next: the deck was awash with rain and no one's shouts could be heard over the thunder. Franky tried to secure the rigging, only to suffer a blow from a bucket pitched by the wind. He fell overboard half-dazed just as lightning struck the mast.

The ocean swallowed him and everything went black.

When he opened his eyes again, it was to a pink dawn. He was floating amidst wreckage, tangled up in rope and bits of splintered wood. Every inch of him ached and his left temple felt afire, throbbing where the bucket had struck him. He called out weakly for his father, for his uncle, for Nico.

There was no answer.

He drifted for a day, the sun baking his skin raw and the salty water splitting his lips. He contemplated attempting to purposefully drown – surely that would be better than death by dehydration, or being eaten alive by sharks.

But even after his catastrophe, and the bitter loss of his family, a small shred of him held out hope that his luck would return.

When the ship appeared in the distance, he was sure it had. He mustered the strength to wave and shout, hoping that the wreckage would catch the lookout's eye, and thanked God for His infinite mercies.

Mercies which started to feel rather finite indeed when he found himself, an hour later, shackled and thrown into a stinking, crowded hold with a slaver's brand burned onto his hand.

"Just be glad you're still alive, boy," an old man with a horribly scarred back reassured him. "While there's life, there's hope."

"Hope for what?" he'd demanded, empty and

aching inside and out.

"Escape. Liberation. Freedom. A kind master. You're a good looking boy – might be you get bought by a fine lady looking for a pleasure slave. That wouldn't be a half-bad life, would it?"

"You know what they call me back home?" he'd said, fighting back tears. "Lucky Franky."

"Luck can be good or bad," said another man with a milky eye. "How long you had good luck, son?"

"I turned eighteen yesterday."

"Eighteen years, huh? Well, most people don't even have eighteen *days* of fair luck. Be grateful you had that, Franky."

"When luck turns, it's a real bitch," said another with a cackle. "Maybe you got eighteen years of shit to look forward to. To balance the scales. Maybe your luck flew away to find another pretty boy."

Franky couldn't argue with that assessment. Especially not after hours turned into days, turned into weeks, turned into months.

But streaks of bad luck break at some point, and for Franky the turn came when his path crossed with the infamous Captain Roberts.

\*~\*~\*

Captain Roberts took a slow sip of her beer, half-listening to her first mate talk about provisions they needed to restock. Most of her attention was across the room, at a half-drunk man who was busy ordering about a teenager in oversized, ragged clothes. The back of the boy's left hand was nearly covered by a swollen red mark — she was certain that if she was close enough to see detail, the mark would prove itself to be a owner's brand.

Across from her, Josephine sighed. "Harriet. You promised."

She didn't acknowledge the comment, and Jo reached across the table to take her hand. Reluctantly, she met her eyes.

"You promised," she repeated, more concern than reproach in her voice. "The boy is not being taken to be sold; he is already owned. His master would not wish to part with such an investment; not for any price that we can afford today. I know you do not wish to hear that fact," she said, when the Captain glared at her. "But it is fact all the same." She squeezed her hand gently. "We cannot save everyone."

"I know," Harry admitted, and though none of the tension drained out of her shoulders, the acquiescence in her voice let Josephine relax slightly.

Then the young man tripped as he was carrying the slave-holder's pitcher to his table, spilling it all over the floor and splashing some onto his owner. The man stood up with a roar of rage and backhanded the boy, sending him sprawling.

Harry erupted out of her chair, and Josephine dropped her face into her hands.

She had been so close.

Jo watched her captain march across the bar and quickly followed. A couple of people raised their eyebrows in amusement, the ones who bothered to look up from their drinks at all. In her haste, Harry bumped into a man who was making his way to the bar. When she didn't stop to apologize, he grabbed hold of her shoulder.

"Now look here, girl—"

She didn't even look at him; just shoved him away and stopped in front of the slave-holder. "How much for the boy?" she snapped.

He rolled his eyes. "More than you can afford."

"I'll be the judge of that."

"Four hundred gold pieces. Would be five if he wasn't so useless."

Had she still been eating anything, Jo would've choked on her food. Four hundred gold pieces was *far* more than they could afford; bargaining from that wasn't even a possibility. That much gold would keep the entire ship in rations for most of a month. She saw Harry's shoulders deflate slightly, and the slave-holder chuckled.

"Told you."

Josephine moved around in front of the man Harriet had bumped into, who was stalking toward her exposed back. "Apologies for my captain," she said, pressing a piece of silver into his hand. "She is in particularly high spirits tonight."

He glared at her for a few seconds, but then nodded. "Happens to the best of us." He then looked to the boy, who was cowering against the wall, and his expression softened a little. "They shouldn't sell them. Not that young. Good luck to her, then. She'll need it against that lout."

He'd barely finished speaking when Harry's

voice rang out.

"Then I will duel you for him."

The slave-holder laughed, clapping one meaty hand on his knee. "Oh, thank you, lass! Today's been a right pain and I thought nothing could improve my mood, but—"

Then he swallowed, looking up very gingerly, the tip of her sword pressed to his throat.

"I do not jest, sir."

"Captain," Jo hissed. "Can I talk to you for a minute?"

"No," she said, not taking her eyes or the point of her sword off her would-be opponent.

"Might want to listen to your friend, there," the man said.

"I issued you a challenge. Do you accept it, or do you admit your cowardice?"

His face grew serious. "Your terms?"

"If I win, I get the boy. No cost."

He grinned up at her. "And if I win, you join him, and wear my brand."

"Captain..."

"I accept."

She withdrew her sword from his throat and nodded sharply at the door. Jo followed her outside. The man walked past them, his slave scurrying after him, out onto the moonlit sand. "I'll get quite a fine price for you," he said confidently.

Jo debated the wisdom of knocking Harry over the head and dragging her back to the ship. She had lost fights before and she always hated to see it; hated to see her friend confined to a bed in the sickbay.

But this time there wouldn't be a sickbay, at least not one on their ship. If she lost tonight, she would walk away at the slave-holder's side.

Josephine clenched her hands into fists. What had she always, *always* told Harry? Never gamble with more than you can afford to lose.

In many of the places they frequented, such a challenge would've drawn a crowd. But here, there were only the four of them. If her captain did lose...

She knew that Harry would hate the fact that she was even thinking it. "I lost a fair duel", she would say, or "Just because I'm a pirate doesn't mean I don't honor my debts".

Honor was all well and good. But there were some things Josephine would not stand for.

She just hoped that if he did best Harry, that she herself would be capable of taking him down. She doubted she could count on much help from the young man. He, understandably, looked scared of his own shadow.

Looking to him, she saw him crouched down on the sand, watching the combatants with wide eyes as the fight began.

The slave-holder drew first blood. And second. Jo watched closely, every instinct telling her to draw her own blade. Instead she held herself still, watching as Harry dodged in low and got in a vicious jab at the man's side. He snarled in pain and lunged again, but too wide, and she easily slipped around him and cut him again.

His teeth bared in rage now, he swung twice in wide arcs. Each time she blocked the would-be blow, and Jo edged closer, worried now that he was no longer concerned with making sure she was alive at the end of the duel. His third strike knocked the sword from her hand.

He smiled. "On second thought, you're not worth the hassle. The sea can have you." He stepped forward, raising his sword, and Jo lunged, snatching up Harry's sword and throwing it back to her. For the second time that night, the slave-holder found the point of her blade at his neck.

"Do you yield?"

"That was... we never agreed on accepting help!"

"We also agreed on the terms of defeat, yet you were more than ready to take my life. Now. Do you yield?"

He scowled, but dropped his sword.

*~*~*

"You're free now, boy," Captain Harry had said when his erstwhile master had gone. She was a lot smaller than he'd imagined − funny how the people of stories were never as towering and impressive as you'd expect. She wasn't a fire-breathing goblin, nor an inhumanly beautiful witch. She was just a slim woman of average height with messy white-blonde hair and a long, ugly scar down one arm. Her trousers were too big, held up only by the thick leather belt she'd cinched tightly around her waist, and one of the feathers in her hat was broken. She also had a snub nose and a perpetually crooked smile − and pale, pale blue eyes that seemed to look straight through you. "You can go wherever you like."

"I... I don't know," he'd said, lightheaded and bewildered.

"Don't know what?"

"Where I am, to start," he'd stuttered. "I don't know how long it's been — I know I was grabbed the day after my eighteenth birthday, but how many years has it been since then?"

"You don't know how old you are?" Harry said, a funny little edge to her voice.

"No."

"What's your name?" the first mate asked. Jo, was what the captain had called her. She was beautiful, too, in a very remote and grim sort of way, much taller than him and no doubt stronger, too. Despite all of the manual labor that had been forced upon him, he still had the reedy build of a teenager rather than a man. Not enough food, and never in regular intervals.

"Francisco Cardinelli. But—"

"But?"

"My family used to call me Lucky Franky," he said wryly, managing a smile. It was strange to smile. Something he had done so frequently, so casually, before, now felt stiff and awkward.

"Well, Lucky Franky, it looks like your name is an apt one again," said Harry. "Come on. We can take you home, wherever that is."

"No, wait. However long it's been, it's been too long. My family must've mourned me, buried me, and moved on. And after everything I've been through... I just can't imagine going back and picking up there again."

"So what do you want to do, boy?" prodded Jo.

"Can I sail with you? I know my way around a boat. And I'll work hard – do whatever you tell me."

Harry looked at him for what felt like an eternity, toe of her boot tapping the dock. "Alright. I'll take you on probation, Franky. You'll sail with us for three months and then I'll decide if it'll be permanent. If not and we part on good terms, we'll leave you at a friendly port with a pocketful of money and our best wishes. If we part on not-so-good terms, you'll get off the boat before we reach a port. Understand?"

"Don't worry too much, boy," Jo reassured him as they set off toward the large ship with *The Sappho* emblazoned across its prow. "She'll only do the latter if you betray us, not if you're a bit messy with the sails."

# RENDEZVOUS

Aveline was sneaking out to meet someone.

Harry grinned and fastened the clasp on her cloak, trying to make as little sound as possible as she crept outside after her. She'd hardly dared to believe it when she'd heard quiet footsteps going past her door, and peeked out to realize it was her sister. Sometimes her mother or father would go sit on the porch late at night, watching the stars and the sea, but neither of them made any attempt to soften their footfalls.

Who was she going to meet? Aveline hadn't mentioned a thing about having a suitor, but when she'd turned around to check that no one was following her, Harry had caught a glimpse of lip rouge on her mouth, and her hair had been done up in an elaborate twist.

After they were out of sight of the house, Harry realized where they were going. Her sister's favorite place in the entire world was by an ancient willow that grew close to the beach; she must be meeting her companion there. Certain of their destination now, Harry stopped concentrating all her focus on which direction her sister was going and started admiring their surroundings a bit more.

She was familiar with this place during the day, but night was more for sneaking into town than wandering out to areas this deserted. Her parents would have conniptions if they knew either of them was in such a desolate place at this hour.

But it was beautiful. The stars glittered above her like diamonds, and all around her the trees stretched their limbs up toward them as if in supplication.

Then she caught sight of a shadow darting between two trees off to her left, and pressed a hand to her mouth to stifle a giggle. There was Aveline's suitor now!

She was tempted to move closer, try to get a look at his face, but reminded herself that if she pressed her luck, she might well be discovered. Besides, she would get a chance to see him soon enough. They had almost reached the willow tree.

Aveline approached the beautiful draping branches and trailed a hand over some of the leaves. She leaned against the trunk, a wide smile on her face.

Stopping a good distance away, Harry watched as the man crept up toward the tree, careful to the very last not to be seen. Finally, he moved into her sister's line of sight.

To Harry's surprise and confusion, her sister's smile faded at once and she straightened up, her delicate hands clenching into fists.

Maybe it wasn't a tryst after all? Maybe her sister had come out alone for some type of negotiation? But Harry couldn't imagine her sister getting into trouble of any sort and not explaining things to mother and father. And if she was out to solve a problem tonight, why would she focus so on her face and her hair?

Harry chanced a few steps closer, trying to hear what they were saying. Both of their voices were low, angry, and all specific words were effortlessly masked by the sound of the nearby waves.

Then the man drew back his fist, and before Harry could even shout a warning, he punched Aveline hard in the side of the head, catching her before she could fall and lifting her over his shoulder. He turned and began moving toward the ocean, his steps astonishingly quick for someone who was carrying another human being, and only then did Harry manage to break through her shock and chase after them, screaming at him to let Aveline go.

He turned, panic flashing across his face for an instant before he took in the sight of her. Then he laughed.

"Go home, child."

Harry didn't even reply, didn't stop running, she just charged straight into the man. To her surprise, he didn't collapse to the ground when she hit him; didn't even seem to budge. He shoved her back with his free arm and she fell, hitting her back and palms against the rocks at the edge of the beach. Flinging herself forward, she wrapped herself around his leg as he began to turn away and did the only thing she could think of. She bit him.

He yowled and tilted slightly, nearly dropping Aveline, who groaned.

Harry tried to gain her feet, tried to pull her sister away from the man, but suddenly there was a cold line running from the top of her left arm almost to her wrist, and she couldn't seem to hold that arm steady at all.

Looking down at it, she saw the blood pouring down her skin and sank back to her knees as the man sheathed his knife and stalked down to the waiting landing craft.

Aveline was still over his shoulder like so much baggage, and Harry tried to get up but the stars were swirling above her and the abnormal chill had gone from her arm and she'd never felt such pain.

They were in the boat now, and he rowed away from the shoreline and maybe he was one of the pirates who worked with the mermaids – greedy and vicious things, she'd heard, always looking for another to join their ranks – or maybe he was taking her to be a slave on a ship somewhere and she didn't *know*; she couldn't see into the fog that covered the dark water and she couldn't get up for a closer view, couldn't swim after Aveline and save her; all she could do was scream.

Then there were hands covering hers, questions rattled off that stopped as soon as the newcomer caught sight of her arm.

"Jo... Josie?" Harry asked, blinking up at her best friend and trying to bring her into focus. "Josie, help."

"I will, I'll get you to the doctor, come on–"

"No, no. Not me. Help Aveline. She's out... he took her out there," she said, waving towards the ocean with her good arm, and the motion would've unbalanced her completely had Josephine not steadied her. Instead of running for the waves, the older girl took off her cloak and wrapped it tightly around her wounded arm.

"No. Why aren't you – didn't you hear–" Had she spoken? She thought for certain that she'd spoken aloud, but maybe she hadn't, maybe she'd just thought–

"I heard you," Josephine said, her voice thick with tears. "I'm sorry. I was late. I'm sorry."

"Late for what?" Harry asked, and then the stars themselves disappeared.

It was only after she was back home, lying in bed with the doctor at her side, pushing a needle in one side of the slash and out the other, that Harry could finally make sense of those words.

Josephine hadn't just come across her as a stroke of luck.

She'd been the one Aveline had gone to meet.

And she hadn't stopped the man. Jo's mom had taught both of them how to fight; there had been things she could've done. Things that she *knew* how to do. But she'd panicked, she'd been stupid and she'd panicked, and now Aveline was–

"Shhh," the doctor said, giving her a sympathetic glance as she burst into tears. "Gotta hold that arm still, girl, I can't get the stitches straight otherwise."

But she couldn't calm down, couldn't hold herself still, couldn't stop.

"Harry. *Harry.*"

She looked over at Josephine, who was on the other side of the bed. Her eyes were red-rimmed and her black hair was a stringy mess.

Harry drew a deep, shuddering breath.

"Ohhh, Jo. I'm—"

Josephine shook her head. "No. Not a word of it. We'll find her. Whether she's a mermaid now or whether pirates took her, we'll get her back."

"But we—"

"No. I want to hear you say it."

Harry swallowed hard, then nodded once. She still felt lightheaded, and the gentle motion after her crying jag made her feel like she might pass out again. "We'll find her."

# MAD IN LOVE

"Have you seen Maddie?"

Harry paused, pressing her finger to the coordinate on the map so as not to lose it – they had to meet *The Charon* there in another week, and she'd heard the reefs in that patch of sea were treacherous – and looked up with a furrowed brow. "No, I haven't. That's–"

"Odd," Jo finished in agreement. "She hasn't been underfoot or tugging at my sleeve or singing off-key. Not her usual self in the slightest. I confess, I'm starting to worry."

"She's obviously not doing her lessons with Miss Euphemia," Harry said, gesturing with her head to the next room, where the old woman was sitting in her chair and crocheting something frilly while humming. "Maybe she's down with Wil, pestering her for a sweet?"

"No, Wil took a lifeboat and went ahead to that sandbar we passed heading into port – the one where the whale was beached? She said she wanted to chart the progression of decomposition or something similarly disgusting."

"Only Wil could be enthused about maggots," agreed Harry, pulling a face. "Well, I feel we would've heard something if she fell overboard."

"And we *definitely* would've heard something if she'd had a fit," Jo said in an undertone.

"Yes." Harry sobered completely. "Well, she *is* a teenaged girl. Maybe she just needed some time alone. If she hasn't popped up by supper, then we'll start worrying."

"Think it's the new boy?"

Harry slid a sunstone to the edge of the map to hold it down and walked over to the cabin window. Franky was sitting on an overturned bucket with a ripped net spread across his lap, able fingers deftly weaving the edges back together with a new piece of rope. He'd pulled off his linen shirt – it lay in a wad by his tapping, boot – and sweat was trickling down his dark neck and chest. He looked calm and focused and even from this distance Harry could see the crisscrossing scars of lash marks on his back and shoulders. There was a second brand burn just above his left nipple and Harry felt another surge of anger directed at those who could do such barbaric things to another person.

"He seems to have settled in nicely – course, it's only been a couple weeks. But he's diligent in his work. Polite and respectful."

"Achingly grateful to finally be out from under the lash," said Jo.

"Yes. And I haven't *seen* any friction between him and Mads. You don't think she's afraid of him, do you? He may be scarred, but he's hardly struck me as a rough lad. After everything he's been through, he's still got a boy's face and soft eyes. He smiles a lot, and it ain't the kind of smile to put your hackles on edge."

"Maybe that's it," Jo said sagely.

"What's what?"

"Maybe you just put your finger on the issue:

he's a good-looking boy. Pretty, even. A pretty boy not too far from her own age, who smiles a lot and has kind eyes. Maybe Maddie's got herself a fancy going."

"Maddie?" Harry considered this. "Maddie's never really given men more than a second glance."

"She's not a virgin," Jo said knowingly.

"How do you know that?" Harry demanded.

"She told me herself. Came to me and asked if I had any advice on how to 'prevent' things. You know."

"And she went to *you* about this?" Harry gaped.

Jo laughed. "The girl's sharp in a lot of ways, but she's still pretty innocent. Remember when she asked Miss Euphemia what the ship's name meant? 'Women? She liked other *women*?' she said. Took a lot to not bust a button with laughing."

"So what did you do when she came to you?"

"I told her to go talk to Hope. Said she has all the pills and potions for that. The Chinese are a lot more advanced when it comes to that stuff than we are."

"Huh," said Harry, nonplussed. "And she didn't even come to me."

"You *are* the captain," Jo said. "Maybe it would be too mortifying to ask you. Maybe she's still a little in awe of you."

"Awed? By me?" Harry snorted. "Doubt Maddie would be awed by the Queen herself if she stepped on deck. She'd just ask her how many rabbits it took to make her fur collar. Well, I guess we'll just keep an eye on her. Either she'll get accustomed to him and lose her shyness or—"

"We'll catch them going at it like the aforementioned rabbits in the cargo hold?"

"Thanks, Jo. I really wanted that mental image today."

*~*~*

Maddie sat on the floor of the crow's nest and glared at the tangle of string in her hands. She was trying to do a complicated cat's cradle Katherine had shown her the day before — her thumb should go *here*, and the pinkie *there* — but the white loops refused to cooperate. Kath had made it look so easy; she said it was a great way to keep your hands busy so your brain could think properly, because it was all about muscle memory. Do the patterns often enough and your fingers would move instinctively without the slightest concentration.

The girl sighed and shoved the string into a pocket, where it would only acquire further knots. It was just a stupid game anyway. Nothing to get frustrated over.

She leaned back against the railing, tapping her head against the wood. The edges of the narrow boards bit into her shoulders. This was her space, the only place on the entire ship that was really *hers*. The others may come up here occasionally to relieve her, especially in bad weather or chancy territories, but everyone onboard acknowledged that it was 'Maddie's nest'.

Marcella had shown her how to sew a nearly

straight line and given her some old canvas and thin leather, which she'd stitched together into a long, thin cushion and stuffed with tufts of raw wool that smelled strongly of lanolin and clean hay. It covered the whole space of the nest, curving around the tip of the mast that rose in the center. There was a hole-spotted bucket up here that doubled as a chair, under which she kept a nub of candle and a small bottle of brandy. A large tarp could be raised on a pulley to erect a tent in the rain, angled in such a fashion that only the most cross-grained winds would catch it, and there was a heavy double-sided blanket: one side waterproofed canvas, the other thick wool.

On days when the water was smooth, the wind fair, and the chances of running foul of someone were slim to nil, Maddie would bring up one of Miss Euphemia's books – always after promising to keep tight hold of them and to tuck them into her belt when climbing up or down – or her latest penny dreadful and read while the wind made a mess of braiding her hair. It would take her most of the day to read any of the stories, because she'd always keep one eye on the horizon as was expected of her, but it wasn't a half-bad way to spend a shift.

With another, heartier sigh, Maddie flopped down across the squashy cushion, rolled onto her back, and spread her arms wide. She stared up at an endless expanse of turquoise blue, unmarked by a single cloud, untouched by a single bird. They were leagues away from land now, and it would be several days more before they'd sight another shore. Out here, it was just the ship, the sea, and the sky. Just the crew. The women she'd been long accustomed to and...

Lucky Franky, as he'd been introduced, was the first man to have a bunk in the hold. He came from Italy, he said, that first night when he'd been introduced to everyone, but he'd been at sea and enslaved for enough years that his accent had changed considerably: there was a bit of an English edge to his words now, and he'd picked up all sorts of slang and turns of phrase as well as the second language. He was very friendly, and made a point of shaking everyone's hand, and it was clear that he carried none of the usual prejudices when faced with a ship full of women.

Indeed, he seemed perfectly content to take orders from one, and he hadn't made any lewd gestures or jokes. He was the picture of a pleasant young gentleman, according to Miss Euphemia, even if he wasn't dressed in a refined fashion.

In fact, he was wearing some of Maddie's spare clothes; they were of an equal height and similar build, and the shirt and breeches he'd been wearing before were fit only for a midden. When Harry had asked Maddie to fetch something for him — "At least until we can buy him something new," the captain had added — she'd grabbed the first things she found and handed them over, unusually tongue-tied.

"Thanks," he'd smiled, and off came the shirt and down dropped the breeches without the slightest hesitation or sign of embarrassment. Her eyes had practically popped from her head and she'd spun around on her heels with flaming cheeks and suddenly sweaty palms.

And ever since then...

Maddie put a hand to her chest. Slipped it beneath her brown shirt and pressed hard against her left breast, fingertips cold on the warm skin. Her heart was thrumming like mad, the pounding of it chaotic and frightening in her ears. She felt as though she'd run at a grueling pace; she was all breathless and flushed and tremble-limbed.

But she hadn't been running. She'd barely done anything today besides climb up here and make a mess of some string.

Why did she feel so wild and strange?

She blinked rapidly in the wind, the pit of her stomach going cold. She wasn't about to have a turn, was she? She'd never had one before without a reason, without something triggering her. There was no reason for her to go mad now. It was quiet and peaceful up here, just as calm on the deck below.

She stared at the sky and took deep, steadying breaths, and thought of the chant Hope had taught her. The words were foreign and odd on her tongue, and she knew she mangled the vowels, but she forced herself to repeat them anyway. It was a meditative prayer, Hope said. Meant to calm the mind and relax the body.

They were words that were once spoken by a god; Maddie had never had much of an opinion about gods, particularly the God so many people nattered on about and wanted perfectly happy naked people to worship, but she had liked the stories Hope told her about the gods of old China. Those gods didn't even look like people all the time. They were shape-shifters and turned themselves into foxes and fish and dragons, and they rewarded normal people who were kind rather than those who were perfectly devout and always went to church on Sundays. Maddie could appreciate a god who understood people were just people and didn't ask too much of them.

She was beginning the chant for a second time when a sudden movement startled her. She leaped up with a breathless shriek that did little to soothe her restless heart and, in the process, frightened the figure climbing over the railing so badly that he almost pinwheeled backwards into nothingness.

"Bloody—!" Maddie shouted inarticulately, lunging forward and grabbing the front of Franky's shirt.

Luckily for him, she was an inordinately strong girl after years on a ship. Luckily for her, he had the reflexes of a cat, and his bare feet caught the grips when his hands slipped. There was no need for a dramatic tableau that could have very well ended with both of them toppling to the far-below deck: instead, she just pulled him closer to the railing while he remembered how to breathe.

"Ohhhh," Franky moaned, clutching at the railing and closing his eyes. His naturally bronzed face had paled considerably under his tan. "That was far too close. Thank you," he added devoutly, after he'd swallowed a couple times and cracked open one eye. "I really appreciate the save."

"What were you thinking?" she hissed. "Spooking me like that!"

"I hallooed when I was halfway up," he said, hooking his leg up and over the railing, recovering more of his usual confidence when both feet were firmly on wood again.

The wind must've flung away his words. Sounds were funny like that out at sea. Sometimes a body could be standing right next to you and you'd hear nothing; other times, a distant cry would be like a slap in the face.

Maddie huffed, raking a hand through her tangled hair. "Alright then," she said finally, begrudgingly. "What do you want?"

"I just wanted to see what it was like up here," he said, face shining with innocence. "And to talk to you."

"Me?"

"Yes. I've had the chance to talk to almost everyone else, but you're still a bit of a question mark. So this is your spot, huh?" He cast an eye over the minor amenities and smiled. "You've got it done up a treat."

"Thanks," Maddie said awkwardly. "It's nothing fancy."

"Fancy is overrated. And very rarely comfortable. This? This is comfortable. And let me tell you, I appreciate comfortable. It's been a long time since I've been able to really relax."

"It must've been awful," Maddie blurted out artlessly. "Going through what you went through. I don't think I could've survived it."

Franky looked at her for a moment, sizing

her up. "Yes, you could've," he said quietly. "You've got steel in you. Or maybe flint. Even sharper."

"How did you bear it?"

"Oh, I had all sorts of tricks. Sometimes I'd pretend it was just a bad dream, and when I made it to the end of the day I'd be able to wake up to the real world. Sometimes I'd count everything around me, or I'd make up little stories about the people I passed. Sometimes I'd imagine a fiery angel appearing like the burning bush to Moses, and the angel would cut my master in two with his flaming sword. I did a lot of pretending. A lot of dreaming. It kept me alive, and I knew so long as I was alive there was always a chance."

"A chance for what?"

"Escape. Freedom. But you know, in all of the scenarios I dreamed up, I never thought Captain Roberts herself would rescue me. That would've been *too* outlandish," he laughed.

"The Cap's a good woman," Maddie said. "The best. She always does right by people; wants the best for 'em. She's a mother and a sister all rolled into one. And she fights like a bleedin' demon."

"Definitely a handy skill in a pirate," Franky agreed. "When do you think I'll start to feel like a real pirate?"

"After you been through a fight," Maddie said with conviction. "Once you've stuck someone with a blade, you'll feel like a pirate alright."

"I..." Franky hesitated, swallowing visibly. "Don't know how good I'll be in a fight. I've never really been in one before, and I don't know much about swords."

"Jo can teach you, or the Cap'n. Jo's mum was a soldier, a real dab hand with a sword, and she taught 'em both how to fight."

"That sounds like quite a story."

"That one's Jo's to tell."

"The Captain said I'm on trial – I've got three months to prove myself, and then she decides whether or not to leave me at a port."

"She tells everyone that. The only people who ever leave go because they want to. She's never forced someone off ship in the years I've been here. Harry's a pretty good judge of character."

"But what if we find ourselves in a fight and I freeze?" Franky persisted. "Or I hide? She won't like that. I mean, who ever heard of a pirate who doesn't like to fight?"

"Most of us don't like to fight," Maddie said. "Just the Cap and Katherine, really. And Cap only when she's riled. And we don't get into too many *serious* brawls. Just the occasional pub roust, or when another captain don't see eye-to-eye with us on something. And if we do cross swords with someone nasty, and you take cover, I don't think Harry will be too hard on you. Better that you get out of the way than get underfoot."

"You must be a really good fighter," Franky said. "You talk so calmly about it."

Maddie looked at him with a queer expression, somewhere between a smile and a frown. Her heart was so loud in her ears she wondered why he couldn't hear it. "Yeah. I'm a good fighter."

"So," Franky said, resting his arms against the

railing. "Anything in particular I should know?"

"What do you mean?"

"Well, you know. Shipboard scuttlebutt. Does anyone have a bad temper, or should I steer clear of so-and-so when they're drinking, and who's a Bible-thumper, and who's touchy about politics?"

"Um." The wind was ruffling his shaggy black hair and his profile was especially arresting against the blue backdrop of the sky. He was, she decided, the most handsome boy she'd ever clapped eyes on. "Well, Katherine sometimes doesn't know her own strength, especially when she's been drinking, so be careful if she tries to give you a hug or shake your hand. Miss Euphemia can be all sorts of odd, but she's not actually crazy — she just pretends she is sometimes. Wil is a, oh, whaddayacallem, doesn't believe in God?"

"An atheist?" Franky supplied.

"Yeah, one of them. She believes in science instead. Marcella and Jo are both pretty religious, though; they read pages from the Bible together every Sunday unless we're in the middle of running a blockade, and Jo's got a cross she never takes off. If you ever need a tool or something fixed, Lizzie's the girl to see. She's like a walking toolbox. Hope's real superstitious, so she'll probably bless you three times a day and give you a dozen lucky charms if you let her. But she's also real smart about herbs, so if you ever get a headache or stomach pain or anything like that, just tell her and she'll give you some pills or tea that'll work wonders.

"Zora's like a magpie: if she sees something shiny or interesting, she'll take it. So just don't leave anything you don't want to part with lying around – she doesn't really mean to steal, but sometimes she can't ignore the itch, you know? But she's good about giving things back if you kick up a fuss. Agnessa is real quiet usually, and keeps to herself, so I've got nothing in particular to say about her. Oh, and Harry threatens to do things all the time – throw you overboard, lock you in the hold, chop off your ears – but she never follows through. Just blusters a lot. It's when she gets all hard and cold and quiet that you need to be careful and jump quick to attention, but I've only seen her like that a couple times."

"You like it here? On *The Sappho*?"

"Yeah," Maddie said, shrugging nonchalantly. "Only real home I've ever had."

"I like it here, too," Franky said decisively. "This feels as good as Heaven. Or, at least, what I assume Heaven feels like. Lord, but it's like you can see the whole *world* from up here!" He leaned forward, hands on the railing, and laughed into the wind.

Maddie smiled, a wide and unselfconscious smile. "It's great, isn't it?" she agreed. "I love it up here – I like being up high. Everything else looks so small and problems don't feel so big or hard to manage. You can do anything here. You feel like you're flying."

"I understand," he said, breathless as he turned to her. "I know exactly what you mean."

Maddie wanted very badly to kiss him. She wanted to grab hold of him and pin him to the cushion and take her shirt off him – but for the first time in her life she felt truly shy.

Was it because she was so attracted to him? Burning in a way she had never burned before? Was she a little awed by his good looks and easy smile?

"Maddie," he said. "It's alright."

"What?" she said, dizzy.

"I want you to."

"To what?"

"Do everything you're thinking right now."

"And how do you know what I'm thinking?" she challenged.

"Because it's exactly what I've been thinking. I can see it in your face. The way you're standing. You're not afraid of me, are you?"

"No, I'm not," she said honestly. "Who could ever be afraid of you, Franky? You smile too damn much."

So she grabbed him by the shirt, pulled him close, and pressed her mouth to his to wipe it off.

As Jo already knew, Maddie was not a virgin. She'd tumbled with a few men in Bogo and other ports. Hearty, pleasant enough men with weathered hands and faces, tattoos on their arms and scars on their chests. They weren't all that gentle, but then neither was she, and they didn't hurt her intentionally, which was all that she'd asked of them.

But they didn't please her all that much, either. It was fun enough for a few minutes, and she could understand why people wanted to do such things, but she never truly enjoyed herself. After a few times, the thrill had burned away and she'd stuck to drinking beer and playing darts at the bar while Katherine and some of the others retired to more private rooms.

She knew immediately, as they fell back onto the cushion, that things would be different with Franky. Those other men, she had let them take charge because they had more experience and she was willing to learn. Why make a fool of herself when they already knew what they were doing? She was content to follow their instructions and be taught the steps to the world's oldest dance.

Franky, though, was making it clear that she was in control. Not because he was unschooled – the way he was touching her made it obvious that he was well-practiced. No, it was because he was *enjoying* letting her set the pace.

It was thrilling. She felt her stomach knot, hot with excitement, and she laughed as she pulled at his sleeves.

"If you wanted your clothes back," Franky said cheekily, "you only had to ask."

"Well, I do," she replied, just as saucy. "These trousers must come off *immediately*." She successfully yanked the shirt over his head before setting to work on unlatching his belt. He lifted his hips as she pulled down the trousers, so obliging, so helpful, and she went lightheaded at the sight of him lying bare beneath her.

"All present and accounted for," he said. "In case you were worried."

"I wasn't," she said. "I saw you the other day, remember?"

"I had hoped you were looking."

"Kinda hard not to, when you're so flagrant

about it," she said. "Did you already — I mean, where you already thinking about—"

"Yes," he said. "Is that so surprising?"

"We'd just met, for starters."

"I already knew you were beautiful and had lovely eyes."

"Is that all it takes?"

"Sometimes," he admitted without shame. "But I'd also felt that little buzz — you know? — that told me there was something there. Between us. Sometimes the body knows before the brain."

"What, like kismet? Destiny?"

"If you like."

He was being completely honest with her, she sensed, and she liked his frankness; it was refreshing to find a man who could be so straightforward. "Do you really think I'm beautiful?"

"Yes," he said, eyes tracing her face, as caressing as a touch. "Very."

"Well, good, because I think you're the prettiest boy I've ever seen." She drew a hand over his stomach, curled her fingers around his cock, and smiled when his breath audibly caught in his throat.

"Careful," he warned.

"I don't want to be careful," she countered.

"No, love, it's — it's been a *long time*," he said meaningfully. "I'm out of practice. And it wouldn't be fair for me to have fun before you have any."

"You really are very polite," Maddie said, hand slipping away. "Since I've gotten a good look, it's only fair to give you one, too," and she pulled her shirt over her head, the effect only slightly marred when her hair got caught on a button.

"Here, lemme help," Franky laughed, pushing himself up and reaching out.

"I'm not cut out to be a seductress," Maddie lamented, frustrated, as he carefully unwound the dark strands and let the shirt fall away.

"Nah, but that's alright," he reassured her, kissing the side of her neck. "Sex is always a little silly, don't you think? It's absurd, really. Especially if you do it right."

He bent his mouth to one breast and she grabbed his shoulders. "Ooh, that's amazing," she said. "No one's ever done that to me before."

Then she shifted over his lap just as he was lifting his head and her chin came crashing into his forehead.

"Ow!"

"Oof!"

"I'm so sorry!" she cried, clapping a hand over her mouth. "I'm sorry! I'm usually not *this* clumsy!"

"It's okay," he assured her, blinking and rubbing at the red mark. "A man should see stars at some point in these proceedings." The restrained laugh was audible behind his words.

"I'm really mucking this up, ain't I?"

"You're making it extra memorable, that's all."

"Lord, Franky, you're the bloody limit. How can you take so much in stride?"

"Perspective, love. I've got loads and loads of perspective. C'mere, just relax and stop thinking so much, you're as skittish as a horse..."

"Alright, wait, wait." She stood up and took a step back.

"If you don't want to go on," he said, "that's fine. We don't have to do anything—"

"Oh, shut up," Maddie said, struggling with her belt. "Just gimme a moment to get this off. I fully intend to ravish you — or as close as I can manage it — so there's no need to be all noble. I just want to take my trousers off without knocking your teeth out or somethin'."

Franky laughed with enough force to shake his shoulders. "Maddie, you are most definitely an interesting girl."

"Alright, there, now, let's try to accomplish something." She pushed him back, hands firm on his shoulders as she slid a brown thigh over his bronze waist and straddled him. "Let's agree: no more talking here on out."

"You don't like your lovers to whisper sweet nothings in your ear?"

"No, I just want my lover to make me feel good enough to scream."

"Fair enough. I'll see what I can do."

He slid a hand between them, fingers plunging through her wiry curls. Parted the damp folds of her skin and rubbed gently.

After only a few strokes she could scarcely breathe evenly. Her inner thighs were hot and slick and the wind had become perceptively colder over her back.

His other hand moved across her stomach, up to her breasts, where he brushed the side of his thumb across a hardened nipple.

Boy, did she like that. She braced her hands against his flat stomach and arched her back.

Those other men had kissed her a few times, squeezed her breasts once or twice, and then promptly plunged themselves between her legs. This was Maddie's first experience with foreplay and she knew with rock hard certainty that *this* was what Katherine liked so much about coupling. (When a woman like Katherine tells a man to do something, he most definitely does it.)

She could understand wanting to do *this* all the time.

Fingers slipped deeper. A shudder coursed down her back and her legs parted further over him. Open and inviting.

His hips bucked up with a twist and all at once his stiff erection was inside her, his palms firm against her waist and fingertips pressed into the curves of her thighs.

"Oh!" Maddie gasped, caught by surprise by the new sensation of fullness. She had never been in this position before, above a man. All the others had pinned her to the bed and thrust down – a thrust up felt entirely different.

She wasn't entirely sure what to do, but her body seemed to know. She rocked forward, then back, on pure instinct. Franky said something under his breath that she didn't recognize; Italian, she assumed. She did it again, slower this time, and felt an undeniable tremor beneath her.

Franky moved slightly and there was a whole new angle, a new feeling to process. She rubbed her body over his, sinking down and then rising up. It felt so good she did it again – and again – and again.

He was gripping her waist, holding her close, and every time she drew away he pulled her back in. Each time with more force and less breath. Each time more quickly than before.

She could feel it rising, like a tidal wave that had only begun to foam and was coming closer, picking up momentum. She was on the verge of cresting the summit, of falling over the edge, and she became overwhelmingly aware of the point where they joined. Every nerve ending strained with tension and begged for release.

She screamed and fell forward, crashing against his chest as their bodies shook together.

"Bloody hell," she swore when her tongue was no longer numb and her lips decided to cooperate again.

"I'm sorry," he said into her hair, voice muffled but the regret audible.

"Sorry?" she demanded indignantly, pushing herself up to glare at him only to find that her arms were still too rubbery. "Oof," she told his chest inconsequentially. "Sorry for what, exactly?"

"I tried to hold out longer but, well, as I said, it's been a long time," he confessed.

"Wait a moment," Maddie said, twisting her head to look at him. "You're apologizing because that didn't last longer?"

"Yes."

"Oh my... Franky, if you're telling me you can usually do *better* than that? Well. I just. Hmm. I need a moment to think about that."

# CURSED

Landon braced himself against the starboard rail of the ship and stretched, the muscles in his arms bunching under his shirt. "We don't get a catch soon, the good Captain's going to have conniptions."

"I know," Junia said. She glanced around, making sure that they were the only two nearby. Nicholas was on deck as well, but he was tending the helm, not anywhere close enough to overhear them. "Still. It's been a good day." She smiled. "Love you."

"Love you, too," he said, and as Nicholas's back was still turned, he gave her hand a quick clasp.

They had been sailing on the *India Marie* for almost a month now. Before they'd left land, she had shorn her hair and acquired a suitable amount of men's clothing. Nothing could help her high cheekbones and aquiline nose, but so far she'd passed herself off as a young man with no one the wiser.

Work on the ship was hard, so much harder than she ever could've anticipated, but there was an odd sort of liberty to it as well. Here, her duty was to scrub the decks and run errands for the captain and help the ship's cook. There was no worrisome nonsense about sharing a man's bed.

She still could not believe her good fortune at meeting Landon, especially after what her first intended had put her through in the gossip circles. Aldric had been carefully selected by her mother and father, a man who hadn't been wealthy but who had been comfortable, in a higher position than the one her family held. The marriage would have been beneficial to both of them – she would have married up, and he would have married 'a lovely young lady of good breeding stock', as her mother had said.

Well into their engagement, she'd had a serious discussion with Aldric. She had agreed that she would bear him children, as was her duty, but had confessed a certain squeamishness when it came to the act of making love. "After our children are born, I would prefer not to engage in such things again," she'd said. "Of course, I understand that my feeling is an oddity you most likely do not share... I know many men who go outside of the bounds of their marriage to satisfy themselves, and I will not mind in the slightest if you do so. You do understand, don't you?" she asked, trying her best to stand straight and composed, like a proper lady, when all she wanted to do was wring her hands.

"I do," he'd said, and the next day he had broken off their engagement.

Women who had never paid her much mind now audibly laughed when they caught sight of her. Men gave her derisive looks.

But nothing had been worse than the reception her own parents gave her, once they'd heard the rumors of how she'd ranted at poor Aldric about how she found his very touch repulsive.

They had evicted her from their home. She'd

at first gone to a house for young women, but the proprietress had explained to her that the women there were orphans or from other unfortunate backgrounds, and they were there until they were sufficiently educated to be able to find a good husband. "Such a thing is quite beyond you, I'm afraid", she'd sniffed.

Eventually, she'd gotten a job at a seaside tavern, working in exchange for a room upstairs and a small bit of wages.

She'd been terrified her first night on the job. Her coworker, Tessa, had helped her to calm down and given her some pointers about who was genuinely friendly and who she needed to avoid.

And she'd done just fine. Despite her parents' insistence that she'd ruined her own future, she'd been happy.

Then one night, amidst a crowd of other sailors, Landon had come in.

Though he hadn't known about her past when they'd first started talking, he'd found out soon enough. It was impossible not to. But instead of giving her a skeptical look and then retreating, he'd asked her what happened.

He hadn't left once she'd explained herself.

They had wed less than a year later. Her parents weren't there, nor were her childhood friends. But the owner of the bar offered her the upstairs room free of rent for a month as a wedding present, and Tessa had grinned infectiously as the two of them had said their vows.

She had taken the room for the month, saving up her wages in preparation for following him out to sea.

Landon had been nervous about the idea at first, but he had quickly warmed to it. The thought of having a wife at port, while common, had never quite appealed to him. There were ships that allowed women on board, though they were few and far between – the *India Marie* wasn't one of them.

"Then it's simple," she'd said. "I'll disguise myself."

Landon had brought her on board the *India Marie* as his young cousin in need of work, and the Captain had agreed to test her out on this voyage as a cabin boy.

It was brutal work, but rewarding. She'd loved listening to the sailors' stories at the tavern, and now she was living some of her own. She'd never seen anything quite so beautiful as a sunrise out on the ocean.

Still, they might have to find a new ship when they got back to shore. They'd barely caught any fish at all, and the mood on the ship was darkening day by day. Depending on his own personal finances, it might be a long time before the Captain of the *India Marie* was ready to head out again.

Perhaps on their next ship, she wouldn't have to disguise herself.

If they struck out on their next voyage together at all. Landon seemed quite content, but how could she be sure, particularly when they were given so few moments of privacy? Thus far he did not seem to mind her aversion to intimacy, but perhaps he was just trying to make her feel better. Despite his station in life, he was far more of a gentleman than Aldric could ever dream of being; he would never wish to be cruel.

It could not be the wish of any man, to never be able to truly touch his wife.

"Tell me," she said quietly. "Do you... do you regret this?"

"Gonna have to be more specific," Landon said. "I spent most of the day up in the crow's nest and I'm pretty sure my *hair* is sunburned."

"All this," she asked, before finally gathering the courage to say what she truly wanted to ask. "Me."

He stepped forward, bending his head down closer to hers. "There are times I wish I could lie with you, yes, but that's because I'm not much good at words. And I can't help but think that if I could show you how I feel instead, then you wouldn't doubt me."

"It's not you that I doubt, Landon—"

"I love you because of your spirit. How hard you work here, the fact that you still smiled back home despite all those simpletons talking about you. There's so much more to you than what's between your legs."

She blinked at the blunt words, and his ears reddened. "Sorry. Sometimes it's easy to forget you were raised a lady." He paused again, scrubbing a hand over his face. "Not that you don't deserve every courtesy that ladies receive, of course—"

"I understand what you meant," she said, laughing.

*~*~*

Junia awoke with a great jerk, and at first she thought the ship had struck something.

Then she realized that someone had yanked at her shirt.

"What is it?" she asked, swatting the hand away, thinking that someone had caught hold of her garment and shook her in an attempt to wake her. "What's happened—"

But the hand returned, and then buttons tore. Her exhaustion disappeared in a flash of anger and panic, and she tugged the torn halves of her shirt together, praying that the man hadn't seen the pale bandages that bound her chest.

A voice above her roared out for the Captain, and she scrambled to her feet, blinking in the dreary light of the crew's cabin. The man facing her was the first mate, a surly, nitpicky sort by the name of Brodbeck.

For the first time since she'd met him, he smiled.

"Knew it," he hissed. "Just knew it."

"What's all this commotion about?" the Captain asked, storming into the crew's quarters even as Landon rushed to her side.

"Believe our cabin 'boy' has something to tell us, sir," Brodbeck said.

"Whatever it is can be said above deck," he said. "Heading into sirens' waters; we all need to keep a weather eye out."

"What do I do?" Junia hissed, as she and Landon were jostled along by the rest of the crew

147

on their way to the deck.

"I–" he began, but then Brodbeck hauled him away from her, the helmsman helping to hold him back when Landon tried to pull away.

"Something this one didn't tell us about his 'cousin,'" the first mate crowed, still grinning. "Tell the lad to open his shirt."

When she didn't immediately comply, one of the crewmen reached out and snatched at her, pulling the fabric out of her hands.

"Who is she to you?" the Captain asked Landon.

"I am his cousin!" Junia exclaimed. "We had communicated through letters, we only met in person earlier this year, he didn't know–"

The Captain's hand cracked across her face. "Quiet, stowaway."

In that instant, for the first time, she was *scared* rather than angry or indignant.

They might well hurt her for this deception. Might hurt her husband.

She had talked him into this foolishness. She had to keep their attention on her. Landon would understand what she was doing and would play along, surely.

"I am no stowaway!" she said, though her split-open lower lip hurt at the words. "I have worked hard for your ship and her crew; you know this!"

"What I know," the Captain said coldly, "is that the weather has been unseasonably poor, and the fishing worse. Now I also know why." He nodded toward the railing. "Send her over."

"No!"

She wanted to shout to Landon, tell him to let them believe her lie. She was a strong swimmer; she could make it to another ship, or perhaps even to land. But she'd barely opened her mouth when he pulled away from the first mate and the helmsman, spinning and punching Brodbeck in the face when the man tried to regain his hold.

He made it two steps toward her before one of the other crewmen drew a sword and ran him through.

Junia screamed, tried frantically to get to him, but then the Captain lifted her off her feet and pitched her into the the ocean. She took in a lungful of water and choked, gagging as she resurfaced, her hands scrabbling uselessly at the side of the ship.

This couldn't be happening.

Couldn't be.

They were supposed to head back in to land next week.

She and Landon would travel just a little further inland, back to her hometown and Tessa's tavern.

They would spend several nights in her old room and figure out where they wanted to go afterwards.

He was fine, he was fine...

"Looking for this?" Brodbeck hollered down at her, laughing as several of the crewmen threw her tall, well-built, handsome husband over the side. His body was weighted down, just as it would've been at a normal burial, had he died of natural causes, and he was gone almost before she realized he was there.

She cried out in protest and dove, wincing as the salt from the ocean seeped into the cut on her lip, but her usual skill evaded her.

She couldn't hold her breath through the tears.

She watched the *India Marie* sail away, the crew hollering and cheering now that they'd 'turned their luck'. Though she knew it was a waste of breath, she screamed after them, shrieking every damnation and curse she could think of.

Curse.

Unable to believe the idea that she didn't want to be with *anyone*, not in that fashion, most of her town had latched onto Aldric's explanation that she must prefer women. And when her parents had evicted her from their home, her mother's voice had trembled, but she'd been steely-eyed as she'd said, "I cannot believe what a selfish witch you've turned out to be. Could you at least have thought of your little sister's prospects? What chance does she have now of finding a good husband, with such a degenerate in the family?" She'd sighed then, turning away. "I pray you'll be just as cursed as you've made us."

Knowing that the siren's lair lay to the west, Junia swam east, but as the sun rose higher in the sky she began to despair of finding another ship or any type of land. There was only water, stretching far and glinting brightly on every side of her.

She floated on her back, closing her eyes against the rays of the sun. Maybe she should stop swimming entirely. It might not be so bad. She could join Landon then, in whatever world lay beyond this one.

No, she decided.

He wouldn't want her to give up. She knew that.

Besides, she thought. She had a ship to burn.

*~*~*

When the voice came, at first she thought it was her husband. Landon hadn't been dead when they'd thrown him over after all; he'd cast off the weights and followed after her and now he was here, was–

No, she thought, blinking in the sunlight. Landon would never allow his hair to get so unkempt, or for a beard to grow. Such things were "quite beneath a gentleman, even a seafaring one", he'd joked.

Then the man moved closer, and she saw the motion of a tail in the water.

Her arms felt as heavy as steel, but panic flooded into her, compelling her to twist away and swim. She'd heard tales of mermaids; how they dragged people to the bottom of the ocean and waited to see if they would turn, then kept those who did as slaves. Perhaps she would drown out here, and perhaps she would be turned, but she would not be beholden to rats like the men who'd left her here to die.

"Are you through?"

She gasped in a breath and glanced to the side. The merman was swimming along on his back beside her, keeping pace quite easily. And she suddenly realized how silly she was being; if he meant to drown her he could've caught hold of her ankle and dragged her under before she had any inkling he was there.

Though her thoughts were foggy, she did her best to gather them into some semblance of order. "My name is Junia Drake. My husband was... was lost to me today. I would be very much obliged if you could get me to dry land."

"I'll do you one better," the stranger said. "I'll get you to Captain Roberts." He held out his hand. "My name is Kaimana."

"Pleased to meet you," she said, thinking woozily that her mother would be quite happy with her manners. She swam alongside him for a few moments, until she realized that when she told her legs to kick, half the time they weren't listening.

"Here," he said. "Hold on to my shoulders." She did so, tucking her knees up close to her chest so that she was largely resting on his back.

He was of the same general build as her husband. Many of the men in town her parents had deemed 'suitable' had been reed-thin and pale. They'd been bookkeepers and the like, politician's sons and fine gentlemen.

She wondered what her mother and father would say if they knew their curse had worked. Would they finally take her back, or would they shake their heads and close the door?

Didn't matter. She wasn't being taken to land. She was going to a ghost ship.

That was the last story she'd heard about

Captain Roberts and *The Sappho*, anyway. That all the women onboard were ghosts, bent on savaging the living.

Maybe she was dead, and Kaimana had been sent to guide her to the afterlife. Would make as much sense as anything else.

He was talking steadily, and she was grateful for the cadence of his voice even if she had no idea what he was actually saying. He was speaking English, she could recognize that, and once in a while she caught what she believed was a name. Probably talking of the people he was taking her to. She tried to focus, but after a moment she gave up and closed her eyes.

*The name of the ship was the* India Marie, she thought. *The captain's name was Absolon Deniaud. The first mate's name was Brodbeck. The name of the ship was the* India Marie. *The captain's name...*

She awoke when the constant rhythm of the merman's voice snapped from something calming into a warning.

"Hold your breath."

Junia sucked in a quick gasp of air and then they were underwater.

Unable to resist, she opened her eyes and looked up, trying to discern what the danger was. The salt water stung her eyes and she quickly closed them again – but not before she saw the enormous shadow of a passing ship.

The merman clasped her hands, holding her in place. Just when the ache in her chest grew unbearable and she thought that maybe he had changed his mind, maybe he had grown tired of carrying her and decided to drown her after all, he tugged her upwards and she kicked hard, taking several grateful breaths as soon as she resurfaced.

She wiped the salt water from her eyes and peered off after the departing ship. "Why did you dive?" she asked. "Maybe they could've helped."

"Not that ship," he said. "*The Blood Moon* collects merfolk tails."

Junia grimaced. She knew that some sailors and pirates caught any mermaid they could, stripping the scales, carving off their tails, mounting their heads and using them for decoration for their flags or belts or to sell on shore. "I'm sorry," she said. "Clearly more ships than the *India Marie* need to be turned to ash."

He stared at her for a few seconds, and then he grinned. Aside from his build, this Kaimana really looked nothing like Landon. He was dark where her husband was – had been – fair, but that smile, bright and sudden and completely honest, reminded her so much of her Landon that she felt like she'd been punched in the chest.

"I think you and Harry'll get along just fine," he said, and to her surprise and mortification she burst into tears.

*~*~*

When they reached *The Sappho*, they discovered that the landing craft was already over the side, waiting for them. Junia wondered how many times Kaimana had brought lost souls to this ship. He lifted her into the craft and then pulled himself in, tugging hard on the rope and calling up to the deck.

Junia looked up as the landing craft rose above the water, and then she looked across to Kaimana. "I thank you, sir," she said. "I am in your debt."

He shook his head. "Everyone in the pod has their job to do. This is mine."

# DISTRACTIONS

Harry didn't think her crew had ever spent so much time in the water. With Kai there to warn them if danger was approaching, they could swim without fear of hostile sharks or merfolk. Many of them took to the water like they were mermaids themselves.

Sometimes, Harry was certain that everyone on her crew was at least a little in love with him. The smitten smiles that came to their faces whenever he spoke to them – or, in Maddie's case, whenever he was even mentioned – were certainly evidence enough.

It didn't surprise her that Maddie had fallen in with him immediately. Despite how violent she could be, in her usual frame of mind Harry suspected that Maddie would call even Wrath Drew a friend if he apologized sincerely enough.

And where Maddie went, Franky followed. She often caught the two of them leaning over the railing, having laughing conversations with Kai late into the night.

Wilhelmina, who had been a trifle nervous around him for the first several weeks – she hadn't had the best experiences with merfolk – had changed her tune right quick one afternoon when he called to them from the water, asking if they wanted to see baby sea monsters.

Held carefully in his hands had been almost a dozen kraken, most no bigger than the coins on

Zora's skirts. Wil had immediately grabbed her notebook and clambered into the landing craft, and ever since had been sure to take time each day to be lowered to the water, asking questions about ocean creatures and writing extensive notes.

Kai had had to do no work at all to win over either Euphemia or Silence; his role in rescuing the young siren had been testament enough. And Hope, their healer, was fascinated by the medicines he had shown them.

Junia so clearly coveted the sword he had brought to Harry back on his island that several days ago he had brought up a dagger for her, a wicked-looking thing curved into a half-moon shape. Junia was so thrilled at the gift that she'd given him a brief hug in thanks, which had startled Harry to no end. Though some members of her crew were tactile almost to a fault – Katherine and her bone-crushing hugs came to mind – Junia was not one of them.

Zora had also been entranced by the things he was able to bring back from the ocean's depths; any time they landed at a port she asked to be shown to any wrecks that were within her own diving distance. Many times ones that close to the shore had already been stripped of everything truly valuable, but Zora's definition of valuable didn't always consist of gold and jewels; she had found countless oddments, including a delicately filigreed hand mirror that she'd spent hours shining up before giving it to her beloved Tessa as a gift.

Even Jo had been drawn into a water fight one afternoon, where she had "battled ruthlessly and well". She'd proclaimed this with a grin, wringing her long braids out over the rail, as Harry arched both her eyebrows in disbelief.

She was glad the crew got on so well with him. She just wished sometimes that he wasn't so distracting.

To the crew.

Right now he was in the landing craft, explaining auras and how each of theirs looked. Maddie listened to him and then stared at her own hand in fascination, as if by focusing hard enough she could also see the bright yellow glow he'd told her of.

"How about the Captain's?" Agnessa asked with a grin. Harry, startled at the sudden inclusion, worked to keep a stern expression on her face as she walked up to the landing craft.

"I'm thinking it's red, with impatience, due to the lack of work being done."

Agnessa laughed, and the others were smiling as they moved back to their posts. Harry gave Kai a brief nod and turned to walk away, pausing when he spoke.

"You're wrong, you know."

"About what?" she asked, though the context of their conversation made it perfectly clear. She wasn't sure she wanted to know a thing about her aura; she already had plenty of suspicions.

"Your aura. It's not red. It's black."

Harry remembered what he'd said about Wrath Drew's aura and felt something in her heart freeze. She started to back away, and something must have shown in her face because he reached out and grabbed hold of her hand.

"That isn't a bad thing," he said. "The color itself is only one part of an aura. There are other considerations. Yours is nothing like oil. It's the black of the night sky. A comfort, if inscrutable. And when you're not at rest, the edges of it catch fire. It's beautiful."

She found herself wishing that he was an expert at cards, was a skilled liar, because then she could tell herself that he was just trying to flatter her. But the words were said with such sincerity that she had no choice but to believe them, and she had no idea what to do with that.

"Well," she finally said. "That's... that's good to know, I suppose."

Feeling utterly off-balance, she tugged her hand out of his and turned to go below decks.

Something, somewhere, *had* to require her immediate attention.

# DOLDRUMS

Four days.

Four days since even the slightest breeze had touched their sails.

Harry paced back and forth across the deck, as if glaring out at the water would get them moving again. Much more of this and the crew would truly start losing patience; even Jo was looking strained.

They had done everything to keep themselves occupied, and Harry was starting to run low on ideas. The ship had been scrubbed from stem to stern – twice. Backgammon and checkers and chess had been played. Supplies had been checked and re-checked. Maddie had taken to giving odd fortune telling readings to everyone with a set of over-sized cards she'd squirreled away in her locker; Harry didn't have the heart to dissuade her anymore.

Kai was sitting up on deck in the landing craft. He'd been telling them stories off and on for half the day, and was now reclining back in the craft, his eyes closed. Harry caught her eyes lingering on his chest and quickly turned away, pacing the other direction.

Junia was leaning against the mast, sharpening one of her knives. Agnessa sat beside her with a book, looking particularly tiny and lost now that she wasn't busy at the helm.

Zora was also pacing, having long since run

out of patience rearranging the baubles on her skirt. She paused to eye Junia's knives thoughtfully, and Harry shook her head. "I remember what happened the last time we had a knife-throwing contest," she said. "Franky just about lost that eye."

"It was his suggestion that we put a lemon on his head and try to knock it off," Zora grumbled.

"Be that as it may be," Harry said. "Let's avoid sharp things, hm?"

"What else are we supposed to do?"

"I don't know," Harry admitted. "Water's calm; we haven't seen any sign of dangerous mers or sharks. Suppose we could go for a swim."

"Mite chilly for that today," Zora said reluctantly.

"Read all your books?"

"Three times over. We need to pick up more in port, assuming we ever get moving again."

"Well, then I don't know what to tell you," Harry said. She was feeling skin-crawlingly restless herself

"Talk to the others, see if they have any ideas. Go braid Kai's hair. Something."

To her surprise, Zora's face lit up and she promptly went to Kai, sitting down behind him. She spoke a few rapid words, and though Kai raised an eyebrow, he nodded with a smile. Zora untied a few beads and coins from her skirt, setting them beside her in a tiny pile before she began to braid.

As she wove the trinkets into his hair, other members of the crew ventured closer, watching. Maddie dropped down next to Zora, staring intently at her fluid motions for a moment before she began to try and weave her own braid.

Junia shrugged and slid her knife into its scabbard, moving to Zora's other side.

"Been a long time since I've done this," Junia said quietly. "Mother's hands had started to grow shaky by the time I reached my tenth year, so I always braided my little sister's hair of a morning."

"How are you even managing to put beads in there?" Maddie asked Zora, frowning. "I can't even get the braid down right! Also, Kai, I may have tied your hair into a knot here. Sorry."

"Here," Zora said, as Agnessa came over to wedge in beside Maddie. "You do it like this."

"Just look at you all," Harry said, trying vainly to hide a smile. "Scourge of the seven seas."

"You can come sit down as well," Kai said. "The ship won't sink if you stop pacing."

"I'll stick to my pacing, thank you," she said. "Besides, it seems crowded over there."

Kai glanced to the side to look at her, drawing an indignant squawk from Maddie as the motion moved the section of hair she was fiddling with. "Still got a free spot, if you want to join us?" he said, grinning as he patted his lap.

An image flashed into her mind – her sitting chest-to-chest with him, his arms wrapped around her waist as she threaded her fingers through his hair – and she blinked quickly, turning her attention to Maddie when she heard a choked-off noise from her that sounded suspiciously like a laugh. "First one of you to snicker, dies," she said.

"Would howling with laughter fall under that?" Maddie asked, a wide smile on her face.

"Because I'm pretty sure you're blushing and I don't have enough self-control to handle that."

"What if we were to just exchange significant glances whilst nudging each other, Cap'n?" Agnessa asked.

"See?" Harry said. "This is what happens when Captains don't flog their crew enough. Sass."

"True," Kai said amiably. "But you still haven't answered my question."

Perhaps it was the challenging smile on his face or the gleeful looks on her crew's faces; perhaps it was the restlessness from the four-day doldrums. But Harry walked over, brushing away a lock of hair the wind blew into her face as she started to climb into the landing craft.

The wind.

"Agnessa, helm!" she ordered. "Kath, Junia, the sails!"

She turned away, and though her heart thrilled at the knowledge that soon they would be sailing again, she couldn't deny a twinge of regret.

# FADING MEMORIES

"How much?" Jo asked, pointing to a quite charming hat with a large red-and-gold feather in the band.

"Twenty drachmas," the vendor said, grinning as he looked her over. "But I'll give it to you for ten, plus a kiss."

Though Jo knew it was a good deal – and there hadn't been any nastiness in the way he'd looked at her, simply appreciation – the derisive look was on her face before she could rein it in, and before he could react, she moved away.

There were some days when she hated visiting the markets.

She heard Maddie whoop with joy and glanced over to see the girl waving three newly-purchased penny dreadfuls, much to Harry's played-up chagrin. Beside her, Franky was laughing.

Jo leaned against the dusty wall of a nearby building, half-watching the crew as they milled around the busy market, most of her concentration on the memory of a night so many years ago, when she'd snuck into Aveline's room and dared to steal a kiss. She'd been emboldened by the fact that Ave was leaving the next day, that she wasn't sure when the two of them would see each other again.

At least that night she had *known* the separation was coming.

She wasn't a fool, at least not completely. She knew that she was holding out hope for a woman who was likely long dead.

Sometimes, in her darker moments, she prayed that Aveline *was* gone. Because most of the alternatives were so much worse.

But until she knew for certain, until she had some kind of proof, she couldn't seem to let go.

Once, she had tried. Tessa had introduced her to a friend of hers, Emerald. She'd been funny and brassy and her hair had been a very particular shade of gold. Jo had picked up drink after drink as the night wore on, trying to convince herself that it had been years since Aveline's disappearance, that no one would fault her for moving on, that she certainly shouldn't fault herself.

In the end, though she had gone to bed with Emerald, she hadn't been able to stay the night, and in fact had been quite brusque with the poor woman when she'd asked her what was wrong.

The next afternoon, she had gone back and tried haltingly to explain herself. When she was only partway through, Emerald had taken her hands, looking up at her sympathetically. "S'alright," she'd said. "You don't have to tell me anything you're not ready to say. We all got our own pains to live with and things we'd rather not dwell on, me included. Unless you think my mother and father gave me Emerald as a legal name?"

Jo had smiled, shaking her head, and Emerald had chanced moving closer, pulling her into a hug. "You seem a good woman, Josephine. I hope your pain lessens someday."

And it had, that was the damnable thing.

As the years went on she could remember

the shade of Aveline's hair, but not the precise color of her eyes. Were they blue-green, or more the blue of the sky on a sunny day?

Her laugh echoed throughout Jo's memory, but whenever she tried to focus on it, it slipped through the cracks like smoke.

And though she doubted she would ever become involved with anyone again, that was one of the few ways that Aveline still affected her daily life. There had been some days when she barely thought of her at all.

Worse still were the situations that *did* make Jo think of her. In every battered face, every horrific story, every rescued woman who trembled and cried or shouted and raged once they were sure they were finally safe, she saw an echo of Aveline.

Aveline had been such a caring soul, and so quick to laugh. She would hate that Jo so often associated her with pain now.

"Present for you," Harriet said, jolting her out of her thoughts by tickling her nose with the red-and-gold hatband feather.

"You paid him the twenty drachmas?"

Harry snorted. "Hell no, I gave him a kiss. Made the blighter's week, if I do say so myself. So," she said, standing on tiptoe to take off Jo's current hat and plunk the new one down on her head, "what are you over here brooding about?" The expression on her face said that she was half-sure she already knew.

"Ave," Jo admitted softly.

"We'll find her, Jo," Harry said, her voice no less determined than it had been the first time she'd said those words.

But it was different for Harry, Jo thought, as the smaller woman pulled her in for a tight, brief hug. Aveline was her sister, her blood.

How could she ever tell her that while most days she would gladly give her own life to have Aveline back safe and whole, there were other days when she wished that she'd never become involved with her in the first place, when – though she hated herself for it – she hoped even for evidence of her death, if only so this limbo would come to an end?

Harry would loathe her, and rightly.

She'd heard so many words used to describe her over the years, but the one that showed up most often was "stoic". The term had always pleased her. It brought to mind strength. Steadfastness. The ability to control one's emotions.

Clearly, the description wasn't accurate at all, but if she was a good enough actress to fool so many people, then perhaps someday the facade would take hold. Become the truth.

Aveline was probably gone, yes.

But someday, they might well find her. If they did, Josephine prayed that she would've formed herself into someone who deserved her.

# MOON-DRUNK

Harry leaned back slightly and rested her weight on her hands, staring up at the moon. She was vaguely aware that she should be in bed by now – it wasn't as if she got much sleep as it was; she couldn't afford to miss out on any – but she was reluctant to leave.

Whether that was because of the pleasant weather and calm seas or because of her current company was a question she refused to debate.

She and Kai sat in the landing craft, tied off so that it rested about three feet above the surface of the water. It was as close to privacy as one could get on a crowded ship, though even now she could hear some of her crew moving around on deck.

She'd heard the phrase "moon-drunk" before; wondered if that was what she was feeling now. Her thoughts seemed a trifle fuzzy and she felt very warm and... relaxed?

Definitely a sign she should get some sleep. Relaxation wasn't a luxury she could afford while at sea. The moment she let her guard down, the weather might change or other pirates would approach or...

Kai flipped the fan of his tail fin lazily back and forth, and she found herself distracted by the motion. She started to reach out, then realized what she was doing and froze. Glancing up at his face, she saw his bemused expression and cleared her throat, drawing her hand back and pressing it to her stomach, as if afraid of what it might do otherwise. "Shouldn't do that," she muttered.

"Why shouldn't you?"

"Well. I don't know how much you might have in common with human men, really, but there are certain... sensitive areas. Particularly below the waist. You can't just put your hands all over someone."

"Sensitive?" he asked. "How so?"

She peered at him, trying to decipher if he was teasing her, but he simply looked curious, the way he did when Jo explained a human custom that he found odd or when Maddie showed the new recruits how to spar.

Wonderful. How was she supposed to explain... "Well," she said again. "Um. There are – you see, there are certain parts of the human body that, when they're touched, it feels – very pleasant."

"Ohh," he said, nodding in understanding. "Like when Agnessa braids my hair."

"Different kind of pleasant," she said, and then she caught sight of the grin he'd been trying to hold back and realized he had been teasing her. She narrowed her eyes and looked away, trying to draw her dignity back around herself. "Since you understand, you can see why that wouldn't be proper."

And all right, that had been a bit too much dignity. She was pretty sure she heard a snort from up on deck. Someone, she decided, clearly wanted to know what it was like to be keelhauled.

"It wouldn't be," he agreed amiably. "So, again – why shouldn't you?"

And his voice was low and warm, a caress in and of itself, but he didn't physically reach out, didn't touch, and she knew that that step was hers to take, as surely as she knew her own name.

"...Kai," she began, voice little more than a whisper, barely audible over the wind and the slapping of the waves against the hull. "Is this a good idea?"

She knew he knew what she meant without elaboration. That she was speaking of more than simply sitting together, late at night, and staring up at the moon.

"I know we have many differences, Harry," he replied, matching her soft tone, expression earnest. "We come from opposing worlds. I can never live entirely in yours, and you cannot live entirely in mine. But we are both clever. We can navigate such obstacles. Together." He hesitated, hand settling beside hers on the wooden seat of the lifeboat. "...If you want to."

"I do," Harry whispered, her inherent boldness asserting itself with a rush of adrenaline. She slid her hand over his, gripping it tightly. "I want *you*."

And with her other hand cupping his jaw, she kissed him fiercely, hungrily, savoring the salt on his lips and the eager passion with which he returned her kiss.

# THE ART OF KILLING

"I want to learn how to kill a man," Junia announced.

Katherine's braying laugh ended on an abrupt note. The other conversations died as quickly. Everyone turned to the figure sitting at the very end of the table. It was the first time she had spoken all night; she sat ramrod straight and stiff, the plate of food before her untouched, the hollows beneath her piercing eyes still black with the bruises of her ordeal.

"Probably a good idea," Harry said lightly. "You'll need to know how to fight – things can get mighty hairy out here."

"Not just fight," Junia said. "I need to know how to kill. They murdered my husband. Stabbed him and threw his body overboard like he was trash. I intend to do the same to them."

She regarded the women – and human man – who had given her shelter, food, and new clothes. They had tended her injuries, listened to her story, and had even offered her a permanent place on board if she wanted it.

What she truly wanted, more than anything else, was revenge. Could they give her that?

Perhaps Lizzie – she had muscular arms that spoke of physical labor. She had to know how to handle herself in a fight. Or Katherine, the logical choice when it came to brawling and bashing a man's brains out through his ears. Harry herself was reputed to be a hellion with a long sword. Or maybe–

"I'll teach you."

Jo regarded her calmly, seemingly unmoved by her passionate pledge. In the few days she had been onboard, the first mate had struck Junia as someone methodical. Precise. Coiled like a big cat about to pounce. She moved with economical grace, every step intentional; she wasn't one to waste energy with wild gestures or emotion.

But there was something Junia sensed beneath her unruffled exterior: a potential for explosive violence that could be unnerving.

She wondered if the others had noticed this, or if she was just imagining it.

"Jo's our best swordswoman," Harry said. "After she's done with you, if there's anything you don't know about handling a sword, then it ain't worth knowing."

"Perfect," Junia said. "When shall we start?"

*~*~*

"Third move," Jo ordered.

Junia adjusted her stance, shaking her head to dash the sweat from her eyes. Her grip on the hilt of her borrowed blade was becoming uncertain – her palm was too wet and slippery from the heat.

*The Sappho* had been sitting on water as smooth as glass for two days now. The wind had disappeared, the waves had abandoned them, the sun was doing its level best to roast them all alive – they might as well have been anchored in a harbor.

Junia had never experienced such a calm ocean before; she would have been more demoralized by it if not for the rigors of her training.

"Fifth stance," said Jo.

The sword fell to the deck with a clatter, slipping free of her fingers like a frantic fish.

"There are ways to adjust for that," her teacher said before she could apologize; those sharp brown eyes didn't miss much. "You can rub powder over your hands to improve your grip and reduce sweating. Chalk dust works well, though that's in short supply on a ship. Barring that, I recommend wearing a glove on your dominant sword hand. We can ask Kai to make you one of shark and sealskin – that will serve a dual purpose. It'll absorb sweat and repel blood, to improve your grip, and also provide a small layer of protection against your opponent's blades."

"I've seen swords before with fancy basket hilts," Junia said. "It must be easier to hold onto one of those."

"Yes, but that type of sword may not be well-suited to your purposes," Jo said patiently. "Most blades made with that type of hilt are intended for fencing or dueling, fine-tipped, meant for inflicting minimal damage. You aim to kill, not wound. And if your opponent is skilled at disarming, your fingers can get caught in that fancy basket hilt and break. If you're determined to be thorough," the first mate added, "we'll find you a fencing rapier and I'll teach you the best way to handle it. But for now, let's focus on the saber and the cutlass – then we'll move to the scimitar and the dao."

"I had no idea there were so many different kinds of swords," Junia said, taking advantage of the brief pause to drink from the bucket of water Maddie had left for them. "I used to think of a sword as a bigger knife."

"Each design has its strengths and its weaknesses. The cutlass and the dao are wider and heavier – better for chopping movements, which is why so many executioners in the East favor them. In Arabia, the punishment for thievery is your right hand, lopped off at the wrist. And if you're convicted of treason, they take your head instead."

Jo swung the sword in a sure arc, and Junia could almost see the invisible convict before her.

"The scimitar and the saber are lighter, longer, better when you want to keep your enemy at a safer distance. These swords slash and stab quicker than the heavier, curved blades. They require less shoulder strength and more dexterity at the wrist and elbow. Now, let's work on parrying and defensive stances."

"Did you pick all of this up on your own, in your travels?" Junia asked as their blades clashed and clanged. "Or did you have a teacher?"

"My mother. As soon as I could stand straight and hold a sword up. She told me it was a hard and dangerous world, and that a woman needed to know how to defend herself."

"And how did your mother know all of this?"

"She was an *amiral* in *La Royale*," Jo said, tongue slipping smoothly around the French, assuming the accent of one taught the language from birth. "She sailed with the French Navy for fifteen years."

Junia almost dropped her sword again. "But how? I thought women weren't allowed to enlist!" she said, wide-eyed.

"They aren't," Jo confirmed. "So she disguised herself as a man. Instead of Francoise Duveau she was Francois Duveau. Worked her way up the same as any man. When she achieved the rank of *amiral*, she decided she was tired of playing pretend and revealed what she really was. They didn't believe her at first – everyone knew Francois 'Le Panthère' Duveau was a brilliant tactician, leader, and swordsman; he couldn't *possibly* be a female – so she tore open her uniform to convince them. She said it made one of the old *commandants* almost swallow his tongue."

"What did they do to her?" Junia asked, dreading the answer.

"They had just promoted her – to strip her of rank and discharge her from the military at that point, to have to admit openly just why they were doing so, would make the entire French Navy look like fools. She had a nearly spotless record and an impressive list of achievements and medals to her name. They sent her on an extremely far-flung mission to the Solomon Islands, assumed that she'd be eaten by the cannibals there, and washed their hands of her."

"But she came back," Junia said with a smile.

"Yes, with a treaty signed by Chief Waganu promising that his tribe would not attack or eat anyone sailing under a French flag. The Navy took the treaty and begged Mum to retire. By then, she was pretty tired and ready to settle down, so she agreed. Left *La Royale* with full honors and a pension. Married Dad, had me, and opened the pub."

"Amazing. Is she still..."

"Throwing rowdy drunks out every night and complaining about the price of English beer? Yes."

"I'd like to meet her," Junia said. She looked down at the sword in her hand. "She was incredibly brave to do all of that."

"No braver than you," said Jo.

"I—" She stopped herself. Thought for a long pause. "I wasn't brave," she said finally. "I was stupid. And it cost Landon his life."

"Junia, look at me." Harry might be the captain, but Jo could be plenty commanding herself. It was a tone of voice that couldn't be disobeyed. "What they did was *not your fault*. They murdered your husband and threw you overboard out of sheer superstitious stupidity and cruelty. Men like that use any excuse to exert power over others. They kill because they enjoy it, and because they believe themselves above the law. And someday they will pay for what they've done. Even if you never find them or put them to the sword, God Himself will give them their due, and they will suffer for eternity. Of that I'm certain."

Jo's dark eyes *burned*, and Junia tore away from them with difficulty. She swallowed thickly, mouth abruptly dry, and blinked away the sting of tears. Her words had rung with truth — she wanted so badly to take them to heart and believe them.

But when she closed her eyes she could still

see Landon's face in that last moment, could still hear the sword as it went through his body and the splash as he sank beneath the waves.

It wouldn't have happened if not for her. Her tall, golden, kind-eyed husband would still be sailing and laughing and whistling if not for her.

His death was a debt that had to be repaid. The men who took it would pay it – and if she died in the process, so be it.

But there would be a reckoning in the end, nonetheless.

"Show me that disarming technique again," she said finally, her voice steady and her eyes dry. "I think I've almost got it."

# STRENGTHENING BONDS

"Do you ever do anything with your hair?" Kai asked, deep voice rumbling pleasantly in the broad chest her cheek rested upon.

They were sprawled in the shallows on the sandy beach, the water lapping up to their waists. Her shirt was plastered to her back and she was wearing her trousers regardless of the briny soaking. "It's fine for you to lay naked in the sand," she'd told a very amused Kai. "You've got scales to protect your intimate bits. I'd rather not get rocks and grit in, well, you know."

"I braid it sometimes," she said sleepily as he combed his fingers through the white strands. "Mmmh, that feels nice..."

"My old matrons said grooming was a way to strengthen bonds," Kai said. "Some evenings, the pod would do nothing but comb and braid one another's hair."

"So when Maddie and the others play with yours," Harry said, "That's perfectly normal to you?"

"Mm-hmm. Your hair is so soft and fine – may I?"

"Alright," she agreed complacently, sitting up. He smiled and rummaged through his ever-present net bag, pulling out a highly polished comb made of a strange fish bone and a corked bottle full of seaglass beads and pearls.

"How on earth have you kept that hidden from Zora?" she asked, taking the bottle and tilting it up to the light.

"Sit," Kai commanded, patting the damp sand next to him. "Look out at the waves."

"Yessir," she saluted. "...So while all of this beauty work is going on, what are we supposed to talk about?"

"Usually we sing, or teach the younglings the history chants. But my language is nearly impossible for a human to learn," he said regretfully. "You simply do not have the right throat."

Harry gently laid a hand on his tail. "I'm sorry – I keep bringing up painful subjects, don't I?"

"You want only to learn about my culture, as I want to learn about yours. And that does not cause me pain. Rather, it makes me happy that you are interested."

"Of course I'm interested," Harry said. "I want to know everything about you, Kai."

The movement of the comb and his steady fingers through her hair was almost hypnotizing, the repetition so soothing. Her scalp tingled pleasantly as he started weaving strands together, slipping the occasional bead or pearl into the slim braids.

"My pod," he began. "My matrons. They died. There was a conflict with another, more violent pod. I was the only one to escape. I was told to flee and hide, and I have always been good at doing what I am told. There was a moment – there was a strange matron, one of the attacking pod – who saw me, who came towards me, and I was sure that I would die. I did not have the will to fight back; I could hear the cries of the others, I could taste their blood in the water, and I knew they were all dying. I almost wanted to join them. But then the matron turned away. She let me go. I still do not know what made her show me mercy."

Harry caught his hand and squeezed it, turning to face him. "I suspected, but... I'm so sorry, Kai. And ever since, you've been alone?"

"Yes."

How terribly lonely he must have been. Merfolk were, by nature, social beings. They required the support of a community. There was no such thing as a solitary mermaid, not that Harry had ever heard of. Bad enough that he had lost his family to violence, but then he had to suffer that loss in silence for God only knew how many months, years...

Small wonder that he had been so happy to see them, so eager to join their odd little tribe.

"It was difficult," he said, reading her expression and following the chain of her thoughts. "But it could have been worse."

"How?"

"They could have taken my voice, as well. And if I had been pair bonded, that loss would have been unbearable. Usually, my people bond for life."

Harry blinked at him. "Usually?"

"Yes."

"And what about – I mean, I'm a human – does that mean..."

"There are certain things we cannot do together, of course. Rituals that would be impossible. But I no longer live under the laws and dictates of my pod. I live under yours," he said, kissing her forehead. "And so I leave such things, such decisions, in your hands. So long as I am with you, Harry, I will be content."

"This is a lot to take in," the captain said slowly.

"You have plenty of time to think on it," he said complacently. "While I finish these braids."

When he'd finished, she ran a curious hand through her hair, brushing over the small pearls and the complicated designs he'd woven with the blonde strands. Most of the hair fell straight down her back, but several braids had been gathered into a spiraling knot at her neck. "All this effort will be wasted the moment I step on deck and face a strong headwind," she said ruefully.

"Then I will just fix it again."

"Alright, you had your turn," she said, smiling. "Now it's mine."

She plucked the comb from his unresisting hand and slid behind him, sparing a moment to slide her hands over his shoulders and press close to his warm back. "Course, I doubt I'll manage anything half so pretty," she confessed readily.

She was debating the merits of rope knots in connection with hair braiding when three cheerful voices approached. "Ah, there you are," Jo said. "Lounging with your fancy man while the rest of us have been hard at work."

"Liar," Harry said pleasantly. "I distinctly remember telling everyone to take the afternoon off. Everyone includes you, madame."

"I'm a fancy man?" Kai asked turning to look up at Franky and Maddie with a smile.

"It's another term for a kept man," Maddie said meaningfully. "You know, a—"

"He knows," Harry said, pinching his shoulder. "He knows a lot more than he pretends to, the cheeky blighter. And what, exactly, do you three want?"

"Oh, we were just hoping to catch you *inflagrante delicto*," said Franky without a particle of shame. "Katherine and Zora have a bet going."

"Oh do they?" Harry said, a hint of warning to her voice.

"That may be *their* motivation," Jo said with a snort. "I was heading over to ask you about the future."

"A serious topic for such a pleasant evening," remarked Kai.

"Sit down, all of you, before I get a crick in my neck staring up at you," Harry acquiesced, shifting in the sand so her knees were more comfortably pressed against Kai's waist. "And speak your piece, Jo."

"Construction's going well," the first mate said. "We'll be done with the lookout tower and storage hut in another day or two. Zora's begging for another, longer stop at Bogo, Wil's asking leave to stay here for a couple weeks in order to properly catalogue the lizard population, the others are itching for a long voyage and something definite to aim for — and we still haven't properly talked about what happened with Wrath."

"You did promise me the full story, Cap," Franky said quietly.

"Yes, I did," Harry said, setting aside the

comb with a sigh. "I keep my word. And perhaps it's time you heard the story, too, Kai," she said, leaning against him. "Years ago, when I was younger than Maddie, my older sister Aveline was taken. Kidnapped by pirates. There were stories that they were working in tandem with a pod of mermaids who turned humans in order to keep them as slaves."

"Unforgivable," Kai said with feeling. "To turn someone against their will. Especially when the change does not always happen. If it fails, it is pure murder."

"Why did you suspect this happened to your sister?" Franky asked, solemn-faced.

"Aveline isn't just physically beautiful – she has a wonderful singing voice, too. Father said it was like listening to an angel. And we all know just how important beautiful voices are to merfolk."

"Those with the purest voices are held in very high regard," Kai said. "Pods with accomplished singers are more respected. But to gain such standing through enslavement..."

"It was a dark night when Aveline was kidnapped, and I didn't get more than a fleeting glance of the man or the craft that took her. And I was injured in the process," Harry said flatly, extending her arm to display the defiant dark scar marring her pale skin. "So it was three days before I was recovered enough to do anything. Jo went out as my eyes and ears and asked around town, and at her mother's pub. Finally, some sailors admitted that they had seen a ship at anchor not far from the cliffs the day she disappeared. *The Barracuda,* captained by a Spaniard named Luis Angel. You could recognize the ship from a league away because its figurehead was a massive, toothy fish."

Jo took up the thread. "It took us some time – more time than we liked – to follow the trail. But eventually we won *The Sappho* off a mean old drunk–"

"He was calling it *Aphrodite's Virtue*, which neither of us liked," Harry interjected. "So we promptly rechristened it."

"So that story *is* true!" exclaimed Franky. "You really did win the ship in a card game!"

"And then we took to sea. We found Lizzie, Katherine, Zora, Miss Euphemia and Agnessa–"

"Picked up a stray brat, and a few others," Harry said, smiling at Maddie.

"And did everything we could to track down *The Barracuda* and Aveline," Jo said.

"Have you found it yet?" Kai asked with concern, brow furrowed and dark eyes somber. Harry pressed her cheek to his.

Jo shook her head. "We learned that Captain Luis was double-crossed by his first mate not long after he sailed from our coast and that most of the crew mutinied – those that didn't acknowledge the new captain were put to the sword and thrown overboard for the sharks. The ship was renamed – but to what, we didn't know. The trail went cold for years."

"Then a few months ago we heard stories of some especially bloodthirsty mermaids that were crossing the ocean and slaughtering everything they found: ships, sharks, even their own kind. A rare survivor of one of their frenzies, a Portuguese sailor Katherine dug up in a pub, said that there was a striking maid with them that looked nothing like the others: the others all had black hair and gray, shark-like bodies, but she was a beautiful blonde with a black tail. A black tail – meaning she had once been human." Harry sounded tired and looked resigned, but there was still a glint in her eyes. So long as there was some hope that her sister was alive, regardless of her current state, she wouldn't stop until she had found her.

"And what will you do," Kai asked slowly; there was a strange, indefinable expression on his face, "if you find her and she *is* that matron? There is no way to reverse the change."

"Doesn't matter if she's a mermaid now; she's still my sister," Harry said firmly. "I won't abandon her."

"Nor I," Jo said quietly.

Franky glanced at her with his bright, observant eyes, realized the unspoken truth, and kept his revelation to himself.

If there was one thing in the world he understood at all, it was love.

"And Wrath Drew knew all of this?" he said instead. "You told him your story?"

"A single ship alone can't canvass the entire bloody ocean," Harry said, grinding her teeth together. "There are a few other captains I trusted enough to tell the truth, and they promised to keep an ear and eye open for me. I thought Wrath a friend; I saved the bastard's life – twice! – and there used to be a time when that counted for something. When a debt like that would ensure loyalty."

"See, I was surprised when I heard you were on friendly terms," Franky continued. "Because I've heard horror stories about *The Charon* for years — how it was a black ship that fired upon anyone, regardless of what colors they sailed under, no matter if they flew a flag of neutrality."

"He's a pirate," Harry pointed out dryly. "Pirates don't always have great reputations. He'd never done anything against me and mine — up until recently, anyhow. And when you're a pirate yourself, you have to take your allies where you can find them. Most naval ships tend to fire on sight."

"So," Maddie said. "What *are* we gonna do about Wrath? If word gets out that we've been double-crossed and didn't do a thing about it, what's that gonna do to our reputation?"

"To hell with our reputation," Harry said, fire in her eyes. "That doesn't matter. What matters is the bastard tried to kill me, tried to sink my ship, and knows something about my sister. I'm putting his head on a spike with my own two hands."

Kai looked at her with some alarm, and she smiled in a not-wholly-reassuring manner. "...Or maybe I'll just shoot him, or stab him, or throw him overboard into a swarm of sharks. I won't be choosy — just so long as the Devil takes his own back."

"Well, to that end, we'll need a plan," Jo said firmly. "Something well-thought-out. Something that takes a number of likely obstacles into consideration."

"Eh, plans," Harry said dismissively. "Too

much time and effort."

"This is precisely why you're so bad at chess," Jo said blandly. "And why you should thank your stars, nightly, that you've got *me* to handle such things."

"You're absolutely right, Jo, I'd be utterly lost without you. So I plan to leave the planning to you, while I enjoy the rest of this lovely afternoon with my fancy man. Tell Wil she has her leave to frolic with the lizards, tell Zora we'll head back to Bogo in a few days, and tell the others to plot a course for some distant shipwrecks. Now that we've got a merman on the crew, it shouldn't be too hard to find some wayward chests others may have missed in their sweeps. You're all bloody dismissed," Harry said firmly with a wave of her arm.

"I *am* your fancy man, then?" Kai asked, curling an arm around her waist.

"You bet your beard you are," Harry grinned. "C'mere..."

*~*~*

"Why'd you join up with Harry?"

Franky's voice was a slow rumble, still slightly drugged from their lovemaking. Maddie rolled over, pushing her tangled hair behind one ear. A leaf caught up in it demanded her attention for a moment and she paused, tongue peeking out of the corner of her mouth, while she extricated it. "I didn't mean to," she said, then giggled at the confusion that flashed across his face. "You get a funny line here when you're bamboozled," she said fondly, reaching over and smoothing her thumb across his forehead.

"Of course I'm bamboozled when you give me a riddle for an answer," he complained.

"I stowed away," she clarified. "Three days out to sea when Harry caught me sneaking out of the galley with an apple in my mouth and three more shoved down my shirt. She looked pretty surprised when she saw me, but she always tells people she suspected I was there all along. Uh-huh. Sure she did."

"Why were you stowing away? The reputation Harry has, why didn't you just march up to her and demand to be taken on?"

"I'd never heard of her," Maddie confessed readily. "And that was early days, anyhow, before she'd had reputation. I just picked *The Sappho* because I liked the look of it. I liked the figurehead and how big it was. I watched it for a couple days and then snuck onboard one night when there was just a skeleton crew on guard and the others were partying ashore."

"How old were you?" Franky pushed himself up onto his elbows. He was looking at her with something very like concern.

"Don't know," she said lightly with a shrug, looking down at the blanket they'd spread over the ground. She picked at a loose thread with her nail. "I don't remember much before Harry and *The Sappho*, really."

"That's a bit of a lie, isn't it, love?" he asked softly. She glanced up, met his dark eyes, and shook her head quickly.

"No. No it isn't. No. I don't – we don't talk about it, okay? I just don't. We all got things we don't talk about. Scabs we shouldn't pick. Bet there's lots you don't think about from before Harry. So don't–"

"Alright, Mads, alright," he said quietly, catching her shaking hands. "It's fine. I'll stop. I won't ask about it again." He drew concentric circles over the back of her hand with the pad of his thumb, spreading out and then back in like ripples in water. Her ragged breathing steadied and slowed; she watched the motion of his hand as if it was hypnotizing. It was the same thing the rest of the crew would do for her when she got upset, and she knew Harry must have taken him aside and told him about it.

"I'm broken, aren't I?" she whispered.

"Oh no, love, no," he said, letting go of her hands to cup her face. "No more than any of us are. We've all got some sharp edges, one way or another, but that doesn't mean we're broken."

"But the rest of you don't go crazy at the drop of a coin," she persisted, tears burning the edges of her dark eyes. "They call me Mad for a reason, Franky. I scare people – I scare myself."

"You don't scare me," he said firmly, wiping away teardrops with his thumbs. He kissed each cheek.

"Only because you haven't seen me in the middle of a fit yet. Just wait."

"It won't stop me from liking you, Maddie. I'm sure it won't."

"I won't be upset if it does. Don't feel like you

have to–"

"Keep making love to a pretty girl who makes me laugh? What torture," he said with a grin. "I'm not a slave any more, so that means I don't do anything I don't want to. I'm here with you because I want to be, Maddie."

She found herself smiling again. "This *is* fun, isn't it?"

"So much fun," he murmured, kissing her. "Fun like I haven't had in *years*."

"You're good at this, you know," she said, letting him draw her down against him. "But then you *do* know that, don't you?"

"I've never heard any complaints," he said modestly.

"Been with a lot of girls?"

"Yes."

"How many?"

"I've never kept count. Why bother? I've known men who keep a tally like it was a competition, but I don't see it that way."

"Oh? How do you see it then?"

"Fun," he said. "An enjoyable thing to do with a like-minded lady. I meet someone, I like them, we laugh, we tell stories, we make love. Simple. Straight-forward. And you?"

"You're the first I've done this more than once with."

"They were that bad, huh?"

"Eh, it was more that we were both too drunk to manage a second performance."

"Their loss," Franky said. "Something like this is best savored when sober. Here..."

# ONE WILD NIGHT IN BOGO

"Ahhh, Bogo!" Harry said with a grin, taking a deep breath. Like all ports, there was a layered richness to its fragrance – unwashed bodies, acrid smoke, dead fish, blood and brine, and most of the pubs were positively redolent of cheap rum, cheaper perfumes, and all sorts of best-left-unnamed liquids. Outside the largest brothel – The Queen Mary, a commanding presence that took up a full two blocks – you'd almost swear the surrounding air was blue with cursing; it also had the wet, sticky, sour consistency of the watered beer served at the front bar.

But over all of this was the heady, intoxicating, unexpected perfume of bougainvilleas. Between every ramshackle building, at every corner, grew huge, thorny, tree-like bushes, lending a bright splash of color to a mixed assortment of tawdry goings-ons. On official maps, this little niche of vice and villainy was called Bougainvillea precisely because of those flowers spilling onto the uneven cobbled streets.

Sailors being what they are, and unable to trust words with too many syllables, the place was colloquially called Bogo in defiance of those high-minded cartographers.

"I've never seen a place like this," Franky said, wide-eyed as they marched down what in other places would be called Main Street but here, in Bogo, was known fondly as Wenches' Way.

"Crazy, innit?" Maddie said with a laugh, hopping nimbly over a drunk as he rolled into the street with a loud groan. One of his companions pounced on him as they passed, rifling through his pockets. "Have you heard the story about the flowers yet?"

"No, what's the story?" Franky shouted as they rushed past a small fight involving six bellowing, shirtless, red-faced men armed with bits of broken chairs.

"There was a sea witch who lived in a cave at the foot of the volcano, hundreds of years ago when the first sailors started using this cove. They made a deal with her: she'd let them build the harbor they wanted, but only so long as they didn't make too much noise and disturb her with their revelries."

"Take it that deal didn't work out too well," Franky said dryly. They were passing The Queen Mary – named not for any royal, but for the legendary Mary Read – and five women wearing nothing but ripped petticoats, their exposed nipples pert in the evening air, leaned from the second floor balcony and blew kisses down at them.

"She warned them that if they broke their part of the bargain, she'd turn them all into flowers. And when the next ship sailed into the cove they found the pub and inn empty and the streets filled with bougainvilleas. So they sailed out again, real sharp, and waited a few decades before coming back, until the old witch had died. Nobody else got turned into a bush, so the curse must've lost its strength, but nobody dares cut into any of the flowers already here, either, in case they start screaming or bleeding like a man," Maddie finished with ghoulish delight.

"Charming," Franky said, eying the lush, beautiful plants in a different light.

"I defy you to find a more superstitious lot than a port full of sailors," Jo said, glancing over her shoulder at Hope.

As always, the slender Chinese woman stood out from the crowd in her brilliant red wrapped blouse and silk pants, hair black and shiny as jet fixed back in a pristine bun, her thin arms draped with bracelets and charms that jingled as she moved. Her face was always so smooth and remote, even in the midst of such chaos – calm with the surety that her gods would protect her, Jo supposed.

Though she didn't rely wholly on divine intervention. A man sidled up through their group and snaked out a grubby hand toward Hope's backside. Quick as a striking cobra, she plucked a sharp silver needle from her bun and drove it into his wrist. The man shrieked and recoiled, freezing when Hope's serene face came within an inch from his.

"If you wish to ever use your hand again," she said in her off-key yet still musical voice, the result of learning English after a childhood of strict Mandarin tones. "You will swear to me to never touch another woman without her express permission. Give me this oath."

"I give it, I give it," the gap-toothed man sobbed, eyes bulging. He'd never crossed paths with a goddess before, and wasn't it just his luck to anger the first one he met? He couldn't feel his hand from the wrist down; as far as his brain knew, his fingers had all fallen off. "I'm sorry, miss. Very sorry. Truly."

"Good." Long fingers tipped with sharp red nails plucked the needle from his flesh and immediately – painfully – his hand started to throb. "Now go."

"It does the heart good," Marcella commented, amused, as Hope fastidiously wiped her hairpin clean on a silk kerchief before returning it to her bun. They had all stopped to watch the scene unfold, sight-seeing being the third-most popular entertainment in Bogo, after boozing and bedding. "Seeing a man get put in his place like that."

"Acupuncture," Hope said, seemingly apropos of nothing, as she began walking again with graceful, delicate steps. "If you know the right spot, you can hold a man in the palm of your hand."

"Don't I know it," Katherine snorted, nudging Lizzie with a sharp elbow.

"So this is your port of choice, huh?" Franky asked the captain as they continued on.

"How could it not be?" Harry countered, putting out an arm and stopping him short just as the closest window exploded in a shower of glass, a limp body of indeterminate age and gender sailing overhead to crash against the far wall, sliding to the alley in a boneless, brown leather heap.

"Tell it to yer bleedin' mum!" shouted a coarse voice from beyond the smashed window frame, the invective followed by a raucous peal of braying laughter.

"Tortuga? Smuggler's Bay? Skull Island? Boring," Harry said with a dismissive wave. "Nah, it's Bogo if you want it all. No government, no law, no rules. Free love and free beer if you know where to go–"

"Don't drink the free beer," Agnessa said in an urgent undertone. "Don't. *Trust me.*"

"A friend in every pub–"

"And three enemies," added Jo.

"Anything you could want to buy–"

"For an exorbitant price," clarified Marcella.

"A thousand different voices and just as many languages–"

"And a third as many working eyes and limbs," Maddie chimed in.

"Yessir: Bogo's the place to go if you're a pirate. Pirate's Paradise, they should call this. And this right here, Lucky, is the pub of all pubs. The Anne's Arms." Harry spread her own arms as if she was a great showman unveiling a remarkable wonder to an appreciative audience.

"Lemme guess: Anne Bonny?" Franky said.

Jo tapped the side of her nose and gave him a rare, genuine smile that didn't have a shred of sarcasm to it. "Got it in one."

"Alright, alright, enough jawing and gawping," Zora said, side-stepping a lurching drunk with her dancer's grace and hurrying through the doorway.

The Anne's Arms didn't have a front door – because someone had recently demolished it upon their untimely exit or because the place was always open, Franky wasn't entirely sure. It didn't seem near as wild or loud as the other pubs they'd passed, those closest to the docks and therefore easier to stagger into. This pub was at the end of Wenches' Way, near the looming bulk of the volcano itself.

"Zora's girl works here," Maddie explained as they followed their impatient crewmate in.

They entered just in time to see the ecstatic reunion. A tall, ginger-haired, extremely voluptuous woman turned from the bar with a tray perched near her bare shoulder, saw Zora, shrieked with delight, dropped the tray back onto the bar regardless of the beer stein that tipped over, and ran straight for the black-haired woman with arms outstretched. The two collided with enough force to make Franky's teeth ache.

"Girl, what did I say!" shouted the beefy, red-faced, middle-aged woman working the taps. "Back to work, else I dock your pay! Plenty of time for that later!"

"But Violet!" the redhead pouted prettily, surfacing for air and clutching Zora to her ample bosom, a position she clearly didn't mind in the slightest. "It's been *weeks* and *weeks*!"

"Be that as it may be, you work to my clock, Tess. Drinks to the gents in the corner, check on Mr. Bright in room three, and *then* you can serve your lady and her mates. *Now*, girl!"

Huffing, Tessa snatched another hasty kiss from her lover and stomped back to the bar to refill the stein. Franky found it just about impossible to peel his eyes away from her — Tessa had an undeniable magic about her. Milk and roses complexion, incredibly impressive breasts, long legs, and a wild mass of flaming hair heaped up in a frizzing cloud that begged to be touched. She wore a green beaded skirt and tightly laced corset that complimented her coloring, displayed her cleavage, and left her shoulders and arms bare.

"She's a lot, ain't she?" Maddie said with a grin. Franky was gawping like a freshly landed grouper. "And her and Zora next to each other, it's like some picture out of the Bible or something."

*Of Lilith and Eve, maybe,* thought Franky, who was far more familiar with a Bible than Maddie. *Or something out of the Song of Solomon.*

But she had a point: the two were a study in contrasts, with Zora's short black hair, olive skin, and dancer's body, all whipcord muscle and petite breasts. They were both of them earthy, lush, and wild, especially now with their proximity charging the air of the room. You could practically smell the lust, and Franky found it hard to concentrate on anything.

*~*~*

"Hullo, boys."

The three men looked up from their notched, battered cards and took in a sight that made the third of the trio with Nordic blood abruptly think of Valhalla. Slap a horned helmet on that regal head, strap a hammered breastplate to that very fine chest, hand her a golden spear and, well, she'd be a Valkyrie worth riding after, he thought, taken utterly by surprise. "Yes, miss?" he

said, catching the hand-rolled cigarette before it
fell from his lips.

"Care to deal me in?" Katherine suggested,
hooking the spare chair with her foot and yanking it
out, sitting with a wide grin. "You need four to play
a really good hand of hearts."

"That you do," said the one with the black
hat tilted over a cauliflowered ear, grabbing up the
cards and shuffling quickly. "Name's John, this
here's Jimbo, and that's Jilly."

"Really?" she lifted an eyebrow at him.

"Short for Jillian," the Norseman by way of
Pruitt Street, London, said without hesitation, long-
accustomed to such a look. "Family name."

"And you three just fell in together naturally?
The three Jays?"

"Been togevver since we was cabin boys,"
said Jim, a compact Cockney with bright gray eyes
and nimble hands. "Thirty years at sea, boy an' man."

"A pleasure to meet you, Jays. I'm Katherine.
What ship do you sail with?"

"*The Corinthian Curse*. Just got in this
morning. You?"

"*The Sappho*. I'll take two more cards,
please," she said, sliding over her discards.

"Cor, really?" said John, sitting back in his
chair to appraise her anew. He had the knotted
hands, thrice broken nose, and maimed ears of a
habitual boxer, but he also had a rich, deep voice
and a crooked smile that was almost boyish. "What's
that captain of yours really like?"

"A hellcat when riled, a pussycat when not,"
Katherine said. "So I wouldn't advise riling her. I'll

raise three bob."

"Always wanted to meet someone who sailed on *The Sappho*," said Jilly. He had thick, shaggy hair the color and texture of hay, pale blue eyes, a squashy nose, and was the tallest and broadest of the trio. A good thing, too, with such a girlish name — he'd probably had more than his fair share of fights over it. He made Katherine think fondly of the boys from back home. Sturdy, dependable lads who could be wonderfully methodical. "Our Cap's always wild to hear stories about your lot."

"That so?"

"Oh, when Captain Thommo finds out we played cards wif one o' ya," laughed Jim, showing a nice set of teeth. "He'll shoot straight t' the moon wif envy."

"This Cap of yours, he a good 'un?"

"The best, the best," said John firmly, to resounding nods and grunts of agreement from his fellows. "Very fair with divvying up the goods. Doesn't hesitate to spend gold on medicines, neither. Member that time half the boys got the grippe somethin' awful, mates? Lots of other captains would've tipped the sick overboard to save themselves, but not Thommo. Captain Thommo ain't afraid of anything."

"Well, krakens," amended Jilly. "And sirens. But then, who ain't afraid of them?"

"Sounds like a man worth sailing under," said Katherine, laying down another perfect run.

"Here, you ain't lookin' to sign on wif us, are ya?" Jim asked, pushing her winnings over.

"No, absolutely not," Katherine said firmly.

"Only way I'm leaving Captain Harry is when the Reaper takes my hand. No, I'm just sounding the waters. See, we had a bit of a dust up with Wrath Drew–"

"Aye, we heard 'bout that," Jim nodded, producing a pipe and setting to work packing and lighting it. "Damn that mutinous dog."

"Drew'd give even a kraken a sour stomach," agreed Jilly.

"Nasty piece of work," contributed John.

"And the captain's made a vow to string his guts across the bow. *The Sappho* may not be quite as big as *The Charon*, and our crew may be smaller, but we're hearty and game as hell." There was a light in the large woman's eyes that would've made anyone but the suicidal and fatally-drunk take heed. "And when going up against a double-crosser like Wrath Drew, it always pays to know who one's real friends are. Savvy?"

"We most certainly do," said John, leaning over the table. "I can have a word with Thommo, see if he might want to have a word with your Harry. How does that sound?"

"That sounds mighty fine to me. We'll be right here for the next two, three days, at least. Damn, seems I've got another straight, boys."

"You're a dab hand at cards, Katherine," said Jilly admiringly.

"Call me Kath, Jilly. That goes for you two, too."

"Alright, Kath. Oy, Violet!" Jim called back to the barkeep. "Bring us anuvver round, would ya, love? Make 'em big uns. Put it on the tab."

"Ta, Jays," Katherine said as she drained her tankard in one go. "That sure does hit the spot. All these pubs in Bogo, and I swear Vi's the only one who doesn't put water or sawdust in the kegs."

"Another game, Kath?" Jilly asked hopefully, shuffling the tattered deck.

"Tell you what," she said. "I've got another idea. Cards and beer are good and all, but I've been on a boat full of uninterested women for a few weeks now."

"And?" John said, a scarred eyebrow lifting so high it disappeared behind his bangs.

"How about we go upstairs and play a different sort of game? You three strike me as adventurous lads."

John, Jimbo, and Jilly looked at one another. They'd been bosom buds since they were ten years old, through cannon fire and siren song and rum runs. Perhaps it had been only a matter of time before they shared this sort of danger as well.

*Cor, but she's a real woman and a half!,* thought John.

*I always say I'm up fer anythin',* thought Jim, lowering his pipe.

*There's certainly enough of her to share,* thought Jilly.

"Alright," they said in almost perfect unison, looking a little poleaxed at this unexpected turn in their fortunes. When they'd come into the Anne's Arms an hour before, all they'd really wanted was a quiet game of cards on a table that didn't move and enough beer to floor a horse.

Instead, they were apparently going to be

carted off to Heaven by a Valkyrie.

*Well*, Jilly thought philosophically as they followed Katherine into room four. *There are ways of getting to Heaven, and then there are ways of getting to Heaven, and who am I to say no?*

*~*~*

"Yer always so bonny to me, Tess," said Mr. Bright, watching her pull up her stocking with glittering eyes. The lamp beside the table was turned down, giving off only the faintest of gold glows to distinguish her alluring curves from the shadows.

"That's because you tip well, Billy," she said honestly.

"I could take you away from all o' this," he said, not for the first time. "I got enough saved up now. I don't have to go back to sea. We could find us a nice little town, settle down..."

"Now, Bill," Tessa said firmly, patting the scarred hand that had slid over her thigh. "I've already told you that I can't. It's a lovely idea, but no."

"You really want to stay here?" he said.

"Maybe not forever," she conceded, gathering up her hair and ramming pins in at random. "But it's good enough for now. It's a lot better than some of the other places I've worked – I keep more of my wages, and Violet makes sure no one's rough with me, and I've got some say in who I service."

"That's good to hear. I'm glad to hear that,"

said Billy Bright, flashing the smile that had earned him his name. A diamond glinted amidst gold-capped teeth. "So you *do* like me, even if just a little."

"Course I do, silly," Tessa said fondly, leaning over to kiss him. "I always look forward to our little interludes. You're probably my favorite regular."

"But you don't love me," he said.

"No. No, I don't."

"Yer the most honest wench I've ever bedded, Tessa, and that's the truth. Yer one of a kind."

"I know," she said with a short laugh. "You sailing out tomorrow?"

"Aye. Just after dawn."

"Well, Zora just got in, so I don't know if I'll see you again before then. So have a safe voyage, Bill."

"You love *her*, don't you?"

Tessa hesitated at the door, looking like some wild nymph out of a Renaissance painting. "Yes. So much I think my heart might burst from it."

"I'm happy for you, then, love. You be careful, until I get back."

"Of course, Billy. Good night."

*~*~*

"...But up until the rule of the Caesars, Rome was an oligarchy," a mountain of a man was insisting. His blond hair was just long enough to curl at the edges and his blue eyes were fringed with dark lashes that would have been feminine if he hadn't been well over six feet tall, hadn't had such broad shoulders, and if his hands had been significantly daintier.

Maddie had to admit, privately of course, that he was extremely handsome. In the belongs-in-uniform-astride-a-charging-horse sort of way. Not her type, not at all, but very striking. And if Agnessa hadn't been so worked up by his previous comments, she probably would've noticed this, too.

"You can't *honestly* believe that oligarchies are the fairest and best way to govern people?" the petite helmswoman retorted, gripping her cup of ale so tightly it was a wonder the wood hadn't cracked.

"Of course," the man said, words clipped. "The many should be governed by the best."

"And who, precisely, determines the best? By best you *actually* mean the most powerful, the richest," said Agnessa. "'Power and wealth corrupts. Great men are almost always bad men.'"

Maddie's eyes flicked from one to another as if there was an invisible ball being lobbed back and forth. She was watching a battle being fought without a single physical weapon.

"I would also say the best includes the smartest, the most practical," the man argued. "Professors and scientists, doctors and mathematicians. Great orators. Those well versed in the management of men – generals. And successful farmers, too, who know the best ways of producing the most food to support the masses."

"And where are the women? Where are the mothers and the midwives? There has never been a place for the female in an oligarchy, which holds that a woman must be subservient to a man because she is seen as the inferior gender with an inferior mind. Women did not vote in the oligarchies of Rome – women were relegated to the same social standing as slaves and cattle. Even war prisoners ranked higher! You speak so warmly of a fallen civilization that was no better than our current state of affairs!"

"If I had me anvil right now," Lizzie said to Marcella in a careful undertone. "I could stick a blade betwixt them, watch it go red hot, then slap it down and hammer a new edge to it. Wouldn't even need me bellows."

"I've got to say, I'm impressed that he's giving back as good as he gets," Marcella said.

"Oh, that's Hugh," Violet said, suddenly plunking down another tray of drinks and startling the trio of onlookers. "Hugh Dawkins. He's quite the big man."

"Obviously," muttered Maddie, grabbing a new cup.

"Real toff when he was young," the barkeep/proprietress went on. She didn't bother to lower her voice – the two combatants were obviously deaf to those around them. "Family rich as Croesus, studied at Oxford, enlisted in the Navy. One of them stories."

"Then how the hell did he end up in Bogo?" Marcella demanded, astounded. Naval men were usually nailed to the posts before they had a chance to set foot on Wenches' Way.

"Seems Mr. Dawkins is a high-minded gent.

His commander, one of them white-wigged arseholes, ordered an unsanctioned raid on a little fishing village near St. Lucia. When he made a bit too free with some of the ladies they found there, Mr. Dawkins challenged the commander to a duel."

"Then what?" asked Maddie, all agog.

"He shot the bastard's head clean off his shoulders, is what. And then he told his mates that he had no intention of sticking around to be court-martialed and hanged for doing the right thing, especially not when none of the rest of 'em had the guts to do it, so he skivved off and ended up on Ol' Thommo's boat. It's a good fit, seeing as how Thommo's one from the same mold as your Harry. Downright golden-hearted for a pirate. Just the spot for a man with morals like Hugh." Violet chuckled, sounding very like a contented hen. "He's sure found a match in Agnessa, ain't he?"

"*Pax!*" Hugh Dawkins said finally, lifting his hands in surrender. "Let us agree then to disagree. It's clear I cannot convince you to see the idea from my perspective, and it's equally obvious you cannot sway me to yours."

"Indeed," fumed Agnessa, draining her cup.

"But I am curious: where did you learn so much about Roman history?"

"I went through five tutors before I walked out of my father's house," she replied.

"Why did you burn through so many? Did they hold views similar to mine?" he asked shrewdly.

"Some. Others tried to teach me only subjects they considered 'safe' and 'proper'. I had no interest in those."

"You wanted politics and rhetoric. Philosophy and the bloody realities of war."

"Something like that," she conceded. "In the end, I just stole my brother's books and made do on my own."

"I'm Hugh, by the way."

"Agnessa."

"May I get you another drink?"

"If you must," she said primly.

"I haven't had such a stimulating discussion in months. My crewmates know every word to a ribald twelve verse shanty but couldn't call up the name of a Greek philosopher to save their lives. Please, it's the least I can do."

"Very well. I'll take a brandy. Thank you."

As Hugh made his way to the bar, he stepped aside to let the fireball that was Tessa speed past. Zora looked up from the game of darts she, Harry, and Jo had started with a few men (Franky was looking on, content to just watch while he drank his beer) and grinned.

"I'm yours for the rest of the night," Tessa vowed ardently, wrapping her arms around her.

"No, you ain't," called Violet. "You still gotta serve the tables, at least until one."

"...I'm *mostly* yours for the rest of the night," Tessa amended. "What can I get you?"

"You can sit right here and kiss me breathless, for starters," Zora ordered, dropping into a chair and pulling her down over her lap. Tessa obliged with a giggle, hiking up her skirt to straddle her dusky legs.

"I know what I'll be dreamin' of tonight," said one of the men at the dartboard, eyes nearly bugging out of his head. "If that ain't the most beautiful thing I've ever seen..."

"Focus, Dugan," snapped his comrade. "I got a bleedin' pound ridin' on this."

"Think I'll sit the next round out," Jo said, pulling out her silver flask and settling in a chair next to Franky's. "Maddie, why don't you come over and spell me. You're better at darts than me, anyway."

"Yessum," the girl said cheerfully, bouncing over.

"Oh no, you're Mad Maddie, ain't ya?" said the man with a pound hanging in the balance.

"Yep."

"That's it. I quit," he said, resigned. "I've heard of you, girl. I don't got that kinda money to lose."

"Are you some kind of a fiend when it comes to darts?" Franky teased.

"Yep," Maddie said with a grin, leaning over to kiss him quickly. "Anyone else wanna leave?"

The other men all exchanged steely looks. The girl looked no more than eighteen, a slim and wiry thing with a smudged face, tangled hair, and bare feet.

Which meant, in their wide experience, they were all about to be fleeced down to their bootstraps.

But they *were* pirates. And what sort of a pirate can resist a challenge or the lure of a pocketful of gold?

"Alright, girlie, let's see what you can do," said the one called Dugan.

After a few minutes, Jo turned away from the massacre to face Franky. "How are you liking your first taste of Bogo?"

"It'll definitely linger," he said. "I've never been somewhere so, so..."

"Intense?" Jo hazarded.

"Robust," he decided. "It reminds me of a bad table wine, the kind my uncle Giancarlo makes. It knocks you on your arse, and it tastes as cheap as it is, but there's just something about it that pulls you back for more."

"An apt description," Jo agreed. "Harry loves this place — simply loves it. It's the only place more brash and unfettered and louder than her, I think. The only place in the world where the average person has *less* self-control in a fight."

"If I didn't think Bogo was dangerous before..." Franky said, eliciting a laugh from the stoic first mate. "I certainly wouldn't want to come here alone, but with you all as guides, I can see the appeal. Though, I simply *can't* imagine Miss Euphemia loose on this place," he added, thinking of the old woman back on the boat with the newest additions, Junia and Silence. The mute siren was absolutely not up for such a crush — and if she *had* stepped off the boat, chances were high that the first people to see her would try to kill her, sentiments for sirens being what they were — while Junia was still recovering from her ordeal, so Miss Euphemia had demurred and stayed behind to keep them company, claiming she was feeling far too creaky "for all that excitement" anyway.

"I pray to God you get to see it at least once," Jo said, taking a pull of her flask. "Last time she was here, there was dancing on the tables."

"On the tables?"

"On the tables."

"At her age?"

"Mmm-hmm. There were high kicks of the like not even Paris has seen," asserted Jo. "Lace and petticoats and those clunky black boots of hers. Then she stabbed a pickpocket with her parasol and got him to return everything he'd taken from the patrons. By the end of her lecture he was sobbing like a lost child, and he swore until he was blue in the face that he was going to turn his life around."

Franky let the whole picture wash over him and shook his head. "Well, that certainly sounds like Miss Euphemia."

Jo offered him her flask and Franky took a pull. "Good Lord," he spluttered, handing it back as his face turned a hectic red. "*What the hell is that*?"

"Pepper whisky," she said. "Make it myself. Something my mother picked up during her travels, from one of the Solomon Islands. Supposed to be the most potent alcoholic drink in the world, or so the chief claimed."

"The Solomons – where the cannibals live?" he coughed.

"Chief Wanganu took a liking to Mum," Jo said. "Said he liked seeing a bunch of white men take orders from someone even darker than him. The chief didn't have a very high opinion of the white man. Did like the taste of them, though. Said they tasted like suckling pig."

"And you can stomach that stuff?" Franky rubbed his hands over his flushed face. He couldn't feel his tongue. Or his lips. And he was pretty sure his teeth were dissolving.

"Don't ever get in a drinking competition with Jo," Maddie advised, sitting down heavily on Franky's knees. "Only one who can come close to out-drinking her is Harry. Lookit my winnings!"

"That is a *very* large purse," Franky said appreciatively. "...And a very nice silver whistle, ivory handled knife, gold compass, and map. Where's the map lead to?"

"Blackbeard's treasure," she replied matter-of-factly.

"Another one?" said Jo.

"Miss Euphemia will like it," Maddie countered. "She collects maps, even shoddy ones. And you never know, do you? Hey, gents, lemme buy you a round of drinks," she called magnanimously to her defeated opponents, who were settling around a nearby table with a chorus of grumbles.

"With our own money, you mean," muttered one.

His neighbor shoved him. "A beer's a beer, mate," he said. "And we can't afford any more *now*. Thanks, missy, it'd be most appreciated."

"Violet, bring these gentlemen some drinks!" Maddie said, sweeping an arm grandly.

"Tess, take those gentlemen their drinks," Violet called.

"Yes, ma'am, right away, ma'am, three bags

full, ma'am," Tessa grumbled, swinging off Zora's lap.

"Don't know why I put up with your cheek," Violet said good-naturedly.

"Because the richest men come to call on me," she retorted, balancing a laden tray with ease.

"Well, there's that," the barkeep conceded.

"Zora, can I ask you something?" Maddie said, leaning over Franky's shoulder.

"Sure, Mads."

"How come you don't get jealous?"

"It's just a job, Maddie," Zora said. "Oldest job in the book, even." She smiled as Tessa slapped away a roving hand, telling its owner that that sort of privilege required four shillings, which she knew he didn't have.

"But don't you ever worry that someone's gonna come in here and sweep Tessa off her feet?" Maddie insisted. "That she'll fall in love with someone else?"

"If she does, I'll be broke up about it, sure," Zora admitted. "I'll be in a black mood, and snap at everyone, and probably do some stupid things. But so long as she's happy, I'll learn to live with it. I can't blame her if one day she gets tired of this work, tired of this place, and accepts someone's offer to escape. That's what I did, after all."

When Tessa had reclaimed her spot on Zora's knee and the two were thoroughly engrossed, Maddie explained quickly to a curious Franky, voice hot in his ear, "Zora used to be a bar wench and dancer, at Port Royal. She and Tess both. But then Zora got knocked around pretty bad by a customer and decided she couldn't do it any more. Harry and Katherine were at the bar at the time, and she just stomped down from her room, face all bloody and bruised, marched right up to Harry, and asked her what it would take to buy a spot on *The Sappho*."

"But Tessa stayed there?"

"Yeah, for a couple months. But then she decided she wanted to go someplace better—"

"Bogo's *better* than Port Royal?"

"For a wench? Absolutely. Port Royal's under British control, with a garrison and governor and everything. Crawling with British sailors. And if they slap around a wench, what's she gonna do about it? She can't complain or else she'll lose her position, and she can't expect the law to do anything. Not when they'll say stuff like that is just part of the job, and she should be a more virtuous lady if she didn't want such treatment. Here, if a wench gets mishandled she can  defend herself with a stiletto, or tell her boss about it and *they'll* bring out a stiletto. Justice is swift in Bogo."

"And the punishment sticks, hmm?"

"Exactly. Nobody roughs up a wench in Bogo, not unless that's part of the deal and it's paid for first."

"When I first went to sea on my father's fishing boat, I had no idea the world was so complicated," said Franky. "It's obvious Tessa and Zora really care about each other—"

"Oh, yeah, they're mad for each other. Tessa's fine with sleeping with men, but she only loves Zora."

"Then why doesn't Tessa sail with us, too? So they can be together?"

"Tessa doesn't like sailing. Says too much open ocean gives her the collywobbles. And Zora jumped ship just to get away, at first, but now she really loves it. Says she can't imagine staying put on dry land. And because neither wants to make the other miserable, Tessa works here and Zora visits."

"Still, it must be frustrating."

"Yeah," agreed Maddie, combing her fingers through his shaggy hair. "Can't imagine having to be apart that long..."

"This place is turning into a regular love nest," Jo sighed, heaving herself out of her chair and leaving the two couples to get on with it. She wandered past the fireplace, where Agnessa and Hugh Dawkins were deep in conversation about the differences between the British and Swedish navies, and made her way to the furthest corner where Hope and Harry were sitting.

"Giving it another try, huh?" the first mate said, surveying the game board laid out between the two.

"Every great leader should know Go," Hope said, hands folded demurely on the table before her. "It is the game of emperors."

"Why are there so many pieces, though?" Harry said, chewing her bottom lip. "And so many *rules*. Feel like my brain's turning into a knot." She reached out hesitantly, selected a polished white stone, and made a move.

Hope's hand flew across the board, collecting several of her captain's pieces. "Your turn again, Captain."

"Sometimes you've just got to accept your weaknesses, Harriet," Jo said, patting her on the back. "Complex games of strategy are simply not your forte." Then she reached over and made a move for her, eliciting a gasp of surprise from Hope. "And I believe that's game over."

"Miss Hope?"

Only with Hope did Violet Bidwell use such a tone. With anyone else she was hearty, or bellicose, or motherly, or exasperated. But when addressing the petite Chinese woman, the florid, expansive barkeep was as deferential as a penitent before a priest. Because the unshakable Violet was in awe of Hope, who she truly believed was a sorceress.

And it paid to be respectful of someone who could talk to spirits and summon fire with a snap of her painted fingers.

"Yes, Mrs. Bidwell?"

"I have the money for your pills. And Amelia's been under the weather again."

"Thought I hadn't seen her tonight," Harry said, sipping her second pint. The Anne's Arms, unlike the busier inns, had far fewer wenches than was typical; normally it was just Violet, Tessa, and one other girl to manage the evenings. Of course, Harry conceded, the clientele here was more select, and Tessa was happy to do the work of three girls just so long as she got paid an equivalent amount. "And where's your other girl – Lucia?"

"Lucia's sister is having another baby," Violet said, "Her fourth. So she went to help until she's on her feet again."

"How bad has Amelia been?" Hope asked.

"Not as bad as she's been before. I haven't had to watch her around the knives. Mostly she's just taken to her bed and been unable to get out of it. Crying a bit, and a lot of staring and silence. I've been doing all the things you told me," she added. "Talking to her, and tempting her with her favorite foods. Making sure she eats every day."

"How long since she fell into the pit?"

"About a week."

"I will see her," Hope said, standing and opening her drawstring bag. "And here are the pills. Three months supply."

"Thank you, Miss Hope." Violet carefully tucked the box into one of the pockets of her voluminous petticoat as if it was worth its weight in gold.

Which, for a lady in her position, it truly was. Plenty of apothecaries and witches in Bogo offered concoctions that did the same thing as Hope's little white pills – namely, prevent the need to see the sawbones on Blood Alley if you were a working girl and found yourself in the family way – but they also charged more for an inferior product. Hope's pills did what they were supposed to without also inflicting awful nausea, splitting headaches, dizziness, or rotten teeth.

The large woman led the sorceress through the hot, steam-filled kitchen and to the back bedrooms, where she and her girls slept when they had the time. Only one of the four doors was closed – they passed Tessa's room, which was wallpapered with the wanted posters of her favorite regulars –

and they paused to knock before opening it. "Ames, it's me," Violet said. "I've got Miss Hope with me."

The light of the kitchen spilled into a dark, simply furnished room. A bed. A trunk. A small table with a basin perched upon it. There was a cracked mirror hanging on one wall and a pretty painting of ships in a harbor – this harbor – on the other. Amelia was a talented artist and a vibrant girl when she wasn't in the grip of what Violet called her 'black spells' and what Hope referred to as 'the pit'.

Hope reflected that the young woman was exceedingly lucky to have found a proprietress like Violet. Anyone else would have thrown her into the street by now, unwilling to believe that she was truly ill and not just being lazy, convinced that she was addled and willful rather than struggling with a very real disease. For all that Violet blustered and boomed, she was genuinely fond of her girls. Not many employers would give their wenches time off for sister's babies or clean their rooms when they were near-comatose from depression. And it was clear that a broom had swept through this narrow space recently.

"Miss Amelia? May I sit with you?"

The lump beneath the blanket moved. A gray, listless face turned towards the light and stared at her. "Alright," she said tonelessly.

"Thank you. Mrs. Bidwell," she said to Violet in a quiet aside. "Would you please bring me a kettle for tea? And something sweet for her tongue?"

Amelia Toussaint was not a beauty. Her teeth were too uneven, her nose too beaky, and her forehead too large. But she had riveting eyes: one brown and one green, with a ring of gold around the pupils. With her black skin and kinky brown curls, that green eye was especially intriguing.

Her eyes were what usually caught a man's attention first; then he would notice how lightly she moved, as if she had clouds beneath her feet, and how well she listened. Amelia had a gift for attention. She could focus on a speaker in a way that assured them every particle of her being was interested and, more than that, she did it in a way that conveyed full sincerity. Men came to the Anne's Arms and asked for her specifically for this very reason. Because after months at sea they wanted someone to listen while they unburdened or bragged. Having a roll and tussle as part of the deal was a bargain, and a perfect way to spend an evening.

So while Amelia was not as physically beautiful as Tessa, or as skilled in the sexual arts as Lucia, she was still popular. She worked hard, she made good money, she ate well, and she usually had time left over for her artistic passions.

But sometimes, without warning, she would fall into the pit. For a day or two, for a week or three, and — when it was truly black — for a month or more.

Until someone like Hope came along, with her magical bag, and helped her climb back out.

"I'm sorry," Amelia said as Hope took her cold hand, squeezing it gently before running a sure finger over her palm and wrist, locating the pressure points. "I'm just so stupid and useless..."

"That is the monster in the pit talking, not

you," Hope said firmly. Cases like this were unique, and the afflicted had to be handled in different ways; with Amelia, she had learned, it was best to be practical. "When the sailors develop scurvy, they do not apologize. They curse themselves as fools, perhaps, and the very stupid may blame imps or black magic, but they understand that it is an illness. So they visit a doctor, who tells them to eat more vegetables and less beef, and they do these things, and by and by they are better. It is the same with your pit. When you stumble into it, you look for a ladder to climb or a hand to reach for."

"And it's always your hand – you must be tired of pulling me up so often," Amelia said, looking away. Hope had taken a packet of extremely sharp pins from her bag and she knew what was coming next. Violet called Hope "The Sorceress", and Amelia reckoned that this was accurate, because what the petite lady in red could do with some fancy sewing needles had to be magic. If *she* stuck pins all over her arms and chest the only result would be blood and dirty needles. When Hope did it, everything tingled and burned in a way that was somehow both invigorating and relaxing.

"Think of it as a form of meditation," Hope said, placing the next acupuncture needle with a deft twist of her fingers. "When things are repeated often enough, we can find clarity and peace. Thank you, Mrs. Bidwell," she added as the barkeep set a stool, a steaming kettle, and a small plate with a pastry on it beside her. "Now, we will have tea and you shall have some of my syrup."

"The one that tastes like dirt?"

"I am afraid so. But Mrs. Bidwell has been kind enough to supply you with a treat to follow, to wash the taste from your tongue."

"She's so good to me," the girl said, sniffing. "I don't deserve it."

"Hush, child," Hope said, to a girl only a handful of years younger than herself. Hope had seen so many strange things in her life, both with her waking eyes and in her dreams, that she often forgot she was still young. There were days when she felt older than Miss Euphemia. After her trances, when she prayed so earnestly she could feel the eyes of her ancestors on her shoulders. When the air was sharp with incense and the smell of home... "You deserve to have friends and be treated with kindness, Miss Amelia. You do nothing that would earn you reproach or banishment."

"Don't I, though?" Amelia countered. "A lot of people would say I'm a fallen, unclean, sinful woman."

"You do a job, Miss Amelia. One that is actually, despite what those people may think, necessary. If you do not wish to do it any more, if you hate it and feel as though you must continue with it because you have no other option, Captain Harry will help you find a new position," she said.

Amelia blinked at her and accepted the fragrant cup she was handed, reaching out an arm that looked like a pincushion. "...No, I don't want to quit," she said finally. "I *like* my job. I like the Anne. Pious prigs may say I'm sinful but I don't really feel like I'm bad. I don't lie or steal or murder."

"You are a saint by most standards," agreed

Hope, sipping from her own cup. "Now, drink that all down. We will give the needles a few more minutes to do their work. Have you any of the medicine I gave you, or have you used it all up?"

"I keep forgetting to take it," Amelia confessed sheepishly.

"Understandable. You are a busy girl with much to remember. Still, you should try to take one small spoonful of powder a day, mixed into a good cup of strong tea. Even on days when the pit seems nothing more than a bad dream. Do that, and the monster in it will find it harder to catch you. I will make you more before we leave again, enough for three months."

"Thank you, Miss Hope." She was an aptly named woman. Amelia still felt heavy and numb, too cold and aching in a bone-deep way. But she would do as she was told, because when she had followed Hope's instructions in the past, things had improved.

She knew better to think she'd be cured; not even the pretty sorceress in red could cure such a sickness. But her powders and advice — to sit out in the sunlight for at least an hour every day, to eat even when she didn't feel hungry, to talk to Violet or Tessa when the pit felt especially deep — could make it bearable.

"You are welcomed, Miss Amelia."

The clock hanging in the common room bonged the one o'clock hour, an asthmatic cuckoo bird popping out to chirp shrilly. An excited squeal, the clatter of feet up the stairs, and the slamming of the door to room two promptly followed.

"Tessa's been pining longer than I have," Amelia said, holding out her cup for a refill.

"Zora's been complaining for days," said Hope. "We were on an island that could be called celestial, and all she could do was frown."

"Glad I'm not in love. I'm exhausted and out of sorts enough as it is." She sighed. "I'll get up and see what Vi needs done."

"Good girl," Hope said approvingly. "Let me reclaim my pins and you can wash your face."

"It'll only be a couple hours," Amelia said, almost to herself. "Just while Tess is occupied. I can manage that."

*~*~*

"How do you manage these laces?" Zora huffed. "I'm good with knots, but these are *infernal*."

"Probably because all sorts of devils have had their fingers on them," Tess laughed. "Here, let me, you're making a mess of it."

"Hmm, you smell so good." Zora bent her dark head to kiss the soft neck and breathed deeply. Unlike most wenches, who bathed in cheap rose perfume, Tessa dabbed vanilla oil at her neck... her breasts... her wrists... "Good enough to eat."

"I should hope so," came the light reply. "Oh, I've missed you, love."

"How much?"

"Every morning I lie in bed, think of you, and *burn*. Nobody touches me the way you do, nobody pleases me like you. They're all dishwater in my mouth and you're brandy. Hot and sweet..."

"Damn these petticoats."

"Mmh-hmm."

They were always too rough and fast and impatient at first. Time apart made them clumsy and desperate. Zora pressed her against the wall, rucking up her green skirts until her questing fingers found their wet, warm goal.

Tessa laughed, a breathless trill, and clung to her shoulders. Lifted a leg to press her thigh against the slimmer waist and give her better access. Kissed the lips chapped from wind and salt and moaned deeply, knowing what her moans did to her lover.

Tessa was a substantial amount of woman, with curves that had overwhelmed sturdy men. She was an armful and a half, they teased. Taller and much heavier than the trim Zora.

Yet the woman with the dancer's grace and athletic arms supported her easily. It was hauling on all of those ropes and climbing up all of those masts, she supposed. That would give anyone arms like iron.

"God!" Tessa cried out as she came with a jolt, the rush of pleasure like a stab of lightning through her core. She'd bedded four men that evening, all perfectly adequate, but what she'd said was true: nobody gave her pleasure like Zora. Those nimble fingers knew just where to stroke and knead. "Oh God, Zora."

"There's too much fabric between us," Zora said. "Too much space."

"Yes," Tessa said, still dizzy and pulsing. "Too much."

Zora's red skirt fell to the floor with a musical crash, the dozens of coins and charms tied to her belt glinting in the lamplight like a spilled pile of treasure.

Her blouse swiftly followed, then Tessa's emerald skirts. Her discarded corset had already disappeared into the corner.

Zora buried her hands in Tessa's mass of red hair, which promptly shed a dozen hairpins – Tessa was forever buying hairpins, having lost an untold number of them to the cracks in the floorboards.

They fell back onto the bed. The springs shrieked in a coarse counterpoint to their laughter. Tessa, Zora knew, was so good that she could coax a symphony from those springs while in the throes of lovemaking. She knew just when to shift and rock to produce the right notes, in both the bed and her partner.

"Any requests?" the wench asked playfully.

"Something slow and memorable."

"I'll see what I can do..." The blue eyes glittered above her as she slid down the taut, tanned length of her body, wild hair caressing her skin and giving her the appearance of a lustful Medusa. Tessa reached the crux between her legs and bent to kiss amidst the curly black hair.

Zora closed her eyes and abandoned herself fully to the sensation of those skillful lips, the sure tongue, the talented fingers.

She balled the blanket in her hands so as not to pierce her palms with her short nails.

Struggled to breathe as her hips bucked and shifted under Tessa's ministrations, smiling as the other woman pushed her legs open wider and laid a firm arm across her stomach to pin her to the bed. Her lover wasn't going to let her rush things, wasn't about to let her set the pace. She was fully prepared to draw this out until she throbbed and begged, until she was half-mad with tension, until she cried and writhed and promised her the world in exchange for release.

And what a release – her body melted and flowed like mercury, the pleasure coursing through her as searing as lava. Zora screamed as she convulsed, her back arching like one possessed.

It was always incredible with Tessa, always unbelievable. The stuff of epic, supremely erotic, poetry. Perhaps because her body had weeks to forget her particular flavor of love, always craved it the way an addict craves the drug. Her own fingers could never reach the plateaus Tessa's mouth took her to.

She was panting, thrashing her head in an attempt to dispel the bursting stars, when Tessa lowered her face to hers for another kiss. She smelled of her own musk now and the way it blended with the vanilla essence was painfully arousing.

"You taste so good," Tessa murmured, voice low and sated. "How was that?"

"I won't walk for a week," Zora replied when she had enough breath.

"Perhaps we can do better than that..."

They grappled and twisted, slid and rolled, intertwining their bodies in a way that would have made the most pious rethink chaste vows. Olive skin against cream, breast to breast, flushed cheeks, bruised lips.

And everywhere was red hair.

So hungry for one another it almost seemed possible that they would literally consume each other, teeth nipping over responsive flesh as moans verged on growls.

"No man could bed me like that," Tessa said finally, splayed comfortably over Zora's chest. "Never. Not if he was God Himself."

"I love it when you're blasphemous," Zora replied, counting the marks she'd left on her pale back and shoulders. "Six, seven, eight..."

"They say God loves everybody, even whores, but He's never paid me a visit," Tessa went on dreamily.

"He couldn't afford you."

"Probably not. I raised my price again, did I tell you?"

"And how has that gone?"

"Wonderfully. I've saved up a king's ransom already. Vi's keeping it all locked up for me. Safe as houses."

"The men been treating you well?" It took a little effort, but she kept her voice even and her face calm.

Tessa, long attuned to her lover's body and moods, twisted to look up at her.

"Haven't laid a hand on me, except to put it where I tell them to," she said.

They'd had the discussion long ago and neither wanted to have it again. Tessa had no qualms about her job; in fact, she enjoyed it. She made good money, she was treated well, and she had shops and people and excitement close at hand. She wasn't interested in the life of a pirate, which was full of long bouts of tedium, hard work of the sort that didn't lead to orgasms, and bloody danger. And the income was hardly reliable. So long as her boss was Violet, she could set her own terms, and she had Hope's little pills and potions to ward off the sicknesses and "results" prevalent in her trade, she was content.

Mostly.

She'd be happier if she could see Zora every day. But she also understood that Zora hated wenching; she'd only turned to it in the first place because it paid better than dancing and she was tired of starving. Zora didn't like being pawed at by men and couldn't stomach playing the game: all the flirtations and coquettishness, the expected script of dialogue and constant smiling. She was happier out at sea on a swaying boat, with dirt under her nails and calluses on her hands.

Zora liked the solitude and silence that could be found at sea; Tessa would go crazy from it. And while Tessa found the hectic life in Bogo energizing, it grated on Zora's nerves after a day or two.

No, they were too fundamentally different to have a perfect life together. So, instead, they settled for what they could get. These moments of compromise were worth the effort and frustrations.

"In fact, I've got a new regular," Tessa said after a pause.

If anyone else had been listening in, they

would have thought such a comment rather heartless. Surely her lover didn't want to hear about the others she'd taken to bed. But Zora knew that Tessa would only bring up the men she serviced for one reason.

"Who?"

"His name's Morgan Yates. He sails with *The Charon*. Works with the cannons."

Zora sat up against the wall. Tessa rearranged herself around her and rested her head on her tanned shoulder. "Be careful," Zora warned, somber as the grave. "Those men are a bad lot. Traitors and slavers. Allied with some very dangerous merfolk."

"I know," Tessa said, a little peevishly. "I've read your letters. I'm not taking any chances. But Morgan's not half-bad. Thick and dull, but not cruel. I know what the cruel ones look like. They've got a sheen in their eyes. Like that Wrath..." She shuddered. "I'm glad he's only got the one eye, because I don't think I could stand to have two of those on me."

"Does he come in here a lot? Wrath?"

"No, Drew hasn't been in for months. None of his crew have. Just Morgan. I think word got round that Harry's a regular. The rest of his crew is avoiding Anne's. Saying this out in public would probably get me in trouble, but," Tessa paused. "I think Wrath's afraid of your captain. Really afraid."

"He should be," said Zora with feeling. "She's vowed to see him dead. And when Harry makes a promise—"

"She keeps it," finished Tessa. "Like when she

promised to find you something better than wenching."

"Tess, things with Wrath are going to escalate. Soon. If that happens, you need to be ready to go to ground. If he knows this place is on friendly terms with us, he might strike here to get back at Harry."

"You really think so?" The smooth brow furrowed with concern. "But everyone knows Violet paid Hope for a blessing, and Wrath's supposed to be real superstitious."

"Even so. If he lives up to his name, he might overlook the threat of incurring bad luck." Zora also spared a moment to wonder: everyone thought Hope was a sorceress, and it was true that she devoutly believed in luck and ancient gods, knew her herbs, and could do strange things to people – like that man in the street earlier – but could she *really* work magic?

Everything Zora had seen her do could be explained away logically; there had been a performing magician in her home village that could create fire with a snap of his fingers, too, but he had shown her it was all sleight-of-hand with black powder and scraps of sandpaper.

Was Hope just another performer? Did she cover simple knowledge with showman's tricks? It would be nice to believe she was a real witch – nice to think they had genuine magic on their side against Wrath Drew's bigger, better armed, better manned ship. But Zora couldn't be sure.

"This talk is making us both cross," Tessa said, cupping one of Zora's pert breasts. "I don't want to feel cross. We don't have time to waste on that."

"You're absolutely right," Zora agreed, licking a lingering bead of sweat from the hollow of her throat. "Lie back. It's my turn to make you scream for mercy."

*~*~*

"Mercy!" croaked the man swaying on the opposite side of the table, tilting until he almost slid from his chair. "I surrender!" He slurred the last word so badly it was nothing but a sibilant 'S' and a rumbling 'R'.

"You did better than most," Jo said to appease the stranger's wounded pride. Empty glasses covered the table between them. The man looked on the verge of coma. And the first mate of *The Sappho* just brushed back a wayward braid and debated on risking Violet's shepherd's pie (which at least had something normally tended by a shepherd in it). All of that beer and rum had given her an appetite.

"See? Told you," said Maddie to an impressed Franky. "Nobody can drink Jo under the table."

"Amy, lass, have you been blue?" asked the unlucky drinker's bosom friend, a man that looked like he was carved from aged teak. He stretched out a hand to the wench passing by with an empty tray. "Ah, c'mere, girl."

Amelia settled on his knee, eyes tired but face calm. "What'll it be tonight, Bruce?" she asked.

"I'd pay a shilling just to see a smile, love.

Here. Thatta girl." He pressed a positively chaste kiss to her cheek and a coin into her palm. "And another five for a song. You sing pretty as a bird, Amy."

"Any requests?"

"'The Moon She be Bold and Bonny'," called a man with a Highland brogue.

"'The Gates of Jerusalem'," suggested another.

"'The Lady of Shallot'," requested the golden Hugh Dawkins.

"Nah, nah," said Bruce, waving these lesser songs away. "Do 'Annabel Lee', Amy. You always bring a tear to my eye with that 'un."

With her arms looped around the man's neck, Amelia sang in a piercing, flute-like tone. The room fell  silent, the drinkers and gamblers and dart-players all turning to stare at the dark girl with mismatched eyes.

And Jo sat back in her chair with a remote, unreadable expression, her hand inching toward her flask.

Harry turned to look at her. Their eyes met for a moment, dark and heavy with understanding, and then Jo looked down. Bowed her head and drank deeply.

"Poor Jo," Maddie said, when the last wavering note had died and the babble of ribald conversation picked up again. "She always gets like that when she's been drinking and someone sings. Especially that song."

"Why, do you think?"

"Miss Euphemia says she must've had her

heart broken by a singer."

"I think I know who," Franky said quietly. "I think when Harry lost her sister, Jo lost her lover."

"You think so?"

"I saw her face when they told the story."

"That would explain an awful lot," mused Maddie. "Poor Jo. Poor Harry."

Franky was suddenly tired. The room felt too hot and crowded, too full of emotion and old ghosts. And the smell of beer was starting to make him queasy. "I think I'm off to bed," he said. "Coming?"

"Alright. It *is* a lot to take in," she added as they climbed the stairs, hand-in-hand. "Bogo, I mean. It can get overwhelming."

"There's only one way I want to be overwhelmed right now, love," Franky said firmly, closing the door to room six and shutting out the crowd below. "Come here."

"Thought you were tired."

"The day I'm too tired to make love to you, Maddie, is the day you can shovel dirt over my head. We haven't shared a proper bed yet, and I intend to make the most of it."

Downstairs, Violet worked the taps and joined in a shanty with a gusto, her voice a brassy baritone. Her old dad and old man had both been sailors, and she knew more of the limericks than her customers. By the fire, Agnessa and Hugh Dawkins had progressed to their opinions on poetry, and the dark-haired helmswoman had pulled her chair closer to his. Hope was reading palms in the corner and handing out charms to anyone who asked. Lizzie was arm-wrestling with a sailor twice her size, her blacksmith's muscles bulging with effort. Marcella had pulled out her bone flute and was accompanying the shanty singers alongside a man with a tiny, creaking accordion and a reedy voice.

And Harry brought a plate of pie and a loaf of bread to Jo's table, where the pair sat and ate in silence.

# NIGHT TERRORS

Silence was having nightmares.

She would wake in the dry darkness – too dry! and why was she sleeping on cloth, why wasn't she in her tide pool padded with fresh kelp; this wasn't the cave she shared with her sisters? – and gasp and cry, longing for the release of a scream. But her throat was too scarred for even that and she would fumble out of the cot and curl up on the hard wooden floor and shake.

Sirens did not dream. They did not have nightmares. The experience was altogether new and incredibly terrifying.

What was happening to her? Was this the result of the foul poison her sister had poured down her throat? Was it her constant proximity with humans; had some of their strangeness somehow rubbed off onto her like a stain, like oil over waves? Was it her distance from the water, the punishment she must endure now that the ocean had repudiated her?

Miss Euphemia would find her lying beneath her cot, cheek pressed to the floor and inky tears on her face, and would draw her out with soft sounds of encouragement and gentle, kind hands. Silence still did not like to be touched by humans, but Miss Euphemia and Maddie were different. Their hands somehow did not feel so rough and alien on her skin, though one had the dry parchment flesh of the old and the other was much callused from hard labor.

She would allow Miss Euphemia to pull her out, like a pearl from a half-closed shell, and drape a soft blanket over her bare shoulders. The old woman would take a bowl of water and a rag and wipe away the black tears from her face before trickling some of the water over her shoulders, onto the blanket, and the dampness would soothe her as nothing else could. She could no longer swim freely in the water, could no longer put her maimed head beneath the waves, but she was still a creature born of the ocean and she thrived best where it was wet.

"Why don't we try something?" the patient teacher said one night as she led her to the desk. "Here is a pen, and here is some paper. Why don't you draw me what is making you cry?"

Silence sniffed loudly and nodded, taking the pen she was just becoming comfortable with holding. Such strange things the humans had and such strange uses they found for them. She bent over the desk, nose close to the paper, and began laboriously etching lines.

Miss Euphemia sat beside her and hummed, as she often did. She was reading a large book covered in cracking red leather. Silence could almost understand the letters stamped across the cover in gold gilt. The first snake shape was an "S" – the same letter that began her new name.

She turned back to her drawing; she had already depicted her sister, and the bone knife in her hand. Then there was the man with the black hat. He had one eye and a wicked smile. And here was the monster fish, the one that was in the room where they threw her before she was dragged across the deck and forced to drink the poison.

Silence drew the creature's teeth with a shudder – there was not a big enough sheet of paper to do it full justice. Each tooth had been longer than her arms; the gaping mouth was great enough to swallow her whole.

When she had seen it in the murky half-light, that terrible day on the black-sailed ship, she had cowered away and pressed to the wall with a scream. It seemed to be coming through the ship itself, a mottled green and bloody red. It gave off no smell, it did not move – not even with breath – and she had been transfixed in pure horror until hands grabbed her and pulled her out of that awful room.

The image of that monster was indelibly stamped onto her memory. Somehow, impossibly, it was even more frightening to her now than the remembrance of what her sister had done. It had achieved a sort of symbolic importance – it represented all of the pain and depravity she had experienced that day.

"My word, what a nasty thing," Miss Euphemia said when she looked over Silence's shoulder. "I'd be having nightmares, too, if I had faced down such a Leviathan. What are you doing now, dear?"

The act of drawing her nightmare had proved cathartic and Silence was feeling much improved. Perhaps if she got every detail out onto the paper it would no longer haunt her sleep. Encouraged by this thought, she was laboriously but carefully curving and slanting her pen beneath the monster.

"Why, this is a word – Silence, do you know what this means? What you've written here?"

The siren shook her head, eyes blank.

Miss Euphemia carefully picked up the paper – the poor girl had pressed her pen down so hard that it had pierced the paper in several places. "This is that scoundrel Wrath Drew," the old woman said. "A most accurate depiction of him, my girl. And is this – is this the one that hurt you?"

Silence nodded quickly, putting a hand to her mouth and throat. She made another gesture that Miss Euphemia didn't understand.

"Wait just a moment, dear," she said, struck by inspiration. She hurried out of the cabin and across the deck, down to the dark berth full of snores and rustling, where she reached up confidently in the dark to tug at someone's blanket.

"Wha, whassit?" Zora mumbled, rolling over.

"Zora, come with me," Miss Euphemia said in her best schoolmarm voice, a tone that went straight to the childish heart and demanded attention. The darker, younger woman pushed herself up and blinked. "I need you to translate for Silence. She's trying to tell me something, and I think it's important."

"Alright, keep your hair on," she muttered, reaching for the ladder and sliding down, clutching a blanket around her shoulders.

"Go on, Silence," Miss Euphemia said when they had returned, Zora dropping down onto the edge of the cot with a squeak of abused springs and a wide yawn.

The siren made the gesture again.

"She said 'sister'," Zora said. "She wanted something to call Maddie that was stronger than just 'friend', so I taught her 'sister'."

"This is your sister?" Miss Euphemia said, pointing at the picture. Silence nodded, eyes sorrowful and lips pressed tighter. "Good Lord. Oh, you poor thing. How absolutely dreadful."

"What?" Zora demanded, finally fully awake.

"It was her sister who did those awful things to her," Miss Euphemia said quietly. She reached over and put her hand on Silence's knee. "I'm so sorry."

Silence nodded, dry-eyed.

"So if that's her sister, and that's obviously Wrath," Zora said, having stood and come around Euphemia's chair to look down at the picture. "What in the nine hells is *that*? And why did she write 'BARRA' underneath it?"

"Where did you see this monster, Silence?"

Silence made an encompassing gesture with both arms that took in the entire room.

"It was in a cabin like this one?" Miss Euphemia asked shrewdly.

Nod.

"That doesn't make sense, though," Zora said, scratching her cheek. "Why would there be a giant fish in a cabin?"

"Zora, these are all things she's actually seen," Miss Euphemia said. "On the day Kai rescued her. On that evil bastard Wrath Drew's boat. She's been dreaming about this because it was all so terrifying. What was this monster doing in the cabin, Silence?"

The siren stood and walked to the wall, putting her hands against the wood.

"It was on the wall?"

She made a gesture.

"'Through' the wall, she said," Zora translated, confused. "It was coming through the wall?"

"Perhaps not — maybe it was a trick of the light. Silence, did this monster make any sound? Did it move? Did it try to attack you?"

The siren shuddered, then shook her head. She made a series of abrupt gestures.

"She says it 'stared'. She says it 'looked hungry'. She says she was 'too scared'."

"I think I understand," Miss Euphemia said. "I think I see. Zora, can you go wake Harry and bring her up here?"

"Really?" Zora said, fixing her with a look. "You really want me to go and drag Harry out of bed? Now?"

"Zora, use your eyes and brain," Miss Euphemia said tartly. "Look at the monster and pair it with the letters Silence has written."

Zora looked again — and paled visibly. "Oh. Oh God." She turned and hurried through the door, blanket billowing cape-like over her shoulders.

Silence looked at Miss Euphemia in concern, and the woman was quick to sit beside her on the bed and take her hand to pat it gently. "It's alright, my dear," she said. "You've done absolutely nothing wrong. Do you feel better now?"

The siren nodded and leaned against the

frail human. She smelled of paper and wax candles and though the scents were strange to her nose they were also oddly comforting.

"What is it, what's happened?" Harry demanded a moment later, hair wild and clothes in disarray from sleep. "Everything alright?"

"We're fine, Captain," Miss Euphemia said. "I'm sorry if Zora's abrupt manner startled you. It's just that I think we've uncovered something you might like to know."

"Yes?"

"It seems that Silence was put into the cabin of *The Charon* before her torture," the old woman said calmly and plainly. "And she was terrified by what she saw hanging on the wall there, half-covered in shadows." Miss Euphemia held out the sheet of paper. Harry had barely glanced at it before she made the connection. She looked up with fire in her eyes. "Yes, dear: I believe you've finally found *The Barracuda* you've been searching for all these years. I'd wager a year's gold that Captain Luis' backstabbing first mate was none other than Wrath Drew."

# THE CLAN OF THE
# BLACK ROCKS

"You know, I think the lizards on this island may be unique," Wilhelmina announced at breakfast.

The others would be setting sail tomorrow – Kai included – and she would be left alone for at least three weeks, probably more. Privately, she was looking forward to the solitude. She loved her crewmates, and she was by nature gregarious in company, but sometimes a woman (and a scientist) just needed to be left alone with her thoughts and her work.

"That so?" Maddie yawned, nearly spilling her mug of tea. Up all hours of the night with Franky, if Wil had to guess. She hoped that Hope would be wise enough to restock certain herbs before they returned.

"Overlooking the obvious facts that they have dorsal frills uncommon in iguanas and six claws on their front legs when there should be only four, they seem unusually intelligent. They also have the chameleon's talent of shifting the colors of their skin. I observed one from afar the other day and saw it shift through six different hues. Such a thing is unheard of in the larger reptiles."

"Fascinating," Zora said dryly, rolling her eyes as she nibbled a biscuit.

"You should talk to Kai about them," Agnessa

suggested helpfully. "Before we leave. Maybe he has some insight to share."

He did indeed. "Are not all *mo'o* like this?" he asked. "I have often talked with them here in the lagoon. You could not find a better pearl diver than Malicky and his clan."

"So you can actually converse with them?" Wil asked eagerly, making a note in her ever-present leather journal. Kai looked up from the piece of seaglass he was shaping with a strip of dried sharkskin.

"Yes," he said, bemused by her excitement. "They do not speak human tongues, of course, but a simple form of ocean pidgin. Mo'o are not as skilled at mimicking sounds the way my people or, say, parrots, can. But they manage some of the more basic songs in rougher tones."

"Could you teach me some of the language?"

"It's a *very* difficult tongue," Kai warned.

"I mastered Latin in two months, and Russian in three," Wil said confidently. "And the Cyrillic alphabet is nothing to sneeze at."

"Wait here," Kai said after a moment's thought, sliding from the rock and sinking into the lagoon. He surfaced a moment later with a curled shell, which he blew into like a horn. The whistle echoed through the palm trees, sending a flock of jewel-toned parrots into paroxysms of annoyance.

A few minutes passed and then an unusual delegation scampered out of the ferny undergrowth. Three large iguanas with mottled green bodies and bright red frills appeared, then froze, fixing unblinking yellow dragon eyes upon

Wil as their blue tongues flicked out nervously to taste the air.

Kai made a series of peculiar chirrups and croaks and the wary trio finally came closer. "Wil, this is Malicky, the Chief," the merman said, gesturing to the foremost and largest lizard, which was easily five feet long and had a crimson frill that stood a foot high. "His brother, Coti. And his son, Tazu. I've told them who you are and that you're very interested in learning more about them."

The one called Malicky croaked hoarsely for quite some time in what had to be quite a speech. Then Tazu, the smallest of the three (at a mere three feet long), crept forward.

"Malicky says that his son will teach you their language as best he can, because he is young and patient and has the time to waste, but that it may be too difficult for a hairless pig to learn. He means no offense," Kai said quickly. "It's just what they call humans."

"No offense taken," Wil said, smiling like a giddy child on Christmas morning. "I've been called worse. This is incredible. Amazing, even. You called them *mo'o* – is that what they call themselves?"

"They call themselves The Clan of the Black Rocks," Kai said with a laugh. "You are *very* excited."

"Kai, no human has ever encountered a species of lizard like this," Wil said breathlessly. "Not even Mr. Darwin. This is – this will fundamentally change the way people look at reptiles. I mean... I could die happy after this. Well, after my paper's been verified and published, anyway. Finding this island almost makes me believe in Fate, and

Destiny, and God Himself. Brilliant! Just wait until my father hears of this! Wait until the British Herpetological Society hears of this! This'll wipe the smug smiles right off their blasted faces!"

Malicky of the Great Claws exchanged a glance with Coti Half Tail. "Hairless pigs," he hissed. "Very strange creatures. Very crazy."

"I like it," Tazu Three Tones said with the burble that signified laughter. "It's funny."

"Good that you like it," Malicky told his son. "Because it is your responsibility. It is friend to Good Kaimana, who will be cross if it comes to harm. So take care of it."

"When did this island get so crowded?" complained Coti. "Not like when I was a hatchling. Could walk from Fire Mountain to Yellow Beach and not even a snake in sight. Now all these hairless pigs and fish pigs at every turn, a body can't sun himself in peace..."

"Tazu likes you," Kai said, holding back a laugh at Coti's curmudgeonly attitude.

"Kai, thank you," Wil said, impulsively hugging him and kissing his cheek. "You've made my whole bloody year."

"You are welcomed?" he said, surprised, as she stumped over to the lizards and clumsily sat down on a rock a polite distance from them.

"Tazu," she said clearly, pointing at her newest subject. Content that this strange hairless pig meant their nephew/son no harm, Coti and Malicky turned and disappeared back into the palm trees.

The remaining lizard ducked his head in what was clearly a nod and made a chirrup sound. Wil obediently mimicked it, and Tazu's mouth gaped open in a lipless smile. "Wil," she said, pointing at herself, grinning at the corresponding sound Tazu readily supplied.

"Guess I'll just leave you to it," Kai said with a chuckle, reclaiming his lump of seaglass and slipping away to a quieter spot.

*~*~*

For a woman who had already mastered five languages, the Tongue of the Clan, as Wil decided to call it, wasn't as impossible as it may seem to others.

It involved complex, harsh tones that the Romance languages disdained, yes, and having air sacs in the jaws and an echo cavity in the sinuses was no doubt helpful. But a determined human could still manage it as long as they kept their throat well-lubricated and didn't mind coughing up the odd bit of phlegm.

"Very smart," Tazu complimented her with pride. "Very clever hairless pig."

"Tazu good teacher," she replied, making him swell even bigger.

As the lessons progressed, Wil realized that Tazu might not be able to speak English – but he certainly understood it. This puzzled her. Perhaps

Kai, in his long period of isolation, had talked to the Clan in a variety of languages, so as not to become rusty.

"How know you my tongue?" she managed to ask finally.

"The Clan knows many things," Tazu said cryptically. "Sun Goddess taught us."

He went on to tell her one of the oldest stories in the Clan's history through a series of short phrases and evocative pictograms he drew across the sand of the beach with his claws and tail.

The Sun Goddess created everything and was mother to all; this was undeniable fact. Didn't the sun bring them warmth to keep them alive and give them strength? Didn't the sun help the eggs to hatch after they were laid? The sun itself was like an egg, fat and round, and rolled across the sky each day to be replaced by her sister, the moon, who controlled the ocean's waves. The Sun Goddess created them, and then the Moon Goddess brought them to this place on the tides.

It seemed The Clan of the Black Rocks had once lived somewhere else, far away, but they had to leave because of some terrible upheaval. A war? A natural disaster? The history was murky. So they dove into the ocean and swam and, just when their strength was at its end and they had resigned themselves to drowning, they found this place. The Moon drew them here on a gentle tide on a bright night, which they remembered every year in a great feast and celebration.

Wil was enthralled. An entirely new civilization, with its own creation mythology – and a matriarchal one at that!

She asked Tazu about his family and how one became a Chief of the Clan.

"You must do a great deed," he said. "My father became Chief when he stopped a rock from crushing the nesting ground. He saw it was loose, would fall, and he built a wall around it. Then he used his great claws to push it away, so that it fell another way. That is also when he got his True Name."

She asked him if he had his True Name yet.

"Not yet," Tazu said with his equivalent of a shrug: a slow and lazy blink of his second eyelids. "I am called Three Tones because that is all I can do now." And he demonstrated, shifting from his usual mottled green (perfect for hiding in the ferny undergrowth) to a sandy yellow that would blend in well on the long stretch of beach. Then he became the startling purple of a ringed octopus; *that* would no doubt frighten any hungry predator. Throughout the shifting, his frill remained bright red. "In a few monsoons, I will do more. I will get better," he promised.

"How old is Tazu?" Wil asked.

"Tazu has forty-two monsoons," he said.

"Tazu is older than Wil."

"No!" he said, tail slapping the ground with surprise. "How many has Wil?"

"Thirty-one."

"Wil is very smart for hatchling," Tazu said. Everything under the age of forty was a hatchling in the eyes of the Clan, where one wasn't considered an elder until they reached two hundred.

While Tazu sunned himself on a flat slab of hot obsidian, Wil sat in a collapsible chair beside it and sketched him in minute detail.

"What I wouldn't give for a daguerreotype camera," she lamented to herself, knowing full well that carting such a delicate instrument on a long voyage, onto an uncharted island, and then expecting successful results with extremely volatile chemicals, was on par with relying only on prayer as a cure for a terrible disease.

"Want to see, want to see," Tazu hissed excitedly when she had finished, climbing up her chair with a scrabble of claws. "Very good," he approved, throat fluttering and frill flicking. He tilted his head one way, then the next, to see the drawing better. "I am handsome, yes?"

"Yes, very handsome," Wil agreed with a smile. "Tazu have hatchlings?"

"No, no, practically hatchling myself," he said quickly. "Not ready yet, plenty of time to find mate later."

"Tazu does not want to settle down," Wil said knowingly.

"I do not understand Wil," he said diffidently, turning away. "Wil use strange hairless pig terms. I am going for swim now."

Like all iguana species, the Clan were excellent swimmers. Wil enjoyed sitting on the edge of the lagoon and watching them dive into its clear, aquamarine depths, their long tails and back legs streaming behind them. Their cheeks puffed out with air, they would pick up oysters with their dexterous front claws and return to the surface with a kick of their legs and a flick of their tail.

Pearls were in high demand in the Clan. The Chief was chosen based upon personal deeds of great valor, but an individual's wealth depended on their abilities as a pearl diver. The most esteemed members of the Clan had the largest, finest pearls in their dens.

"Do you know what pearls are?" Wil asked Tazu one day, when his dive had resulted in an exciting find: a bright purple pearl. It was only of average size but the color was unique, and Tazu had been beside himself with glee when the rest of the Clan gathered around to examine it with appreciative hissing.

"The Moon Goddess' tears," he replied promptly, rolling onto his back and pressing the pearl to his leathery, spotted chest the way a child would hug a beloved teddy bear. "She must have been very sad indeed to cry such a tear. I will polish it every night, so she knows I am thinking of her. Then she will not be so sad."

And Wil, who had always felt a driving need to be factual, who had never before resisted the urge to disprove some superstitious belief with scientific logic, held her tongue for once. Perhaps the Clan thought that if they gathered enough pearls and treated them with enough respect, the Moon Goddess would never cry again. There was something touching in that.

As belief systems went, there were far worse.

When she felt she could speak confidently without embarrassing herself too badly, Wil asked

Tazu if he could call a meeting of the Clan. She had something she wished to discuss with them.

"I am Wil One Leg," she said, introducing herself in the formal way. "I am a sage of my Clan." The Clan did not have scientists; the closest equivalent was a sage, or One Who Knows Things. "Tazu Three Tones has taught me much about you, and I ask for permission to share your stories with my Clan."

"Do we want hairless pigs knowing our secrets?" Coti asked, grumpy as always.

"Why does Wil One Leg wish to do this?" an elder demanded, a huge and impressive female called Woi of the Cracked Frill. Her eyes were clouded and her scaly skin had dulled to a uniform gray, but the entire Clan deferred to her decisions. Tazu had told Wil that in order to succeed, she would have to convince Woi.

"My Clan knows nothing of yours. I have traveled far to find people like you, so that my Clan may know more of the world. As a sage, my dream is to understand all."

"A mighty dream," said another elder female, Poly of the Hundred Hues. "An impossible dream."

"But a dream worth having," Wil said firmly.

"Yes," agreed Woi. "I see you, Wil One Leg, though my sight has dimmed. You burn with bright light. The light of a dreamer. Where would we be without dreams? Did not Chief Jupaca of the Old Land dream of this island, and listen to the Moon's song to bring us here?" The others all nodded and hummed, claws clicking against the rocks.

"You may tell your Clan of us, sage. But do

250

not bring death upon us. Good Kaimana has told us your Clan, the ones who came on the big log, are to be trusted. But we have no wish to see more hairless pigs on our island. So you may tell others of us, and perhaps a hatchling like Tazu may wish to journey with you, to see other hairless pigs. But you will not bring those outside of your Clan here. Yes?"

"Yes," Wil said, thinking of how many delicate ecosystems had been destroyed by man's carelessness. The islands where invasive rats, snakes, and rabbits devoured rare fauna and wiped out species of birds. Huge tracts of land razed for human habitation. The sicknesses that wiped out native populations. "I agree to this."

"Good." Woi turned to regard Tazu, who bent his head to her. "Tazu Three Tones is a great teacher," she said, to the surprise of many. "He will be a great sage and elder one day."

"Such praise!" Tazu said to Wil later, still giddy. "To be so praised by an elder!"

"She was right. Tazu is a *very* good teacher."

"Woi sees all, though she is half blind. She knew I wish to go with Wil."

"Go with me?"

"Yes, when you sail to other lands. I would like to see these lands, too."

"Then Tazu will," she promised with a smile.

When the others returned, still flush from their latest adventure, it was to find Wil sitting on a rock, her wooden leg lying in the sand, hard at work writing in her journal. A large iguana sat on the rock over her shoulder, hissing and croaking in her ear as she nodded thoughtfully.

"'Being An Examination On The Physiology, Psychology, and Social Hierarchy of The Great Black Rock Iguana'," Agnessa read, peeking over her other shoulder. "'With Additional Notes On Their History, Language, and Belief Systems'. Phew, Wil! Sounds like you're writing a book!"

"Most likely," the scientist agreed cheerfully, focus still on her pen. "Nessa, this is Tazu."

"Hello," the helmswoman said politely, bobbing a curtsy that would have brought a tear to her father's eye before she realized she was greeting a lizard. "Um..."

The lizard made an odd burbling noise, and Wil laughed before croaking something at it. "He says you're graceful for a hairless pig. It's quite a compliment."

"Yes. Alright. Good," Agnessa said slowly, taking a step back. "You *are* feeling alright, Wilhelmina?"

"Very well, thank you for asking. Oh, how did the trip go?"

"Good. It went... good. Um. I'll just go tell Harry you're over here, shall I?"

"As you please."

Agnessa found Harry, Kai, and Katherine in the lagoon washing their hair. "I think we stayed away too long. Wil's finally cracked," she announced. "She's talking to a lizard."

"Must be one of Malicky's people," Kai said. "I should see if they want to join us for supper, now that Wil is probably an honorary member of the Clan."

"She is?" Agnessa said, feeling lost.

"I knew they'd take to her," the merman added. "In fact, I wouldn't be surprised if one of the Clan wants to join *us*."

"You wouldn't?"

"With a merman and a siren already on the crew," Harry said complacently, having been forewarned by Kai. "I don't see the problem with a giant lizard or two."

"I'm just going to ask Hope if she can make some tea, then," Agnessa said faintly, wandering off.

"Can you help me with these pins, Kai?" Katherine asked, having coiled her wet braid around her head. "It's so much easier to do this with another set of hands."

# REMEMBER

She couldn't *breathe*.

Aveline kept her mouth tightly closed, her body solely focused on the burning in her lungs and the way her vision was going dark; her mind solely focused on the way the stranger's sword had flashed and her little sister had screamed.

Was Harriet still alive?

Of course she was. She had to be. Jo was coming to meet her and she'd find Harriet, she'd get her to the doctor–

Jo.

She was never going to see her again. Either she'd turn into one of these *things* that the stranger had thrown her to or she would die here, and they would leave her body to rot right along with all the other skeletons she'd seen pinned to the ocean floor; her family would never know what became of her.

The creature holding her arms tilted its head, its eyes somehow registering mirth even though they were entirely black. Aveline kicked out again, her foot uselessly striking against the thing's scaly gray skin.

She couldn't fight. Couldn't get away. All she could do was take a breath, and hope.

She would change, and escape as soon as she was able. Find her way back to shore, find Harriet and Josephine, let them know she was safe.

It would be all right.

Even telling herself this, she couldn't make her mouth open, couldn't consciously decide to take a breath of the water she knew would kill her. Only when her lungs couldn't hold on anymore did she give in. The ocean rushed into her body, and everything went dark.

*~*~*

"What should we do? I've never seen one react this way before."

"I have."

The women spoke in guttural, wordless noises that Aveline nevertheless understood as words. She tried to focus on the voices, tried to open her eyes; found she couldn't do both. She reached out toward the people she heard, and found her hand enveloped in a rough grip.

"Don't get too attached," the second voice said. "Last time this happened, the mer was useless. Couldn't talk anymore and could barely even swim. Just had to leave her and let nature have its way."

"That won't happen," another voice said, and something in it was so familiar that her heart ached at the sound. Forcing her eyes open, Aveline saw a brown-skinned girl who couldn't be real. She wore a deep blue dress (her birthday, she'd saved up all her money and bought it for her for her birthday last year) and her black hair hung dry around her shoulders, though they were deep underwater. "You'll be all right," the girl said. "Just rest."

Though Aveline knew the other girl had to be imaginary, her presence still made her feel safer somehow, and she closed her eyes.

*~*~*

"You are awake, sister?"

She opened her eyes, waving her tail
experimentally. It didn't quite look right. It was a
deep iridescent black, and of course it was
supposed to be there, it was her tail, but it still
didn't look right.

Shouldn't there be legs?

She looked up at her sisters, who looked so
different than she did – entirely gray bodies, wider
mouths with serrated teeth – and tried desperately
to cling to the ideas that seemed to be flitting away
as quickly as fish did when they sensed a predator.

Predator. They were predators. She was...

She was also a predator?

They were her sisters. She traveled with
them. She was like them.

"I... yes, I'm awake," she answered. "What
happened?"

"The humans attacked you," one of her
sisters said. "We saved you."

"It isn't true," a new voice said. Aveline
quickly looked to the side, her mouth falling open
when she saw something that didn't, couldn't exist.
Something horribly familiar.

There was a dark-skinned human floating
there, black curls flowing around her face, staring
at her solemnly. "It isn't true," she repeated.
"Remember?"

"I... I can't – remember what?"

"Remember me."

"Remember us," another voice said, and Aveline watched in disbelief as a skinny, pale girl with white-blonde hair appeared next to the tall young woman. The blonde hair matched the shade she could see floating around her own face... was she old enough to have a daughter? And if she was her child, why did she have legs?

Wasn't she herself supposed to have legs?

"Who... who are... I don't know you. I don't know anybody," she said, abruptly feeling close to tears. She couldn't remember any of them, couldn't remember herself. She did remember a man. A human, grabbing hold of her arm. Pain. Screaming for help. Then water. "You saved me."

"Of course we did," one of the sharkmaids said, swimming closer to wrap her arms around her. "You're one of us. I'm Anahera. Remember?"

"No," she said. "But I will."

*~*~*

Anahera was the leader of their pack. She found new hunting ground, and provided for all of them. On nights when they weren't able to find much to eat, Anahera was the one who went hungry, making sure that all the rest of them went to sleep with full bellies.

Kalea was Anahera's sister-by-blood. It was rare to find such a thing, Kalea had explained. Most pups died before the age of eight, when they grew old enough to properly defend themselves. Other mers killed them on sight simply because they were sharkmaids, hated oceanwide because they were reputed to be vicious and cruel. Many, Anahera had told her, confused them with sirens. Sharkmaids were not even given names until they reached their sixth year. It was fortunate enough to reach adulthood, let alone have a sibling survive alongside you.

Only one of Kalea's pups was still alive, and she had not quite yet reached the age when she would be given her own name. She was simply known among them all as Pup or Young One.

Uilani had never spoken a word to her. It wasn't out of cruelty; Uilani never spoke to anyone. She had asked Anahera about it one day, and her expression had darkened before she told her shortly that Uilani had been captured by humans when she was barely older than Pup. They'd managed to rescue her, but she hadn't spoken a single word since. When Aveline sang, Uilani looked at least close to contentment, so she made sure to sing whenever asked.

Maata did have a streak of cruelty, at least when it came to feeding. She would play with whatever animal she'd selected as prey, torturing it before dealing a death blow. It was a frightening thing to see, even more so because Maata was so chipper and sweet otherwise, forever telling jokes and hugging the others and trying to make sure that she felt comfortable in the group.

Chausiku was young and flighty, always darting off alone even though Anahera lectured her every time. Anahera had told Aveline privately that she knew Chausiku wouldn't always be with their pod, that she was too restless to be anything but a loner, but that she wanted to protect her for as long as she could. Lone sharkmaids so often ended up diced into pieces on some cruel fisherman's ship, after all.

Desta was the oldest of their group, and Aveline knew that she would never have a chance of surviving without their pod. She could still hunt, but barely, and oftentimes Anahera would cripple her prey before letting her finish it off. She was a devoted podmate and a superb storyteller, but Aveline worried how much longer she would be around, even with their help.

Subira was the most serene person she'd ever known. She never lost patience with the Pup, even when she refused to settle down to sleep or darted amongst them asking the same question over and over again. She knew which seaweeds and other plants could be mixed to make healing potions, and even when Maata was thrown into a wall of coral and got her back sliced up so badly that Aveline had been certain she would die, Subira had remained calm, singing quietly to her as she applied her salves.

The only thing Aveline didn't like about their routine was the hunts. She knew, of course, that they had to kill to survive, and no one could say that the fish or seals that they killed didn't die quickly (well, save for Maata's). But the sight of blood in the water always made her squeamish, even as it excited her podmates, and she wondered if she'd always been this way, or if it was something that had only recently developed. Hopefully, if it was a new development, it would be something she could overcome in time. She didn't have Subira's healing talents or Anahera's leadership qualities. They had been kind enough to take her in, to protect her. She wanted to be able to pull her weight.

But the first chance she got to prove herself, she failed miserably.

Their pod came upon a great cloud of blood in the water, with chunks of fish already in near to bite-size pieces slowly sinking toward the bottom. Maata and Chausiku and the Pup darted forward, eagerly gulping down the bits of meat, even as Anahera called to them to be careful, that they needed to assess this situation before they ate. But even she swam forward as the scent of blood invaded her nostrils, and Aveline watched as her expression changed, became something feral.

Aveline was the only one to see the silver of the fishhook.

She screamed a warning and swam forward, trying to pull the others out of there, but a great squall of pain overpowered her cries and she turned to see Kalea, clawing uselessly at her face, her cheek torn through by a curved, barbed hook. Aveline darted for her side, as did Subira, but before either of them could reach her she was pulled upward by a great unseen force, screaming as the metal tore further through her cheek.

"No!" Aveline cried, swimming as hard as she could, even as Subira turned to get the others out of the way, to make sure no one else was captured. She grabbed hold of Kalea's hand and thought for a brief wonderful second that she might be able to do it, that she could pull Kalea free. Her cheek would be torn to pieces and she would have trouble eating for a time, but Subira could help her heal and they could slice her food into small pieces; she'd be all right–

But the strength on the other end of the line was too much for her, just too much, and she found herself pulled upward as surely as Kalea was, and both of them broke the surface.

There were three men standing in the vessel, pulling Kalea up, shouting in glee at the sight of her pained, bloody face. They yanked her into the boat, one of them tearing the fishhook out of her cheek. She opened her ruined mouth in a snarl, tried to bite them, but a fourth man lifted a rock and bashed in her head with it.

Aveline cried out at the sound of the wet crack, and the men turned to her. Their smiles were horrifying things and she dove, screaming for help. Subira had gotten Anahera and the Pup out of the cloud of blood, and was swimming back in to rescue the others. Aveline swam to their leader, pointing to the surface.

"It's your sister, they trapped her, she's–"

She didn't have time to finish the sentence before Anahera tore past her. Aveline followed, almost shouted that it was too late, that there were four men and she would just end up getting herself killed, too, but of course there was no point to that, Anahera wouldn't listen–

Of course she wouldn't. That was her sister.

A memory forced its way into her mind – pale blonde hair and bloody arm, a frightened furious cry – and then was gone just as fast, leaving Aveline shaken. She shook her head to clear it and then took off after Anahera, who had reached the surface. One of the men in the boat had grabbed an enormous spear, and was just taking aim with it when Aveline grabbed hold around Anahera's waist, dragging her back under the water. The spear cut through the ocean just to the left of them, and Anahera struggled out of her grip.

"Stop!" Aveline cried. "The others; we *have* to get the others. We can't fight them alone!"

Anahera stared at her, barely seeing her, and Aveline had trouble believing there had ever been a time when she'd believed those black eyes incapable of showing emotion. She wanted to pull her into a hug, wanted to console her, but knew that now wasn't the time. Kalea might be gone, but that didn't mean they had to let those brutes keep her body.

Finally, Anahera nodded once and swam back to where Subira had gathered the others. "They have Kalea," she said simply, and as one all of the other sharkmaids rose from the ocean floor, following Anahera and Aveline toward the humans' ship.

They were headed toward the safety of a larger vessel, but Aveline and the others intercepted them just as they reached it. All of them hit the side of the boat at once, upending it.

Once the humans were in the water, they were easy prey. Anahera thrust her head forward, tearing out one man's throat with her teeth. Chausiku grabbed one of the men's legs as he tried to climb on top of the overturned boat.

Blood enveloped them again, and Pup nearly bit down on Aveline's arm in her frenzy. Aveline had to tap her sharply on the nose to bring her back to her senses, and she clung to her tail briefly as an apology, and then swam to one of the sailors' bodies.

"Kalea!" Anahera yelled.

Aveline looked around. Her body should be floating there, should be—

There were only three sailors. She had counted four in that boat.

They hadn't gotten there in time. One of the murderers had gotten back onto the ship, and had taken Kalea's body with him.

Anahera let out out a shriek of rage and ripped into one of the already-dead sailors so viciously that Aveline would normally have been terrified. As was, she stared up at the enormous shadow of the ship, knowing they could do nothing to save Kalea's body from whatever indignities were coming, and sobbed.

"We'll ruin them," Anahera hissed, her voice so ravaged with grief that it was barely understandable. "The humans. The mers who help them. We'll ruin them." Then she curled in on herself, wrapping her arms around her midsection tightly, and Aveline held her close. Several moments later, as the blood dissipated enough to release the rest of the pod from their feeding frenzy, they approached as well, all of them trying to hug Anahera or at least rest a hand on her shoulder.

"I'll follow the ship," Desta offered. "I'll

discover its name." Though Desta couldn't read any human tongues, she was excellent at remembering symbols down to the final line and curve. There were some mers in other pods who could translate such things, who could tell them what name to ask for when they captured humans for information.

But finding a translator would be unnecessary this time, Aveline realized. Desta could copy it down when she returned, and they would have the name that very day. She knew how to read.

*~*~*

One by one, they tracked down the sailors who worked on *The Siren's Blood*. But they couldn't find them all – four of them, learning that they were being hunted, retired and moved inland where the sharkmaids couldn't reach them – and for every one of them they found, they discovered tales of other ships that did even worse things, other men and sometimes even mers who tortured sharkmaids for sport, who wore their teeth as necklaces.

Hunting fish and seals became rarer. They survived almost entirely on human flesh now.

The Pup had her naming ceremony. They named her Kalea'lii, or Little Kalea. She stared up at the grown sharkmaids around her solemnly, and said, "I will honor her memory, I promise," and Aveline tried in vain to hold back tears, her arm around Anahera's waist, the other woman's head resting against her shoulder.

*~*~*

"It was a group of mermaids!" the sailor cried, as Uilani held a jagged piece of broken coral close to his left eye. "In the cove on the east side of that island!" he said, barely inclining his head to nod to the left. "They... they were the ones who told us to hunt you! I promise! We never had such an opinion ourselves; we never even knew you existed! They said you were dangerous, they did! That you would make your way on board and kill us in our sleep! Please. Just let me go, let me go and I'll tell my crew, I'll tell them how merciful you are, we'll never hunt you again..."

Anahera stared at him for a long moment, and then nodded once. "Let him go."

The man tugged out of Maata's grip and swam hard back to his vessel. His crewmates were leaning over the rail, calling for him, fear written clearly on their faces. Aveline watched as he reached the landing craft the other humans lowered for him and climbed in, shaking.

"Aveline," Anahera said. "The name?"

"*The Devil's Rose*," she said. If they reached the cove and there were no mermaids to be found, or if they heard tell of any of the crew of that ship continuing to hunt sharkmaids or other mers, then the man they'd just released would beg to be let off with something so trivial as a missing eye.

"All right," Anahera said. "Come on. To the cove."

They didn't look like murderers, this pod. But then, some of them didn't. The men who had stolen Kalea away; they had looked like murderers, like bad men. All sneering grins and mocking laughter and blood on their hands.

These mermaids just looked frightened.

An act, Aveline knew. She had witnessed interactions between mers herself, where one gave information or even offered payment for the teeth of a sharkmaid, only to whine and cry and claim innocence the moment they were confronted.

Kalea had done nothing wrong. Her only wish had been to eat, to keep herself safe and play pranks on her sister and help raise Pup with the rest of their pod.

Had one of the women here sent out word that sailors would be rewarded handsomely for every confirmed kill of a sharkmaid?

They attacked swiftly, Chausiku slicing open two throats with her well-sharpened claws before a full warning could even be sounded.

The mermaids panicked and tried to swim away, but none got far.

Anahera and Desta had fashioned her a spear, its spike formed from the sharpened bones of one of the sailors they'd killed. Aveline had never used it, but she liked the way it felt in her hand, the way it made her feel more like one of her sisters even though she possessed no sharp teeth or tough skin.

She stayed at the outskirts of the fight, as she always did, searching for any who may have escaped and tried to call in reinforcements while her podmates were under their bloodlust.

Normally she never found anyone – her pod was very thorough – but today she saw movement, half-hidden behind a large stone. She swam over to investigate, and found herself face-to-face with a half-grown merman.

Aveline knew what she needed to do. What she had to do. They couldn't let anyone escape; any survivors would get in touch with their contacts in the human world, and then the hunt against them would grow even worse.

She could do it. Stab out with the spear quickly, hit the boy in the neck. It would be over; he wouldn't suffer. The oceans would be just a little safer for her and her pod.

Aveline's grip shifted on the spear as her mind trying to prepare her for a killing strike, and then suddenly there was someone between her and her target.

The young girl with the white-blonde hair. She hadn't seen her in months.

"No!" the girl said, holding out her hands in supplication. "Aveline, please. You can't do this."

She started to argue, started to explain to her that she had to, but then a name floated into her consciousness, and suddenly it was all she could focus on.

"*Harriet*?" she whispered.

Then the girl disappeared as the ocean around Aveline turned black, and her eyes began to burn.

Octopus ink. The boy must have opened a vial of it.

She swam back out of range, rubbing at her eyes, and several moments later, once her vision had finally begun to clear again, Anahera swam up to her, her teeth red with blood.

"Did you find anyone?"

"Were – Anahera, were there ever any mermaids in this pod named Harriet?"

"No," she said. "What an odd name. Did you find anyone?" she asked again.

Aveline hung her head. "I'm sorry."

"What happened?"

She thought about bettering her role in the story, saying that he surprised her, that she never had a chance to act. But though she didn't know much about her previous life, she did realize that she wasn't that good of a liar. "I couldn't do it," she whispered. "I hesitated. He was..."

Was what? Was terrified and young and had had the same pained look in his eyes that she remembered seeing in Anahera's when her sister was pulled out of the water?

"Was what?" Anahera asked quietly. "Was more important than the safety of our pod?"

"No, no, of course not–"

"After we took you in!" she shouted, drawing the attention of the others, and Aveline wrapped her arms around herself as she was surrounded. "Shared our food, protected you from the humans! You couldn't even get rid of *one* of our enemies? Maata took down five!"

"I'm sorry," Aveline said, unable to meet her eyes. "I'm so sorry, I had the spear, I just couldn't..."

Anahera sighed, and then put a hand on her arm, tugging her close. "No, I'm sorry," she said. "It's all right. I shouldn't have been so hard on you. You'll do better next time, won't you?"

"Yes."

"And don't fret about this one escaping. Ink vials are a defense used by younger merfolk. Now that it's alone, it won't survive long."

# THE TRAGIC END OF THE PRINCESS ILSA

Letter received June 7th, sent by Agnessa
Gärd of *The Sappho* to Hugh Dawkins of *The
Corinthian Curse*:


*Hugh,*

*How like you to not properly warn me in
advance — we all received quite the shock when your
messenger landed on the fore deck this morning.
Hope immediately let out a wail as if she had seen
her own ghost and rushed to fetch incense to purify
the ship. Albatrosses are not good omens for the
Chinese, apparently, and half the crew was
convinced we were targets of a curse.*

*Then Maddie — bless her sharp eyes — saw
your missive strapped to the bird's leg and everyone
calmed down. I expect you to explain how you (or one
of your crewmates) managed to tame and train such
a wild bird. Wil is most interested to hear, too. And be
grateful that your feathered friend is returning to
you of sound body, for Wil's lizard friend Tazu
wanted badly to eat him.*

*I received the book you left for me with Violet
and must confess that I cannot develop a taste for Mr.
Dickens, no matter how many times I try him. I will
grant you that he has a decided gift for outlandish
names, and a few pretty turns of phrase, but too*

many of his stories boil down to moralistic muck (in my opinion).

Have you tried the Currer Bell volume yet? The last third is a little trying, but it has a satisfactory conclusion. I am eager to hear your thoughts on it, and how Jane herself struck you. I will refrain from voicing my opinions here, for fear of ruining the narrative for you. I would never wish to prejudice your thoughts on such matters.

Captain Harry asks me to inform you that we will be anchored off Breaker's Ridge the last week of the month, and she would like to speak with your captain then if possible.

I hope all is well with you and that this letter finds you in good health and spirits,
Agnessa

Letter received June 11th, not far from the reef known as The Grinders:

Agnessa,
I hoped Socrates would cause a stir; he earned his name due to his love for incessant debating, his penchant to perch on the railings and yammer at anyone who passes in his quarrelsome way. We discovered him floating in some flotsam several weeks ago, half-dead for lack of fresh water, and my friend Jilly nursed him back to fighting strength.

(Jilly wishes to be remembered to your crewmate, Katherine, as do John and Jim, who say they think of her often and very fondly.)

After his recuperation, we decided to make

Socrates a productive member of society. Hence his training as a messenger, which to all appearances he enjoys. Captain Thomas has been his primary handler, as he has previous experience with strong-minded fowl. I would almost swear the man speaks the feathered creature's tongue; he certainly has no trouble making his wishes understood, and Socrates found you like a shot judging by the date on your last letter.

I finished the Bell book this evening and concur with your sentiments regarding the last third. The interlude with the poor yet noble family of a religious bent — who coincidentally are revealed to be long-lost relatives — sorely tried my suspension of disbelief.

But as a whole, the so-called autobiography was engrossing and diverting. Miss Eyre reminds me of you in several ways: firm in her beliefs and opinions, unwavering in her course, kind-hearted and honorable beneath whatever hardness she affects. I was pleased that she had a happy ending, reunited with a man who had finally learned to properly appreciate and care for her.

I will not chastise you for improperly appreciating Dickens. Our tastes, as we already know, are not similar. Given your recommendation of Bell, I assume you have read First Impressions? I would be interested to learn of your thoughts on that work.

Captain Thomas is adjusting our course as I write; we will be at the rendezvous on time so long as the wind remains fair.

I am, as always, in high spirits — they are at

their highest when I receive a new letter from you, so please continue to write. I greatly miss our discussions, and look forward to seeing you again soon. Until I do, best of luck to you and yours.

Your obedient servant,
Hugh

POST SCRIPT: Socrates prefers sardines but will take any fish he can snatch — so keep an eye on him when hauling up nets.

Letter received June 18th, the writing much scribbled and the parchment dotted with blots of ink:

Hugh:
Something has happened and we will not make the appointed meeting. We have changed course and are camped on the north side of Laia Island. I do not have the time to go into further details now, but we are none of us hurt and the ship is undamaged.

Agnessa

Letter received June 21st, on Laia Island:

Agnessa:
We will be there in three days. I send all of my strength to you in advance.

Ever yours,
Hugh

*~*~*

He had been trapped in a nightmare for so
long that this sudden change must surely be
another dream.

He moved with a sleepwalker's clumsiness,
unable to trust his own eyes. Hadn't they been lying
to him for weeks, plaguing him with terrible visions,
haunting him with the faces of dead men?

His ears, too, had become unreliable. They
rang with the whispers of ghosts, with shrieks and
sobs, when he knew the ship must be quiet now.

Quiet as the grave. Everyone else was dead
– perhaps he had finally joined them in death.
Perhaps he was just a ghost now, shattered and
broken and doomed to pace the deck. A revenant.

Through the fog, he felt hands touch him.
Was it the ferryman, searching for his fare? "I
haven't any gold," he heard himself whisper, the
words scraping painfully out of a throat that had
gone desert dry days ago. "I haven't any silver. I
don't even have any copper. I cannot pay for your
ferry. I will have to stay here forever."

"He's delirious," a voice said above him in
English. "Badly dehydrated. Bring the water here."

Someone was supporting his head and
pressing a cup to his cracked lips. The first trickle
of water burned his mouth like acid and he coughed
so badly he nearly choked.

"Drink," a second voice begged, a voice he
felt he should know. "Please, you have to drink." It
was a woman, a woman pleading, a woman crying.
But there were no women on board – not since

Celeste, the cook's little girl, had died. Not since her face turned purple and her lips turned black and flies gathered on her swollen, bleeding eyes.

The memory made him retch.

"You need to drink," the faraway voice insisted. He couldn't disappoint that voice, though he didn't know why. He forced his mouth to open and swallowed the water tipped into it. Drank and drank until there was nothing more. The cup was drawn away, and then it was back at his lips, and he repeated the process.

"It's alright," the voice said. "It's going to be alright. You're safe now, and I'll take care of you."

"What a nice dream you are," he said as consciousness slipped away.

*~*~*

"It's a plague ship," said Jo.

"Not according to the flag, or the ship's log," Wil said, scanning said log. "*The Princess Ilsa* set sail two years ago, bound for the Horn of Africa on a scientific survey. A royally-funded mission."

"Not even royal funding helped these poor bastards. Is anyone else still alive?"

"Miss Euphemia and Silence found three down in the hold. Another day and they would've been gone." Wil closed the heavy leather book in her arms, face somber. "Grim reading in here."

"Everything about this is grim."

The two turned to watch as Katherine and Lizzie emerged from the hold that reeked of putrefaction, handkerchiefs tied around their mouths and goggles over their eyes to protect them from the massive cloud of flies buzzing over the hatch. In their arms were two men that already looked like cadavers, wasted away and skeletal, the only sign of life the rasping rise and fall of their chests. They laid the pair down on stretchers and Katherine turned back to bring out the last survivor.

A half a league away, Maddie leaned over the railing of *The Sappho* and peered through her spyglass. Franky stood beside her, stiff with tension. "It looks bad," she said. "Very bad."

"So Jo was right? Sickness?"

"If I had to wager, yes. Kai said the hull's intact — no other reason a big boat like that would just be sitting in the water, sails furled and nobody moving on deck."

"Any survivors?"

"Maybe. Hard to tell."

"What if they bring someone back and we catch whatever it was?"

"Harry wouldn't have let anyone go aboard if she didn't know a way to prevent that," Maddie said, her trust in the captain absolute. And Harry had called half the crew into the cabin to discuss the situation before the lifeboat had been lowered and rowed over; they'd been in there for close to an hour, so they must have made some sort of plan. "Wait, it looks like they're done. There must be survivors, because I can see Katherine putting people in the boat."

"Why aren't they rowing back here? They're not rowing all the way to Laia, are they?"

"That's exactly what they're doing," Harry

said behind them.

Franky jumped. "Oh, Cap, didn't hear you walk up."

"Before they get back on *The Sappho* they have to disinfect everything. Including themselves. And those men are in no condition to go into water this deep – they're heading for Laia and the shallows where they can bathe them properly. C'mon, Mads, I need you up in the nest. I'll be sailing us in after them, and I'm not near as good at steering as Nessa. You'll have to sound out anything that might scrape the hull."

"Aye, Cap'n."

*~*~*

It was a strange party that arrived on the small, black beach of Laia Island's north face. As soon as the landing craft was dragged above the tide line, the women stripped completely naked and threw their clothing into a pile. Four unconscious men were laid out on the sand, likewise stripped, and their tattered, stained uniforms were added to the pile. Wil took a bundle of waterproof matches from the compartment in her leg and lit the bonfire.

Then bottles of alcohol and fat cakes of red carbolic soap were taken from the boat. Everyone lathered and scrubbed until every inch of skin stung and their hair was full of suds. The men, too, were washed by hands that were as gentle as possible but painstakingly thorough. One regained consciousness enough to scream as the disinfectants burned his open wounds, but thankfully subsided back into a coma before he was dipped into the seawater. Wil even wiped down her wooden leg with a cloth soaked in rubbing alcohol.

Finally, the boat itself was doused and scrubbed. They would take no chances – they couldn't afford to.

As this was being done, Harry maneuvered *The Sappho* into place and Marcella dropped the anchor. Hope and Junia finished loading the supplies into the second lifeboat and headed for the beach, where several naked people were in dire need of new clothes and warm blankets.

"Drink three sips of this, each of you, and then pass it to the next," Hope ordered after they had wrapped up the sick men and began dressing themselves. She thrust a large green bottle into Jo's hands. "And you will wear this – absolutely no argument about pagan witchery," she added, dropping a necklace around the first mate's neck. "We must do all we can to keep the demons of sickness at bay."

Each obliged her without a word of protest, bending their heads to accept the charms.

"Set up one tent here," Miss Euphemia told Junia. "Silence and I will sleep in that, with these poor souls, but the rest of you are camping on the other end of the beach. Until we're certain, we need to keep them as quarantined as possible."

"Are you sure you want to stay with them?" Junia asked.

"I'm old and I've seen enough, girl – if I'm to die of the plague here, then so be it. Better me than one of you girls."

"And Silence?"

"Silence will be just fine," the old woman said firmly.

Silence, in fact, was kneeling beside one of the men with an expression of such rapt concentration Junia doubted she was aware of the bustle around her. Unlike the others, she was still naked, her long black hair plastered to her back — the sharp bones of her spine stood out prominently in a disturbing way, in a way no human spine would.

Her hands were pressed flat to the man's chest. She had unbuttoned his new shirt in order to touch his bare flesh and there seemed to be a glow radiating from her fingers, a faint light shining through the translucent webbing between her joints.

As Junia watched, the man's breathing became less labored. It no longer rattled ominously in the back of his throat. The deep lines of pain etched across his sunken face were smoothing and fading. An open boil on his neck began shrinking, closing, healing before her awestruck eyes.

Silence sat back abruptly on her heels, head twitching up in an almost birdlike manner, the movement so uncanny and inhuman that Junia took a step away. Eyes as black as pitch met hers and she knew that she would never be entirely comfortable around the siren. She believed the others when they said she would not harm her, and she was sympathetic for the barbaric treatment she had suffered at the hands of her own sister. She would always show her nothing but kindness and polite respect.

But like her? That might be impossible.

Silence tore her eyes away from Junia's blanched face and scrambled sideways, like a crab, to the next man, where she settled into her previous position and repeated her unusual treatment.

When she reached the fourth man, she hesitated and looked first at the woman kneeling beside him. Agnessa, a blanket over her shoulders, was holding his hand so tightly she was on the verge of breaking bones, but he felt nothing. Like the others, he was insensible of the world around him.

"I'm here, I'm right here," Agnessa was saying repetitively as tears trickled down her face, a face so like the one lying before her. "I won't leave you, Alvar. I'm here."

When Silence tapped her arm – the quickest and lightest of touches, meant only to gain her attention – Agnessa startled as if she'd been shot. The siren attempted a smile and pointed at the young man.

"You're going to heal him?" Agnessa said, voice brittle with desperation.

Silence nodded. She was tired from curing the first three; her skin was beginning to burn and felt too tight, and her head ached badly. But she had strength enough for this last man, the one who was so important to Agnessa.

Strength enough, at least, to keep him from death tonight.

When it was done, she crept away to leave Agnessa to cry in privacy. The crying of humans unnerved her.

She made it to the shallows before her legs gave out, where she lay in a panting heap, the water splashing over her feet.

Kai was suddenly beside her and she couldn't recall hearing him approach. Perhaps she had slept. Yes, the water was over her hips now. Kai was looking at her with such concern on his face.

"You pushed yourself too hard," he said, sliding a strong arm beneath her shoulders. "Little sister, you need to be careful. Here. Drink."

He held a bottle to her lips, another one of his potions, and she drank until it was empty. Soon her skin was no longer feverish and sweating. Her head and hands stopped aching so badly. She could stop squinting in the bright afternoon light.

*Thank you*, she signed, swallowing until the bitter taste was gone.

"There you are, child," Miss Euphemia said. She had a white cotton shift draped over one wrinkled arm. "I lost track of you while I was helping with the tents. Here, let's get you dressed. Did Kai tell you that he found us some lobsters for dinner?"

*No, he didn't*, she signed. *What about the ship?*

"We're taking care of that tomorrow, or the day after — tonight, we're focusing on those boys and ourselves. And Agnessa will need some company, too. This has been a bad shock for her."

*He's alive*, Silence signed. *Her brother. I healed him.*

"And that's something she'll never forget.

You did a wonderful job today, dear. I'm very proud of you."

*~*~*

By the unsteady light of the fire, with her twin sleeping fitfully on a pad of blankets beside her, Agnessa wrote a short note, tied it to an albatross' leg, and, for the first time in years, prayed.

*~*~*

*Well*, thought Wil the next morning, *at least the worst is over now. My dreams are going to be full of bloated bodies for the foreseeable future, but at least I'm confident that my disinfectant methods will prevent the spread of the disease.*
*Pretty confident, anyway.*
*Relatively confident.*
"Is Wil going to eat that?" Tazu croaked, a large yellow eye fixed on the bowl she'd set down by her knee.
"You can have it," she said, the last word drowned out by the crunching of his jaws. "Doubt I'll have much of an appetite for a while."
"Hope, I believe you when you say that stuff will keep away the demons," Zora said between coughs, waving at the incense smoke that hung around the fire like an earthbound cloud. "It'd keep away gods, too. But at this rate, I'm going to hack up a lung from all this smoke."
"Three days," Hope held fast. "The fire must

burn for three days. We will all drink three times a day, three sips each, of my potion. And then we will be safe."

"I thought Silence healed the sailors, though?" said Maddie.

"Whatever disease struck that ship – and it wasn't one that I immediately recognized – could be passed any number of ways," said Wil. As was often the case, her helpfully provided information was more worrying than reassuring. "Through contact, which we did our best to prevent by washing and burning everything, through the air, or through insects. There were so many flies on that ship, any one of us could have been bitten by one carrying the illness. And if it was passed through the air, we could have been contaminated purely by getting too close to the dead. Which was unavoidable, as we couldn't just leave the survivors."

"If we were more pragmatic and selfish, we could've," said Franky wryly.

"It was Agnessa's brother's ship," said Maddie. "We really couldn't've."

"The chances that any of us are infected are slim though, I think," Wil said as confidently as she could. "Diseases that result in pustules and suppurating wounds usually start to manifest within forty-eight hours of exposure. If we're all fine after three days, we should be out of the proverbial woods."

"And by then, Silence should be recovered enough to heal others," Harry said. She and Kai had had a long conversation at dawn, and she was going to keep a closer eye on Silence in the future when someone required her help. "Until then, we'll do whatever Hope and Wil tell us to do, keep our spirits up, and focus on getting those men back on their feet. Miss Euphemia promised to fetch me when any of them are coherent enough to talk."

"What I want to know," Jo said thoughtfully. "Is how did they end up here? They were supposed to be hugging the African coast. This is off course even for a blind, deaf steersman."

"And Agnessa's brother was the steersman, wasn't he?" said Maddie. "He taught her, didn't he? So he must be good."

"There must be some reason he brought them out here," Junia said, sharpening one of her swords. She'd found it impossible to sleep and had spent the entire night putting new edges on her blades; it was the only thing that really soothed her. "We'll just ask him when he wakes up."

"What we gonna do 'bout the *Ilsa*?" asked Lizzie. "Can't just leave her there, for some'un else ta find."

"I know exactly what we should do," said Marcella. "Burn it."

"Like the Vikings of old," said Katherine. "Perhaps those poor souls will end up in Valhalla and find some peace, then."

"Miss Euphemia always says fire prevents infection," Marcella went on.

"It is the purifying element," said Hope.

"That strikes me as the best option. No one else should ever set foot on that boat," said Jo. "Taking the bodies off to bury them would be too dangerous."

"Yes, that would be an extremely bad idea," Wil agreed. "Meat buried on an island doesn't stay buried for long, and the disease may be able to jump from species to species. We don't want to infect the boar population here and have it decimate the ecosystem."

"So we'll burn it," Harry said. "How are we gonna burn a ship that size? The fire will need to be big enough to consume the whole thing, where it sits in the water, without us dousing everything in kerosene. Difficult trick, that."

"We can use Greek fire," Miss Euphemia said, cresting the small dune separating the main camp from the nursing tent. She stopped several feet away, still intent on distancing herself from the crew to prevent any further contamination. "I think I've a book with the recipe somewhere. Harriet, Agnessa's brother is awake. He's not entirely cogent – he's convinced he's either dreaming or in Heaven – but he's speaking in sentences."

*~*~*

A strained voice was speaking Swedish as they approached, a language Harry had never picked up, so she didn't understand the exact words.

But the tone was one she recognized. It was the weak, fearful pleading of a broken child, and it made all of Harry's dormant maternal instincts stand up and scream.

"Agnessa, you really need to get some sleep," Harry said, sitting down beside her; the strained vigil she had held all night had weighed so heavily on her shoulders that her back was bent with it. "Hello, Alvar, it's lovely to finally meet you. I've heard a lot about you. My name's Harry."

The face that stared up at her was so like Agnessa's. The same nose and eyes and chestnut hair, though his had been cut just below the ears. The only stark differences marking Alvar as the masculine half of the pair were his squarer, bearded jaw, prominent Adam's apple, and thinner lips. There were bruised hollows beneath his eyes and the gaunt lines and loose skin that only extreme deprivation can cause.

And then there was the stare. It was a look Harry had seen many times before, on the faces of slaves and beaten women, on survivors of shipwrecks and soldiers broken by war. "A thousand league stare", Jo called it, a phrase she'd picked up from her mother, and it told the world that this was someone who was too well acquainted with death.

"Harry Roberts?" he said, wonderingly. "Captain Roberts?"

"The one and only. Are they talking about me even in Africa?"

"Yes. I had a penny dreadful about you," he said. There was a distant, almost dreamy quality to his voice now. "A yellow pamphlet, with an etching of you on the front, looking like Mary Read with your shirt torn open. You were holding a severed head."

"Severed heads make poor trophies; I just leave them where they fall. And I hardly ever go into battle half-naked. What cheek! To publish something like that and not even pay me a commission. If they'd only asked, I would've been happy to grant them an interview. The truth of my exploits is probably more interesting than whatever dreck they concocted."

Agnessa looked at her captain and found she could still smile.

"Is there anything I can bring you, Mr. Gärd? A particular fruit, perhaps a book? You'd be surprised at the size and quality of our library. Our scribe, Miss Euphemia, has put a lot of work into it."

"You have a scribe? Pirates with a scribe?"

"Of course — most of us don't have the patience for long words, so it pays to have someone on hand who can read the really interesting wanted posters to us."

The boy was relaxing in slow increments; Harry decided she could sit there and play the wit all day if it would dispel some of the shadows still clinging to him.

"Or would you prefer a musical interlude? I remember Nessa telling me that you played the violin — we haven't a fine instrument like that on board, but Miss Euphemia *does* have a fiddle. Only slightly warped from that time we spilled a bottle of rum on it."

"A fiddle. I haven't touched strings in months..."

"I'll just pop out and fetch it then, shall I?" said Miss Euphemia cheerfully, bustling away as if she was nothing more than a society dame in a nice manor house rather than a weathered lady in a ragged petticoat with sand in her white hair.

"And why don't we have a cup of tea?" Harry suggested. "Nessa, could you put the kettle on? Which do you prefer, Mr. Gärd: Chinese, English, or Indian blends? Black or green? I hope you don't take yours with cream or milk, because we're fresh out of cows or goats at the moment. We've got a lizard, but it would be difficult to milk him, seeing as he's a he."

"I — I'm *really* awake?" Alvar said, putting a hand to his temple.

He must have been the last Silence healed. He still had a faint sunburn darkening his forehead and cheeks, and a large crack across his bottom lip.

"Yes, you're awake."

"You brought me here from the *Ilsa*?"

"Yes. And your mates."

He turned his head to look at the three other men laid out in the tent, still deeply unconscious but breathing easily.

"I thought I was the only one..." he murmured. "Only one still alive. I thought everyone in the hold was dead. I hadn't the strength to climb down the ladder again. I knew if I did that, I'd never come back out again. And... And I wanted to die where I could see the sun and smell the sea. Dying on deck seemed better. And all those flies..."

"Mr. Gärd—"

"No. Please. Alvar. Call me Alvar. Mr. Gärd is my father, and I'd rather not think about him now."

"Alright," Harry relented easily. "Alvar, you don't have to think about what happened on your ship, and you don't have to talk about it. At the moment, I'd rather you put your energy into your recovery. That'd be best for you and best for your sister. Until you're back on your feet, Nessa will fret herself sick, and we can't have that."

"No. No, we can't. But Captain Roberts—"

"If I'm to call you Alvar, I'd like you to call me Harry. Everyone does. Everyone who's worth more than ten pounds, anyway."

"Harry, I need to know," he said urgently, reaching out to grab her arm. His hand was little more than bone. He could barely lift himself up from his blankets. But his grip was like an iron manacle. "You're going to destroy the ship? You're not going to salvage anything from it?"

"No. We aren't setting foot on that deck again. We only came aboard to look for survivors. All that we took away from that blighted craft were you and your mates."

He released her with a fervent sigh of relief. "Good. I was afraid... You *are* pirates. And there is gold locked in the chests of the commander's cabin. Weapons and bolts of cloth. But it's all tainted now. It has to be. None of that is worth your lives. Worth my sister..."

"This is cool enough to drink now," Agnessa said, ducking back into the tent with a pair of cups. "I put in three sugars already."

"I take my tea plain," Alvar started to say.

"No, you don't," replied his twin firmly. "You only started doing that when we were twelve and your friend Søren teased you. Said that men always take their tea unsweetened. I *know* you like it better with sugar, so I put the sugar in. There's no room for mannish affectations out here, Alvar. It's stupid to put on such airs."

"I'd listen to your sister," Harry advised.

"This is what comes of being the youngest," Alvar said. "I'm always mollycoddled."

"Youngest?" asked Harry.

"By fourteen minutes," clarified Agnessa.

"Aggie always was in a hurry to go places," said her brother as she helped him sit up and sip his tea.

*~*~*

It was late afternoon and wavering music was echoing down the black beach. Alvar was coaxing a melody from Miss Euphemia's fiddle that brought tears to their eyes, a plaintive song that made Zora think of her homeland, of the families in big red wagons pulled by hardy ponies, men with thick beards and dark eyes and gold coins dangling from their belts. Franky, too, remembered passing tinkers with huge packs on their backs, who would whistle and sing such tunes as they tramped from village to village.

"Where did he learn a piece like that?" Zora wondered aloud.

"How is something that beautiful coming out of Miss Euphemia's fiddle?" said Maddie. "It was missing a string last time I looked."

"Someone who can play like that was wasted at sea," said Marcella, the most musically-minded of the crew. "He should be performing on a stage, for nobs who paid a year's wages for the privilege."

"Mads, how are you feeling?" Wil demanded,

limping up with opened journal and pencil in hand.

Maddie paused to give herself a once over. "Alright, I think. No sneezing, no coughing, no itching, no headache. I don't feel hot like from a fever, and I'm not sweating more than usual."

"Good," Wil said, making a note on her page. "Zora?"

"Same."

"Franky?"

"Likewise."

"Marcella?"

"I've got a tickle in the back of my throat, but I think that's more from Hope's holy smoke," she said. "Either that or it's sheer nerves. When you're sitting around waiting to develop a terrible sickness, your body starts to play tricks on you, doesn't it?"

"Yes, and that's why we need to keep ourselves occupied," advised the scientist. "If you focus on a task, your imagination won't have the time to concoct false symptoms. So I suggest we all work on making this camp more comfortable. Let's act as if this is going to be a new operational post, even if it means overdoing things. Better that than developing false positives."

"I like Wil," Marcella said as she stomped away to confer with the others. "But I swear: I don't understand half the things that come out of her mouth."

"I'm gonna go gather more wood," announced Franky, standing and brushing sand off his backside. "Build up the pile."

"I'll help," said Maddie, popping up.

"I remember gathering wood at that age," Zora said as the pair loped into the trees. "Her name was Nina and she had eyes like jet."

"Those two make me feel old," said Marcella. "Old and boring. I'm going to go meet this brother of Agnessa's. I haven't had a good conversation about music in donkey's years."

Down near the tide line, an odd conversation was happening. Silence stood with a long stick in hand, listening intently to Miss Euphemia's questions, before sketching out her responses in the damp sand. Harry, Kai, and Wilhelmina looked on thoughtfully.

SOMETHING BAD IN BLOOD, the siren wrote.

"So it's a blood-borne illness," said Wil, making a note. "Meaning it could be passed on through biting insects. Hmm..."

THREE MEN SICK, Silence went on. LAST NOT.

"You mean the first three you healed had the disease, but the fourth didn't? Agnessa's brother wasn't sick?" asked Harry.

NO. NO WATER. NO FOOD.

"So he was dying of dehydration and starvation, not from whatever killed the others," said Harry. "Well, that would make sense, considering he was in the best shape of the survivors and seems to be recovering more quickly. He must've been nursing the others until he collapsed on deck."

"It might also explain how they sailed this far," said Kai. "If they were supposed to be many,

many leagues away. As the steersman, Alvar could have sailed the boat off course."

"Either on purpose or because he was hallucinating and unable to maintain a steady heading," added Wil. "Silence, can you, hmm, how to phrase this? Can you *feel* that sickness in anyone else? Do you think any of us are infected?"

Silence looked at her for a long moment, puzzling out the meaning of her words. She knew what the rot of the sickness smelled like, the way the air around the men had pricked at her skin. She hadn't smelled or felt that again – yet.

A sudden touch on her foot made her look down sharply. It was the scaly creature, the *mo'o*, Wil's near-constant companion. He had put one of his many-toed front limbs over her bare foot; his flesh was dry and rough and very warm. He looked up at her, throat pulsing hypnotically. And then he withdrew, scampering to Wil with his swinging, undulating gait, tail whipping back and forth.

"I see, I know," he hissed and burbled. "I go and check."

"...Alright?" Wil said, confused.

"What did he say?" Harry demanded.

"That he was going to go check everyone," said Kai. "Apparently he knows what he's looking for."

"How?" Wil asked.

"I do not feel it is my place to say," Kai said mysteriously. "I'm going to check the nets."

"I find it intriguing that Alvar did not succumb," Wil said after a moment, her mind, as always, focusing on the greatest mystery. "Perhaps he has some natural immunity..."

"Wilhelmina," Harry said in her firmest captain voice. "You are not to poke, prod, test, experiment on, or interrogate that boy until he is completely recovered. Am I clear?"

"Yes, Harry."

*~*~*

Junia had nodded off with a sword in her hand. Just as she was about to roll over onto it, she was startled awake by the caress of a very wet tongue over her nose.

Her shriek brought Lizzie and Katherine running. They found her sitting in her tent with a hand clasped to her heaving chest and Tazu at her knee looking amused.

(How a lizard could look amused was beyond Lizzie, but there was no denying that expression. His yellow draconic eyes were half-lidded, his mouth slightly open, and he was hissing in a way that was very clearly laughter.)

"What is it?" Katherine demanded.

"I was taking a nap and Tazu just *licked me*," Junia spluttered.

The big lizard croaked something, turned, and trotted out of the tent. The three just stared after him, utterly unenlightened. If they'd had Wil's gift for languages, they would've known he had said, "You are not sick," but they didn't — and so they were left to wonder just why the iguana had abruptly decided to act like a dog.

*~*~*

The next day, while Miss Euphemia and Silence were occupied with feeding the Swedish sailors broth and small mouthfuls of boiled fish, Agnessa helped Alvar take a short walk to the water's edge. She had an arm around his waist – so narrow, so much thinner than hers! – and a hand at his elbow. She half-believed that it was only her grip that kept him from being blown away by the wind. Her brother was a skeleton beside her and she had almost bitten through her lip.

When his legs could go no further, they sat on the sand and stared out at the waves. The ill-fated *Ilsa* was just visible to their left, near the line of the horizon, but *The Sappho* dominated the scene, swaying gently, tethered by her anchor line.

"There aren't many black beaches in Africa," Alvar said when he'd recaptured his breath. "Just the normal gold and yellow."

"According to the merfolk, black beaches are holy places," Agnessa said. "They're places to journey to when you know death is near. When Kai was very young, one of the wisest of his matrons left his pod to come to a place like this. She wanted to die somewhere sacred."

"Fitting, then, that we ended up here," Alvar said. "Why didn't you ever write to me?"

"I turned pirate, Alv," she said. "I didn't think it was safe for a good sailor in the Royal Navy to get letters from a known pirate. It would have gotten you into trouble."

"Do you think I cared about trouble? I cared

about *you*. When I left, I worried so much about what would happen to you. I knew Father wanted to marry you off to that old brute, the one who'd already buried two wives, and I knew you wanted no part in it. I didn't sleep for two weeks – and then Father wrote to me that you had walked out of the house with only a bag and had disappeared. That you'd disgraced the family. Do you know what that news did to me? I almost deserted and came home to look for you."

"I'm sorry," Agnessa said. "I'm sorry, you're right. I should've written to you then, to tell you where I was going. I was just so angry and so afraid and so determined to escape, I didn't think. My head was just screaming to run."

"It was months later, when we stopped at a town and I had three days of shore leave, that I finally heard you'd joined up with Captain Roberts. There was a man in a bar who was talking about *The Sappho's* new helmswoman. 'Pretty little thing only yea high,' he said. 'Used to be some fancy noble lady. Swedish, I think, or maybe Dutch. Traded her lace gloves for calluses. And you'd never believe it till you saw it, but she can haul that big ship around as if it were nothing more than a dog on a leash.' I knew it was you – how could it be anyone else?"

Alvar shook his head. "I couldn't stop thinking of how many dangers you had to be facing. Murderers and typhoons and thieves and krakens. But I never thought of sickness – isn't that funny? I never worried you'd catch some tropical plague."

"I'm a hardy woman," she said. "We're both of us made of strong stuff."

"Has it been worth it?" he asked. "Turning your back on Father and his money, living like this? Are you happy, Aggie?"

"Yes, I am. Happier than I ever would've been as some Lord's wife. At the very least, I haven't followed in poor Agathe's footsteps. Or Mother's."

"Yes. That is true," Alvar said heavily. The hissing of the waves as they crashed onto the beach, their white foam swirling and displacing tiny blue crabs, was so soothing. A far cry from the horrors of the past weeks.

He started to speak like one in a dream, remote and calm. "One of the botanists brought it on board. The sickness. We'd stopped in a remote bay to refill the water tank. He wandered off to explore, as they always did when we landed, and found a strange animal he didn't recognize, dead, and he lead the naturalists to it to examine it. They did a dissection and talked excitedly about its unusual anatomy. When they came back to camp that night, they were all infected. Within a day or two, they were coughing badly.

"It strikes the lungs first. Fills them with water until it's impossible to breathe. Then the fever and headache sets in, until the afflicted are bashing their heads against things. I watched a lieutenant crack his own skull open, he was that desperate to relieve the pressure. Blood and brain matter flying everywhere..."

Alvar paused, swallowing convulsively. He reached over blindly, eyes still on the ocean, and grabbed her hand. The touch steadied him and he continued.

"Then the blisters. They moaned about the itching, how their skin was too tight, and they started to scratch themselves raw. At that point, it was only me and a handful of others still on our feet. We tried to bandage up everyone's hands so they'd be unable to scratch. The commander was dead by then, and most of the lieutenants, and I was in charge. Me. I've only ever been good at taking orders, not giving them. You know this."

"You headed out for open sea, rather than land somewhere," Agnessa said. "Because you didn't want to spread it to anyone else. Rather than look for help and start an epidemic, you did the honorable thing and tried to quarantine the ship."

"We were all dead men," Alvar said tonelessly. "How could anyone possibly cure something like that? By the time the blisters appeared, coma wasn't far behind. The fever cooked their brains, destroyed whatever made them people. There was nothing left at that point but pain. They suffered so horribly, Aggie. The blasted illness took everything from them, and then it didn't even let them die in dignity."

Agnessa thought of the other three in the tent, the infected men that Silence had healed. They were speaking now, faltering and stuttering with their words, but they were getting better. They remembered their names, where they had come from, what they had been doing before everything had gone hot and black.

If what Alvar said was true, they should only be empty shells now. Puppets. The fever should have destroyed everything. But they weren't babbling or blank or dumb.

Because of Silence? Could a siren heal even a damaged brain? Agnessa's already high estimation of her rose higher.

"But you didn't get sick?" she said.

"No," and Alvar was bewildered. "No, I didn't. I kept waiting for the cough, the fever and the blisters. Days went by and they didn't come. I tended the dying, tried to make them as comfortable as possible, tried to keep them clean and gave them water. And then one of the men threw himself into the water tank – because he was so feverish or because he preferred drowning to lingering any further, I don't know. And that was the end of the water. The food ran out two days later, and I decided there was no point in fighting the inevitable any longer.

"I managed to haul myself out of the hold, went to the tiller, and wished there was a way I could warn anyone who found us. I thought of prying up a board and painting a warning on it with some pitch, but I didn't have the strength to use the pry bar. I just sat by the tiller and stared at the sky. I thought of you, and the stories I'd heard of Captain Roberts, and I wondered if the ship would disappear and become a ghost ship like *The Flying Dutchman*. If we'd become a story people would tell, or if we'd be forgotten completely."

He turned to face her. "It was pure, impossible luck that you found us, Aggie."

"Perhaps Hope is right, then," his sister said, squeezing his hand. "And Lady Luck favors us."

*~*~*

"I can't believe we all just let a lizard lick us," Marcella said. She wasn't fond of Tazu – she wasn't fond of anything that had scales and double-lidded eyes. As a child, she'd been greatly affected by a painting of the serpent tempting Eve; she'd had screaming nightmares for two weeks, and afterwards had the deepest, most abiding mistrust of reptiles.

"A small price to pay for peace of mind," Jo said. "If Tazu and Silence both say we're free of infection, I'm willing to believe them."

"Tazu, how did you know what to look for?" Wil demanded.

"The Clan has many gifts," he said. He shifted slightly, clicking his claws together: a sure sign that he was hiding something.

"Tazu, Wil won't tell your secret. I swear on all the pearls in the world."

Tazu was impressed by such a pledge. "Very well – the Clan can touch a person and See."

"See?"

"Behind their eyes. I touched the siren and Saw what she knew."

Wil absorbed this. If she was understanding him properly, Tazu was confessing that he could read someone's thoughts. That sounded awfully unbelievable – then she sternly reminded herself that Tazu belonged to an intelligent, hitherto unrecorded lizard species and that evolution could work in unexpected ways. If mermaids could see auras and sirens could heal with a touch, why couldn't an iguana read minds?

Well, that would certainly explain how he understood English, even if the structure of his mouth and throat didn't allow him to speak it. One small, lingering question answered.

"...that the men we took off that boat are out of the woods and we've all been given a clean bill of health, our next task is to take care of the dead," Harry was saying. "To that end, Miss Euphemia has been going through her books and she's pretty sure she's found the ingredients to make Greek fire. The only problem there is that it doesn't seem we have enough whale oil or sulfur. Some of us may have to take *The Sappho* to the nearest port–"

"Actually, Captain," Agnessa interrupted, holding up a small scrap of parchment. "We may not have to do that. *The Corinthian Curse* should be here within the next day or two. I've just gotten word from Hugh. They may have what we need. In any case, we should wait until they arrive."

Harry was visibly relieved. "Oh, brilliant! But we'll have to keep a weather eye out for them, and make sure they don't stop to examine the Ilsa before heading in. Kai, can you keep watch tonight?"

"Of course."

"Excellent. Well, let's eat, then. And Hope, no more incense on the fire. There's no need for it any more, and I'd like to actually taste the fish tonight."

*~*~*

Agnessa woke just as dawn broke. Alvar had

rolled over in his sleep and was nestled against her, his hand clinging to her shirt. She was painfully reminded of their childhood, when he had crept into her bed every night against the express wishes of their Father and Nanny. He did it because he was terrified of the dark and because he had absolute faith in her ability to protect him from whatever may lurk in it; for that, he was willing to risk their father's ire. It was one of the only ways he had ever challenged the man's absolute rule; even as a child, Alvar had always followed orders. She had been the wayward and headstrong one, forthright when he was hesitant, obstinate when he yielded, unforgiving when he was tolerant.

What a shame for her father: to finally have his perfect heir with Alvar, but to be saddled with Agnessa in the bargain.

She wondered now, as she carefully unhooked his fingers from her clothing, if Alvar had curled against her in such a way in the womb. If the position was so comforting to him because it was his oldest memory, on a level that was deeper than memory.

Before she stood she tucked a curl behind his ear – his hair was longer than it had ever been; she should offer to cut it for him – and kissed his warm, bearded cheek. He made no sound and didn't move as she pushed back the tent flap and stepped out into the cool morning air.

The contrast of the pink light of dawn against the black sand of the beach was beautiful. For several minutes she simply stood and stared, thankful that she was alive – that her brother was alive – that her crew had taken no harm in their selfless act of rescue.

Then she stretched the kinks and knots from her back and arms and went down to the water to splash her face.

She was straightening and gathering up her hair when there was a flurry of white wings and a harsh squawk. Socrates the albatross wanted breakfast. The bird had perched himself on a tent pole after supper the night before, far out of Tazu's reach, and promptly gone to sleep with his head tucked under one immense wing. No doubt he had been exhausted from his strenuous flight, goaded to exert himself more than usual by a worried handler.

Now he was strutting across the wet sand towards Agnessa, who he associated with both pieces of paper and pieces of fish. One was a responsibility, the other a reward, and as he had accomplished the first last night he fully expected the second – repeated often – until another piece of paper was tied to his leg.

The pair walked to the pit where the coals from the night before still glowed dully and smoked fitfully. Agnessa took the lid off a small bucket filled with water – there was a flash of darting silver within – and stepped back. With another squawk, Socrates sidled up and dipped his sharp beak inside, scooping up the tiny fish and swallowing them whole. Kai had collected them the night before; even without Socrates, there were some nights when Silence or Tazu craved a light snack.

The messenger appeased, Agnessa sat down

and picked up a stick to poke the fire back into life. After a moment's pause for careful preening, and with a wary look around for Tazu, Socrates strutted over and sat down by her knee, settling his massive wings against his back. She debated reaching over and scratching his head, and then thought better of it. That beak was awfully sharp, and the bird's wingspan was nearly six feet. An angry albatross could inflict quite a lot of damage.

Hugh's ship should arrive today. She felt in her pocket for his last letter, just a torn scrap of paper with a handful of words. But it was still a reassuring talisman.

For a moment, she thought about the tall, golden Hugh Dawkins.

Then, feeling discomfited and restless, she set to work building up the fire and began making breakfast for those who didn't have feathers and a taste for live fish.

*~*~*

The morning passed uneventfully. Dishes were washed, more wood was gathered, sand was shaken from blankets.

Miss Euphemia and Franky started cracking coconuts, one armed with a machete (Euphemia) and the other wielding a mallet and a wedge (Franky). The old woman poured the milk into a large jug for future use in a lotion recipe, something to prevent sunburns and rashes.

Hope was sitting in a trance – probably communing with the spirits and thanking them for driving away the pestilence — and Kai was scrubbing a burbling Tazu with a strip of sharkskin; the lizard was going through an uncomfortable molt, and there were large patches of itchy skin on his back that he had trouble reaching.

With Franky occupied and the woodpile large enough to last them a week, Maddie was sitting on one of the taller rocks and keeping watch. She absentmindedly suckled on stinging fingers; she had tried to catch some of the periwinkle crabs scuttling about the swirling foam, but the crustaceans were in a snippy mood and had shown her no mercy. She was examining a particularly painful welt when a flash of movement caught her eye. A ship rounded the point from the east, a ship with yellow sails and a huge black flag emblazoned with the traditional skull and crossbones over a rising sun motif.

"*The Corinthian*, Cap!" Maddie shouted, scrambling to her feet. "Ship ahoy!"

Harry threw aside the piece of wood she'd been half-heartedly whittling and sheathed her knife at her belt. "Sound the welcome, ladies!"

There was no doubt that *The Corinthian Curse* had sighted them; it honed in on the small beach like a bird to its nest. There was a magnificent splash as the anchor was dropped a safe distance from the tethered *Sappho* and, in the space between blinks, a landing craft packed with men was lowered. The little boat positively flew across the water, propelled by four rowers who were enthusiastically putting their backs into it.

Captain Thomas "Thommo" Grey himself

stood at the prow. A good-looking, well-built man in an unbuttoned black coat, he had his shoulder-length brown hair pulled back in a tight queue and a smile already fixed on his tanned, liberally freckled face. The red gold of his beard was a striking contrast with his darker hair and blue eyes. "Hullo, Harry!" he called as soon as they were within hailing distance.

"Hullo, Grey!"

"Can't wait to hear what the commotion's all about! We've all of us been frettin' for you!"

But Captain Grey wasn't the first ashore – before the landing craft had even been pulled out of the waves, Hugh Dawkins dropped his oars and bounded through the surf, his long legs carrying him out of the water in four great strides. "Agnessa?" he demanded breathlessly of a bemused Harry.

"Went to fetch water, I–"

She didn't bother to finish the sentence; his gaze had sharpened on a point over her shoulder and she knew he must have caught sight of her helmswoman. He rushed past the captain as she turned.

Agnessa had scarcely stepped out of the trees, a laden bucket dangling from each hand, when she was suddenly caught up in a pair of wet arms as firm as iron.

The buckets clattered unheeded to the ground.

Water splashed over the sand.

And for the first time in her life she found herself being kissed – and with an astonishing amount of passion.

She was so surprised she was kissing him back before her brain caught up to what was even happening.

"Dawkins!" Captain Thommo bellowed. "You've got to let the poor lass *breathe*, son!"

"Apologies," he gasped when they'd parted. "I'm sorry – I should've asked permission first–"

"Yes, you should've," she agreed, cupping his face.

He was trembling! Hugh Dawkins, the shining paragon of moral virtue and physical brawn, the Oxford intellectual, the noble son and nobler pirate, was trembling! "And you should put me down, you ox."

She hoped her feet would be steady enough to support her when he did.

"Well, I'm glad he got that out of his system," Captain Thommo told Harry, shaking his head. "Boy's been as wound-up as an alarm clock since he got that letter. He did nothing but pace the deck and brood the three days it took us to get here. Still, you've got to make allowances for youth."

"And first love," Harry said with a snort. "I can practically see the stars in Nessa's eyes from here."

"Alright, Harry, tell me what's going on. Does it have something to do with that ship?" he asked shrewdly, pointing to the horizon.

"It does – I'm relieved you tacked in from the east; we were worried you'd stop there first."

"With Hugh practically chewing the lines and pining for his lass? Nay," Thommo said with a chuckle. "We were coming straight for this beach like an arrow from a bow."

"Let's have a seat by the fire and I'll tell you the whole sad affair. Have your men eaten yet?"

"Nay."

"Then we'll see to feeding them – *after* our story. Better to lose an appetite than lose a good breakfast..."

*~*~*

"A sobering tale, to be sure," announced Thommo when it was over. His men nodded grimly. It hadn't been that long ago when influenza had burned through their own ship, taking seven men's lives before it was finally conquered. They knew they'd been lucky – the *Ilsa's* fate could very well have been theirs. "And we should have plenty of oil and tallow in the hold. Jays!"

"Aye, Cap?" the trio looked up sharply from their conversation with Katherine.

"I want you three to go back to the ship and bring back three casks of the whale oil and one of the tallow. And we should still have the barrel of sulfur we liberated from the Portuguese man-o-war, stored with the gunpowder, so bring that as well. Report to Miss Euphemia and Miss Wil and do exactly as they say, understood?"

"Clear as crystal, Cap," said John, sketching a salute and climbing to his feet, offering a hand down to Jim.

"Now, while yours and mine are busy cooking up Greek fire," Thommo said to Harry.

"What was it you wished to talk about at Breaker's Ridge?"

"I've learned something about Drew that may prove useful," she said, unsurprised by the reaction her words caused. Thommo's face had hardened with purpose, his jaw tightened, and his laughing pale eyes had gone cold and hungry.

When Harry had first been properly introduced to Thomas Grey, after years of hearing tales about him, she'd liked how the real man measured up to the legend. He was strong physically and mentally, with a code of honor that paralleled her own. He had an iron control over his hand-picked crew and treated them with the respect a good captain should. Under his sharp eye there would be no raping, no torturing, and no mistreatment of those who surrendered under his terms – but he was also a brutal fighter and would kill without hesitation. He didn't favor any one style of combat, using a sword, a pistol, and bare fists in equal measure, whatever method would get the job done the quickest. He had a particular grudge against the Portuguese for undisclosed reasons – the only figure he hated more was Wrath Drew.

That night in Bogo, with a dozen empty cups between them, Harry had listened as Thommo spoke of his son. He had been illegitimate: the result of a youthful week's carousing in Trinidad with a wench named Rita.

Thommo hadn't learned of the boy's existence until two years later, when he crossed paths with the woman again purely by chance. She had shown him his son – a laughing boy with a healthy pair of lungs – and he had given her enough gold to set them both up in a decent house.

There could be no doubt that Paul was his son: the boy had his eyes. But even if he'd been unsure, he would've done the same. Rita was a woman who had left quite a mark on him, and he knew how difficult life could be for a wench who chose to raise a child rather than abort it.

He went back to visit as often as he could. Every five months, once a year. He looked after them, made sure they were eating well and kept in good clothes. When the boy was twelve, he begged to go with Thommo. The sea was calling to him. He would work hard and be a good cabin boy. And he longed to have adventures like his father.

But Thommo didn't want his son to follow in his footsteps. His gold had bought Paul and Rita respectability – no one remembered that Rita had once been a wench (she was known as 'Mrs. Grey', though she had no legal claim to that name) and no one openly called the boy a bastard. Paul could be an apprentice in the proper way. He could become a chandler or a blacksmith or perhaps even a doctor. Better any of those options than to turn pirate like his old man.

When Thommo visited next, almost a year later, it was to find only a somber Rita waiting for him. Paul had run away, she said. He had hopped aboard a ship four months ago and disappeared. She had no idea where he was, what condition he was in, or if she would ever see him again. She didn't even know the name of the ship.

And a year after that, Thommo returned for a funeral.

There had been an incident in a bar. Paul had been beaten badly, stabbed twice, and left for dead. But he'd held on just long enough to tell the barmaid trying to comfort him that his father was Captain Thomas Grey.

"What happened?" Thommo had asked, dry-eyed and stony faced, when the news reached him through a network of gossip.

"The boy tripped and spilled his beer on a man," the barmaid told him as she shrunk away, afraid not of him but of the rage she could feel he was barely holding in check. "A man all in black, with a jeweled eyepatch. The others called him Wrath, I think. And the man grabbed him. Beat him. Called him a mongrel cur and stabbed him. My old man pointed a pistol at him and chased him out, but there was nothing we could do for the lad. I'm sorry."

"Where did they bury him?"

"Pauper's field, two streets over. Under the cross that says 'Black Boy'."

So Thomas Grey dug up his son, who had been buried in a flimsy wooden box, and took him home to his mother. He told her, as Paul was lowered back into the ground in a proper cemetery, that he would not see her again – but that he would find the man responsible and carve his heart out.

"Ever since the day he killed my son," Thommo had said to Harry, "that bastard has been living on borrowed time."

Indeed, meeting Thommo had felt a lot like the touch of Destiny – if Harry believed in such things, anyway. She had no doubts about his loyalty and commitment to their shared cause, no fear that *this* ally would ever turn traitor. And Kai had seconded her opinion of him.

"His aura isn't pure," her merman had said after they were introduced. "I believe he is a man capable of great violence. But it isn't rotten, either. It isn't the aura of a man who lies or cheats. There is no malevolence in him."


"Do you know where he's hiding?" Thommo asked in the present, looking rather like a hawk that has spotted its prey.

"No, not yet," Harry said regretfully. "But I've learned that he's looking for something in particular. Have you ever heard of the Emerald of Tococo?"

"Of course I have," said Thommo, a scholar of great treasure if of nothing else, as so many pirates were. "It once belonged to a Mayan king. It was used in blood sacrifice rituals. Thought to be as big as a dragon's egg, and also thought to be lost forever. It went down with Willis the Bloody's ship, *Maelstrom*, a hundred years ago. Legend says the ship sank because of a massive whirlpool created by a kraken, but no one knows exactly where this happened."

"Don't you find it interesting that we know such things?" Harry said. "All of these ships supposedly sinking with 'all hands on deck' – but *someone* must have survived to tell the story, right?"

"You're off the subject, Harry," Thommo warned.

"Yes. Right. Well, legend also says that the Emerald has certain magical properties. That it can preserve its owner from all evil, for starters. Protect them from bad luck, physical attack, even the wrath of gods. The stories say that Tococo was a powerful king and undefeated warrior *until* he lost the Emerald — because he didn't treat it with enough respect, so it abandoned him."

"Willis the Bloody must've used it as a doorstop, then, if it made his ship sink," Thommo said dryly. "Why is any of this relevant? It's all just pubroom stories."

"It's relevant because Wrath Drew believes the stories. He's become obsessed with finding it, according to my source. It's part of the reason why he's allied himself with so many vicious mermaids."

"So they can scour trenches for him?" Thommo paused for thought. "That does make sense — but where are you getting this information?"

"Zora's girl, Tessa, wenches in Bogo. One of her regulars is on Wrath's crew, and the man's tongue gets awfully loose around her."

"Tessa of the Anne's Arms?" Thommo asked with a grin. He'd visited her once himself, on the recommendation of a good friend. She had most certainly lived up to her reputation. "Aye, I could believe that. That woman has a real gift for lowering a man's defenses. So, what are we to do with this knowledge, Harry?"

Harry grinned. "We find the Emerald first, of course. And then we use it as bait to lure Wrath in."

*~*~*

"I could tell something was wrong from the tone," Hugh said. "And your hand was practically illegible. Are you surprised I was so concerned?"

"No, I just – I suppose I hadn't expected you to be so, well, *demonstrative*," Agnessa said.

They were sitting a distance away from their crews, large mugs of tea in hand as rather a lot of unspoken communication happened between them. She was almost *too* aware of him; of the coiled tension still thrumming through his body, grounding itself in the smallest of gestures. The way his fingers tapped against his mug. The tightening of his jaw and the darting glances he cast at her.

"I apologize, again. I took a liberty and that was wrong of me."

"I've already forgiven you, Hugh."

Now that the first rush of elation and relief had passed, they were both feeling awkward and embarrassed. For several minutes there was only silence between them, as they looked at the ground, the sky, their hands – anywhere but at each other.

Agnessa finished her tea and cleared her throat nervously.

"Yes?"

Had his eyes always been so earnest and pleading when he looked at her? "Oh, um, nothing. I just had a... a tickle in my throat," she said lamely.

"Socrates will be pleased to see you."

"Where is the feathered nag?"

"Probably hiding in a tree somewhere, avoiding Tazu. I had Wil give him strict orders not to eat him — that Tazu couldn't eat Socrates, I mean. But he still looks at him longingly..." She paused, seeing a similar emotion on Hugh's face, and finished in a rush as her cheeks flushed red, "and Socrates doesn't like that one bit."

"No, I expect he wouldn't."

Oh, this was *ridiculous*! She'd never had trouble speaking her mind before — why was she mumbling over such inanities? And she'd always known just what she wanted (or *didn't* want) — so why was she so confused on that score now?

"You *are* alright, aren't you, Agnessa?" Hugh asked quietly. He had listened to Harry unfold the harrowing events for his crew, but sensed that there was something *The Sappho*'s captain had left out. Something to do with the slim woman sitting in front of him. Something that had affected her in a significant way, because she seemed smaller and paler than he remembered. Older, even.

"My brother," she said. "My twin brother. Was on that ship."

"Good Lord." He swallowed. Reached out for her hand. "I'm so very sorry—"

"He's alive," she said, just before their fingers brushed. He froze instantly, forcing her to bridge the short gap. Her hand looked like a fairy's against his. Everything about Hugh was almost too big to be allowed, including his heart. "He'll be fine, with time and care. He's sleeping right now, on the other end of the beach, with the other survivors. His name is Alvar."

"I look forward to meeting him." He sounded oddly formal, as if they were sitting in a parlor in someone's townhouse. Perhaps because she'd slid her fingers between his and all of his focus was concentrated on the sensation of her skin pressing against his.

"You were trembling," she said.

"Pardon?"

"When you were holding me. When you kissed me. You were trembling all over."

"I... I was so relieved that you were safe," he stuttered. "My imagination was cruel, had dreamt up all manner of horrors that might have befallen you. I was just so glad to see you. I know I was behaving irrationally–"

She leaned forward and kissed him.

Just because she was curious to see if it would feel as good the second time, she told herself. Just because he was so embarrassed. Just because...

She wanted to. She really wanted to kiss Hugh Dawkins, she finally admitted. And kiss him often.

It appeared they were of the same mind on that count. For the second time that day he wrapped his arms around her. He held her as if nothing, not even a cannon, could separate them. And she half-believed it – the man was an unshakable titan.

Unless she was in danger. Then he suddenly became the most mortal of men, frail and breakable and liable to explode.

He began shaking again, clearly overwhelmed, and she put her arms around him as if she alone would be able to hold him together.

When his hands clenched around her shirt, and she found her fingers unknotting the handkerchief around his neck, she realized belatedly that this wasn't the best time nor place to lose her last inhibitions. It was midday, on an open beach, and, by this point, no doubt a dozen eyes were avidly watching them with interest. She pulled away with an effort, lips bruised a bright red and hair disheveled. "Wait, wait," she said, pushing against his chest. "Not here."

"Oh. Yes. Um." To the left, five of his crewmates were grinning at them, waggling their eyebrows and whistling encouragement. And to the right, Katherine and Zora sat like cats who had just swallowed extremely fat canaries.

"If you need any advice, Nessa, just ask!" Katherine called, to assorted laughter.

Agnessa hastily re-buttoned her shirt, but she was grinning. Pleased rather than ashamed, he was grateful to realize. "Later," she said, making every one of his thoughts screech to a halt. He stared at her. "We can pick up where we left off. If you're still interested by then, of course."

"I can assure you, I will be," he said firmly. "Uh... would now be a good time to meet your brother?"

"Why don't we go see?" she said, standing and straightening her trousers. "Follow me."

"To the ends of the earth," he said, devoutly

and mostly to himself.

*~*~*

All her life, Agnessa had been content to only read of love. She'd never met a man who could kindle a spark in her breast; had, indeed, never exerted the effort to find such a man. She'd had better things to do and didn't feel as if she were missing much.

Besides: loving a man was dangerous and could lead to her greatest fear. She was more than willing to lead a celibate life and forgo any fleeting physical pleasure so long as it meant she would never swell with child.

Not for any amount of gold nor lustful excitement would she ever be a mother. Thus, she reasoned, her bed would by necessity remain empty. And never would she marry, because men expected – nay, *demanded* – children of their wives.

Or so she'd been taught and had always believed.

But two years at sea had been very enlightening. It turned out there were plenty of women in the world who shared her sentiments. There were men who cared nothing about securing heirs or accruing daughters that could later be sold to the highest bidder. And there were ways to lie with a man and still be assured that nothing but pleasure would come from the experience.

So that night Agnessa stepped into a tent with the first man who had ever made her burn, more excited than nervous, with a pocket full of pills from Hope's medicinal chest and a smile on her lips.

A smile that remained as Hugh undressed himself, then her, and pressed his mouth to her body.

A smile that lasted as their bodies aligned and slid and rocked.

A smile that only slipped when she sighed, and moaned, and cried out her release at the end.

"So you ran away to the sea," Hugh said later as they discussed their personal histories, rolling over beside her. His hand lay heavy and warm on one of her thighs and it felt unexpectedly natural. "Because you didn't want a marriage – especially not one arranged by your father purely for his own benefit."

"Precisely," she confirmed.

Hugh laughed, and her forehead wrinkled with confusion. "What about that amuses you?" she demanded.

"Just that that's precisely why I joined the Navy," he explained. "My father talked constantly of how I was of an age when I should be turning my thoughts towards matrimony. And didn't he just have the perfect young lady picked out for me – it was her first season, she was already a celebrated beauty at eighteen, such masterful needlework, what an adornment she'd be for the house in Town, think of what pretty children she'd deliver with her blue-blooded pedigree! It was revolting. The way he talked – as if a flesh and blood human woman was comparable to a hunting dog to breed, or a porcelain vase to put on display. It angered and disgusted me, and finally I lost my patience. So I signed my oath, took the Queen's shilling, and sailed away as quickly as I could."

"Really? Truly?"

"Really and truly," he swore.

"I never suspected that men were similarly pressured," she said thoughtfully. "Father never tried to force Alvar into a marriage, but then perhaps there was no young lady suitable enough and he was simply waiting for one to appear."

"From what you've said, I suspect our paters would be bosom friends," Hugh said dryly. "Though, it is somewhat ironic, isn't it?"

"Hmm?"

"My father's a Lord. Your father's extremely wealthy. If circumstances had been different, if you'd come to London or I'd gone to Stockholm, our families might have thought us a suitable match."

She had to laugh at that. "Quite. And if they had tried to arrange it, both of us would've been obstinate and hated each other on sight just to spite them."

"Choked on the bit and dug our heels in like recalcitrant horses."

"They would've had to physically drag us down the aisle."

"And then, after five or ten years, we would have unbent enough to actually get to know the other and found that we liked each other."

"Sounds like novel fodder," Agnessa said. "For a really purple romance."

"We should write it," he suggested. "And sell it to a publisher for an outrageous sum. It would shock the ton and make us notorious."

"We're already notorious," she pointed out. "Lord, if my Father could see me now, he'd swallow his own tongue."

"I'd rather not imagine your disapproving Papa peering in on us right now," Hugh said, kissing her for the fortieth time – she found herself unconsciously keeping track. "I'd rather resume our previous debate..."

"I *have* always found our discussions very stimulating," Agnessa sighed against his cheek in the darkness.

*~*~*

The Greek fire was ready by mid-afternoon the following day. Jo took *The Sappho* out with a skeleton crew and five pots full of the mixture carefully sealed and strapped to the deck. Lizzie's catapult – a contraption she'd made months ago purely as a means of filling an especially tedious three days on a becalmed sea – was attached to a pulley system and lifted out of the hold. Once the range had been accurately determined with test barrels, the first pot was loaded into the basket.

"Do you wish to say anything before we fire?" Jo asked Alvar.

He stood at the railing and leaned heavily on his sister, his face the color of curdled milk. Agnessa had tried to convince him to stay back on the shore but he had held firm: he needed to witness the immolation. He owed his dead crew that much.

"I said everything I needed to say the last

time I was on that deck," he said quietly. "God's already heard it all."

Jo nodded and pulled the lever without another word.

It only took three of the five pots; Miss Euphemia's recipe proved to be a powerful one. Once the ship was fully alight, Jo signaled to Agnessa to pull *The Sappho* back further. They couldn't chance a gust of wind sending any embers into their sails.

Then they stood in a line at the railing, a mixed collection of faces in a variety of hues, all sharing the same somber expression. They watched for close to an hour, and then *The Princess Ilsa* and her ill-fated crew was gone, the last flickering bits of wood sinking beneath the water with a hiss.

"We'll be heading out in the morning, then," said Thommo that evening at supper. Socrates was perched on his crossed knee and taking hunks of meat from the man's fingers. Everyone sprawled around the fire enjoying a stew full of crab, lobster, and whitefish. "We'll take the Swedes to London – won't be hard for them to get back home from there."

Unlike *The Sappho*, *The Corinthian Curse* could sail openly into English ports because Captain Thomas Grey was, in British eyes, a privateer commissioned by the Queen herself. Out in these waters, he was considered a pirate just like Harry, but back home he was a national hero with official standing. The distinction was a vital one.

"Let's meet again at Bonefish Cove," said Harry. "That'll give us time to do some research."

"Research?" Miss Euphemia and Wil echoed with interest.

"Yes, ladies, just the task for you – and Nessa, too. Poring through dusty old books."

"What fun," Zora said sarcastically.

"It's the sort of research that'll lead us to treasure," Harry added, which recaptured the others' interest. "Treasure *and* revenge, if we're lucky."

"Only my favorite combination," Katherine said.

"Pardon, but Captain Grey? Captain Roberts?"

The two turned as one to stare at the only person on the island who rivaled Katherine in size and strength. "Yes, Mr. Dawkins?"

"I think I would be of more use to Captain Roberts at this juncture," he said, meeting his captain's eyes steadily. "I was hoping to be given leave to sail with *The Sappho* for the time being."

"I've no problem with that," Thommo said easily. "Harry, what do you think? Got enough room on your tub for Mr. Dawkins?"

"I'm sure we can find the space," Harry said, catching Agnessa's eye. "Only temporarily, of course. Wouldn't want to steal one of your best and brightest, Thommo."

"And me," Alvar said, surfacing from the image of a burning ship. "Do you have room for me as well, Harry?"

That request *did* make her pause, and seemed to take his twin by surprise as well. "Are you sure about that?" Harry said. "You've been through hell, Alvar, and you've more than earned the right to go home. Back to an easier, quieter life. Sailing with us, nothing's ever easy or quiet."

"I can't go home," Alvar said in a stumbling rush. "Not right now. Not after what I've seen. I can't go back to that big, empty house and listen to my father yell about unimportant things. He'll expect me to be the way I was before, and I'm not that boy any more. I'm never going to be that boy again. But he won't understand, and he'll push and pry and make demands... I can't face that, Captain."

"In that case – you do realize you don't *have* to go home?" Harry said gently. "Thommo can take you anywhere you like. You can stay in London, or go somewhere quiet out in the countryside. We'll give you enough to make a new life for yourself."

"Or I could make a new life here, with you," he said. His jaw was set. He was already resolved. "With my sister, who I understand better now than I ever did before. If you'll give me a bit more time to recover, I'll prove myself a hardy seaman, Captain. I swear it."

Everyone looked from the young man still disturbingly marked by sickness and tragedy to the pale and thoughtful captain – everyone but Tazu, who took the moment of distraction to stretch out a clawed hand and tweak the albatross Socrates' tail feathers. The bird shrieked like a banshee and took off with a thunder of buffeting wings, shattering the moment and leaving Thommo cursing and clutching a leg pricked by avian talons.

"I've never been one to deny someone so earnest and decided," Harry said when peace had been mostly reclaimed. "If you're sure you want to sail with us, Alvar, then I welcome you to the crew. For at least the next three months – you're on probation, same as any who signs on with us. We'll decide how permanent your position is after that."

"I wouldn't worry, mate," Franky confided, shaking his hand with a grin. "She gave me the same line, and she made up her mind not even a month later. I'm sure you'll do just fine."

# THE KIDNAPPING OF LADY CAVENDISH

Deborah, Lady Cavendish, was in the middle of composing a letter to her grandmother when all hell seemed to break out on deck.

"What on earth...?" she exclaimed, setting aside her pen, stoppering her bottle of royal purple ink, and pushing back her chair. She went to one of the windows of her tidy cabin and stared out at the dozens of men running pell-mell in a frantic state of extreme alarm. Guns were being passed out from the powder room, the steersman was gripping the tiller with a grimace of resignation, and Captain Fulsome was shouting himself hoarse.

His coat hung crookedly, Deborah noted, because he had buttoned it in a hurry and missed one. And his white wig was on backwards.

Taking up her sky blue parasol – the one that perfectly complimented her current gown – she opened her door and stepped out into the sunlight. An ensign rushing past with a rifle almost as big as himself saw her, did a comical double-take, and rushed over.

"Oh no, m'lady, you should stay in your cabin," he said breathlessly, overlarge Adam's apple bobbing madly. The boy looked like someone had hung a uniform on a lamppost: he was mostly ears. "Lock and barricade your door."

"What is going on?" she demanded coolly,

opening her parasol. "I'm not moving one centimeter until you explain this chaos."

"Pirates, miss," he said miserably, skinny shoulders slumping under his despair. "They'll likely kill us all and sink the ship!"

"Nonsense," she said, reaching out a lace gloved-covered hand to pat his shoulder. "Chin up, boy, and have faith. Most pirates are nothing but ruffians who prey upon the weak – so long as we show them proper English courage, they'll realize we're not worth the effort and leave."

The ensign stared at her open-mouthed. He was young, and green behind the ears, and extremely hesitant to argue with an aristocrat – but he couldn't help thinking that Lady Cavendish was madder than a march hare. "But, miss, they've got more cannons than us," he pointed out.

"What do pirates want? Gold and jewels and cargo. They won't sink us before trying to board us and taking stock of our inventory," Deborah continued blithely. "And when they try to board us, we'll show them what we're made of."

"Same bits every man is made of, miss," the ensign said. "Blood and tubes and wobbly things. And I'd prefer all of my bits stay inside where God intended."

Sensing that she was getting nowhere with this young man, Deborah huffed, squared her shoulders, and set off across the deck towards Captain Fulsome. Several men carrying weapons and spyglasses had to quickly adjust their course or else collide with the determined Lady.

"Yes, what is– Oh, good God! Lady

Cavendish!" The Captain's Romanesque features were cartoonish with surprise. He looked like an especially lop-sided Punch puppet after a good thrashing. "You need to take cover immediately!"

"I hear we are being harassed by pirates, Captain Fulsome," Deborah said, spinning her parasol.

"So we are, which is precisely why–"

"I've dealt with pirates before, Captain," she continued on smoothly. "Twice, in fact. Both times the scoundrels intended to kidnap and ransom me for the family fortune."

"And what happened?" Fulsome asked, curious despite the manifold pressing distractions.

"The first lot were rousted by a few shots from the crew and the second rethought their plan after I put a pistol to their captain's head," Deborah said sweetly. She flashed a perfectly proper society smile. "Now, how do you intend to handle this bunch?"

"We've only just sighted them, miss," Fulsome said. "Once we know just who it is we're facing, we'll plan according–"

"I see the prow, Captain!" one of the lieutenants at the railing shouted, a spyglass pressed to his face. "It's... It's *The Sappho*, sir!"

The wave of relief was palpable. The mad rush of activity ceased immediately. Men sighed and rubbed their faces, setting aside their guns and leaning against the masts. Some even started to laugh.

"I don't understand," Deborah said, bewildered. "It *is* a pirate ship, is it not?"

"Oh, yes, my lady, most definitely," said Captain Fulsome, pulling out a white kerchief to mop the beads of sweat from his tanned brow. He dislodged his wig in the process, and had to stoop quickly to catch it. "Apologies, miss, I'm usually not in such a disarray."

"Then why are your men lowering their weapons? Shouldn't we be readying ourselves for battle?"

"We've no undue quarrel with *The Sappho*," the captain said, looking a little uncomfortable. He was unaccustomed to well-bred young women in voluminous petticoats being so, well, *bloodthirsty*. "They'll only levy a minor tax and let us go peacefully on our way."

"Levy a tax?" Deborah said, voice rising in both volume and pitch. "This is the *HMS Williamson*, and they are pirates! Since when has the British government made a habit of giving in to the demands of thieves and murderers?"

"Lady Cavendish, please. The world out here does not always abide by the same rules as the one we left in London. Sometimes certain... allowances must be made. For the good of everybody. Far better that we part with a few pounds and a barrel or two of preserves than with our lives! Surely you can see that?"

"I can see, Mr. Fulsome, that cowardice is easier than chivalry," Deborah said, head held high. The pirate's vessel was very close now, close enough for them to see individual faces grinning along the railing. Tightening her jaw, she turned to face the silent, staring men of her ship. "Gentlemen, are you men or mice? Give no quarter to these vultures! They can't bloody kill us all!"

"What did she say?" Marcella asked Lizzie.

"Somethin' 'bout us bein' vultures, I think," the blacksmith replied, grinning.

"Girl's got sauce," Zora said, admiring the figure striding across the deck in a froth of blue muslin, satin, and lace. "And she must be cooked alive in that get-up, just look at it all."

"She's beautiful," Katherine said dreamily, sliding the gangplank across. "A real lady, you can tell."

"She's certainly ordering them about like a toff," Harry said, amused by the entire scene. "Franky, ladies, let's go see just what we're dealing with here."

"...cower in the presence of their military might? No! Did David back down before Goliath? Of course he didn't!" the lady in blue was shouting, swinging her furled parasol just as a general would use a baton. "So gird your loins, gentlemen, pick up those guns, and defend this ship from the forces of unlawful tyranny!"

"We've never been called tyrants before, Cap!" Franky said with a grin, making the woman startle sharply and spin to face them, her dark curls swinging in her wake. Her face was flushed from delivering her rousing call to arms and her shoulders heaved with the force of her breathing – it must be exceedingly difficult to breathe deeply in such a tight corset. Katherine found her eyes glued to the heaving breasts framed in lace and felt breathless herself.

Full lips, a firm nose, and brown eyes that flashed with anger while glaring at them. This lady in blue definitely had the face and bearing of an aristocrat — and was obviously of the type that led men into battle rather than remained home at the manor to quietly embroider seat cushions.

"No, usually we get called smug, interfering bitches," Harry agreed. "Hullo! I'm Captain Roberts. These are my miscreants. We'd like to take a look in your hold, if you'd be so kind."

"We'll let you do nothing of the sort!" shouted Deborah Cavendish, swinging her parasol like a club and catching Franky a real ding against the left temple. He yelped and ducked, raising his arms against the onslaught. "Scoundrels! Ruffians! Thieves!"

Katherine reached over and caught the makeshift weapon in mid-swing. Deborah tugged once, twice, and then glared up — and up — until she finally met her enemy's eyes.

In the heat of her indignity, Deborah hadn't looked properly at the scruffy boarding party. She had noticed, somewhat dimly, that Captain Roberts was actually a woman, but hadn't given much thought to the others. Now she stared up at a towering figure she had automatically assumed was a man and found the opposite.

Eyes the blue of cornflowers looked down at her with obvious amusement. Hair the gold of corn silk was braided into a crown atop her head. Pink lips smiled at her, and the plain white shirt at her eye-level was only half-buttoned, revealing a defiantly much-tattooed, undeniably female chest.

"...Oh," Deborah said, blinking rapidly. She released the parasol. "Um."

"I'm Katherine," the figure spoke, low voice pleasantly rounded by a Scandinavian accent. "And you are?"

"Lady Deborah Cavendish," she replied promptly. She smoothed the front of her ample skirts self-consciously.

"Honored," Katherine said, inclining her head. "Sorry – I'd curtsy, but Agnessa hasn't gotten around to teaching me yet."

"Quite alright," Deborah said. "We aren't in court, and this isn't a ball."

"No, it isn't."

"Well, uh, what exactly is it that you intend to do today?" she said finally, straightening her back.

"We just wanted a quick look in the hold," Harry said, holding back laughter. The lady had been thoroughly and immediately cowed, all of her righteous fire banked beneath embarrassment. All thanks to a single sizzling look at Katherine. "Might help ourselves to a little of your gunpowder, any spices you might have. We're running a tad low on those and haven't had an opportunity to visit any shops lately. You understand how it is."

"Yes, well, that doesn't sound unreasonable to me," Deborah said, glancing at the boggled, silent men behind her. Her inner fire flared up momentarily. "In fact, help yourselves, Captain Roberts. Obviously, these men don't deserve the luxury of well-flavored meals. Cowards should be grateful for mere bread and water."

"Indeed," Harry snorted, waving for Marcella, Zora, and Lizzie to follow her, leaving Franky to rub his aching head and Katherine to continue her unabashed appraisal of the outspoken Lady Cavendish.

"You have a low opinion of pirates," Katherine commented.

"Those I've met haven't impressed me much," Deborah said. "Also, I assumed you were here to kidnap me."

"Kidnap you?" Katherine raised an eyebrow in surprise. "We've never been ones to kidnap people."

"Be that as it may be, the last two sets of pirates I encountered attempted to do so. I'm quite the ransom prize, apparently. Old family," she explained in a private undertone. "Pots of money, sweeping ancestral estates. You know."

"Ah. I see. So if it's so dangerous for you to sail, what are you doing on this boat?"

"Just because some rotten-toothed men assume they can use me to milk money from my family, that doesn't mean I intend to hide myself away," Deborah said stubbornly. "I am going to see the world and enjoy my youth – there will be plenty of time for boring safety when I'm old and grey."

"That sounds perfectly reasonable to me."

"Besides, staying at home doesn't guarantee safety, either. Someone tried to grab me on my way to the opera last winter – eager for a large payout, no doubt – and I convinced them that they had made a bad choice."

"How did you do that?"

"I stomped on his foot hard enough to break several bones and thrust the end of my umbrella into his manhood," Deborah said proudly. "Left him sobbing on the street and continued on. I'd been looking forward to *La Boheme* for a month."

"Do you always travel alone?"

"Oh yes. No one can keep up with me."

"That sounds like a challenge," Katherine said.

"Oh? Did it?"

"I've seen a lot of the world, sailing with *The Sappho*," Katherine said, nonchalantly. "We've traveled just about everywhere. Uncharted islands. Distant cities."

"Is that so?" Deborah's full lips began to curve into a smile.

"I would just like to say," Harry announced as she and the others emerged from below-deck, a small chest in her arms. "That you've got a *lovely* hold, Captain..."

"Fulsome," the man supplied, staring. It felt as if he hadn't blinked since the pirates had stepped aboard; how could he? If he did, no doubt he'd miss something unbelievable. The whole afternoon had become something out of the strangest dream. There was Lady Cavendish, the most headstrong woman he had ever met, talking politely to a giant she had only moments before been hellbent on seeing shot dead. And now she was smiling at the pirates she had so soundly denounced, and giving him a look of pure exasperated annoyance.

"Captain Fulsome." Harry adjusted her grip on the chest to free up a hand and reached over to companionably slap his back. "Beautiful boat, this. Tidy. Well-organized. Very clean and nicely polished. You do a credit to yourselves and your country. Keep up the wonderful work. And don't worry: we left it all as nicely ordered as we found it. Just helped ourselves to some gunpowder and the spices, as I said. Oh − and that little bag of sapphires you had tucked in the back of your roll-top desk. You don't mind, do you?"

"No, of course not," Captain Fulsome said weakly.

"Good man." Another slap; this one sent his wig flying. "Then we'll just be on our way."

"Uh, Cap?"

"Yes, Katherine?"

"Perhaps we should take Lady Cavendish as well?" Katherine suggested. "She's worth an earl's ransom, after all." The look she shot at her captain was a pointed one.

Harry played dumb. "That so? Well, I don't know, Kath. Taking hostages is always risky−"

"I'll fetch my trunks," Deborah said abruptly, turning and rushing for her cabin.

"Lady Cavendish!" Captain Fulsome shouted, driven to act. "My lady, I must protest!"

"Mr. Fulsome, I don't believe you have a leg to stand on," Deborah said haughtily from her doorway. "Think of this as the price you pay for not heeding my orders."

"Oh good God in Heaven," the captain said mournfully as *The Sappho* pulled away, a figure in blue satin waving cheerfully back at them. "How on *earth* am I going to explain this to Lord Cavendish?"

"The good news, sir," said a lieutenant helpfully, "is that we'll have three months to get our story straight."

# GLAMOUR

He had seen them for the first time when they'd all come ashore at the Whitehaven Harbor. His own family had grown too familiar and rather boring; always the same things. One ritual or dance after another, tricks played on humans, time spent speaking about their long family history.

After three or four centuries, it got tedious.

He'd begun spending more and more time with the First People, whom his family had tolerated. Eventually new people had come in from the sea, people with paler skin and different weapons, and a strong desire to build pathways of iron across the land. He and the other Fae families had tried their best to sabotage the pathways, but they'd eventually bisected the country anyway, splitting apart Fae territories that had existed for centuries.

Some Fae had moved away entirely, taking the form of the humans they so despised in order to seek passage on great wooden ships, intent on reaching safer lands. Others had gone into hiding, seeking solace among only others of their own kind.

He, meanwhile, had grown more and more interested in the humans that unwittingly traveled by their home.

His parents said that his fascination with humans, particularly sailors, was a phase (one they didn't approve of, because he used his talents to help them rather than confound them or steal their children). And he'd believed they were probably right; he'd been content to wander around human establishments and listen to their wild stories of life at sea, and that had been enough.

Then *The Sappho* had arrived.

He'd never met a crew entirely made up of women before; judging from the looks on the other sailors' faces, it was equally odd to them. He'd been charmed by Captain Roberts, so much so that he'd been half-convinced that she had Fae blood in her somewhere.

By the time he'd spent a full hour in their company, he'd known that he wanted to leave with them.

He hadn't said a word about it to his parents or other relatives, save for his cousin Aurelia. He knew that Aurelia would keep his secret for as long as need be, while his mother and father and aunts and uncles and siblings would merely argue with him endlessly – or, worse, put a curse on the ship in order to keep him home.

At that point in time, Kai hadn't yet been with the crew, nor had Lucky Franky. Believing that one had to be a woman to sign on, Marcel had cast a glamour, shifted form, and come aboard as Marcella.

She had relished every day of her life on the ocean, finding it to be everything she'd been unconsciously longing for for years.

Though she knew now that Captain Harry was purely human, without an ounce of true magic in her blood, she still had a way with inhuman creatures that she felt might even impress her stoic great-grandmother. Not many sea captains could claim the loyalty of a Fae, much less that of a Fae, merfolk, and a siren.

The only complaint she had was how much the former blacksmith, Lizzie, still liked to work with iron. She'd even forged herself a ring made from the stuff, which kept a necessary distance between them. She always made sure to speak to Lizzie very nicely, so that the other woman wouldn't think she had a grievance against her; she just didn't get close physically.

Which kept in line with how she was with everyone else anyway; physical closeness wasn't something she was always interested in. Two centuries of being in small crowded homes with all of her extended relatives, sleeping in tight rows and sometimes messy piles on the floor, and the ship seemed like a spacious haven. It was quite freeing, to have space to herself.

Even if Katherine did insist on giving hugs that might have crushed a lesser Fae.

It was a pity, she thought, that her family was so disdainful of humans in general. If they chose to, they would find many commonalities between themselves and this crew.

Maddie was every bit as sweet and kind as Marcella's mother – and every bit as terrifying when threatened. Imriska had Berserker blood in her; though she didn't sense the same about Maddie, she was certain her mother would appreciate the fast, brutal way that she dealt with those who meant her or her crew harm.

When she'd first seen Katherine, she'd been

half-sure she was part Giantess. Grandfather's cousin had married a Giant, and despite how supremely crowded their home always got, she loved when they visited. They were very much like Katherine, all booming laughter and lewd jokes and claps on the back that nearly sent you tumbling.

Deborah reminded her of a Pixie — a creature that was much like a Fae, but smaller and more refined, possessing higher voices and committing fewer tricks. They were, however, capable of unimaginable cruelty when wronged. She hoped to never find out if the Lady was like a Pixie in that way as well.

She knew that Wil would want to hear about all these creatures and more... the moment she found out what Marcella truly was, she would surely ask a myriad of questions. If she didn't take off her wooden leg and pummel her with it for not revealing herself right away. Aurelia would love that about her; they shared the same insatiable curiosity.

She didn't know who Alvar reminded her of. She'd spent a good deal of time trying to figure it out before finally letting herself realize that he hadn't taken over her thoughts because of any mere resemblance to someone she'd once known.

# MEMORIAL

By the time he reached their ship, a beacon of fire in the cloudless night, it was already far too late.

Kai swam through the debris-thick waters, searching for anyone who had survived, anyone who had turned. He encountered several bodies – including that of the cabin boy, a lad so young that it broke his heart – but either all had died in the fire on board their ship or, in their drowning, whatever controlled these waters had not seen fit to give them the gift of continued life.

He thought of Harry's ship, of the state it had been in when he'd first encountered it. With their ship, the fire had been put out and they'd found safe harbor. This...

He wondered who had been on this ship, where they had been going.

Resurfacing again, he scanned the waves for any signs of life. A couple of bodies were braced against debris, but no light emanated from them; they blended seamlessly into the cold water.

Then, only a short distance away from a small patch of land, he caught sight of a very faint glow. Pale orange, flickering like a dying candle. Kai swam quickly to it, realizing as soon as he saw the elderly woman that drowning would be her only chance.

She blinked at him, smiled. "Hello," she said, her arms wrapped around a charred piece of the ship. Her hands were blackened and scarred, as was her face, and Kai was surprised she was even conscious, let alone speaking. Her face registered no pain, and as he watched, the light extinguished completely before immediately flaring up again.

"Hello," he said back, carefully taking hold of the driftwood. He was afraid to touch her; just because she felt no pain now didn't mean she wouldn't if he jostled her. He swam slowly, aiding the driftwood along on its journey to the beach. Once they were on the sand, she still clung to the piece of the ship, resting her head on it as if it were a pillow, staring at his tail.

"Well," she breathed. "Of all the things I never thought I'd live to see." She reached out a shaking hand, resting it on his hip, staring at the individual scales with bleary eyes. "Oh, Florence and the others should be here. They helped make an entire society about you, you know."

"About me?" he asked, smiling. "I'm flattered."

She laughed, the wide smile crinkling up her face and in that instant she looked so much like Euphemia that he almost had to turn away.

"Mermaids. And I suppose mermen, too, if they'd been sure you existed. Bit harder to find." She coughed, a wet, rattling sound. "Society for Mermaid Safety. Ten members on the ship. Did they turn?" she asked, trying to raise her head. "Anyone?"

"Yes," he said, because what good would the truth do? "I'll check on them again soon. Right now – Miss, I can't do much to help you here. If you come back into the water–"

"No." She said the word so fiercely that she coughed again, so harshly that her light almost faded out.

"It's your only chance," he said. "Please. Let me help."

"Wouldn't be helping," she said, her grip tightening on the driftwood. "Always been scared of the water." Seeing the look on his face, she laughed again, a smear of blood showing at the corner of her mouth. "Can't even swim! Yet I'm the one who made it."

"The others are—"

"You're a terrible liar, lad."

He didn't try to argue. Harry had told him as much on multiple occasions; he'd hoped it wasn't so much a flaw with his ability to tell a falsehood so much as it was her being supernaturally perceptive.

"What's your name?" he asked.

"Minerva Claire Harper. Going to see my son, you know. Moved such a long way away from us. Never understood it. Wanderlust. Never had it myself. Thought I'd die in the house I was born in."

"You don't have to die here," he said. "If—"

"Can you promise?" she asked. "Can you... can you guarantee, that if I go back into that water and drown, that I'll wake back up?"

He closed his eyes. "No."

"I know I said I wouldn't try and talk you out of it, and I'm sorry, but... no, please, just listen. You don't have to go."

Kai started to ask what she meant, and then he saw the faraway look in her eyes, the way that her aura was flashing, switching from one shade to another so rapidly that he could barely keep track of the colors. He had seen this before, memories before death taking hold of a person so completely that they were their younger selves again for a moment.

"Minerva?" he said, snapping his fingers in front of her face, but her eyes remained unfocused.

Holding her hand, he knew this was his last chance. He could drag her back into the water, hope that a tail and gills developed so that he could get her back to the Sappho. She would get on wonderfully with Euphemia.

But she had asked for a guarantee, and he couldn't give that to her. Even if he could, it would be going against her wishes. She was at least lying still now, her expression peaceful. She wouldn't be granted that peace if he took her back into the ocean.

Then the embers of light faded, and this time they didn't rekindle. Kai squeezed her hand, praying that he'd made the right decision. Maybe the momentary panic would've been worth it, justified, to have her still be alive.

He couldn't bury her. He had nothing to dig with, no way to make a hole deep enough to keep her body away from predators. But knowing she had feared the water, dragging her out to sea seemed wrong.

Kai slid back into the water, gathering rock after rock up from the ocean floor, making dozens of trips, until her body was completely covered. It wouldn't last; he knew this. Eventually, through the tides or a storm, the water would claim its own. But at least this would delay it for a while.

He had set aside the driftwood she'd clung to, and now used one of the sharper stones he'd retrieved to carve into it. Though Euphemia and Wil had been trying to teach him how to read and spell in their language, he was far from an expert, and doubted he could spell the woman's full name correctly. But it began with an 'M', and that he did know how to carve.

Even with the marker for her name on it, her cairn looked barren, plain. Though he hadn't known Minerva long, he doubted she would approve.

He dove again, searching until he found a shell bigger than his fist. It was an opalescent silver-white on the outside, and what was visible of the inside was a sunset-toned orange that reminded him of the aura she'd displayed before it had begun flashing.

Kai set this on top of the board, staring at her cairn for several long moments before he turned and dove back into the water, swimming hard for *The Sappho*.

When he arrived, he didn't call up to them as he usually did, though he'd been intending to. He'd rehearsed everything he could possibly say, just a lighthearted "didn't find anyone tonight" and then he could let himself be distracted by Maddie's antics or one of Wil and Hope's spirited arguments. But no words would come, and the way Harry stilled as soon as he came into sight told him that everything wrong was showing his face.

"Kai?" She approached slowly, as one might a wild animal, keeping her eyes on his as she climbed into the landing craft. "What's the—"

He didn't let her finish the question, nor did he answer it; he simply hauled her into his arms, holding her tightly – too tightly, if her breathless squeak was any indication.

He knew he should let go, should apologize, should go back into the ocean until he'd managed to calm himself down. Instead he held on to her, his ear to her chest, the beat of her heart as rhythmic and steady as the waves on a beach. Kai closed his eyes, trying not to dwell on the sight of an aura flaring brightly for just an instant before disappearing altogether, trying not to dwell on how easily that could have been Harry and her crew, their lights extinguished in the midst of uncaring waters.

After a moment, her arms slowly went around him as well. She gave no platitudes, no reassurances – he hadn't expected them. She simply held him, anchored him, and finally the terror and anguish faded enough to allow him to let go.

Harry stayed where she was, one hand reaching out to hold his. A slight motion over her left shoulder drew his attention, and he realized half the crew was standing around the landing craft, looking worried. Maddie had bitten her lip so hard it had drawn blood, reminding him of the bloodstain at the corner of Minerva's mouth. He quickly looked away, focusing his attention on Harry's hand in his.

"Who was it?" Jo asked softly.

And he told them.

# ISABELLE

Isabelle grimaced as she chewed on a piece of seaweed and once again debated the merits of trying to catch a particularly slow-moving fish.

But even if she could catch it, how was she supposed to kill it? She was far enough away from the small island that the water rose well over her head; she couldn't hold the fish up into the open air. And she most certainly couldn't eat one raw. She would have to drag herself up onto the beach in order to try and start a fire – how, she had no idea – and that meant she could well be discovered.

In all the times she'd secretly wished to be a mermaid, she'd never once pictured this.

Biting her lip, she looked down at her tail. She didn't know what precisely had happened to the ship, whether a lightning strike had taken them down or whether a fire had started in the room that held the supply of gunpowder. All she knew was that the wall she had been leaning against had suddenly blown apart in a shower of light, and the pain in her legs as she'd plunged into the water had been indescribable.

The next thing she remembered was resting in the rocks and sand at the bottom of the ocean, and being able to breathe. She'd lain there in wonder, just breathing, before everything came rushing back and she'd sat up, intent on searching for other survivors.

Half of her body was dead weight.

She'd looked down at her tail, at the way it had formed into a bent, misshapen mess in a mimicry of the way her legs had broken in the shipwreck. It didn't hurt anymore, but neither could she truly swim. If she put all her energy into it, she could make it a couple of feet using the strength in her arms before her bottom half dragged her back down.

She'd pulled herself along as best she could, searching the wreckage that littered the ocean floor.

Bodies. All she found were bodies, trapped and pinned in the remnants of their ship. No humans-turned-merfolk searching for her, no survivors diving again and again in hopes of finding someone. Only her.

Cursing, she'd headed upward, intent on reaching the place where the sand disappeared above water before she realized that showing herself on land in this state was probably a horrible idea.

She knew what people did to merfolk. She had even witnessed it once. Wasn't that why she and Florence had formed the Society for Mermaid Safety in the first place?

Florence.

She might have survived. There had been bodies trapped in amidst the sunken wreckage, but none of them had been hers. Maybe she was on the shore, exhausted and resting, waiting.

But, as cowardly as she knew she was being, she couldn't make herself get out of the water.

She wasn't sure how long she'd been sitting

there among this patch of seaweed; only knew that her stomach was growling and her efforts to hold back panic were less and less successful with each passing minute.

Then she saw motion in the water—something much larger than a fish—and instinctively ducked down, the word 'shark' ringing through her head like a scream.

But it wasn't a shark, and she peered out amongst the seaweed, staring in awe. She and Florence and the other members of their society had spoken to four mermaids over the years, but they'd never been fully in the water with them. And seeing one dive into the water or swim lazily at the surface was nothing compared to seeing one fully in the ocean.

So mermen did exist, she thought. She and Florence had had an ongoing bet for the past six months; when they arrived at port they were to have a meeting with a group of mermaids who lived around the Cape and they'd intended to ask them...

Many people, her own mother included, had felt that creating the Society was a foolish mistake, trying to actually contact mermaids even more so. They'd told horror stories of drownings, both intentional and not; of slavers who drew innocent souls under the water to work their mines; of merfolk who hated humans and delighted in torturing them.

But she wasn't a human anymore, she reminded herself. She didn't have to worry about any of that.

She did, however, have to worry about

trespassing. Mermaids were extraordinarily territorial creatures, they'd discovered, and could grow quite violent with others of their kind. One of the mermaids Florence had spoken to had been missing an eye for precisely that reason.

Damnation, she thought. At least as a human woman, she'd had training in how to defend herself.

She edged further back into the seaweed, wondering what the odd glow was around the merman. She'd never seen it around mermaids, was it something only the males of their species had? Or was it something she could only see now that she was one of the merfolk herself?

If that was the case, then was she herself sending out a beacon of light?

The thought had scarcely occurred to her when the merman focused directly on her hiding spot.

She scrambled backwards, dragging her useless tail along and letting out a stream of curses that her mother would've fainted at. Seeing her panicked motion, the merman stopped approaching.

"My name is Kaimana," he said. "Yours?"

"Isabelle," she answered, her hand slowly closing around a good-sized rock. The fact that he wasn't moving any closer was somewhat reassuring, but she wasn't taking chances. She couldn't kick, couldn't run, and couldn't swim. That left punching, throwing things, scratching...

Florence would be asking her what the hell she was thinking. If her friend would've even remembered her existence at this point.

In the first place, he proved the reality of something they'd never seen before, so Florence's inborn caution — of which she didn't have much — would've been easily overwhelmed by curiosity. And in the second place, she'd been blissfully free with her affections, with someone waiting for her in every port — usually tall men with black hair. If she were here, Isabelle would've teased her about having a type, and Florence would've rolled her eyes at her, grinning before she swam straight up to him, an excited chirp in her voice as she asked a thousand questions.

Florence had always been the one to take risks, to trust quickly, and it broke her heart that such a spirit could be gone in one awful moment.

"Were you on the ship that burned two nights ago?"

"Y... yes," she stammered, coming back to herself. "*The Chastity.*"

"I sail with *The Sappho*," he told her. "I saw the fire and came to look for survivors."

The fact that he wasn't saying, "I found dozens; they're taking shelter on that island" unsettled her, and she quickly latched onto his first sentence. "*The Sappho*? I heard that was a ghost ship."

He smiled. "They're as real as you and I, and a more goodhearted crew you won't find."

She thought of *The Chastity*'s crew, and her throat grew tight. "Have you found anyone other me?"

"Yes," he said, his own expression growing somber. "Her name was Minerva."

"Miss Harper?" His phrasing sank into her mind. Her name *was*. "She... is she..."

"I'm afraid so."

"She's wonderful," Isabelle said. "She was... she was going to see her son. Oh, God. He won't know. It was a surprise. He didn't know she was coming."

"Do you know his name?"

"Yes. Samuel."

"We can ask Harry to make a detour to where you would have docked. Her boy deserves to hear such news in person."

"We?" she asked quietly.

"Well, yes," he said, as if this was obvious. "Surely you do not wish to stay here by yourself?"

And she didn't. At home, she'd always had her parents and siblings; she'd loved the noisy markets back home and their Society had been a constant blend of conversation and laughter and questions. Privacy was almost unheard of on the ships she'd traveled on, including *The Chastity*. Every day of her life, there'd been the bustle of people, the joy of company. Solitude was something she loathed.

"I..." She scrambled for some way to delay the answer that she knew she'd have to give. "Why are you glowing? Am I?"

"Yes," he said. "They're called auras. A life-light, that can give merfolk information about who we're speaking with."

"I can't see mine."

"We can't see our own."

"How do you tell what they say?"

"It takes years of practice," he said. "Colors are the major component, but there's also the way the light plays through them, the brightness, the—"

"Okay, okay," she said, scrutinizing him closely. His aura was ocean-blue, bright as the sunlight through water in some places and in others melding with the deep blue-black of the inlet where she rested. It was a calming, gentle color, but the ocean could be terrifying, too; how well did she know that now?

"All right," she finally said. "Unfortunately, I'll need some help," she told him, looking ruefully down at her tail.

"I've never seen such a thing," he said as he moved to her side.

"My legs — I think my legs were broken in the wreck."

"We'll figure something out," he promised, but she didn't take his hand.

"I'm honestly not sure I should go to a ship," she admitted. "What good can I do like this? I would simply be a mouth to feed, a drain on—"

"You would not," he said firmly. "In fact, once you've recovered, perhaps you can come out with me the next time a ship finds danger."

"Me? Why?"

"I fear I am too intimidating to do as much good as I'd like. I do not wish to frighten anyone, but..."

She shook her head, trying to put a reassuring smile on her face as she belatedly remembered to let go of her rock. Now that she was fairly certain he meant no harm, her initial panic seemed silly.

He smiled back. "A few moments ago you nearly tried to bury yourself in the sand. And poor Junia would have led me on a merry chase had she not already been exhausted. Perhaps I wouldn't cause such a fright with you by my side."

"I'd be glad to help," she said. "But first, I have to relearn how to swim..."

# IN THE FIRELIGHT

Kai grinned as Isabelle slid down the beach toward him, shrieking with laughter as she tested out the runners on the new wheelchair that had been built for her.

"Izzy!" Wil shouted, lowering her half-full bottle of rum from her mouth. "It doesn't work in the water, remember?"

Isabelle made an exceptionally rude gesture at her, but she made it too wildly and overbalanced, upending herself into the sand with a whoop of laughter. She rolled to a stop a few feet away from Kai, pushing her now sand-caked hair out of her face as Agnessa and Katherine strolled over to upright the wheelchair again.

They were two of very small number on the beach who could still walk a reliably straight line. The weather had been much calmer than the last time they'd pulled into port here, but it had still been a tense journey, and between that and the map they'd just gotten hold of, by the time they reached the shore everyone was more than ready to relax and celebrate.

Harry and her crew had built up an enormous fire on the beach, which warmed him even at the distance he sat from it. Isabelle squinted as she looked to the flames, and then she scooted down into the shallow water beside him, grinning as she watched the crew busy themselves with drinking and telling wild stories. Then her eyes widened as Miss Euphemia picked up a fiddle and began to play with such vigor and speed that Kai was half-certain that her bow would set the fiddle aflame.

"She never mentioned she could play the fiddle!" Isabelle said.

"I'm coming to believe that Miss Euphemia is an expert at everything," Kai said. "She's just too modest to tell us about it."

Zora and Maddie danced and whirled around the fire, holding each other's hands as they spun. Katherine and Franky followed suit, joining their circle, and when Euphemia was done with her song, Katherine let out a roar of a laugh and pulled each of them in for a quick kiss one by one.

"Sorry, Maddie," Katherine said as she caught sight of the startled look on Maddie's face after she'd kissed Franky. "No harm meant."

"Of course not."

Kai watched Katherine curiously. The flame around her aura, that hint of attraction, stayed precisely the same whether she was speaking to Franky or Agnessa. "Is it common?" he asked. "For a human to feel lust toward both the females and males of their species?"

"Not common, that I know of," Isabelle said. "But it happens, yeah. You talking about Kath? Dunno if she likes both, at least seriously. She just kisses everybody. It's kinda her thing. Not shy."

"No," he said, grinning at the memory of how she'd removed her shirt without hesitation so he could give her a tattoo. "Not at all."

"And that's what that part of her light

means?" Isabelle asked. "It means she cares about someone?"

"In a way," Kai said. "There's a difference in the light between wanting to bed someone and caring for them. When the two combine, of course—"

"Just look at them," Isabelle said, sounding so dazed he doubted she'd heard a word he had said. "They're all as bright as the fire."

"That they are," Kai said, his gaze focused on Harry. Then Maddie passed in front of her, and he realized how she'd begun to worry at her lower lip with her teeth. He had thought nothing could affect any of them on this night, but clearly he'd been wrong. Franky flirted with other members of the crew frequently, and this never seemed to be a problem. Both he and Maddie seemed to recognize effortlessly that there was nothing serious in the offers, simply a more elaborate form of teasing.

But once in a while, when the women teased back, Maddie began chewing at her lower lip and didn't talk quite as loudly for a while.

He didn't fully understand it; simple words — or, sometimes even actions — didn't mean feelings for another weren't true.

Junia's unusual situation proved as much. She felt no desire for her late husband — on the rare occasions when she spoke of him, there hadn't been a flare of anything in her aura that signaled as much. Due to this, he had briefly assumed their relationship had been a marriage of convenience; but then he'd listened to the way her voice sounded instead of just watching her light. There may not have been desire there, but she had loved Landon deeply, and the grief lay over her aura like a cloak.

She came to him some nights, simply asking to be held. There was nothing in her request to make him think he was betraying Harry, or that she was betraying her slain mate — it was a harsh world, and he reminded her of the one she'd lost.

Though Franky was young, he had not been spared the world's cruelties. And so he gave most of his focus over to things that weren't cruel — laughter and good friends and a beautiful woman's smile. No harm was intended in his attention to the last, and most of the time Maddie obviously understood this, laughing along with him when he was given yet another teasing rejection.

"Maddie," he called, waving her over. It wasn't any of his business, truly, and he probably wouldn't talk it over with her now if he hadn't had several cups of the liquid that Harry had called "rum" and Jo had called "an extraordinarily bad idea". He could help; he was sure of it. Why in the world wouldn't he have done so before?

"You needn't worry about him," Kai confided, once Maddie had moved a little closer. "There's a light to him when he's with you that doesn't flare with anyone else."

Maddie smiled a little at that, her own aura flashing brighter, but his voice had apparently carried further than he'd intended, because Agnessa was staring at him with wide eyes.

"You can see things like that?" she asked him.

"Like what?" Jo asked.

"Who has feelings for who," Isabelle said. "Ohh, that would have been a useful skill to have when I was a girl."

"Kaiiii," Franky said, flopping down onto the sand next to him and slinging an arm around his shoulders. "You are my *best friend.*"

"You are to give him no information," Harry said, "upon pain of death."

"Awww, you're just saying that because you're sweet on me and don't want me to know," Franky said, turning to give Kai a hopeful look. "Right?"

"Her aura around you is far more maternal than sexual."

Franky clutched at his chest as though he'd just been stabbed, while Harry spluttered out a litany of offended words.

"How dare − I am in no way *maternal*, I will have you know−"

"Of course not," he said, smiling fondly up at her. "You merely take people in as casually and as wholeheartedly as others would wounded strays."

She blinked at him, struck silent, and then turned away. "I... I'm going to get some more rum from the ship."

There was an entire case of it sitting on the sand mere feet away, but even in his apparently-addled state he knew better than to mention that.

"Shouldn't you go after her?" Maddie asked worriedly, staring off after the captain who, in fact, was walking in the direction of the lagoon, not the beached landing craft.

"No," he said. "She's not upset, merely

surprised."

"And you can tell that? From her aura-thing?" Maddie asked, dropping down into the sand beside him, taking another swallow from her bottle.

He grinned. "No. Because if she had been upset they would be able to hear her three ports away."

Maddie snorted with laughter. "You're not wrong." Then the laughter faded as abruptly as it had appeared, and she looked at him with seriousness bordering on tears. "Need to ask you something. Franky, can you... can you go be over there?"

"Why?" he asked.

"'Cause I have to ask this but I don't know what the answer's gonna be and if it's bad you don't—"

"I firmly believe that nothing can be bad where you're concerned," Franky said, scooting over so that he was sitting behind her, wrapping his arms around his waist. She gave him a look that bordered on panic, and he leaned forward, resting his cheek against hers. "You sure?"

"Yeah."

"Okay." He got to his feet, moving just barely out of earshot.

Kai had heard Harry say that there were cuddly drunks, maudlin drunks, and mean drunks, but he didn't think any of those fit Maddie. She seemed to flit from one emotion to another as quickly as a minnow. Now, the panic she'd shown an instant before was entirely gone, and she looked at him with a mixture of fear and stubbornness, as if preparing for a physical blow.

"All right. I need you to tell me the truth."

"Of course."

"My life-light thing. Aura. Whatever you called it. I know it's yellow, you told me, but color is just that. Color. Some parts of the body turn yellow when a cut gets infected enough. I need to know. Am I *good*?"

He reached up to take her hand – he missed on the first try, apparently this "rum" made two of everybody appear after a while – and held it tightly. "You're beautiful, Maddie."

She grinned, tears falling, and he felt a quick jolt of confusion. That had been good news; why was she crying? He wasn't sure he would ever truly understand human behavior.

Then Franky was sitting back down in the sand next to Maddie, giving her a loud, smacking kiss on the cheek. "Everything okay?"

"Uh-huh."

"See? Of course it is. I keep saying I'm always right but none of you believe me..."

Then he and Maddie and Isabelle let out surprised squawks as the ocean, which until now had been content to lap gently at their feet, decided to splash up almost over their heads. Kai watched them, nonplussed and smiling, as they scrambled further up the beach closer to the fire.

Harry still wasn't back. She hadn't been upset when she'd left, true, but he clearly had surprised her, and perhaps not in a pleasant way.

Leaving the crew to their revelry, he slid back into the water and swam for the lagoon.

# A SONG WITHOUT WORDS

"Why do you always pull away from me, Harry?"

"I don't—"

"Yes. You do." He looked at her, unflinching. "You tell me you appreciate how honest we can be with each other. You tell me you trust me, because you know I would never lie to you or lead you astray. Yet in this we are never open. Every time I begin a conversation with this inevitable conclusion, you cut it off or stop talking. I have let you do this for weeks, because in my culture there are things the women control. I always defer, because this is what I was taught to do. But living among humans, I know that is not the only way to act."

"Kai, I don't know what you're talking about," Harry said, looking away. She shook her head and stood. "I should go and see—"

"You are attracted to me," he said bluntly, calmly. "Physically attracted. I know you are. We have kissed, we have touched, and I know you desire more. You cannot hide something like that from me. And I have hardly been hiding my own attraction to you. Yet you refuse to act fully upon it. Is it because of what I am?"

"No," Harry said sharply, reacting rather than thinking. She crossed her arms over her chest. "No, Kai. It's just been... confusing."

"Because you are human and I am not."

"Well, a little, but... I've never felt like this before," she confessed in a rush. A blush spread up her chest and neck until it burned her cheeks and she was unspeakably grateful that the rest of the crew was on the far end of the beach. Bad enough that Kai saw her so embarrassed, red as a schoolgirl and twice as awkward. "It's been so distracting. It's impossible for me to focus on other things when you're around, because I find myself concentrating instead on how close you are and the smell of your skin and how big your hands are... I'm having trouble sleeping, and my skin feels two sizes too small, and I constantly have to fight the urge to stare at you. It's, well, it's enough to drive a woman mad. I'm the captain," she finished just shy of a shout. "I can't be going to pieces over one of my crew!"

"This sounds very serious," Kai said solemnly.

"Yes, it is."

"We will have to do something about it."

"Yes, we will."

"Come swim with me."

She blinked at him, nonplussed. "I'm sorry?"

"Swim with me." He held out a hand. "Please, Harry. Do you trust me?"

"I trust you," she said hesitantly.

"Then oblige me."

Harry stared at him while her heart did its best to thrash its way free of her ribcage. The wild pounding in her ears — was that her own heart, or just the music of the waves crashing into the lagoon? He was looking at her so intently, as if she was the only thing in the world, and the water around his broad chest rippled and flashed in the bright moonlight like liquid silver. It was hypnotic: the combination of his dark eyes and the glinting light.

How could she resist? And he had always asked so little of her. To deny him such a simple request would be cruel...

She stepped to the edge of the rock. Reached for the buckle of her belt with fingers that had started to shiver. Why was she so nervous? She *knew* he had already seen her naked, before they even knew each other's names, and she had never been shy about her body. It was just a body, after all, basically the same as any other woman's. Unique only in its scars. How many times had she cast aside her clothes for comfort or practicality?

Yet in this moment she felt dizzy as she kicked aside her trousers and pulled the loose red shirt up over her head, because she recognized the significance of this disrobing: this was the first time she was doing it expressly for someone else, at their request.

The water was shockingly cold on her legs as she slipped off the rocky ledge, and her breath caught in her throat in a painful gasp. She let herself sink until she was fully submerged before bobbing back up, hair plastered to her face and teeth chattering.

"Before I left home," she said, as Kai drifted closer. "Jo's mother warned me to never swim with a mermaid, and that I was to make sure Jo was never tricked by one of their songs. She said even a kindly-disposed mermaid was liable to drown us, because they'd forget that humans weren't built the same way and might accidentally kill us in the midst of sporting. All these years, and I've never been tempted to test her warning."

"Until now," he said, close enough for her to touch.

"You're not a mermaid," she said quietly

"No, I am not." Close enough for her to feel his breath on her face

"What are you going to do?"

"What do you want me to do?"

Her mind was a chaotic mess of want — too many kinds to decide on just one. To touch and be touched. To feel his mouth here, and there, and here again. To know what it was like to have his arms wrapped around her, to bury her fingers in his hair, to truly understand the strength of his hands, the sensation of his full body against hers...

She was so used to giving orders. So accustomed to having them followed without question. And she knew she could say anything and he would obey readily, but that somehow didn't appeal to her. Every day she had so much control over him as a captain with her crewmate.

Right now she didn't want that power. She didn't want to be his superior because she had never felt less superior than she did now. No, she was unsure and confused and nervous and a dozen other things, and more than anything she wanted someone else to make a decision.

"Surprise me," she whispered, and the next breath she took was his as he pressed his mouth to hers.

Before, Harry had never understood the appeal of kissing. It looked awkward and a little grotesque, with both parties having to contend with lips, tongues, teeth, and noses. How was a kiss romantic or enjoyable? How did one person not accidentally bite the other, and when did one know when to breathe? And while everything was going on with the mouths what did you do with your hands?

Now? With Kai's right hand at her neck and his left arm around her waist? With his tongue sliding over hers and his chest hot against her bare breasts?

Now, she was starting to understand.

She held onto his shoulders and followed his silent instructions, tilting her head just so, dragging her teeth across his bottom lip, catching her breath when she could.

God, it felt good. Perhaps she should have tried this earlier – though something whispered that it wouldn't have been like this with anyone else. Without the frisson in her stomach every time a glance was exchanged, no chance she'd be this lightheaded and giddy. Yes, giddy. The infamous Captain Roberts reduced to a giggling girl by one merman with an infectious smile.

"I have wanted to do that to you for weeks," he said in a pleased rumble.

"Was it what you expected?"

"I did not expect – I merely hoped."

"Aren't you going to ask if I enjoyed it?"

"No need to. I know."

"I feel you have a rather unfair advantage

over me, with the auras and pheromones," she complained.

"I cannot help that my senses are more heightened than yours. Or that I have become so adept at reading your body." His hand trailed downwards, the pads of his fingers caressing her side until she shivered.

"From anyone else that would have sounded creepy," Harry warned.

"I do frighten you a little, don't I?" he asked quietly.

"Yes," she admitted.

"Why?"

"Because you have power over me. Everyone else in my life, I intentionally gave them that right when they earned it. But you? From the first, you had a sway over me. I didn't understand it — I still don't, to be perfectly frank."

"Humans do not have pair bonds? You have never met another person who felt like someone you had always known?"

"Well, Jo," admitted Harry. "But I literally *have* known her my entire life. I've never questioned it because it was always there."

"I believe that had you met later in life, it still would have been the same. You and she were born podmates; you have a connection in your souls. And I think it is the same for us."

"That sounds suspiciously mystical," she said.

"Perhaps. But you must admit," he kissed her again, very persuasively. "That our bodies are very comfortable together despite our differences."

Harry absolutely couldn't argue with him.

Not when he was touching her like that, not when his lips were doing positively arcane things across her chest. She was starting to lose track of her surroundings, beginning to forget that she was actually floating and not just metaphorically.

Was this a good idea? She was the captain, after all, and fraternization was usually a bad policy. It could go wrong and cause trouble – though it was hard to imagine things going wrong when everything felt so *right* at the moment.

And what if this just made the constant sense of distraction worse? Stories claimed that merfolk could bewitch sailors in a multitude of ways; perhaps she was literally becoming addicted to Kai. Maybe there was just something about him that was dangerous to her, something neither of them could control.

"Wait," she gasped. "Wait."

His hands immediately dropped away and she felt her heart flip. He would never touch her without her permission; he was fundamentally unable to ignore her wishes. With him, she would never have to worry about that. "What is it?" he asked, gauging her expression. "I am sorry—"

"No, don't be sorry," she said. "I've just never... It's overwhelming," she finished lamely, staring at his chest rather than meet his eyes.

"Then we shall be slow and careful," he said, pressing a kiss to her forehead. Even that chaste gesture made her skin flush and heart race.

She looked up and grinned her crooked grin. "Not *too* slow," she countered, pulling him closer again.

As a girl, listening to the stories in Jo's father's pub, Harry had puzzled over the appeal of mermaids in an academic fashion. Growing up as she had, she'd learned plenty about the ways of men and women by the time any of that should have meant something to her.

The way she looked at it, without the vital parts required for the act of coupling, the whole affair should be a non-issue. Even if a mermaid had a beautiful face, a lovely smile, and an enchanting song, what sailor would try to make love to her if all she had below the waist was a fishtail? The idea that men routinely drowned – either through their own stupidity or because the mermaids luring them in were wont to drag them under – in the pursuit of such romantic dalliances was incredible to her.

Then, when she'd set out to sea herself, she'd learned that there were all sorts of unusual ways people made love. Sometimes the bits she'd once considered required weren't involved at all. It was surprising and a bit boggling, listening to Zora and Tessa discuss it all one night during an especially bawdy evening in Bogo. When she'd left, she'd had an entirely newfound respect for wenches and the ways they earned their keep.

"Hold onto me," Kai said suddenly in her ear.

She wrapped her arms around his shoulders.

"Close your eyes and hold your breath."

The waterfall was incredibly loud this close; she pressed her cheek to his as they passed under it, the cascade of water almost bruising against her bare skin.

Unable to restrain her curiosity, she looked

around. The small, dim cave behind the fall was coated in pale green moss, the air inside much cooler and scented with some indefinable wild tang.

"Why are we—"

"Privacy," he said, kissing the side of her neck. "Do you ever find yourself listening to a music no one else can hear?"

It was becoming increasingly more difficult to concentrate on his words when his hands were sliding over her body like that. "Music in the wind? On the waves?"

"Yes. A song without words. A melody you feel in your very bones?"

"Yes! God, I mean, yes. Sometimes I – I can." Her back was pressed against the wall of the cave, the sharp edges of the rock cushioned by the soft moss.

"When I saw you, I knew. I could see it in the way you swam, how the water welcomed you. You have the sea in your blood. Humans usually can't hear its song, but you can."

"Here, right here," Harry said breathlessly, guiding his hand. She was incapable of getting her legs to cooperate any more, and surely would have sunk to the bottom if he wasn't bracing her so effortlessly. "Oh, God, Kai..."

"I have you," he promised, so warm and powerful against her.

"Yes, yes, you do."

He helped her hook her legs around his waist as he rubbed and swayed over her, whispering something, another language, something so musical no human could repeat it, and she felt as if she was melting and flying and drowning all at once. The green light of the cave, the rain-like patter of the waterfall, the hot weight of him against her, the scrape of his beard on her cheek, the delicious pressure of his fingers and tail, his inhuman voice in her ear: it all bled together in an overwhelming rush.

And afterwards, when she had time to reflect, she would swear that yes, she heard the song of the sea. She felt it as if it were an inextricable part of her, an impossible sixth sense that told her where the whales sang in the deepest trenches and how the light glistened on the backs of breaching sharks. In that moment, with Kai, she had a sense of the magnitude around her and how her single note fit into the wild symphony.

# PORTRAIT

"There's another reason why I can't go home," Alvar said one hot, placid afternoon. Agnessa was at the tiller, navigating the ship around a series of sandbars. He sat cross-legged behind her, his back against one of *The Sappho*'s three masts, a book opened over his knees.

"Oh?" she said, half her mind preoccupied by thoughts of Hugh and the things they had discussed the night before. Her lover was currently sitting in the landing craft at the other end of the boat, deep in conversation with Kai about the mythology of merfolk.

"Father wants me to marry. To start fathering children of my own, in order to carry on the family name."

"Yes," she agreed. "He's a traditionalist that way, and you *are* the heir."

"I can't do it," Alvar said quietly.

"Give in to Father's demands any more?"

"Marry a woman. Sire children."

The next sandbar was a safe distance away; she risked a quick glance over her shoulder. Alvar had begun to hunch over his knees, physically drawing in on himself. "Not because you don't want to," she said, "but because you *can't*."

"Yes."

"I've always suspected," she said. "But I didn't want to pry. I was hoping you'd tell me when you felt more comfortable about it."

"Well, here I am. Telling you."

"It doesn't matter to me, Alv. You're still you. You're still my brother. And I still love you. No one here will judge you if you choose to be open about it — the ship's called *The Sappho*, after all, and we've all sorts here."

They both fell silent. Agnessa turned her attention fully on the tricky maneuvering required to avoid beaching the ship. These sandbars hadn't been here last time they passed this way, and it was both puzzling and worrying. Had some immense creature created these to ensnare passing vessels? Did the earth really shift, as Wil claimed, and was this evidence of new islands growing? Surely something like that would take longer than a year to achieve. Or maybe black magic was involved, a curse upon this stretch of sea that would claim any too unwary or impure.

"I lost someone on the *Ilsa*," Alvar said suddenly, shattering the quiet. "His name was Sven."

Agnessa was torn — it was clear her brother was in turmoil and needed comfort from her. But she couldn't slacken her focus, not with the entire crew depending on her. She bit her lip with indecision, knowing either choice could prove disastrous.

"I'll man the wheel," Hugh said suddenly at her shoulder, having appeared as if summoned. "I'm not a bad hand at a tiller, never fear. I'll get us through."

"Thank you," she said earnestly, relinquishing her hold to his much larger hands and going to kneel beside her brother.

Poor Alvar — the marks of his ordeal were taking so long to fade. He was still gaunt in body and haggard in the face. She had cut his hair two weeks ago but it was still long enough to tangle in the wind. He refused to shave, and his beard had filled in to the point where, if he'd been wearing more ragged clothing, he would've looked like a typical castaway.

"Tell me about Sven," she said, taking one of his hands and chafing it between hers. During those long nights on the black beach she had sensed that there was something her twin had been holding in reserve, something he was unwilling to share. And ever since they had set sail, she could feel a deep pain festering in him, peeking out at one moment only to be ruthlessly suppressed the next. Surely this was its source.

"He was a botanist. So intelligent, so well-spoken. But he was also innocent, despite all of his education and traveling. When we realized we cared for one another, he was surprised that I found him desirable — and he was so handsome, Aggie. Long ginger hair and serious eyes; he looked like someone da Vinci might have painted."

"You became lovers?"

"Yes." He fixed anguished eyes on her. "In secret — we had to be so careful — because if the commander found out I could have been summarily discharged and Sven could have been expelled from the research party, left at the next port. That seems like such a small consequence, when most men would have to worry about their own crew turning against them. But it was nerve-wracking, and... I loved him so much," he said, tears spilling down his cheeks, the drops catching and glinting in his beard. "And he loved me. He told me he loved me, that he'd never been happier with anyone else. When the voyage was over, we were going to go away together. I was going to turn my back on Father just as you had. Sven had money, from his mother and his books, and we were going to find a place where we could live together and be happy. And then that damn plague—!"

"Oh, Alv, I'm so sorry," Agnessa murmured, holding him tightly as he sobbed.

"He was one of the first to die," he said after the full force of emotion had been spent. "And that is such a small consolation: that he went quickly. He didn't linger like some of the others, he didn't have to watch the entire group burn up. When he was gone, I didn't care any more if I got it. I didn't care. I just pointed the ship out to sea."

"And if you hadn't, you would be dead," she said, combing her fingers through his hair.

"I don't even have anything to remember him by," Alvar said. "None of his notes, no daguerreotypes – everything was left on the *Ilsa* when it burned. It all had to burn."

Agnessa mulled this over. "But you can describe him," she said.

"Yes, of course. But what does that matter?"

*~*~*

Silence listened to Agnessa's request with wide, unblinking eyes. They were in the cabin, which was shadowy and gloomy after the bright open air of the deck. Since the siren could no longer properly swim or fully submerge in water, she avoided the deck during the hottest, sunniest hours of the day; her skin dried out too quickly and the light reflecting off the waves hurt her eyes.

Eyes which glinted blood red in the dim cabin, when she tilted her head and peered avidly at Alvar. It took some effort not to shudder and draw back; a part of his brain knew that she was a predator, a threat, someone who might attack at any moment. It was hard to overcome that primal impulse to flee, try as he might to remind himself that this woman had saved his life when his organs were failing from dehydration.

*Silence is part of this crew,* he told himself sternly, straightening his back. *She means well. She cares for us. It isn't her fault that she can be so frightening to humans.*

"It would mean a lot to Alvar, Silence," Agnessa finished. "And to me."

The siren nodded. Went to Miss Euphemia's roll-top desk and selected a large pad of paper and a pen. Then she unexpectedly knelt beside Alvar's chair – pressed the tip of the pen to the paper – and stared expectantly up at him, huge eyes fixing on his with all of the hypnotic force of a cobra staring down a mongoose.

"He had a square face but a pointed chin," Alvar heard himself begin, voice echoing down a long tunnel. He was vaguely aware that he was talking, could almost hear distinct words, but it was all far, far away. He could only stare into Silence's eyes, eyes that never blinked, never moved from his, even as her hand skittered across the page over her knees, pen charting the familiar, well-loved, now-lost lines of Sven's face.

It was strange, but the longer he spoke to Silence, the easier it became. Words flowed from his mouth. The ache in his chest faded to a bearable sting. The great sense of loss was no longer clawing its way up his throat and threatening to choke him.

When he'd run out of things to say, he blinked. The room snapped back into focus and he became aware of a crick in his neck, how dry his mouth was, and that Silence's empty hand had reached out at some point and clasped his leg, not far above his ankle. The moment he realized this, she pulled it away in a clumsy, jerky motion.

The pen slipped from her fingers and rolled across the floor, stopping only when it struck the edge of a loose floorboard. She held out the pad, glancing away as if embarrassed.

Alvar took it gingerly with hands that shook only slightly. Because there was Sven, smiling out at him. Somehow, between his words and her pen, the man had appeared on the page as clearly and perfectly as if he had sat patiently for a professional daguerreotype.

It was so exact a likeness that Alvar began crying again — this time out of pure reaction rather than pain, because his heart didn't ache as badly as it had even minutes ago. He could look at this portrait and remember the warmth of the love without feeling the sting of the loss.

"It's perfect," he said through his tears to a

siren who seemed confused and taken aback by his violent display of emotion. "It's him. You did a beautiful job, Silence. You made magic here. Thank you so much."

She nodded again, flashed a hesitant, serrated smile, and retreated to the bed and the books Miss Euphemia had given her to study.

"We'll get Lizzie to make you a nice frame for it — or maybe keep an eye out for a really fancy one, in gold or silver," Agnessa suggested as they exited the cabin, the drawing pressed to Alvar's chest.

"Thank you," he said, wiping away tears with the heel of his hand. "Now that I've told others about him, it doesn't hurt as badly. Keeping him a secret — keeping *us* a secret — felt like I was still dying. He deserves to be remembered; he should be mourned openly."

"If you ever want to talk about him, I want to listen. I'd like to know more about this man who made you so happy. If he won your love, he must have been a great man indeed."

# THE SPINSTER
# AND THE PIRATE

From a very early age, Deborah knew her own mind.

She woke knowing what she wanted from the day. She ate only what she wanted to eat, read only what she wanted to read, went only where she wanted to go. She wore the clothes society dictated a woman of her means and standing should wear, yes, but even then she wore only what suited her tastes. Her dresses were of the finest silk and satin, in flamboyant colors and with daring necklines where other young ladies were demure and maidenly.

As a child, she was called "precocious", "insatiably curious", and "a handful". As she aged she became "opinionated", "headstrong", and "a bloody nuisance". And with each passing day she took more and more delight in defying expectations.

When she went to the breeder to select a new horse, she ignored the docile, tame little mares with the dainty, feathered fetlocks and instead chose the fire-eaten half-mad stallion with a propensity to buck wildly.

She paid no attention to the safe little books about polite women coming of age, finding a kind husband, mothering doe-eyed children, and leading quiet, peaceful lives – instead, she devoured novels of scandalous adventure, travelogues that spared none of the grimy details, and other hot-blooded volumes that would have given the average society miss an aneurysm.

And while other young women of the *ton* committed every waking moment and thought to the avid pursuit of an eligible (and rich) husband, Deborah Cavendish wasn't in the slightest hurry to secure a man.

Because – knowing her own mind as she did – Deborah had decided long ago that a husband would never satisfy her appetites.

No, what Deborah *truly* wanted was a partner. A cohort in crime. Someone to travel with; to share madcap adventures with. She wanted someone who would never demand – nor even ask – that she change a single particle of herself. Someone who could match her madcap pace and passion.

And, ideally, this partner would have fantastic breasts.

But Deborah knew such a thing would be frowned upon in her genteel, ordered, polite world. Ladies were supposed to marry Lords, or even Dukes. Women went to bed with men, and only after a ceremony in a crowded church, officiated by a pompous windbag in expensive drapes.

That was the natural order of things.

That was the way of the world.

This was extremely frustrating, and would be cause for great concern in most, who might understandably suffer sizable amounts of angst regarding hiding their true nature – and who might lament that they would be forever unable to express love in a public fashion.

Deborah, however, was not like most ladies, even amongst "singular" ladies, and carried on in spite of this. At the age of twenty-five, she merely resigned herself to the life of a spinster – which didn't feel like a poor second choice in any way, shape, or form.

As a spinster, after all, she would remain her own mistress. No one would have the right to give her orders or make demands on her time; as a lady of wealth, independent of a man's clutches, she could spend her riches however she wanted, keep her own hours, and travel to her heart's content.

Hardly an unfortunate or unhappy life. In fact, it suited her right down to the ground.

So this was Lady Deborah Cavendish: a figure of much gossip and whispered intrigues; a constant target for kidnap and ransom; a pariah of polite society by personal choice; a passionate spinster and world traveler; a would-be adventuress always eager for the next horizon.

And, above all else, a woman who *has* always and *will* always do exactly as she pleases.

*~*~*

It took her roughly four hours aboard *The Sappho* – and oh, how she had reveled in that fortuitous name; clearly this was a good omen – to make up her mind on several counts.

*Firstly*: these pirates were nothing like the pirates she had encountered before, and if more pirates were like this lot, she would have let herself be shanghaied long ago.

*Secondly*: the life of a pirate was vastly superior to life in London, if only because it did not require corsets or three layers of petticoats.

*Thirdly*: that Katherine struck her quite forcefully as a lady worth knowing.

"...and this is the cargo hold," Katherine was saying, having usurped Maddie's usual role as tour guide. "Not a lot to look at right now, since we're sort of in-between hauls at the moment. This space is mostly used by Lizzie and Marcella, our blacksmith and seamstress. When they're working on one of their projects. And that's basically it," she said in closing, making a sweeping gesture with her arms that took in not only the work table bolted to the floor and various tools hanging from the walls, but the entire ship. "All that's worth seeing on the good ship *Sappho*. We could go see what Wil's cooking in the galley now, if you're hungry."

"Oh, I am hungry. But I doubt she'll have anything that would satisfy my current craving. I'd be more than happy to stay here for a while longer..."

Katherine gave her a look. It was an amused, appraising look. It was a look that said, *I know exactly what you're doing, because it's exactly what I'd do in your place.* It was a look that said, *I'm definitely not saying no, but you might have to convince me a little more.*

It was the look of someone who was unused to a so-called nob being so forthright.

"I'd like to see the rest of your tattoos," Deborah said, all innocence.

"I've only just met you, Lady Cavendish," said Katherine thoughtfully. "Usually I only show off my ink to friends. Good friends."

"I would like us to be good friends," she said. "More than that, actually. You know, you're the most striking woman I've ever met."

"And how do I strike you?"

"As someone who could teach me a lot of things. I've always been a glutton for education — it's part of the reason why I travel."

"I'd be happy to teach you anything I know," Katherine said blithely. "But you *have* had an unexpected day, what with the kidnapping and all — perhaps you'd rather settle in first, find your bearings, get a good night's sleep under your belt?"

"I'm not wearing a belt," Deborah countered. "And I thrive on excitement. In fact, I'm insatiable when it comes to excitement — one can never have too much of it. Now, Katherine. Are you going to continue undressing me with your eyes, or are you actually going to follow through on those promising glances?"

"You don't like to dance around the bush, do you?"

"Why bother? We're allotted a finite amount of time on this planet. I believe in speaking plainly and acting without hesitation. Enjoying life as thoroughly as possible. If there's one thing I cannot abide it is tedium, and I was up to my neck in that on the *Williamson*. I'm counting on *The Sappho* to satisfy my need for excitement."

"I can promise you excitement here," Katherine said. "Of all sorts."

"Wonderful. Why don't you start delivering on that promise now?"

"You like to order people around, don't you?"

"I'm an aristocrat. It's what we do."

"Well, I'm not an aristocrat. I'm the illegitimate daughter of a wench, and an avowed pirate. Are you so sure you want to tussle with a low-born peasant and criminal?"

Her tone was light; there was no malice or anger behind her words. But it was also clear – in the set of her shoulders, in the serious lines of her face – that it was an earnest question. Katherine was making it clear that she had no interest in indulging a toff who had an inclination to "go slumming" for the novelty of the experience. She wouldn't let a titled Lady get away with treating her badly just because of their disparate classes. She was most definitely attracted to her – her body language was screaming her interest quite loudly – but she would refuse to indulge that attraction if she suspected she would be made a fool in the process.

"Most people look at me and see the title, the money," Deborah said by way of answer. "They don't see *me*. Back home, I'm a chess piece in a game played by old society dames who cultivate bloodlines the way breeders produce champion racehorses. I'm a walking chest of money to the men eager for a quick payday. I'm my father's daughter but never a mind in my own right. And because of all of that, I'm constantly running away to sea where I can be something more, something different, something free. My own woman. Free to learn whatever I want about life. And right now I want to learn all about you."

"...How attached are you to that corset?"

"How do you mean?"

Katherine stepped closer. Reached out and began calmly unbuttoning the front of Deborah's dress until the tight laces of the corset beneath were revealed.

"I ask," the much taller woman said conversationally, "because I don't have the patience to untie laces like these. Much easier to just cut through them." A small knife was suddenly in her hand, and there was a smile on her face that was positively wolfish.

Deborah found she was having difficulty swallowing. "I can always buy new laces," she said, hoping her voice didn't sound as shaky as it felt in her throat.

The sharp edge of the knife made a whispering *shhh* as it sliced cleanly through the white ribbon laces; then the blade had disappeared back into a pocket and Katherine was pushing the sleeves of the satin dress off her shoulders while the mangled corset slid to the floor.

"Have you ever done this?" Katherine asked next as she brushed Deborah's long dark curls away from her pale neck, continuing in the same even, casual tone. It was a reassuring voice, very matter of fact, and Deborah felt her painfully thrumming heart begin to steady under its influence. "Been with a woman?"

"No," Deborah confessed. "I've never been with anyone. Never had the opportunity."

"But you've wanted to?"

"Oh, yes. Very much so."

"I'll try to make this worth the wait, then."

Katherine bent her head and caught Deborah's waiting lips with hers. The pirate's large hands slid down from her firm shoulders and across her chest, cupping and kneading and caressing her full breasts.

Deborah shivered, a violent full-bodied tremor, and reached up to put her arms around the bended neck. She stood on her tip-toes and balled fistfuls of Katherine's shirt in her hands as their tongues slipped over lips and rubbed against teeth. Her nipples were painfully hard in the cool air of the hold, beneath Katherine's knowing touch, and she felt feverish all over, skin too tight and hot and pricking with sweat.

"How does that feel?" Katherine asked, pulling back momentarily.

"Marvelous," Deborah replied ardently.

"If I do anything you're not comfortable with, anything you don't enjoy, tell me and I will stop," she promised.

"You're wearing too many clothes," was her response. "I said I wanted to see your tattoos — show me all of them."

Katherine readily complied, casting off her loose shirt and unbuckling her breeches. It took both of them to unfasten Deborah's petticoats and skirts and they were laughing by the time they puddled around her feet.

"Damn to the depths whoever decided women's clothing should have so many buttons and buckles and ties," Katherine said with feeling, before scooping Deborah up without a sign of strain and setting her down on the edge of the long work table. "Lie back," she told her with a grin and an arched eyebrow.

Deborah obeyed, breathless again as Katherine threaded the fingers of her hand through one of hers and placed the other on her knee, kneeling before her.

She had always suspected the things female lovers did together – through extensive experimentation she knew what to do to pleasure herself, and she knew the principles involved to stimulate another with the same type of body.

But understanding a concept and experiencing it in action were two entirely different matters.

As Katherine's tongue licked and rolled, Deborah clenched at the hand she held. She bit the edge of her bottom lip. She stared up at the dim ceiling of the hold, then closed her eyes and discovered the sensations became sharper, more exquisite without sight to distract her.

She found she could only breathe in short, labored gasps – then only by panting. There was an almost frightening pressure building beneath her stomach, a tightening knot of fire.

"Please," Deborah heard herself beg. Katherine's movements had slowed, almost stopped completely, and she felt as though she'd go mad if she didn't quicken her pace. Her ragged request spurred her lover onto greater heights, fast and brutal and unrelenting.

Then, just when it became too much and the pleasure began to verge on pain, the muscles in her legs and back seized, spasmed, and abruptly relaxed as the knot exploded in a dizzying, overwhelming rush of ecstasy.

"Oh, oh Lord," Deborah whispered, rolling her head to the side. She was shivering uncontrollably beneath the aftershocks. Sweat had pooled in the hollow of her throat and was cooling rapidly, heightening the illusion that she had a newly-broken fever.

She had never felt quite so giddy or unhinged.

Katherine straightened. Pulled herself up onto the table. Straddled the shaking hips and lowered her body over Deborah's, until her tattooed breasts pressed firmly against her flushed, paler chest, pert nipple brushing over nipple.

"How was that?" Katherine asked, voice husky, mouth hovering above her ear.

"Unbelievable," Deborah replied, putting her arms around her and turning her head to meet the playful eyes and kiss the smiling lips. "I thought," she said between kisses, savoring the strength of the body draped over her, "I was content to be a spinster. Content," here she lost herself for a minute in the skillful manipulations of Katherine's tongue, "to never know physical love of the kind I craved. I thought," and she dared to slip a hand between the long legs, to plunge fingers into the curled blonde hair and wet skin she found there, to stroke Katherine's center in a way that made the pirate's breath hitch audibly, "I could be happy with the pure aesthetics of travel. Seeing new places and people," Katherine gently bit her shoulder, making her gasp, "learning of strange cultures and languages. I thought that would be enough."

"And now?" Katherine asked, eyes glazed and lips bruised.

"After you? Everything else will seem weak tea indeed."

They rocked together. Fingers pressed against soft, yielding buttons. Pale hair mingled with dark. Sweat-slicked skin slipped and glided. Two voices called out as one.

"And to think," Katherine said later, when they were dressing. "This morning you were on a boring ship full of boring men."

"Fortunes can change in the space between hairpins," Deborah said, finding several of the aggravating things strewn about floor and table. She seized one and thrust it into her limp, damp curls at random, fully aware that she looked like what she was: a woman who had been thoroughly ravished to within an inch of her life.

"Don't bother with those, love," Katherine said, putting her hands in her hair and kissing her again very firmly. "They'll never stay put long enough to be useful, anyway. Not while I'm here."

# A FORBIDDEN GIFT

How could something feel both right and completely wrong?

In the weeks since the reunion with Agnessa and the rescue from his blighted ship, Alvar had found it difficult to step out of the shadows and back into the light. The loss of Sven, of his whole crew, weighed so heavily upon him. Such an experience was not one that could be easily shaken off.

And then there was the profound and very familiar shame that had been dormant for months, only to burst back into full flames: shame that he had never been as strong as his sister.

Agnessa had always refused to blindly submit to Father's orders. She had dared his displeasure, defied all polite society, and run away to sea rather than accept the unacceptable. She had been true to herself no matter what it cost her, willing to toil and endure all manner of distasteful things, because she had a core of steel, of granite.

And Alvar? Was all jelly and no spine.

When he should have raised his voice, he whispered. When he should have stood firm, he stepped back. And when he should have accepted who and what he was, when he should have been proud of his feeling, passionate heart, he hid it all beneath bland smiles and obedience.

The only time he had ever been truly brave had been with Sven. For the first time in his life he had embraced his nature and dared to love another man, and had been well loved in return. It had been impossibly freeing, for all that they had been forced to keep their love secret. Just being together had been enough, even with all of the subterfuge and snatched moments.

Now, with the portrait of Sven that Silence had drawn hanging on the wall of his compact bunk as a talisman of comfort; with all of his secrets bared to a sister who understood and accepted; and with all of the pain and horror receding further into the past, Alvar was trying to reclaim his sense of self.

Or perhaps he was trying to discover who he truly was now that he was no longer suffocated by Navy or father.

For the very first time, he could live without strict regulations. He could openly show his feelings and desires.

So why was it that his desires were now muddled and confusing?

All his life, he had found himself drawn to men. His most passionate dreams had involved large hands, muscled torsos, and... other pieces of anatomy. He enjoyed the rasp of a bearded chin when he was kissed and the heavy pressure of firm thighs against his.

Since puberty, such things had been exceedingly attractive to him – and on the flip side of the coin, he found himself completely uninterested in all things female. Women were too soft, too curved, too sweet scented. The idea of laying down with one thrilled him not at all; in fact, he was certain that he would be unable to perform with one, at least not in the way society expected. He might be able to touch a woman, perhaps even kiss her, but he would never be able to make love to her. That would require a stiffening of certain muscles that would refuse to cooperate unless properly aroused. And no woman had ever aroused him.

Until Marcella.

It happened so gradually he hardly noticed it. That first week on the black beach she came to sit with him every day to discuss their shared interest in music. She showed him how to play the pipes she carried with her at all times – rather like the panpipes of ancient Greece and carved from whalebone, she told him – and he in turn taught her how to coax a melody from a stringed instrument.

They discussed composers and their preferred styles. Debated the merits of classical training (him) versus being self-taught (her). She told him about the sirens and mermaids she had seen while sailing on *The Sappho* and described the unique sounds of each pod and tribe; some merfolk sounded like choirs of celestial angels, others like loud parrots, and some clicked and screeched like dolphins. She had a rich singing voice and an incredible range; she would often accompany him when he played by the fire after supper.

Little by little, he opened up to her – and she returned the favor. She told him of the chaotic, sprawling family she had left behind when she took up with Harry's crew, the dozens of aunts and uncles, the hundreds of cousins. He shared embarrassing anecdotes of his private school years: how he was frequently taunted by bullies and even more frequently sought solace in the quiet music classroom with an understanding, if ancient, professor. She showed him the piece of eight threaded on a leather cord that she wore around her neck at all times, a bit of luck her favorite uncle had given her as a child. He explained how his fear of heights had started after being chased up onto the roof of the naval academy by the other cadets, a prank that ended when he very nearly fell through the crenellations.

In a matter of weeks, Marcella had become an intrinsic part of his life. Yes, the entire crew was a part of his life now, too – but none of the others came close to approaching the importance she had unexpectedly gained. He would wake in the morning and one of his first thoughts would be about her: a question to ask her, an opinion to share, a thought to discuss.

They would sit together by the fire, at the trestle table in the galley, and share loaves of bread and glasses of ale. No matter what mood he was in or how the day was faring, his spirits would always lift at the sight of her. A thrill would shoot up his spine when she approached or flashed him a quicksilver smile. He became acutely intuitive of her thoughts, able to read the slightest expression on her face; he learned that her pointed chin would cant to the right when she was worried, and that her left eyebrow would arch up when surprised while the other remained fixed in place.

"You and Marcella are thick as thieves," Agnessa commented one cool night as they tacked eastward through a sharp wind. Both of them were at the helm that evening to keep *The Sappho* on her course as a gale brewed on the horizon. They were only a couple of hours away from Nalani and everyone was hoping to make landfall before the rain fell. "I'm glad."

"Because I've made myself a friend?" he said with a laugh. He'd always found it difficult to make friends; Agnessa had never had that trouble. Funny how that was, given that he was forever eager to please while she was obstinate and outspoken.

Perhaps it was more because he was afraid to fully trust people, with so much of his life a secret, and others could sense that reticence, while Agnessa didn't care what anyone thought and so was wholly unaffected, her sincerity and honesty drawing people in like moths to a flame.

"Yes, but I was thinking more that *she* finally has a friend," his sister replied to his surprise.

"She's been on the crew for years," he said, confused.

"Yes, and the rest of us have always been friendly to her," Agnessa explained. "And she's been friendly back — but none of us have ever truly been taken into her confidence the way you have. She and Zora are fond enough of one another, but they're not exactly close. And Lizzie, well, you know how welcoming Lizzie is. But even with her there's a distance, as if she's afraid of her. She and Jo understand one another, I think, because of their faith, but they're both so stoic. It's hard to tell if they share anything more than Sunday prayers. I tried to talk with her, the first few weeks I came aboard, and it was like trying to hold onto an eel. She was always slipping out of our conversations, finding something that she needed to do. She's an extremely private person — I know next to nothing about her beyond the fact that she's a Christian and plays the pipes."

"She's never spoken of her family? All of her mad aunts and uncles?" Alvar said. "Or how she's afraid of reptiles, even Tazu?"

Agnessa shook her head. "All news to me, brother."

He mulled that over. Clearly, Marcella had trusted him when she trusted very few people — that was a warming, giddy thought. She'd chosen to confide in him, to befriend him, when none of the others had managed to scratch beneath her surface; he had never been someone's first choice before. Unlike his father, she valued him as a person, as Alvar, rather than just as a necessary heir and banner upon which an entire family history would hang.

For a moment, he felt special.

He hadn't felt special since Sven.

And that was when it hit him: he was falling in love with Marcella.

But how had it happened? Surely, he couldn't be attracted to a woman — but no, that wasn't entirely true. He *was* attracted to her, he realized with a gulp. She had such arresting eyes, and thick black hair, and skin that was golden and smooth in the sun. As he mentally assessed her he felt his cheeks flush and his heartbeat quicken. There was an electrifying energy about her when she moved and the features of her face could be staggeringly beautiful in the right light, in the sway of her quicksilver moods. That pointed chin, the full bottom lip, the rounded cheeks – she was so youthful and vital and yet she could smile or laugh or frown and everything would sharpen to a razor's edge. Even the crescent scar high on her cheek was appealing, a reddened curve that would darken when she was angry and blanch when she was worried.

Alvar knew that some people felt attraction for both genders – he had heard Wil and Katherine in enough bars to know the truth of that – but never, not once, had he felt even the slightest of stirrings for a woman before. He didn't know how to handle this revelation.

In fact, he even wondered if there wasn't some external force causing this. Perhaps a bit of Hope's magic had gone awry, or one of the many blessings she'd given him over the weeks had had unforeseen side effects. Could it have anything to do with the healing Silence had done to save his life? Could the siren have unintentionally reworked some fundamental part of him?

He began to doubt his own feelings; they were so contrary to his past experiences. In his emotionally fraught state after the burning of *The Princess Ilsa*, had he latched onto Marcella in an unhealthy way? What if this love was only misplaced gratitude and friendship? After all, the loss of Sven was still fresh and sharp; he couldn't possibly be in love again, not truly, not so soon.

Because if he was, what did that say about his heart? That it was inconstant and weak. That he had never deeply loved Sven, not in the way he deserved.

With these heavy, dark thoughts to brood upon, Alvar hardly noticed the anchoring at Nalani and the clamor of the crew disembarking. He found himself jostled along in the general bustle, climbing out of a landing craft with no recollection of who else had been rowing beside him.

In the months since discovering this particular spot of paradise, *The Sappho*'s crew had done much to entrench themselves. There was now a tiny village of wooden huts on raised stilts dotting the beach, more permanent protection and far sturdier than tents, especially in a downpour. The watchtower had been ringed in a tall protective fence. Bamboo shoots were being cultivated at the edge of the tree-line, to provide cover and windbreakers for a small vegetable patch that flourished without any human assistance.

As the two-footed crew ran across the beach with their arms laden with supplies and heads bent against the whipping wind, a scaly delegation appeared to greet them. Tazu's people made a point of welcoming them every time they landed; Wil said they claimed it was a sign of respect, but she suspected they worried about one of their hatchlings and wanted to assure themselves he was still whole and able. The Chief ducked his head and flicked his back frill at Lizzie with a pleased burble – ever since she had carved a huge stone altar for his impressive pearl collection, she had earned herself an honorary position in the Clan, not to mention his undying respect.

"We will feast tomorrow," Wil promised the Clan as thunder crackled overhead. "A huge feast, with many stories."

"We shall begin preparations," the Chief agreed, before turning sharply and disappearing back into the trees. The other iguanas followed, glad they had done their duty and eager to reach their warm caves at the base of the volcano before the rain began to pour in earnest.

"Alv, are you okay?" Agnessa asked, catching his expression as everyone dispersed to their respective huts.

"Of course," he said, flashing a quick smile. "Stay dry. Good night."

He ducked quickly into his shelter as the sky opened with a roar. It would be a cold and solitary supper tonight. Some of the other huts had been polished enough that they had fire pits or tiny charcoal braziers to cook meat and boil water over, but his was a very simple, somewhat ramshackle affair, being more recently erected than the others. He hadn't had the time yet to add creature comforts beyond a roof, floor, door, and four walls, so he would just make do with day-old biscuits, an apple and carrot, and some dried beef.

As he chewed on the apple, he considered lighting a candle end and reading for an hour or two. But he was tired from the day's journey and didn't want to risk falling asleep beside a lit candle – with his luck, the hut would catch fire. So he made himself comfortable on his thin pallet of blankets and took up his violin.

It was an old, battered instrument he had rescued from a market weeks ago. With Miss Euphemia's help, he had restrung and tuned the strings, but it still had a plaintive whine that was more suited to folk music than classical compositions.

But that mattered little to him: it was music. He could coax sincere emotion out between bow and strings. And he could play in the dark, without a candle or audience.

He knew that he was one of the few alone right now; Agnessa had Hugh to keep her warm, Maddie had Franky, Deborah and Katherine would be very warm indeed, and Lizzie and Zora shared a hut – though not a bed – so they at least had companionable conversation to fill the evening. Harry had a little nook on the edge of the lagoon where she could sleep close to Kai (and Isabelle); Miss Euphemia was no doubt continuing Silence's lessons, tempest be damned; and Wil had Tazu and her books for company.

All he had was a violin and his thoughts, and the latter was very poor company indeed. He was caught in a spiral, constantly circling the same point, going nowhere while he exhausted himself. He tried to break free, tried to focus wholly on the melody he cut from the strings beneath his chin, but he found he could not abandon himself wholly to his playing as he so often had in the past.

When the knock rattled the very hinges of the door, he was almost relieved. Anyone would be a better distraction right now. "Come in," he shouted over the drumming of the rain and the crashing of thunder overhead.

The door swung open, revealing a cloaked figure momentarily silhouetted by a flash of lightning, and then banged closed. The darkness filled with the sound of heavy breathing; whoever it was had made a mad dash through the storm. "Agnessa?" he asked, unsure.

A match flared with a sharp pop and hiss and was pressed to a candle. By the flickering light it was obvious that it wasn't his sister.

"Is it alright if I sleep here tonight?" Marcella asked, pushing back the hooded waterproofed cape she was wearing. "There's a huge crack in the roof of my hut and the whole floor is already inch-deep in water."

Alvar forced himself to swallow despite his dry mouth. "I've only two blankets," he managed to say in a deceptively steady voice.

"We can share," Marcella said blithely. "We're both of us scrawny enough. What were you playing just now? I heard a snatch of it over the storm before I knocked."

"I don't know what it's called," he said. "I picked it up in Cameroon. When I heard it, it was played with drums and pipes. I've been trying to fine-tune it for the violin for months."

"Play a little of it and I'll try to join in," she said eagerly, pulling out her panpipes.

He started from the beginning and was halfway through when she began to accompany him, an octave higher and in a counterpoint that made the music feel wilder and untamed. It was what had been missing. A second voice to carry the raw energy.

The musicians who had played it in Douala had been part of a welcoming committee when the *Ilsa* had docked for minor repairs; the language barrier had prevented either group from being eloquent, but the music had spoken volumes. This was a song about unfettered joy and excitement; perhaps it was played at weddings or feasts, to chase away evil spirits and bad energy. With Marcella's accompaniment, Alvar could feel the rhythm work its way into his bones. He wanted to get up, to move, to do something worthy of such an ecstatic beat.

"Did you feel that?" Marcella asked, breathless, when he stilled his strings abruptly. "It was like I could feel the drumbeat in my chest. Was that a ceremonial song?"

"I don't know," he said shortly, setting aside his bow and looking away from her face. She was too bright in the candlelight, her eyes glittering and smile crooked. The effort of playing had darkened her cheeks and lips a ruddy red. Wet tendrils of ink-black hair clung to her forehead.

"Alvar? Is something wrong?"

"No, I'm just tired," he said. He could hear the frown in her voice but refused to look up and meet her gaze. "I was actually about to go to bed when you knocked. It's been a long day."

"Yes, but it'll be a long night, too," she pointed out as another clap of thunder made the hut shiver around them. "I don't think any of us will be getting much sleep."

"I still intend to try," he said, for lack of a better excuse. "Here's your blanket."

"Alvar, what is it?"

"Nothing. I'm fine."

"Something's bothering you," she said with firm assurance. "Your voice is too brittle. And you've got that crease in your brow that you always get when you're upset. I can go bunk with Junia if you'd rather be alone—"

"I'd rather not be confused!" he said loudly. He looked up, caught a glimpse of the surprise on her face, and closed his eyes tightly. Pinched the bridge of his nose and took a deep breath.

"I don't understand it. I've always known what I wanted, even though I rarely tried to have it. I was never brave enough to pursue it, but at least I knew. And now you... You've got me so confused, Marcella."

"What have I done?" she asked.

"Nothing you need to apologize for," he said quietly. "I'm sorry, I'm making it sound like you've done something wrong, like this is your fault, and it's not. This is my problem."

"Alvar, if I've done something to make you uncomfortable, if I've overstepped a boundary, please tell me. I like you too much to cause you pain."

"And I love you," he said before he could stop himself. "That's the crux of it. I realized today that I'm in love with you."

After a long moment had passed without a response, he finally looked up from the floor. A wine-dark blush had suffused her neck and cheeks. There was a strange light in her eyes – they seemed to gleam silver in the uncertain candlelight, like a shadowed mirror in a dark room. Her lips parted and a soft sigh escaped her.

"You love me?"

He nodded, dizzy. "But I... I... Marcella, I don't love women. I never have. I'm an invert. Do you see why I'm so confused? It was only a handful of years ago that I finally came to terms with what I am, when I finally decided I wasn't unnatural or broken, just different. And now I meet you and I don't know what happened, I don't know why I'm suddenly feeling like this–"

"Is that it?" she said, eyebrow arching. "You're upset because I'm a woman?"

"Well, yes," he said softly. "I'm sorry, I know it sounds mad."

"But that's no obstacle at all, Alvar!" She laughed, reaching out to lay a hand over his. "Just this morning, I decided I was going to tell you the full truth about myself. About how I joined the crew and why. In fact, I came here tonight to tell you everything."

"Then your hut isn't flooded?"

"Yes, actually, it is, but that's besides the point."

"What do you mean 'the full truth'?" he added quickly. The strangest thrill of hope was creeping through his veins; but what the hope was for, he had no idea.

"The truth is that I'm not a human woman," she said, eyes boring into his. "I'm Fae, one of the elfkind. And I haven't always looked like this."

The candlelight flickered, threatening to go out completely, and in the fluttering of shadows there was a strange shift in the air, a sense of space expanding and contracting, and suddenly the face staring at Alvar was different.

Marcella was gone. In her place was a masculine face and fuller body. The same eyes smiled at him, but the jaw was wider and the hand against his was bigger, heavier.

Alvar felt his mouth sag open and couldn't stop blinking.

"This is what I used to look like," a slightly deeper voice said. "Back when I was called Marcel."

"I don't — but why?" Alvar spluttered.

"*The Sappho* came to my family's island to make substantial repairs after a rock gouged the hull," Marcel began. "I watched them every day and came to like them from afar. I was feeling stifled with my family; I wanted desperately to strike out on my own, to have my own adventures away from their prying eyes and interfering affections. I decided *The Sappho* would be my escape. But in my observations, I noticed that the entire crew was female. I decided that must be a requirement, so when I revealed myself and asked to sign on, I cast a glamour over myself. I became Marcella."

"So for all of these years, you've been pretending to be something you're not?"

"Well, not exactly," he said slowly. "I forget that you humans tend to see things as either/or... I'm Marcel *and* Marcella. Male and female. And sometimes I'm neither. I just *am*."

"And you've never told the others?"

"No. At first, I didn't tell them out of fear: I worried they would maroon me, or even attack me. Humans and Fae haven't always gotten along. Then I came to know them and learned they were more open-minded than some, but by then I'd been keeping my secrets for so long that I was afraid revealing them would hurt everyone's feelings. Not knowing wasn't hurting anyone. So I just kept quiet."

"But you wanted to tell me."

"Because not telling you was keeping me awake at night. I felt like you needed to know — when I've never felt that way about anyone else. I knew I could trust you. And hearing you tonight, seeing how bewildered you've been feeling, I knew the truth had to come out, for your sake."

Alvar's head was spinning. So many things suddenly made sense. The way Marcella had always shied away from cold iron, the cannons, Lizzie when she was working with her tools. Her love of and skill for music. Her unearthly singing voice and boundless energy. His confusing attraction for her — no, *him*.

If Marcella had been surprisingly arousing, Marcel was a revelation. He could feel heat flooding his cheeks and knew he would have to shift soon before the positioning of his trousers became too painfully tight.

"You should tell the others," Alvar said finally, when he felt he had a grip on solid ground once more. "I know what it's like, hiding what you really are. It can eat away at you. It can do things to your state of mind."

"I'll tell them tomorrow," Marcel promised.

"Do you, which do you prefer?" he asked hesitantly. "Marcel or Marcella?"

"It depends on the day," he said with a shrug and small smile. "But with you? Marcel. Definitely Marcel."

"Oh, that's wonderful," Alvar said fervently, grabbing handfuls of his wet cloak and pulling him close.

Marcel's lips tasted like copper, a cool metallic tang over the wet heat of his tongue. Knowing what he was explained the shocking sizzle, like static electricity, that passed between them. It was as if the Fae were living batteries; perhaps they absorbed energy around them in order to cast their glamours, perhaps there was something about cold iron that disrupted that energy and that was the cause of their aversion. Alvar didn't waste much thought on such musings then, though, too absorbed in experiencing the flow of energy between their bodies.

When he pushed the wet cloak off his shoulders and tugged the loose shirt over his head, Alvar discovered that the zing he felt in a kiss was nothing compared to drawing his hands over Marcel's bared chest. The skin, the slight scattering of dark hair that he caressed, was so hot that the palms of his hands tingled.

"I don't know if I've mentioned it before, but I love your beard," Marcel said, voice low and husky as he unbuttoned Alvar's shirt, then unbuckled his belt. "The way your hair curls. The color of your eyes. And your hands... I've been dreaming about your fingers, and I've never thought of fingers as particularly desirable before. But the way you hold that violin..."

Alvar buried said fingers into Marcel's thick black hair, brushing against his ears. And yes, they were a little pointed, weren't they? How had no one else noticed the signs before?

But perhaps Marcel had completely dropped the glamour now; perhaps this was the first time anyone had seen what he – she, they – really was, all of the otherworldly details.

"Wait," Marcel said, pulling back. He ran his tongue over his bottom lip; it was swollen and bruised by the edges of Alvar's teeth. "You're sure about this, aren't you? You're not worried I put a spell on you?"

Alvar blinked at him. "You haven't, have you?"

"I don't like to use my magic on anyone but myself," Marcel promised, leaning his forehead against his. "Yet another thing my family and I didn't see eye-to-eye on."

"I thought as much. Although..." Alvar hesitated. Struggled to draw in a shaky breath. "It's only been a couple months since..."

"You had a lover," Marcel said, enlightenment dawning abruptly. "On your ship."

Alvar nodded and his brow furrowed.

"What was his name?"

"Sven."

"Alvar, he wouldn't want you to mourn him forever. He would want you to be happy. To live your life. Don't feel guilty for doing that. I understand if you're not ready, but you shouldn't cling to a ghost forever."

"You don't think I've a fickle heart?"

"No, I don't. I think you've a very loving heart, if you found space in it for both me and Sven."

Alvar nodded and swallowed back the tears. Marcel was right: Sven would have wanted him to find someone else. He was dead and gone and nothing would ever bring him back. He wouldn't have demanded eternal fidelity to the memory of him. He wasn't going to hate him for loving again, for being happy.

When Marcel moved to kiss his cheek, Alvar surged forward and caught his lips with his. His momentum carried them both to the floor. Trousers were unbuttoned and kicked away, and Alvar learned that the Fae may be different from humans in many ways, but their bodies were still shaped the same in all of the important particulars.

"I've never been with a human," Marcel panted beneath him. "Is it always this... overwhelming?"

"I honestly don't know," Alvar confessed, stroking and squeezing in a way that made Marcel moan, sliding his fingers inside to stretch him in preparation. "But I can promise to try my best every time."

When Alvar thrust into Marcel, the Fae stifled his cry by biting down on his shoulder — hard. But instead of the expected flare of pain, a wave of euphoria crashed over him. It left him shivering as forcefully as the Fae beneath him; it took innumerable breathless minutes to regain his senses and remember the rhythm his body wished to sway with.

"Can you... can you hear it?" Marcel gasped. The sweat trickling down his neck smelled of sandalwood.

"Yes," Alvar groaned, dropping his forehead to his lover's chest before sharply pivoting his hips, drawing a hiss from Marcel as his back arched off the floor. "The song..."

He had known since that first meeting that they could make incredible music together. They always slipped so easily into tune... This was no different.

Save for one vital detail: Alvar now felt the melody through his entire body. This was music made physical; they had become the embodiment of their song. He was the bass to Marcel's alto and the crescendo was coming ever closer.

Their timing, as ever, was in perfect unison. When Alvar slumped bonelessly forward it was to fall straight into Marcel's waiting, shaky, arms.

"I feel scorched all over," Alvar mumbled.

"I enjoyed it, too," Marcel laughed weakly. "How can you hide all of that passion? Outwardly you're so quiet and calm, and underneath it all is this wild creature."

"I'm not an exhibitionist. Some things should stay private. Like what we just did. What I want us to do later."

"What do you want to do later?"

"You'll just have to be patient," Alvar said

pertly. "Give me enough time to catch my breath."

"Oh, but I like you breathless. Your hair all wild. My teeth-marks on your skin."

"That *was* some bite. Bet it wouldn't feel half so good for you if I returned the favor."

"Well now you *have* to test that hypothesis."

"I think you've been spending too much time around Wilhelmina," Alvar chided. "Making love shouldn't be reduced to a scientific method."

"No, you're right. I like the way we do it better. Spontaneous and fervent. Do you always like to be on top and in control?"

"Not sure how much control I really had," he confessed. "As we've already established, you tend to put me off-balance."

"I don't mean to," Marcel said earnestly. "You took me by surprise, too. I've always felt so detached from humanity. But you drew me in like... like the Church. You made me burn with a fire that felt almost zealous."

"I didn't think the Fae believed in God — at least not the singular one."

"We don't, as a rule." He propped himself up on an elbow, shifting into a more comfortable position against Alvar. "At first, it was just another sort of glamour. I started attending services with Jo — borrowed her Bible, got a rosary — because she'd impressed me with her strength. The others always deferred to her, never questioned her, and I decided part of it had to be her faith. So I mimicked her piety to give myself that same aloofness. But the more I read, the more I heard, the less it became an act."

"You started to believe?" Alvar's family had never been an especially devout one, though a branch of cousins had been of a monastical bent. He had attended holiday services in his youth and had owned a Bible – which had burned with the rest of the *Ilsa* – but he rarely thought of God. He had prayed over Sven, over his last captain, over the cook's little girl. But had never sought a conversation with God before or since. He had always looked at the truly religious with a mixture of awe and embarrassment: some had clearly found strength, solace, and purpose in their faith, and he was envious of those lucky few, but others had struck him as loud hypocrites or dangerously imbalanced.

"I started to feel God's presence," Marcel said quietly. Sincerity rang in his voice like a bell in a steeple. "I felt His hand stretch over me. When I pray, when I sit in a Church, I feel a peace and wholeness I've never known elsewhere."

Alvar was quiet for a long, thoughtful beat. "And how do you reconcile yourself with the priests and preachers who claim people like you are demonic? Unclean? I've heard priests denounce merfolk, elfkind, magicians, inverts – so many groups as sinful and worthy of stoning, damned to Hell and irredeemable. How can you bow your head and count your rosary when such venom is thrown in your face?"

"I pray and listen to Him. I know He is a loving God, an accepting God. He welcomes anyone into His presence. Those who choose to preach hatred and division have strayed from His true

411

message. No one is truly innocent or pure, which means every person, regardless of what they are, is equally important and valuable to Him."

"You don't think we're damned, then? For being what we are, for loving the way we do?"

"I can no more change what I am than you could, Alvar. I may put on a glamour at times, and you may keep your passions private, but that doesn't change what we are beneath. It's how we were made, how *He* made us. Believing God would shape us this way only to condemn us to eternal damnation is to believe that He is fallible or cruel, which is impossible. He's a force of love, not hate."

"I'd like to believe that," Alvar said softly, struck by Marcel's conviction. "I really would. But I just can't." He had only to close his eyes to see the suffering of the sick – how could a loving God allow something like that to happen? How could He turn his back on such pain without a shred of mercy?

"We all find our truth in different ways," Marcel replied. "Some paths are longer than others, some destinations look different from other perspectives. I understand."

The Fae reached out to draw his fingertips along the curve of Alvar's bearded jaw. To bend his head and press another kiss to the slightly parted lips.

"All of the stories I've heard," Alvar said after a pleasant, warm lull. "Said that the Fae were as changeable as mercury, with mad tempers and feet that barely touched the ground. That they didn't so much walk as flit; that they could never stay settled, and had thoughts so fast that they could never focus on one thing for long. That they could be as selfish and cruel as a child. I always imagined that someone like you would be capricious and unpredictable. But you're nothing like what I expected. Are the stories all lies, or are you an exception to the rule?"

"I suppose, in my youth, I was little thought and all feeling," Marcel mused. "Much of my family is what you would expect the Fae to be. But in my years on *The Sappho*, living around humans day and night, I think I've settled into patterns. My people hate patterns. They thrive in surprise and confusion. But I think there's something to be said for routines and repetition. And God has been a steadying influence, too; He's grounded me. I doubt my family would recognize me now. They'd probably say I've 'gone human'."

"Does that bother you?"

Marcel smiled crookedly. "I love my life here. I don't regret a thing. And I don't see 'human' as the insult they think it is. There's a lot to be said for humanity. You have some very fine qualities."

"Such as?"

"Your music. Your soft clothes — cotton and wool can be far more comfortable than leaves and plaited grass. Your art and beautiful buildings. Your books and languages. And now that I can speak from experience, the way you make love is very fine indeed..."

He didn't put the specifics into words, but he did his best to convey everything with his body: how Alvar's skin felt like silk against his, how his kisses tasted almost alcoholic on his tongue. Aunt

Cressidian had once seduced a human and told him they were like chalk, flavorless and dull, to warn him off of the experience.

But Alvar was sweet and heady and soft, as warming as the coals of a fire, and he was utterly intoxicated as they grappled in the dimming candlelight.

"Do you know how beautiful you are?" Marcel sighed in Alvar's ear as the human slid deeper, filling him up to the hilt.

The candle flickered out and in the darkness every movement became more intimate and overwhelming. It was difficult to discern where one body ended and the other began.

Alvar's teeth grazed the edge of Marcel's ear and the Fae cried out with the pleasure of the sensation. He clung to the sturdy arms, fingernails biting tiny half-moons across the pale, freckled skin, and pressed his thighs to the tapered waist as they rocked together. The friction left them gasping and sweat-slicked, unable to speak as they became creatures of instinct.

It felt like falling and flying at the same time, Alvar thought in broken fragments. Being with Sven had been thrilling, wonderful, but being with Marcel was something else entirely. The way their slim bodies aligned, the strength behind the pressure of their lips, the sense of fullness – it was profound. This felt like a ceremony, like some sacred act.

Somehow, he wasn't surprised by what came next.

"Open your eyes," Marcel said, voice ragged yet as commanding as a king.

It would have been impossible to disobey, and Alvar had no intention of denying him anything. In the humid darkness Marcel's eyes were the silver of liquid mercury, the only light in the room. He could feel himself falling into those eyes, even as his body hovered on the edge of oblivion.

"I give you power over me," Marcel said. His breathless words seemed to echo from a great distance. "No magic cast will bind you. You will see all as it truly is. I give to you as you give to me."

He could feel the bolt of power striking, grounding itself in his bones, spreading through his veins, as they came together in a dizzying rush. He turned his cheek to Marcel's damp chest and shivered as he spent himself, certain that it would be days before he would move again, weeks before he could trust his legs to support him.

The storm outside was dying. The thunder receded to the east. The wind no longer howled and tore at the planking of the hut. The rain remained steady, a rhythmic tattoo against the roof, but it had gentled. Nature's fury had been spent. Very soon now it would be quiet and peaceful across the beach.

"What you did," Alvar said finally, surfacing from a lazy drowse. Marcel's fingers paused in their gentle combing through his hair. "That meant something, didn't it? For us, I mean. You did it to show me you truly trust me."

"I unclouded your eyes," he said, confirming his suspicions. "No Fae glamour will ever work on you again."

"That isn't a gift that's often been given to a

human, is it?"

"No," Marcel agreed. "It's taboo to give a man that sort of power over us. The only reason my people have not been wiped out yet is because we can hide in plain sight with our glamours."

Alvar managed to push himself up. He could make out the shape of Marcel's face in the darkness, the glitter of his eyes, though there wasn't a shred of light in the room. "What would your people do if they found out you'd done this for me?"

"Kill me." His voice was so calm. A hand crept up to cover the crescent scar on his cheek and Alvar's heart twisted as if pierced by a knife.

He pressed his own hand over Marcel's, the question unspoken. "One of my cousins stole the blacksmith's wife as she was washing in the creek, after her husband made the village protective horseshoes to hang above their doorways and bar us entrance. Feegan was angry because it kept him from playing his spiteful pranks, so he stole the woman to punish her husband. I pitied the girl, who was being tormented through no fault of her own. I set her free and guided her back to the safety of the village. When Feegan learned I was responsible for thwarting him, he took up an iron nail and marked me as one not to be trusted."

Alvar kissed him fiercely, putting his arms around him in a protective embrace. He held him tightly until he felt the Fae relax, the tension elicited by the old memory fading until he was supple once more.

"No wonder you wanted to escape," Alvar

murmured. "How could you ever be truly comfortable around someone willing to do that to his own family?"

"Fae do not forgive or forget easily. We have codes, laws, that must be adhered to. For the good of all. And part of that code is to never trust a human. But I can't help but trust you."

"I swear to you, Marcel, that I will never do anything to betray that trust."

"I know you won't."

They drifted off to sleep, warm enough in each others arms that nothing else mattered.

*~*~*

The sun rose, as it always did at Nalani Island, in a glorious burst of pink and orange. Harry woke before Kai, crept out of her nook quietly so as not to disturb Isabelle, stretched comprehensively, and set off along the edge of the beach. Doubtless there would be some repairs to tend to after last night's squall, and she wanted to make sure nothing unexpected had washed up with the jetsam.

Junia, Jo, Wil, and Silence were already sitting by the fire, having rigged up the huge stewpot and set it to boil. Wil was laying out biscuit patties on a hot stone. The air smelled delicious and the sky above was serene. They had a beautiful day ahead of them.

"After breakfast, Jo and I will take stock of the huts," Harry announced, helping herself to a steaming biscuit. "The morning will be spent on chores and any repairs, but everyone can have the afternoon free..."

She trailed off, eyes narrowing as the door of a nearby hut swung open and a stranger stepped out, clad only in a loose shirt that fell to his knees. His skin was a pale golden hue not unlike Hope's, his short hair black and sleep-tousled, sticking out at odd angles. He walked toward the fire with a definite bounce to his step and a crooked smile on his angular face.

"Morning!" he said brightly to the staring, silent quintet. He crouched down, flashing a *lot* of bare skin, and deftly flicked two biscuits from the stone and into his hand. With a wink and a whistle, he straightened and walked back the way he came, hooking a foot on the edge of the door to pull it closed behind him.

"Who in blue blazes was that?" Harry demanded, the first to unfreeze. "And why the hell did he look so familiar?"

"Better question is: why was he wearing Alvar's shirt?" Wil asked.

# REUNION

"There they are," Anahera said, motioning to the two mers swimming in the water close to the human ship. One, a female, had a gnarled, twisted tail, and Aveline was baffled that she could move through the water at all, even with help.

They had heard tale upon tale of *The Sappho*, a ship where humans and mers worked in tandem. Anahera had been obsessed with it after first hearing of it, insisting that they would bring down every human on the ship and every mer who betrayed their own kind by sailing with them.

Aveline was unsure of this goal – none of the stories said that *The Sappho* killed mers, after all – but she did well know that whenever humans and mers interacted, things always went horribly wrong, and mers were most always the ones who suffered for it.

"Aveline," Anahera said. "Circle around to their front; keep them from reaching the ship. Uilani, Kalea'lii; to their left. Subira, Maata, to the right. I'll come in from behind."

Uilani nodded her understanding and darted off through the water. Aveline swam as well, diving underneath the two strangers and coming up in front of them. She started to speak, to tell them that they had a moment at most to defend themselves and give her some reason to let them live – but then she saw the man's face.

She had seen him before; had spared–

Seeing recognition cross his face as well, she opened her mouth, unable to think of any words. And then the merman was past her, dragging the younger mer with him, and lifting her into a small craft that dangled a few feet out of the water. He hauled himself in afterward, and still all Aveline could do was stare.

"What's wrong with you?" Anahera snapped. "You were supposed to distract them until we—"

"I know him, Anahera," Aveline said. "I recognized—"

"Never mind that now; they're getting away!"

Maata hissed in anger, and leapt for the small boat.

*~*~*

"What's the matter?" Isabelle asked, as Kai started to haul them back up to the deck. She'd barely had time to catch a glimpse of the small blonde mermaid – used to be human; had a black tail just like hers – before Kai had practically flung her into the landing craft.

"I've seen her before," Kai said. "She travels with—"

Isabelle screamed as something gray vaulted out of the water, and instinctively threw her arms up to defend her face. The sharkmaid's teeth sank into her forearm rather than her neck. Kai yelled for the others to haul them back up, the landing craft dropping a couple of feet between when he let go of the ropes and when the crew caught hold of them again.

Kai struck the sharkmaid hard in the side of the head and she released Isabelle's forearm, turning on him with a snarl. Isabelle flailed at her with her uninjured hand, punching the sharkmaid's shoulder. She hissed in pain as her knuckles scraped against the rough gray skin. Then Kai lashed out with his tail, knocking their attacker over the side.

"What happened?" Jo asked, helping Isabelle onto the deck. "Hope! Silence! Need you here!"

"Sharkmaids," Kai said, as Harry raced up to them. She peered over the side, ready to shout a challenge down to their attackers. But amongst the gray faces and toothy snarls, there was—

"Ave!" she screamed. "Jo! Jo, they have Aveline!"

Even as she and Josephine scrambled into the landing craft that Kai and Isabelle had so recently abandoned, time seemed to slow down. All she could see was her sister's face, confused and panicked, staring up at her from the water.

She was a mer, then. Enslaved by a sharkmaid pod, most certainly terrified but *alive*, her sister was here; if she had to kill every one of those sharkmaids she would—

But even as the landing craft hit the water and she raised her spear, Aveline was screaming. "No! Don't!"

"It's all right," Jo said. "Ave, come on! We'll get you out!"

"I'm not... they're not — no!" she cried, when one of the sharkmaids swam too close and Jo stabbed out with her own spear, striking the creature in the side.

One of the sharkmaids, the largest, bared her copious teeth as the wounded one swam back to the safety of the pod. "Kill them both," the leader hissed.

"Don't!" Aveline yelled, grabbing hold of two sharkmaids' arms as they started to swim forward. "Anahera, this is Harriet! Remember? The girl I've seen!"

"One of the humans who left you to die, no doubt!"

"No, I don't think so," Aveline protested, even as Harry let out a barely-intelligible curse. "I think she's safe."

"She's human!"

"So was I, once!"

"And you're lucky you no longer have to bear such a curse," Anahera said, touching her cheek gently. "Ave, dear, you have always been too soft. If seeing this will disturb you, you have my permission to leave until we are done. Maata. Uilani," she said, saying their names like an order as she nodded toward the landing craft.

The two glided forward again, teeth bared, and as Jo and Harry readied their spears Aveline darted forward, too, stopped only by Anahera's tight grip on her arm.

Aveline spun, striking Anahera across the face with her free hand.

Immediately, she froze, looking just as stunned by what she had done as Anahera did. Even Uilani and Maata turned, wanting to see what had made the remaining sharkmaids gasp in horror.

For a long moment, both Aveline and Anahera were silent, staring at each other. Finally, Anahera reached out, pulling her into a brief hug before pushing her away.

"Go, then," Anahera said quietly. "Go with them."

"But I wasn't – that wasn't what I meant, I'm sorry, I–"

"Your choice is made, Aveline."

"You can't. Please. I don't know any of them, not truly, I don't–"

Anahera didn't say anything else, didn't blink, and finally Aveline turned, swimming past Maata and Uilani, who each gave her a tight hug before letting her close to the landing craft.

"We will not strike this vessel," Anahera said. "In deference to your choice. Goodbye, little sister."

"Goodbye," Aveline said, her voice thick with tears, and then she was clinging to the side of the landing craft as the sharkmaids circled nearby, watching them warily.

And though Harry's's self-preservation instinct made her want to keep an eye on the sharkmaids and make sure they didn't change their minds about attacking, she couldn't take her gaze from her sister.

Aveline stared up at her and gave her a hesitant smile, and then looked to Jo.

"I... I have seen you as well," she murmured. "We were friends, weren't we? You were my friend."

"Yes," Jo whispered, her own voice hoarse. "Yes, I was."

# ABOUT STEPHANIE RABIG

When not writing, Stephanie can be found hanging out with her kids, making steampunk hats, or trying in vain to buy every pint of Ben & Jerry's in the store. Loves include fairy tales, mythology, tea, chocolate, and The Avengers.

The co-author of the novel *Faerietale* with Angie Bee and Colleen Toliver, she has several short stories published in anthologies. Her previous novels are available on Amazon.

Follow her on Twitter: **@stephrabig**
Check out her website: **stephanierabig.weebly.com**

...And for supplemental content and inspiration from the Sink or Swim universe, find the Pinterest storyboard at: https://tinyurl.com/4pwbwwx9.

# ABOUT ANGIE BEE

Angie Bee is a novelist, freelance writer, and pop culture pundit. She has five tattoos (so far), has lived in the Midwest and New Zealand, wrote a thesis on the socio-political commentary in zombie films, rescues cats from cemeteries, keeps skeletons in her car, and dreams of one day meeting Guillermo del Toro. Her ultimate goal in life is to be the lady all the neighborhood kids suspect is a witch (but a good witch, who gives out full-sized candy bars every Halloween). By day, she's a bookseller at a major retailer.

She reviews books and movies under the name Angie Barry on CriminalElement.com. The co-author of the novel *Faerietale* with Stephanie Rabig and Colleen Toliver, she has several short stories published in anthologies. Her previous novels are available at Blurb.com.

Follow her on Twitter: **@therealzombres**
Check out her website: **theangiebee.tumblr.com**

Printed in the USA
CPSIA information can be obtained
at www.ICGtesting.com
LVHW042013080823
754630LV00001B/6